Praise for these bestselling authors

VICKI LEWIS THOMPSON

"Vicki Lewis Thompson is one of those rare,
gifted writers with the ability to touch her
readers' hearts and their funny bones."
—*New York Times* bestselling author Debbie Macomber

"*Talking About Sex*...sizzles with sexuality and will
have you turning up the AC to cool down."
—*Writers Unlimited*

JULIE ELIZABETH LETO

"Nobody writes a bad girl like Julie Leto!"
—*New York Times* bestselling author Carly Phillips

"Sizzling chemistry and loads of sexual tension
make this Leto tale a scorcher."
—*Romantic Times BOOKclub* on *The Great Chase*

KATE HOFFMANN

"Kate Hoffmann traverses the minefield of
relationships...and comes up a winner."
—*Under the Covers*

"Kate Hoffmann pens an amazing story!"
—*Romantic Times BOOKclub*

Signature Select™
COLLECTION

VICKI LEWIS THOMPSON
JULIE ELIZABETH LETO
KATE HOFFMANN

A FARE TO REMEMBER

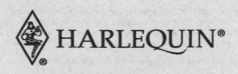

HARLEQUIN®

TORONTO • NEW YORK • LONDON
AMSTERDAM • PARIS • SYDNEY • HAMBURG
STOCKHOLM • ATHENS • TOKYO • MILAN • MADRID
PRAGUE • WARSAW • BUDAPEST • AUCKLAND

ISBN 0-373-83708-9

A FARE TO REMEMBER

Copyright © 2006 by Harlequin Enterprises S.A.

The publisher acknowledges the copyright holders of the individual works as follows:

JUST WHISTLE
Copyright © 2006 by Vicki Lewis Thompson

DRIVEN TO DISTRACTION
Copyright © 2006 by Julie Elizabeth Leto

TAKEN FOR A RIDE
Copyright © 2006 by Peggy A. Hoffmann

www.eHarlequin.com

Printed in U.S.A.

CONTENTS

JUST WHISTLE
Vicki Lewis Thompson

CHAPTER ONE

IF HANNAH HADN'T PACKED twenty-seven cans of tuna in her suitcase, she would have taken the bus from JFK.

She'd researched it, and the bus stopped a mere two blocks from her hotel. *Her hotel.* Just knowing she had a room reserved in a New York City hotel almost gave her an orgasm. She'd flown in on a red-eye, which had two things going for it—the el cheapo price and the 7:00 a.m. arrival, which meant she wouldn't have to worry about muggers.

Besides, muggers weren't a problem if you walked with purpose and didn't wear your hair in a ponytail they could grab hold of. She'd left her hair loose and she always walked with purpose, so she wasn't the least bit afraid. But the flowered suitcase weighed close to fifty pounds thanks to the tuna, and wrestling it on and off a bus didn't fit her picture of how she wanted to make her Big Apple entrance.

Logically she should be exhausted after being up all night, but she was wired and ready for the adventure of a lifetime. She, Hannah Robertson, was lining up at the taxi stand outside JFK, waiting for a bright yellow cab to take her to the place she'd dreamed about ever since reading the *Eloise* books as a kid.

She'd finally made it! So what if she wasn't staying

at the Plaza? Her hotel was in Manhattan, and that was all that mattered. So what if her first deep breath of genuine New York air made her cough? She wasn't expecting clean, dry Arizona air. She'd had her fill of clean, dry Arizona air.

She wanted this place, gasoline fumes and all. She wanted Times Square, Central Park, the Empire State Building, Fifth Avenue, the Statue of frickin' Liberty! It was all she could do not to spread her arms wide and shout *Hey, New York! Hannah's here!*

OUT-OF-TOWNER. After spending all his sixty years in NYC, Mario Capelli could spot a newcomer with one eye closed. But any fool could see that the redhead wearing a taxi-yellow sundress and pulling a flower-print suitcase hailed from somewhere other than New York. For one thing, she was smiling. New Yorkers didn't smile while waiting for a cab, especially coming off the red-eye.

For another thing, she had all that color going on— yellow dress, blue-and-yellow purse, gaudy flowered suitcase. Mario counted the cabs in front of him and the people standing in front of the redhead. Unless he'd miscounted, she'd be his fare. Perfect. From the minute he'd seen that smile and that cloud of dark copper hair, he'd started thinking of Zach.

Mario didn't believe in coincidences. He did believe in fate. For six months he'd wanted to find somebody for Zach, somebody who could save him from becoming a jaded corporate hack, somebody whose glass was not only half-full, but seriously overflowing. Mario thought he might be looking at her.

As he inched up to the head of the line, so did she.

The more he studied her, the more he could see her with Zach. She was stacked, and Zach liked stacked women. It didn't hurt that she had a pretty face, either. Mario even liked the way she stood so straight, with her shoulders back. Too many women slouched these days, trying to look like a magazine model or a bored superstar.

Her red hair was a bonus. Adrienne was blonde, and Mario didn't want to introduce any echoes of Adrienne into the equation. Anyone who'd dump a guy like Zach for somebody with a bigger bank account wasn't worth remembering, but Zach was sensitive enough to remember, and he might be off blondes for the time being.

Of course, Zach would object if he knew Mario was trying to fix him up. He would hate it, in point of fact. So Mario would have to be sneaky about the whole deal. He could do that. He hadn't spent thirty-five years with the NYPD for nothing.

Reaching for his cell phone, he speed-dialed Iris, who would have opened her coffee stand by now. Iris Rivera made the best espresso in the city, but that wasn't what kept Mario coming back. It was more about the whiteness of her teeth against her olive skin and that dimple when she smiled at him.

She was a kind person, so he wasn't sure if she really liked him, but he thought she might. That was a miracle, that a woman like her could be interested in a guy with more gray than black in his hair and the beginnings of a paunch. He hadn't decided what to do about his feelings for Iris, so until he did, buying coffee was a good excuse to see her a couple of times a day.

"*Sì*, Mario!" She always yelled into her cell phone because she couldn't believe the thing worked in the first place.

He didn't care if she yelled. He just loved hearing her Puerto Rican accent, which made him think of swaying palms and swaying bodies. "Has Zach come by for his espresso yet?"

"No! But I expect him soon!"

"When he comes by, can you stall him until I get there? I want to talk to him about something."

"I'll try! Zach, he's in such a hurry these days!"

Exactly. That's why Zach needed a girl. "Sell him a *pastelito* and he'll have to stick around to eat it." Thinking of those pastries made his mouth water.

"Okay! Are you trying to fix him up?"

"I am, but don't you dare tell him." The taxi in front of Mario pulled away from the curb, so Mario eased his foot off the brake and coasted to the front of the line. "Gotta go!" Snapping his cell phone closed and throwing the cab into Park, he jumped out and came around to help the redhead with her flowered suitcase.

"Be careful," she warned. "It's really heavy."

Mario had guessed as much. "No problem." He gave the redhead an indulgent smile. Out-of-towners always overpacked. They hadn't caught on to the concept of basic black, which meant you could get away with a much smaller wardrobe. Flexing his knees, he lifted the suitcase.

Shit, it really *was* heavy. A little flowered job like this wasn't designed for this much weight. "You got bowling balls in here?" he asked.

"No. I just brought—"

She was interrupted by the rip of fabric giving way and the clatter of cans hitting the pavement. Tuna cans. Mario dropped the suitcase and grabbed a couple before they rolled under the cab. By the time he stood, the redhead was frantically trying to stuff the cans back through a fifteen-inch-long tear along the seam.

Her face was the color of a stoplight. "It wasn't an expensive suitcase."

"I'm glad to hear that." Mario ignored the impatient honk from the cab behind him as he adjusted his Giants baseball cap and surveyed the situation.

"We're holding up the line."

"I know. Don't panic. If I lift the suitcase up flat, it'll go in the trunk without spilling. When we get to where you're going, I'll throw some duct tape on it."

She blew out a breath in obvious relief. "Thank you." Still blushing, she stood back while he maneuvered the ripped suitcase into the trunk of the cab. He only lost one can.

Snatching it from the pavement, she threw it in the trunk before he closed it. "Okay, let's go." She wrenched open the back door and got herself into the cab in short order.

Mario hurried around to the driver's side. *Tuna?* As he pulled into traffic, he wondered if his instincts had been off. He didn't want to saddle Zach with a nutcase. "Where to?" he asked.

"The Pearson Hotel, please. It's on— " She gasped as Mario cut across traffic.

"Hey, don't worry." Mario usually had to reassure first-timers. "I know what I'm doing."

"I'm sure you do." She took a deep breath. "They say that New York City cabdrivers are the best drivers in the world."

"And they would be right. Anyway, I know where the Pearson is." Her choice of hotel told him a little more about her. The Pearson was on the seedy side, but safe enough for a woman traveling alone. The combo of the Pearson and the tuna meant that his passenger was pinching pennies.

In the backseat, the redhead cleared her throat. "Uh, Mr. Capelli?"

That startled him, until he realized she'd taken the time to read his name on the license displayed on the dash. "I usually go by Mario."

"Okay, Mario. You—"

"I know. I changed lanes kinda fast back there, but trust me, it's how you have to do it if you want to make good time."

"I wasn't going to say anything about your driving. I thought you must be wondering about all those cans of tuna."

"I'm sure you have a good reason for them." He hoped to hell she wasn't a skinflint. A skinflint wasn't the right personality type for Zach.

"They're for the homeless."

"Oh." Okay, so she had the generosity gene. That was good, although most of the street people he'd known would prefer a fifth of vodka to a can of tuna.

"See, I knew that I'd want to give them something, but if I gave them cash, they might use it to buy booze. At least the tuna's nutritious."

"Provided they can get it out of the can."

She sighed. "I know. I thought of that, too, but I couldn't afford to buy a can opener to go with every can of tuna, so I hope they can figure that one out."

"It's a nice idea, cans of tuna." Mario wondered what Zach would think of such a thing. He'd probably say it was impractical to be hauling tuna cans all over creation, but Mario hoped the generous impulse behind it would impress Zach. Still, Mario decided that when he mentioned this woman, he wouldn't lead with the tuna.

"They were having a big sale on it at the Safeway near my apartment in Phoenix."

Phoenix. Mario made a mental note. Zach might be intrigued by somebody from Arizona. If Mario remembered his geography, Phoenix wasn't too far from the Grand Canyon. Surely Zach had some interest in the Grand Canyon. Everyone did.

Time to trot out one of his stock questions. "What brings you to New York?"

"I'm interviewing for a job in publishing."

Mario smiled. She wasn't a tourist. She intended to get a job and stay, which meant his instincts were still working. "Who are you interviewing with?"

"I was able to get appointments at two of the houses, and the others I'll try to set up while I'm here. I just got my English degree at ASU. I probably seem a little old to be graduating, but I had a few interruptions. Oh, look! The *skyline!*"

Mario's heart squeezed at the reverence in her voice. He didn't have to ask if this was her first trip. Or whether she had the faintest idea how competitive the job field was. He was no expert on publishing, but this time of year a hoard of Ivy League graduates descended on the city looking for jobs. And they all had connections.

"Do you know anybody here?" Mario hoped she knew somebody. Or maybe Zach had clients in the publishing world.

"Nope. I've lived in Arizona my whole life. My brother and sister thought I was nuts to want to move here. But I love books, and if you love books, New York is the place."

"That's a fact." Mario decided that even if the redhead didn't take to Zach, or vice versa, she could use some help with this job quest. "I know somebody who might have a connection at one of the publishing houses." That was stretching things a bit, but odds were it was true. A glance in the rearview mirror told him the redhead was smiling again.

"Look at that," she said. "I'm already networking."

"This guy I know is an investment counselor. Name's Zachary Evans, but he mostly goes by Zach. I'm pretty sure one of his clients works for a publishing house." Put that way, it sounded kind of lame. Mario wondered if she'd question the value of talking to Zach.

Instead she seemed eager. "Great! Do you have his number?"

"Not on me, but I should be seeing him this morning. I can give him your name and have him call the Pearson."

"That would be terrific. My name's Hannah Robertson. I don't have any business cards, but I could write it down for you." She rummaged in her purse.

"That's okay. I'll remember." As a cop, Mario had been famous for his recall. He still prided himself on that.

"All right, then. I'll look forward to hearing from Zach Evans."

They rode in silence for a while. Mario could have asked a bunch more questions, but he'd learned that too many questions could make a passenger suspicious of his motives. So he waited for her to make the next conversational move.

Finally she spoke again. "You know, it's nice that you have pictures of your family taped on your dash. It makes the cab look homey and cheerful."

"They're not exactly my family." So she'd been

studying his pictures. Ordinarily Mario was happy to talk about his matchmaking hobby, but not when he was in the process of trying to hook people up. People got hinky if they thought he was doing that. "Just a bunch of good friends."

"Well, that's still nice. Everybody looks so happy in those pictures. You must have a lot of good-natured friends."

"Life's too short to have bad-natured ones." Mario only matched up people who were pleasant. Maybe that was why he had such an astounding success ratio, ninety percent.

"Is Zach Evans in one of those pictures?"

"No, I don't happen to have a picture of him yet." *But if everything works out the way I'm hoping, I will soon.*

IRIS DIDN'T USUALLY GIVE Zach a hard sell, so he wondered why she was suddenly pushing the *pastelitos* and urging him to buy a second cup of espresso. He hoped she didn't have money troubles. A woman as fiercely independent as Iris would die before admitting that she had problems in that area, but she might increase the sales pressure to generate better cash flow.

What the hell. He'd started going into the office an hour early, so it wasn't like he'd be late to work if he hung around the coffee stand a little longer. There'd be another bus along later. And two espressos might be exactly what he needed today to nail his monthly quota and secure his move to that corner office Drake Medford had promised him.

An image of Ed, the guy currently in that corner office, flashed through his mind. Ed had been around for years and no longer seemed to care about his monthly quota. If you worked for Drake Medford, that was a bad thing. Zach told himself not to think about where Ed would end up. That wasn't his responsibility.

So he drank his second espresso, munched on a flaky *pastelito* and listened to Iris's favorite Celia Cruz CD while some guys in dreadlocks went strolling by. At times like this he wondered what the folks back in Auburn, Illinois, would make of it all. No one in his family had expressed any desire to visit, so he'd had to make trips home in order to see them.

Because that only happened about once a year, he'd constructed his own little support group in Manhattan, and Iris was definitely included. He would hate to think she'd fallen on hard times. Maybe he could smoke out some information on her financial picture and see if he could guide her in some way.

He waited until she'd served a couple who looked like they might be honeymooners judging from the way they held hands and couldn't stop gazing at each other. Their obvious affection sent a pang of regret running through him. Adrienne had never looked at him that way, which should have given him a clue.

When the coast was clear, he wandered closer to the coffee stand. "I hope your tax guy advised you to take a deduction for your CD player and the music you buy," he said. "That's an integral part of your business."

Iris nodded as she tucked money in her cash drawer. "I have many deductions, *mijo*."

"That's good. Keeping a business afloat isn't easy these days. You need all the breaks you can get."

Iris smiled. "*Si*. I'm lucky that people like my

coffee and my *pastelitos* so I won't end up a beggar when I'm old."

She said it with such confidence that Zach had to believe she was solvent. That left him still wondering why she'd urged him to spend more at her coffee stand this morning.

"Aha! Here's Mario!" Iris sounded delighted, as usual. No doubt there was a romance blossoming there.

Zach was also happy to see the guy. A chance cab ride with Mario about a year ago had resulted in a growing friendship, and Zach considered Mario part of his New York family, too. Mario had introduced Zach to this little piece of espresso heaven, and Zach always enjoyed running into him here.

"Hey, Mario." Zach brushed the crumbs from his fingers and held out his hand. "How's it going?"

"Can't complain." Mario shook hands before glancing over at Iris. He touched the brim of his Giants cap in greeting. "Morning, Iris. That's a good color on you."

"*Ai,* this old thing?" Iris blushed like a teenager as she looked down at her red blouse. "Your eyes are tired from being up all night. You need coffee so you can see better." She reached for the small porcelain espresso cup she kept especially for him.

"My eyesight's fine, but I'll need that coffee to go," Mario said.

"Oh." Iris's smile faded.

"I'm giving Zach a ride to the office. I'll be back."

"*Oh.*" Iris's smile returned.

"You don't need to give me a ride." Zach didn't want to get in the way of this flirtation. "The bus is almost here. I'll just—"

"Ah, get in the cab and pretend you're a rich guy."

Mario picked up the foam cup Iris handed him and used it to gesture toward the curb where he'd parked. "I need to discuss a little matter with you."

Zach shrugged. "If you insist." He didn't mind the expense once in a while, especially when the money went to a guy like Mario. Besides, riding in Mario's cab was an experience. He drove the cab the way he'd probably driven the cruiser when he was a cop, except now he had to substitute the horn for the siren.

Because they were friends, Zach rode in the front, which gave him an excellent view of all the happy couples taped to Mario's dash. Mario's romantic streak was touching. Zach had asked him once why he wasn't married, considering how much he supported the institution.

Turned out Mario had lost his wife some time ago, and still seemed to be hurting. But time had passed, and he definitely seemed interested in Iris. Zach thought the two of them would be good together.

Mario climbed behind the wheel and set his cup in a plastic holder before starting the engine. Then he turned off the meter.

"Hey, I want to pay," Zach said.

"Nope. This one's on the house." Mario gunned the engine and tires screeched as he plunged into traffic.

Zach held on to the armrest for balance, but he wasn't the least bit nervous. Mario drove fast, but he never wrecked. "If you want a hot stock tip," Zach said, "you'll have to wait until I get to the office. But as of last night, your portfolio was looking good. I wouldn't change anything, but if you want to add, then—"

"This isn't about the market." Mario surged through a yellow light, honking the horn to warn off anyone who dared get in his way. "It's about a woman I picked up at the airport."

Suddenly Zach understood Iris's strange behavior and Mario's offer of a ride to work. "Oh, no."

"What do you mean, *oh, no?*"

"You're ready to fix me up with her, aren't you?"

"Hell, no, I'm not!" Mario veered sharply around a parked van. "She needs some help looking for a job, that's all."

"Yeah, sure. Listen, Mario, thanks, but no thanks. I know this is your mission in life, but I have no interest in getting taped to your dash. Forget it."

"But I only thought—"

"Nope. Nix. *Nyet. Non.* Negative. Not going there, Mario. You'd better dig deep in your Bag o' Bachelors and come up with another candidate, because I'm so not meeting the woman you picked up at the airport."

"How can you make a statement like that? Sheesh. And I didn't even tell you about the tuna!"

CHAPTER TWO

THE PEARSON HOTEL LOBBY wasn't much bigger than Hannah's living room back in Phoenix, and there were exactly two armchairs available. She probably should have guessed that her room wouldn't be ready at eight-thirty in the morning, but she hadn't spent much of her life in hotels and wasn't totally familiar with the routine.

Both lobby chairs were occupied, one by an elderly man reading a newspaper and the other by a young woman filling out a job application. So Hannah stood, being careful not to jostle her duct-taped suitcase. The desk clerk had offered to keep the suitcase in a storage room, but Hannah was afraid it wouldn't survive being manhandled by a bellhop. She hadn't seen a bellhop, but this was a New York City hotel, so there had to be a bellhop somewhere on the premises.

Well, this was awkward. The desk clerk had predicted it might be another hour or two before a room became available. She could feel the hum of the city just beyond that lobby door, and she was desperate to get out there and take her first New York City walk.

On the drive in she'd spotted some homeless people who probably could use her tuna. At this point she could use some of that tuna, herself. The peanuts and Coke she'd had on the airplane had worn off quite a while ago.

But she had no can opener and she'd also promised herself a hot pretzel from a street vendor once she hit the pavement.

The lobby door opened and she turned to see if it might be the bellhop returning from a coffee break. Whoops, not a bellhop. Not even close to being a bellhop. Instead she was eyeball to eyeball with a gorgeous specimen of New York manhood tricked out in a crisp gray suit, power tie in red-and-gray stripes, and a shirt that looked white at first but upon closer inspection displayed fine vertical lines of gray running through the fabric.

She wondered if he'd dressed to match his eyes, which were the color of campfire smoke. Add to that a movie-idol smile and wavy brown hair. If this guy was staying at the Pearson, she had definitely picked the right hotel.

His gaze moved from her face to the duct-taped suitcase at her feet. "You're Hannah."

Her mind clicked rapidly through the possibilities. She only knew one person in New York, and that was the man who had duct-taped her suitcase. He'd promised to mention her to his friend. She wished he'd left out the part about the duct tape.

She swallowed. "And you're Zach."

"Right." He held out his hand. "Zach Evans."

"Hannah Robertson." She shook hands with what she hoped was the right amount of firm, businesslike pressure. He was so delectable that she wanted to hang on a while longer, but she didn't dare. She was supposed to network with this Adonis, not jump his bones.

"I called the hotel and they said you weren't registered. That got me worried, so I decided to come over and make sure you were okay."

Hannah's faith in the desk clerk slipped a notch. They darned well knew she was standing in the lobby. "I tried to register. The room wasn't ready." Surely the desk clerk could have said she was here, couldn't he? Maybe not. She didn't know New York City hotel procedure.

Zach glanced around the small lobby. "So you're kind of stuck."

"Oh, not at all! I was just about to ask them to store my suitcase so I could leave the hotel and explore the city." To hell with the suitcase and the potential for tuna cans all over the storage room. She was not about to appear helpless and stranded in front of her network, all one of him.

"Oh! Well, that's a good idea." He eyed the suitcase. "I guess."

"It'll be fine. I know the suitcase looks a little…"

"Compromised?"

"You could say that." She wouldn't mind being compromised by Zachary Evans. But she had to cool it. There were probably lots of guys like him walking around this city. He happened to be the first certified NYC hunk she'd seen, so she was probably overreacting. And she was starving, too, which didn't help.

"You could ask them to tie something around it," Zach said.

"I'll do that." She realized that the networking hadn't begun yet, and maybe it was up to her to do something about it. "Mario mentioned that you had a contact in publishing."

"I do. He's an editor."

"Really?" Hannah hadn't expected to be this lucky. "For what house?"

"I can't remember the name, but I have it at the office.

I know they mostly do cookbooks and travel guides. Is that what you're interested in?"

She was tempted to say yes, just to make the connection stronger, but she hadn't come all this way to work on cookbooks and travel guides. "I have a degree in English literature. I'm hoping to edit fiction."

"Oh." He rubbed the back of his neck. "Then Percy might not be the guy to help you."

"I'd be glad to talk to him, even so." Maybe she could learn to love cookbooks. No, probably not. She was a nuke-'em-and-scarf-'em-down kind of person. Her theory was if you took enough vitamins and ate tuna once in a while, you'd be okay.

"It could be a waste of time if you're into fiction." Zach checked his watch. "Look, I have to get to the office, but I can ask around. Someone else might have a better lead than I do."

"I hate to put you to the trouble." Actually, she didn't. Anything that would keep that tenuous connection between them worked for her. But she had to give him a graceful way out if he wanted to let this go.

"No trouble." He paused. "If you don't have other plans, we could go to dinner tonight. I could tell you what I've found out."

Other plans? She'd arrived in the city less than two hours ago! She knew no one! How could she possibly have other plans? But she hesitated, as if considering her packed schedule. "That might work."

"Seven?"

"Seven would be okay."

"I'll ring your room."

"Great. See you then." She watched him walk out of the lobby and controlled the urge to jump up and down.

Her first night in New York and she had a date! Not only a date, but one with a guy who came recommended by her very friendly taxi driver. Even better, this highly recommended, date-worthy person looked like he'd stepped out of the pages of *GQ*. New York was going to be *incredible*.

MARIO RETURNED TO THE coffee stand feeling smug. Maybe he shouldn't take credit, though, because he'd been wrong about not leading with the tuna. The tuna had made all the difference. He only hoped this Cupid operation wasn't too late.

After finding a parking spot near Iris's stand, he sauntered over, unable to hold back a smile of triumph. He waited until Iris had finished serving an espresso to a long-haired college student toting a heavy backpack.

She counted out change to the student. *"Gracias, señor."* Then she turned to Mario, her dark eyebrows arched. "Well?"

"He's calling her this morning."

"Bueno!" Iris clapped her hands together. "That boy needs a sweetheart."

"You're telling me. He's so focused on success after Adrienne worked him over that he's ready to bulldoze some poor guy out of a corner office."

"That's bad."

"It's not so much him as that boss of his." Mario took the small porcelain cup of espresso Iris handed him. "Thanks, Iris." He reached in his pocket and pulled out some money, but she waved it away. "Hey." He tried again to give her the money. "You can't be serving me free coffee."

"You can give free taxi rides but I can't give free coffee?"

He met the challenge in her dark eyes. She had spirit, and he admired that. "Thank you."

"*Da nada.* So Zach will take away someone's job?"

"I don't know about that, but he definitely has his eye on a big bonus and a better office, which is currently occupied by a guy named Ed. Ed's older and isn't producing like he used to. Zach thinks the big boss wants to squeeze Ed out, even though he's a nice guy and treats his clients great."

Iris clucked her tongue.

"Yeah, it sucks. I know it happens all the time, but I hate to see Zach buying into it. If he doesn't watch out, he'll get as ruthless as the boss."

"This woman, you think she'll be good for him, then?"

Mario pictured Hannah Robertson in her yellow sundress and flowered suitcase held together with duct tape. "Oh, yeah. She's exactly what the doctor ordered."

ALL THROUGH THE DAY Zach kept telling himself that just because he was taking Hannah Robertson to dinner didn't mean he'd end up taped to Mario's dash. If and when the time came for him to find someone and settle down, he would do the picking, not some guy who'd seen *Fiddler on the Roof* once too often. Although matchmaking was cute when it happened to other people, Zach wasn't about to fall for that program.

But a guy would have to be made of stone not to be kind to a woman who brought cans of tuna to New York so she could pass them out to the city's homeless population. It also didn't hurt that she'd looked like a ray of sunshine standing in that dingy hotel lobby. Her red hair was glorious, a deep copper color. She also had brown eyes, which might explain why her sundress had revealed a golden tan rather than pale skin dotted with freckles.

Taking Hannah Robertson to dinner would be no hardship. Getting her the right publishing contacts might be. Zach had asked around, and the consensus seemed to be that Ed had a client who was a publishing bigwig. This was the day that Drake Medford would inform Ed that he would probably be losing his corner office come the first of the month. Under the circumstances, Zach thought asking Ed for a personal favor today was just wrong.

So he'd called his cookbook guy and milked that contact for a couple of tenuous leads. It wasn't much, but it was better than going to dinner empty-handed.

Partly because he didn't have much to tell her and partly because he kept thinking of how good she'd looked in yellow, he bought a bouquet of daisies and yellow roses before hopping on the bus that would take him to the stop closest to the Pearson. Going to dinner with Hannah was turning out to be the best part of his day. Every time he'd passed Ed's office he'd cringed at the idea that he was driving the guy out. Although he'd told himself not to worry, he was worrying, anyway.

So dinner was a terrific distraction. He'd made reservations at a Thai place on Restaurant Row, and they could walk there and back from her hotel. He wasn't opposed to taking a cab, but Mario wasn't on duty yet and Zach had become picky about his cabs after riding with Mario.

Fire trucks drove screaming past the bus as it stopped where Zach wanted off. When the sirens abruptly quit, Zach paused at the front of the bus, bouquet in hand, to lean down and peer through the bus's windshield to see where the trucks had ended up. Damn it, the fire trucks, lights flashing, sat smack-dab in front of the Pearson!

Galloping down the steps to the pavement, Zach headed off at a run. The Pearson wasn't as tall as some hotels, but tall enough, more than thirty stories. The fire escapes were probably old and rusty. A horrible image of Hannah dangling from a rope made of knotted sheets made his stomach churn.

Hotel guests came streaming out of the tiny lobby as the firefighters went charging in. Zach couldn't see any smoke, but that didn't mean anything. The fire could be in a hallway or an elevator shaft. Now he could hear the hotel's fire alarm, a grating beep, beep, beep that sent sweat running down his spine.

Then Hannah—barefoot and wearing a thin flowered bathrobe—came out of the hotel. Relief emptied his lungs, making him dizzy as he stood a few feet away catching his breath. Now that he could see she was fine, he felt a little silly. He'd pretty much overreacted, considering he barely knew her.

What was that all about? It was probably Mario's fault. The guy had portrayed Hannah as an innocent plopped down into the big, bad city. The message had been clear—Zach was supposed to be her knight in shining armor.

He'd thought that message had rolled right off his back, and yet the evidence said otherwise. When he hadn't been able to reach her this morning he'd hopped a bus and dashed over to make sure she was okay. Then he'd raced to the hotel because a couple of fire trucks were sitting there. And he still hadn't seen any smoke.

Hannah looked upset, though. Wending her way

through the guests, she padded over to a fireman stationed by the front door and started an earnest conversation, waving her arms as she talked. Zach couldn't help but notice how sexy she looked standing there in her bathrobe and bare feet, her hair catching the glow from the revolving lights on top of the fire engine.

Finally he decided to walk over and make his presence known. Everything she owned could be going up in flames right now. He pictured himself taking out his credit card, just like in the commercials, and buying her a new wardrobe while "My Girl" played in the background. It was a stupid idea, but it ran through his head, anyway.

As he walked toward her, she stuck her hands in the pockets of the bathrobe and gazed up at the fireman. "So I'm really, really sorry," she said. "But the room smelled so stale and musty."

"Next time, buy some Glade, lady." The fireman turned away and clicked a button on the walkie-talkie clipped to his shoulder. "Sammy, check out Room 538. Seems one of the guests was burning sage as an air freshener. That could be the problem."

Zach groaned. Far from being the victim, Hannah had been the perp.

At the sound, she turned and gasped. "Zach! Omigod, is it seven already?"

"Five after." Zach tried not to stare at her cleavage, but the bathrobe had gaped open and he could see…a lot. He now knew that she was wearing a black lace bra with a front clasp, that she had no discernible tan line so she might have been out in the sun topless, and that she had a cute little mole on her left breast.

"I am *so* embarrassed. The room didn't smell good,

so I found a little shop that sells incense and stuff. Sage works great at home. I was afraid the smoke was a little too heavy, so I tried to get the window open but it was painted shut." She gestured around her. "You see what happened."

"I see." He was seeing way too much for a first date, that was for sure, but that didn't mean he couldn't enjoy the view.

"And you brought flowers." The way she said it sounded as if he'd brought her the Hope diamond.

He'd forgotten he was clutching them. In the two-block dash to the hotel, he'd broken a couple of daisy stalks, and the blossoms hung their little heads. "Uh, yeah." He plucked the blossoms off and stuck them in his pocket. "Here."

"They're beautiful." She buried her nose in the bouquet and one of the naked stalks almost poked her in the eye.

"Hold on a minute." He jerked the bouquet back.

She looked startled. "What's the matter?"

"Stalks." He pulled them out and handed it back to her. She was showing signs of being accident prone. In a place like New York, that wouldn't be good.

"I don't mind a few stalks." She held the bouquet out and admired it. "I'll bet you bought this from one of the sidewalk vendors."

"I did, actually."

"I love that. I've been in New York a mere twelve hours, and I've already eaten a soft pretzel, passed out five cans of tuna and received a bouquet from a sidewalk flower shop." She threw both hands in the air like an Olympic athlete at a medal ceremony. "I've arrived!"

"I guess so." Zach wasn't used to dramatic displays

in a crowd of people. He glanced around to see if anyone was staring. They were. "I'm glad you like the flowers."

"I don't like the flowers."

"You don't? I thought you just said—"

She laughed. "I *love* the flowers."

"Oh." Zach couldn't remember the last time he'd been with someone who had this much energy, and according to Mario, she'd come in on the red-eye. "I guess you took a nap today, huh?"

"Are you kidding? Who could sleep on their first day in New York? I've walked up and down Fifth Avenue and through most of Central Park. I would have gone up to the top of the Empire State Building, but I ran out of time."

"All clear, folks!" said the fireman stationed at the door. "You can return to your rooms now!"

Hannah produced her key from the pocket of her bathrobe. "Come on up with me while I finish getting dressed. The lobby's too small to hang out in. Well, my room's not very big, either, but I can't make you wait in the lobby. Someone's usually sitting in the chairs."

"That's okay. I can wait in the lobby." Zach was already on sensory overload with all those peeks at her black bra. Being alone with her in her room might bring on some unwanted developments, like a woody. He prided himself on having more control than that, but Hannah pushed all his buttons.

Had Mario known that would happen? Maybe Zach had seriously underestimated the taxi driver's skills when it came to matchmaking. Nah, not even Mario could have predicted that Hannah would end up on the sidewalk in her bathrobe, which turned Zach's thoughts to bedrooms, and soft sheets and naked bodies.

"Oh, come on up," Hannah said. "I won't compromise your virtue. I'll get dressed in the bathroom."

If he didn't go along with her suggestion, he'd look like a prude. "Okay. Sure."

The ride up in the elevator posed no temptation. The elevator was crowded with people returning to their rooms.

A cross-looking woman standing next to Hannah glanced at her. "Were you the one who set off the fire alarm?"

"I was." Hannah looked repentant. "And I apologize."

"I should hope so!" The woman looked indignant. "I was watching the Yankees, and Derek Jeter was up to bat. I hate it when I miss one of his times at bat."

"Here." Hannah pulled a rose out of her bouquet. "Take this as a gesture of peace."

The woman blinked. "Um, thanks." She took the rose and brought it slowly to her nose. "Smells good."

"Anybody else want a rose?" Hannah held up her bouquet. "I'm the bad guy here, but thanks to my friend, I have a way to make amends."

"I'll take one," said a guy in a T-shirt and jeans.

"Me, too," said an older woman in a baggy sweat suit. "I'm twenty minutes late for my medication. I need some aromatherapy for the stress."

"Be my guest." Hannah presented a rose first to the T-shirt guy and then to the lady who'd missed her meds.

"I wouldn't mind one," said a young woman sporting several tattoos. "I just broke up with my boyfriend so this fire alarm makes a bad day even worse."

"Then here you go," Hannah said. "By all means."

Zach wanted to protest. Four of the six roses in the bouquet were gone, which made it look a lot less festive. But he'd given her the flowers, so he no longer had any say-so as to what happened to them. Fortunately nobody else made a bid for a rose.

One little girl wanted a daisy, but he didn't mind that so much. He'd trashed two himself. Then they reached the fifth floor, and that was the end of the flower giveaway.

"I hope you don't mind," Hannah said as they walked down a hallway covered by a faded carpet. "It really was my fault, and I felt the need to make amends."

"No problem."

"Oh, now, see? You're hurt because I gave away your beautiful flowers. But I'll find a way to make it up to you."

His imagination danced through that possibility for at least ten seconds. Surely she hadn't meant it to sound as suggestive as it had seemed. Or maybe she had. What did he know? Mario had thrown him into the deep end, and he was hoping to hell he could swim.

CHAPTER THREE

HANNAH FELT COSMOPOLITAN and daring, inviting a man up to her room on her first night in New York. It wasn't a particularly elegant room, but she couldn't imagine making him wait down in that cramped lobby. He was her new best friend and she wanted to treat him right.

He'd brought her *flowers,* too. Even with a few of the roses and a couple of daisies missing, it was a fabulous bouquet. She'd been a little worried that he was watching out for her as a favor to Mario, but if so he wouldn't have brought flowers. She'd tuck one in her hair for the night and put the rest in the ice bucket. A daisy would look great with the peacock-blue-and-yellow dress she'd planned to wear tonight.

"Here we are, home sweet temporary home." She pushed her card key into the lock and opened the door. The minute she stepped on the carpet and it squished under her bare feet, she suspected a problem. When she glanced at the bed where she'd laid out all her dry-clean-only, sale-priced interview clothes in preparation for ironing them, she knew disaster had struck.

"Sprinklers," she said, moaning as she walked across the drenched carpet to her equally soaked clothes. "The smoke set off the automatic sprinklers."

Zach closed the door and stared at the mess. "Can't you just dry them somehow?"

"Not these. I mean, look at them." A sick feeling settled into the pit of her stomach as she picked up what used to be a bold purple-and-kelly-green-striped dress. Purple and green oozing together made brown, something she'd learned in kindergarten with finger paints.

A neon-green suit decorated with big white tulips had rust splotches all over it. The rust had probably descended when the old pipes disgorged their supply of water all over the room. Her peacock-blue-and-yellow dress, a combo of silk and rayon that had been a steal at fifty percent off, was covered with ugly water stains and seemed to be shriveling before her eyes. That left her with the yellow sundress, which she'd hung in the closet after taking it off this afternoon.

She turned to him, determined to be a big girl about this. "Well, I'm clothes-less! Down to my underwear, a sleep shirt, my yellow dress and this bathrobe. Know any cheap stores?" Her voice barely quivered. She hoped he couldn't tell that she was close to tears.

From the way he was looking at her, he probably could tell. "There are some resale shops in the Village."

"Yeah?" She was determined to maintain a brave front. "Shopping in the Village would be very cool. I've always wanted to. Now it looks like I have a great excuse."

"If you want, I could go with you during my lunch hour tomorrow."

She was touched that he'd offer, but there were limits to how much help she could accept. "That's sweet, but you really don't have to. Shopping for clothes can't be your favorite way to spend free time."

"I don't mind. I'd be happy to do that."

"Because you feel sorry for me."

He hesitated. "Look, it's natural to feel a little sorry for somebody who just had her entire traveling wardrobe sprinkled into oblivion. But that aside, I'd like to help. And the fact is, you need me."

She was afraid that might be true, for a variety of reasons, but she wasn't ready to admit it yet. "Why is that?"

"I drive a hard bargain. No offense, but knowing how you pass out tuna and roses, I'm guessing you don't."

That made her laugh. "You're right, I don't. My sister refuses to take me to garage sales with her because I pay whatever's marked on stuff, which she says violates the basic law of garage sales."

"That's absolutely true. It's settled, then. Did you know your message light's blinking?"

She glanced at the phone, and sure enough, the red light was flashing. "But I don't know anybody."

"You know the people in the hotel."

Her tummy churned. "Oh, God. Do you think they're going to charge me for this disaster?"

"No, but they might want to talk to you about it."

She stared at the blinking red light and wondered if she could pretend she hadn't seen it. If Zach was wrong and the hotel wanted to charge her for the inconvenience and water damage, she'd rather not find out right before her first big night in New York.

But she'd worry about that blinking light all evening, so she might as well get it over with. Picking up the phone, she punched the message button.

An official-sounding male voice came on the line. *Ms. Robertson, we understand the sprinklers discharged in your room.*

Hannah closed her eyes and hoped that her shaky financial situation wasn't about to get a whole lot worse.

We apologize for the inconvenience. When you're ready, we'll transfer you to another room.

She let her breath out in a whoosh. "They want to switch me to a different room. That's all."

"As well they should," Zach said. "You can't sleep in that bed tonight."

"Guess not. I hadn't thought of that. But I don't want to take the time to change rooms now. I don't know about you, but I'm starving."

"And our reservations are for seven-thirty. I could call and change them, but—"

"No, don't. I'll let them switch me while we're gone." With no choice in the matter, she hurried to the closet and took out her yellow dress. Draping it over one arm, she pulled a rose from the bouquet. "Be right back."

Then she stuck the rose between her teeth, flung her free hand in the air and cocked her hip in a flamenco dancer's pose before dashing into the bathroom. His startled laughter was exactly what she was after. She might be a clueless newcomer who had trashed her clothes immediately upon arriving, but she didn't want Zach to think she was totally pathetic. She still had flair, damn it.

FOR SEVERAL SECONDS ZACH stood staring at the closed bathroom door as he processed that last provocative image Hannah had given him. There was no getting around it, the woman was hot. Hot and generous. Zach's imagination latched on to those two attributes and came up with one obvious conclusion. He wanted some of that.

But just because she aroused him didn't mean he'd end up taped to Mario's dash. It didn't even mean he and

Hannah would end up in bed together. He had no idea if he was the only one thinking about sex, although the rose between her teeth suggested she might be having thoughts along those lines, too.

He ran a hand over his face and took a deep breath. The rustling sounds coming from the bathroom did nothing to calm him down. He pictured the black bra and panties and realized she would have to take off the bra in order to wear the thin-strapped sundress. If she had spent some time sunbathing topless, which he suspected, her breasts would be golden and gorgeous.

This was insanity, standing here on a squishy carpet imagining what was going on behind that bathroom door. He should have waited in the lobby. At the rate he was going, he was liable to do something inappropriate, like grab her and kiss her the minute she walked out.

And then what, genius? Throw her down on that soggy mattress? Very classy.

Actually it sounded kind of kinky and exciting. The wet sheets might feel interesting against their hot bodies. He'd never had sex on a soaked mattress before, and the experience might prove educational and moist.

Oh, for God's sake. He'd invited her to dinner, and they would have dinner. Then he'd walk her back to her hotel and go home like the sophisticated urban professional he was. He would not spend the entire meal wondering if she'd invite him back up to her new and improved, much drier room afterward. He would not hope that he could get her to do that routine with the rose one more time.

Mostly to give himself something to do, he pulled out his cell phone and moved the reservation ahead fifteen minutes so they wouldn't lose it. There shouldn't be a problem on a weeknight, but he didn't want to take any chances. The evening had already had its share of detours.

As he was closing the phone and clipping it back on to his belt, Hannah came out. She wore the same dress, so the sight of her shouldn't have affected him, but it did, anyway. Maybe it was how she'd done her hair.

After piling it loosely on top of her head, she'd tucked daisies into her curls so that she looked like a wood nymph, or at least what Zach thought a wood nymph might look like. He felt as if they should be running hand in hand through a meadow in slow motion before settling down on a bed of soft grass to…yeah, to have sex. *Face it, Evans, you're officially obsessed with the subject.*

As a hormone-driven teenager he'd devoured a copy of *Lady Chatterley's Lover,* and daisies had been involved in one of the sex scenes. He'd forgotten that until this very minute and wondered if the scene in the book had anything to do with his own fondness for daisies.

Hannah smiled at him. "Ready?"

You have no idea. "Sure. Let's go."

"I put the rest of the flowers in the ice bucket. Wait a sec. I should probably throw my undies and makeup in the suitcase and put the wet clothes in the laundry bag."

"Probably should." And he shouldn't watch her do that, either. But he did, anyway, torturing himself with a view of silk and lace in various colors being tossed from a drawer into the duct-taped suitcase she'd taken out of the closet.

She ducked back into the bathroom and returned with her cosmetics bag. Then she grabbed two cans of tuna and dropped them in her oversize purse. "For tonight, in case we pass any homeless people." Finally she turned to him. "Now I'm ready. You've been extremely patient."

"It's easy." And it had been, which should have surprised him. Normally he didn't like waiting for people.

"It's not easy for everyone. A lot of people are very impatient. They have to have everything happen right this minute, but you don't seem like that. You seem like the kind of person who's willing to delay gratification."

"That probably depends on the gratification." He was very much afraid that everything he was thinking was showing on his face.

She met his gaze and a becoming pink tinged her cheeks. "I suppose it does."

He wanted to kiss her so much he ached. But it was too soon. "Let's go get some dinner."

"Yes, let's."

As he followed her out the door and closed it behind him, he wondered if this was the way things had gone for those other couples taped to the dash of Mario's taxi. A feeling of inevitability was settling over him.

THE EXCITEMENT OF SHARING a restaurant meal with a certified New York City bachelor wiped out any lingering sadness Hannah felt over the loss of her clothes. They hadn't been practical in the first place, being drycleanable, but the price had lured her into buying them. Tomorrow she'd look for washable clothes and let Zach drive his hard bargain.

And didn't that sound sexy? She kept admiring how good he looked as she sat across the table from him at the Thai restaurant. He made her chicken with peanut sauce taste like the best meal she'd ever had. The restaurant had chosen blue neon as the light of choice, and the eerie glow turned the customers into a crowd of the undead, but Zach was the most handsome zombie in the room.

She was developing a giant crush on her one-person network. Standing in her hotel room talking about delayed gratification had nearly done her in. How embarrassing if she'd jumped the gun and planted one right on him.

That would have been jumping the gun, too. Instinctively she knew that. She didn't want to come across as some eager hick from Arizona who didn't know the rules. Of course she'd seen *Sex and the City,* but that was all about sophisticated New Yorkers getting involved with other sophisticated New Yorkers. She didn't want to come off as green as grass or hopelessly lacking in subtlety.

She could do subtle. She would let Zach make the first move toward getting physical. From the way he looked at her, she thought he wanted to, but he was restraining himself. That was her cue to restrain herself, which she was doing.

"Mario said you're an investment counselor," she said. "That seems like a very New York thing to be."

He made a face.

"What, you don't like it?"

"I like working with clients, but…the atmosphere of the company is very competitive, especially lately. There's this guy named Ed, who's in his fifties, been there a lot of years, but he doesn't push like he used to."

Hannah nodded. "Seems like people deserve to cut back at some point."

"Not according to my boss. He's ready to kick him out of his primo office location and put a top producer in there."

"Would that top producer by any chance be you?"

"Yeah, it would." Zach took a sip of his Thai iced coffee and set it down on the table. "And I appreciate the recognition, but I feel crummy about taking that office away from Ed."

"So don't take it away."

Zach laughed and shook his head. "You don't know Drake Medford. He'd see that as a sign of weakness. I'd lose all the ground I've gained."

"Excuse me for saying so, but your boss doesn't sound like a nice man."

"Nobody's ever accused him of being nice, that's for sure." Zach reached into his pocket. "Before I forget it, here are some people to contact about job interviews. It's not a huge list, but—"

"Are you kidding? This is great!" She glanced at the three names and numbers he'd written on the back of his business card. She didn't recognize any of the publishers listed after each name, but she might have to start at a small house and work her way up to the big boys and girls.

Even better than the numbers on the back was the info on the front. Now she had contact points for Zach, something she'd been missing. She should give him contact points in return.

Reaching into her purse, she pulled out the little notebook-and-pen gizmo her little sister, Cara, had given her before she left. "Here's my cell phone number, in case you should need it." She hoped he'd need it. Desperately.

"Thanks." He tucked the piece of paper in the inner pocket of his suit jacket. "Are you up for some dessert?"

"No place to put it." But she didn't want the night to end. "Could we take a walk, instead?"

"Sure." He signaled the waiter. "Where to?"

"Times Square!" When she saw his tolerant smile, she reconsidered. "Too corny, huh? I suppose real New Yorkers don't go to Times Square unless they're headed for a play."

"No, but let's go there, anyway."

"You're sure? I hate to make you endure the tourist thing, but I promised my brother and sister I'd get my picture taken in the middle of Times Square, and I...brought my camera." She pulled it out of her purse.

The waiter paused next to their table. "Would you like a picture of the two of you?"

Hannah imagined them as a couple of grinning corpses surrounded by a ghostly blue light, and she started to laugh.

Zach looked offended. "What's so funny about having our picture taken together? Do I have a piece of rice stuck in my teeth?"

"No, you look great. It's a wonderful idea." She couldn't say what she thought of the lighting in front of the waiter, so she handed him the camera. "Thanks."

The waiter backed up and motioned them to get closer together. Zach angled his chair sideways and reached across the small table to put his arm around Hannah.

When he cupped his warm hand around her bare arm, her heart began to beat so loud she was afraid he'd hear it. The waiter waved her closer, and she leaned in, putting her head almost next to Zach's. That gave her a delicious whiff of his aftershave. In no time she was imagining what it would be like to kiss him, then snuggle against that soft white shirt and loosen his silk tie.

The camera flashed, blinding her. At that moment,

whether it was a reflex or intentional, Zach's fingers tightened around her arm. Warmth coursed through her, and she didn't want to move…ever. "How about a second shot?" she asked.

"No problem." The waiter aimed the camera again.

This time Zach stroked her arm gently as the camera flashed. That was no reflex. That was intentional. He was touching her as if he liked the idea. Well, so did she. A lot.

"Those are two winners." The waiter handed the camera back to Hannah, and she had to move away from Zach to take it. Bummer. But her skin still tingled, reminding her that they'd made their first physical connection. She stayed high on that sensation as Zach paid the bill and they left the restaurant.

Still thinking of his hand stroking her arm, she shivered.

"Cold?" Immediately Zach took off his suit coat.

"Um, no…" Then she felt the cocoon of his coat settle around her shoulders and changed her mind. "Maybe a little."

"I thought so. We're not in Arizona. It's probably a hundred degrees there right now."

"So Mario told you I'm from Phoenix?" She'd secretly hoped Zach would take her hand as they walked along the sidewalk, but he made no move to do it. Well, holding hands in public was a statement, after all. Stroking someone's arm while having your picture taken was not. She could understand if Zach wasn't ready to make a statement.

"He mentioned you were from there. He thinks you're a hop, skip and a jump from the Grand Canyon."

"Not quite. Things aren't quite so close together in the western part of the country." She hugged his jacket close and inhaled *Eau de Zach*. He was right that she hadn't expected chilly weather. Tomorrow she might need to buy a light jacket, but for tonight, this was perfect. Romantic, even.

That made her remember the pictures the waiter had taken. "Do you want to see what our pictures look like? It's a digital camera."

"First I want to know why you laughed at the idea of taking a picture in the first place."

"You'll see." She pulled the camera out of her purse and clicked a button to turn on the tiny screen. Sure enough, they looked like two ghouls on Halloween. She handed him the camera. "Check it out."

"Whoa." He stopped walking and moved to the inside of the sidewalk. "Now, that's scary."

"I can erase them." She reached for the camera.

He pulled the camera out of reach. "Don't you dare! My nephews back home would love this. The Uncle Zach freak show. I want a copy."

"Great. I'll be the laughingstock of your hometown." But he wasn't worried about showing her around, which was nice. "So you're not from here, either?" Knowing that made him less intimidating.

"A little town in Illinois called Auburn. It's near Springfield."

"That explains why you don't sound like Mario."

He grinned and handed her the camera. "No, but I'm working on it. Promise you won't erase those pictures."

"I promise." As she was putting the camera back in her purse, a tattered young guy with long hair approached.

"Can you spare some change?" he asked.

Thrilled to be able to help, Hannah rummaged in her

large purse, searching for a can of tuna. "I have something even better."

"Folding money?" the guy asked hopefully.

"This." She held out the can. "Loaded with omega three."

The young man blinked and took it. "Huh." He stared at the can as if trying to decide what to do with it. Then he brightened. "Cool! This will make an awesome puck for street hockey! Thanks!"

"But I intended for you to…." She let her protest trail off as the guy sauntered away, tossing the can in the air and whistling.

"You can't save 'em all," Zach said gently.

"I know." Feeling deflated, she gazed after the young man as he crossed against the light, all the while juggling the can from one hand to the other. "This afternoon one person asked me if there was some way you could distill tuna. I told him I didn't think so. But three others seemed really glad to get it, so I don't think it was a total waste of suitcase space."

"It was a great use of suitcase space."

Something in his voice made her look up at him. One glance into his eyes and her heart started pounding again. Giving away tuna might have reaped an unexpected reward. Zach Evans was about to kiss her.

CHAPTER FOUR

ZACH HAD HELD OFF AS LONG as he could stand it. He'd been wanting to do this for two hours, and seeing the earnest way she'd offered up her can of tuna to the vagrant had sent him over the edge. Taking her firmly by the shoulders, he drew her close.

She came willingly, which was a good thing. If she'd resisted, it could have been very awkward. But she looked as ready to be kissed as any woman he'd held in his arms. He couldn't remember a time he'd anticipated the moment more, either.

Her eyes fluttered closed, and he took the time to savor the view of her face tilted up to catch the light from a nearby streetlamp. He took it all in—the daisies in her hair, the graceful sweep of her eyebrows, the pert shape of her nose, the generous fullness of her mouth. Her lips were parted just the slightest bit, which made him believe this kiss could progress nicely into something hot, wet and French.

She opened her eyes. "I thought you were going to kiss me."

"I am."

Her brown eyes were soft and dreamy. "Isn't everything supposed to move faster in New York?"

That made him smile. "You don't think this is fast? We just met this morning."

"Are you having second thoughts?"

"Oh, yeah. Second, third and fourth thoughts." And they all centered on Mario's dash.

She frowned. "Then you think kissing me is a bad idea?"

"No."

"Then what's wrong?"

"Nothing, and that's what worries me." He leaned closer. "Everything is exactly…right." And with a soft moan he gave himself up to her velvet mouth.

He should have known he'd find paradise there. The warning signs had been flashing from his first glimpse of her in the hotel lobby. Whoever had said that a kiss was just a kiss had never locked lips with Hannah.

She welcomed him with more enthusiasm than any poor mortal deserved. But deserving or not, he was going to take advantage of that delicious, moist and erection-producing welcome. He kissed her from one angle, then shifted to capture all that perfection from another, deeper, angle.

Although he longed to pull her tight against him, he didn't dare chance it. Once that happened, they'd never make it to Times Square. So he clutched her shoulders and centered all his attention on her marvelous, incredible mouth.

He supposed passing pedestrians stopped to stare. He and Hannah must be putting on quite a show, and normally he wasn't the type to do that. But this morning he'd met Hannah and his type might be about to change. Now he didn't give a damn what anyone else thought. He was too busy kissing a woman with daisies in her hair.

"Well, well, Evans. Quite a bit of salesmanship you have going on there."

It was the only voice that could have cut through his fog of passion. Lifting his head he found himself staring into the steely-blue eyes of Drake Medford. Medford's salt-and-pepper hair was perfectly styled and his suit impeccably pressed. Of all the sidewalks of New York, he had to walk down this one. Shit.

Slowly Zach released Hannah and straightened the jacket around her shoulders. He probably had lipstick all over his mouth. He resisted the urge to wipe it away. "Hannah Robertson, I'd like you to meet my boss, Drake Medford."

She glanced quickly up at Zach and crossed her eyes. He choked back laughter as she turned and held out her hand to the tall man standing behind her. "Hello, Mr. Medford. I've heard so much about you."

"Whereas I've heard zilch about you, young lady." He took her hand in both of his. "Evans, you've been holding out on me."

"The fact is, we've just—"

"Just reconnected after a long absence," Hannah said. "Zach and I kept missing each other, but here we are, united at last."

"You seem to be having quite a reunion party," Medford said. "And maybe I can give you even more reason to celebrate. Ed Hasbrook gave me the key to his corner office this afternoon. I know the reports aren't finalized for the month, but I see no problem with you moving in there tomorrow, Evans."

"Uh, that's great." Zach felt his curried beef turn to cement in his stomach.

"Try to contain your excitement, will you?" Medford looked annoyed. "The corner office is only the obvious change. I'm promoting you to vice president."

"That's very good news." Zach wished he could feel more jubilant, but he'd been a lot happier two minutes ago when he'd been kissing Hannah. "Of course, I can't help wondering where you're stashing Ed."

"I'd relegate him to a coat closet if I could, but we don't have an empty coat closet. I'm using some portable partitions in a corner of the outer office. Maybe he'll get the hint. It's one step closer to the front door."

"How long has he been with the company?" Hannah asked.

"Too long, Hannah." Medford had always been good about picking up on names. "He was good once, but he's lost a step. Your guy Zach, here, that's the kind of go-getter I'm looking for." He shoved back his cuff and glanced at his designer watch. "I'm late. Nice meeting you, Hannah. Zach, bring her around to the company picnic next month, why don't you? She looks like she'd play a mean game of volleyball." He winked at Hannah and hurried off.

"So there you have my big, bad boss." Zach sighed. "Poor Ed."

Hannah turned to face Zach. "You need to quit your job."

ZACH LOOKED AT HER AS IF she'd murdered a close relative. "Are you crazy? I've put eight years into that job."

"You've tolerated Drake Medford for eight years?" If so, her estimation of him would take a serious nosedive.

"Well, no. He came on board last fall. The office was underperforming and he was sent in to straighten things out."

She frowned. "By humiliating people like Ed?"

"Look, I may not like what's happening with Ed, but

Medford's done what he was sent to do. Everyone's working harder and making more, the ones who've stayed, anyway. All except for Ed, who's close to retirement."

"And is everyone happy? Except for Ed, of course, and you."

"I'm happy!" He flung out both arms. "I'm ecstatic! I'm making more money!"

"Are you happy? At dinner when I asked about your job you made a face."

His gaze was wary. "I don't know that I made a face, exactly."

"You most certainly did. Like this." She pulled her mouth down at the corners and scrunched up her eyes.

"That didn't have to be about my job. Maybe I bit into something I didn't like right at the moment you asked."

"It was about your job."

"Okay, so maybe it was about the job. Nobody's career is fun and games all the time. I can see now I wasn't working up to capacity. I'll bet that's what Adrienne meant when she—" He stopped, coughed and looked away. "Are we going to Times Square or what?"

Although Hannah wanted to finish the discussion, especially now that a woman's name had been thrown into it, she could tell that Zach's heels were dug in on this issue. She shouldn't have come right out and told him to quit his job. That wasn't her place. But he kissed like an angel, and a man who kissed like that didn't belong in an office with the devil himself.

She'd suspected the boss was bad news when Zach had told her about him during dinner. But now that she'd met the guy she knew for sure, and not just because he'd interrupted what had been the primo kissing experience of her life. Drake Medford was completely unacquainted with the concept of human kindness. He would kill himself laughing if he knew about her tuna project.

"Let's go to Times Square," she said.

"Good." Zach sounded immensely relieved. He still made no move to take her hand.

She thought he might have, especially after that kiss, except that his boss had come along and messed up the mood. Hannah thought Medford took pleasure in messing up other people's moods. He could have walked on by and left them to their kissing, but that wasn't in his nature.

No, she really didn't like the man. Neither did Zach, but he wasn't going to admit it. "Would you do me one little favor?" she asked.

"Sure, as long as it doesn't involve courting economic disaster."

"It doesn't." She must have really scared him, suggesting that he leave his job. Maybe because she had no financial stability at the moment, she'd forgotten that most people liked to know where their next paycheck was coming from.

"Then ask away," he said.

"When you're in the office tomorrow, I'd rather you didn't mention the thing about me giving away tuna."

He glanced at her. "What makes you think I'd do that?"

"Oh, you know."

"No, I don't." His voice had gone quiet. "Explain it to me."

"Water cooler stuff. Medford makes some reference to catching us kissing, and you tell the very entertaining story about me giving away tuna to a guy who's going to use the can for a hockey puck. I can understand how—"

"You think I'd make fun of what you're doing to get a laugh from the people I work with?"

Whoops. "Obviously not," she said quickly. "Sorry to imply that you might."

"Apology accepted."

She snuck a peek at his firm profile. She'd insulted him, no doubt about that. But she'd found out some valuable info in the process. The deeper she probed into Zach Evans, the more she liked what she found. It wasn't realistic to think that the first eligible man she met in the city would become someone very special, but she couldn't throw off the premonition that Zach was special.

TWENTY MINUTES LATER, Zach posed Hannah smack-dab in the middle of the gaudy, crowded, most neon-infested section of Times Square. Even so, she was the brightest thing in the frame. Her natural glow put the glittering lights to shame.

She'd taken off his jacket so her relatives wouldn't get the idea that it was cold in New York. If she was cold, she didn't act like it. Instead she flung her arms out and turned this way and that like a high-fashion model at a photo shoot.

He was fascinated with her. Too bad she thought he should quit his job, because he knew she really did, even though they'd dropped the subject for now. Well, he'd cut her some slack on that opinion. She was still very naive. Let her struggle in the big city for a while and see how she felt about throwing away perfectly good jobs just because the boss wasn't a sweetheart.

Without his job, he wouldn't be able to buy bouquets of flowers or take a date out for a nice dinner. He was finally making the money that Adrienne had thought he should make, not that he was doing it to prove anything to her. She'd never know.

So what if he didn't play as much racquetball? The guys he'd played with had decided to leave the company, anyway. One of them was still in town and struggling to make ends meet. The other had left New York completely. Zach wasn't about to run home to Auburn because his boss wasn't sensitive to the needs of his employees.

Granted, a part of him would love to tell Medford to take the job and shove it. The guy was an unfeeling son of a bitch to be treating Ed that way. But this was the business world, not *Sesame Street*. Ed knew the score and was choosing not to play Medford's game. Ed would have to take the consequences for that.

Zach took pictures of Hannah until she called out that they had enough and ran back over to him. He wouldn't have minded taking a few more. Watching her perform for him as her personal photographer was more fun than he'd had in a long while.

"I don't want to overdo it." She accepted the jacket he held out. This time she put her arms in the sleeves, which were too long and made her look adorable.

"Why not overdo it?" He thought about the meager supply of pictures he sent home to Illinois. "My experience with families is that you can't overdo the snapshots. You need some for Mom, Dad, brothers and sisters, grandmothers and grandfathers, aunts and uncles."

She gazed at him wistfully. "It must be nice, having all those people to give pictures to."

"You don't?"

She shook her head. "Just my brother and sister." Then she smiled. "Don't look like that, all pitying. It's okay."

"I'll accept that it's okay. You're living proof." But his heart went out to her, anyway. "What happened?"

She tucked the camera back in her purse. "I was thirteen when my mom died, which was lucky because I was old enough to help Dad with my brother and sister, who were only four. Poor Dad was never the same after Mom died, and I had the feeling he was hanging on until I was eighteen, so the twins wouldn't end up in foster care. He died a month after my eighteenth birthday."

He was beginning to understand her need to take care of the whole world after conditioning like that. "But what about other relatives? Grandparents, aunts, uncles?"

"Both my parents were only children, nerdy types who married late in life. I barely remember my grandparents. My mom had me at the age of forty-one, and then, because she was always ready to buck convention, decided to try having a second child at fifty. She ended up with the twins. Who are both brilliant, since you asked."

"I'm guessing you're no slouch in the brains department, either."

"I do okay, but nothing like the twins. They kept me on my toes, but they've turned into adults who can actually take care of themselves now. It's a miracle."

He thought she might be the miracle for weathering all those hard knocks and keeping her sunny disposition. "Did you feed them lots of tuna?"

She laughed. "Good one. Yes, I did. Brain food." She gazed around at the crowds milling through Times Square. "This place is amazing. I had great plans to stay up until midnight seeing more of the city at night, but I'm starting to fade."

"You mean after thirty-six hours with no sleep, you're tired?" He grinned at her. "What a wimp."

"Embarrassing, isn't it? But I think we'd better start making that trek back to my hotel or you might have to carry me."

That didn't sound so bad, although from a practical standpoint he probably couldn't make it, which wouldn't play well.

But he had a better idea. "Hang on a minute." Unclipping his phone from his belt, he dialed Mario's cell. "You available?" he asked. Having Mario drive them to the hotel would keep the lid on Zach's libido.

He also didn't want to be accused of taking advantage of a jet-lagged woman. As an added advantage, after they dropped Hannah off at the Pearson, Zach could have a chat with Mario about Hannah's views on his current job situation. Mario would understand that a guy couldn't just up and quit a steady job, especially after being promoted to vice president.

"Yeah, I'm available," Mario said. "I just delivered Barbra Streisand to the Plaza."

"You did not."

"I did so. Ask anybody. She was supposed to meet James Brolin there for some shindig. You need a ride?"

"Yep. I'm in Times Square."

"Alone?"

Zach glanced over at Hannah. "Nope."

"Who?"

"Mario, I'm gonna make you wait in suspense."

"I'll be right there."

Zach clipped the phone to his belt. "Mario's on his way."

"But that'll cost money. I can walk."

"It's not that much, and I'm sure Mario would love to hear how your first day went."

She relented with a smile. "It would be nice to see him again. I—" She was interrupted by an earsplitting whistle about ten feet away.

A cab swung over to the curb and the whistler jumped in.

Hannah watched the process and turned to Zach. "Can you whistle like that?"

"If I need to."

"I would love to learn how. I don't expect to be taking cabs much, but if I could whistle like that I'd feel like a real New Yorker."

"Then I'll teach you. I don't take cabs a lot, myself, but—"

"Aha!" She pointed a finger at him. "Because they're expensive, right?"

"Because a bus or the subway can serve the same purpose and I'm promoting mass transit, okay?"

She nodded. "I buy that argument, but I'll also bet that once you live here full-time, you consider your pocket-book and learn to do without taxis except in emergencies."

"Which this is. You're exhausted."

"A little." In fact, her legs trembled from the effort of holding herself upright.

"I don't think you can be a little exhausted. It's like saying you're a little pregnant."

"Then I'm a lot exhausted."

He couldn't help himself. He put his arm around her and tucked her against his side. "Lean on me."

"Okay." She nestled close and laid her head on his shoulder. "This would be the cue for your boss to happen along."

"Not unless he's stalking me. I've been eating on Restaurant Row for years and I've never once seen him there."

"I think it was meant to happen that way."

"Why is that?" He gazed into her tired but contented eyes and wondered if this was how she'd look after a round of excellent sex. Highly inappropriate thoughts. He was taking her home so she could get some sleep. He hoped to God they'd already switched her to a dry room.

"I think I was supposed to meet your boss," she said.

Her reasoning was pretty transparent. "So that you could point out to me that he's the devil incarnate and if I value my soul, I will leave that firm before I'm damned forever?"

She gazed at him dreamily. "Something like that."

"I'm not quitting my job, Hannah."

"You should." She covered a yawn. "You're a fantastic kisser."

CHAPTER FIVE

HANNAH KNEW SHE NEEDED sleep when she started babbling things that were better left unsaid. Fortunately, before Zach could ask her what she meant about quitting his job because of the way he kissed, which must have made her sound like a lunatic, a horn bleated right beside them.

"That would be Mario." Zach kept his arm around her as he guided her over to the waiting cab. "Time to get you to bed."

"Sounds wonderful." She was tired, but not *that* tired. She wanted a bed, all right, and Zach in the middle of it. It wasn't going to happen, not tonight, at least. That was for the best. She intended to be in New York for the rest of her life. She didn't have to have sex on her very first night. Their outstanding kiss was memorable enough.

"Hi, Mario," she said as Zach handed her elegantly into the backseat of the cab. "Thanks for picking us up."

"Glad to do it." Mario's wide grin was reflected in the rearview mirror. "Whatcha been up to?"

"Zach took me for Thai food."

"Nice."

"It was nice." Zach got in and closed the door. "But this woman's exhausted."

Mario chuckled, obviously in a very good mood. "Tried to do everything in one day, did you, Hannah?"

"Sort of. Zach's going to teach me how to whistle for a taxi." She settled back against the seat with gratitude.

"You know, New York Survival Skills 101," Zach said as he climbed in beside her. "But not tonight. She's had enough for one day."

"Right." Hannah had sort of hoped Zach would put his arm around her after he climbed in, but he didn't. She could understand it, though. It wasn't as if they were going to make out in the back of Mario's cab.

But then Mario took off with his usual speed, throwing her into Zach's lap. "Whoops." She reached for the armrest to steady herself, but Mario whipped around another corner and she was thrown against Zach again.

This time Zach wrapped his arm around her and held on. "I'd forgotten that the ride is wilder in the backseat," he murmured.

"No problem." She was grateful for Mario's driving if it meant being close to Zach for the trip back to her hotel.

"How'd the tuna go over?" Mario asked.

"Some liked it and some didn't." Hannah paused to see if Zach would add anything, but he stayed silent, letting her control the conversation. She gave him points for that. "One guy said the can would make a good puck for street hockey," she said.

Mario laughed and shook his head. "It takes all kinds. And that doesn't mean he won't eat the stuff after he's banged the can around for a while. You did a good deed, bringing the tuna."

"Most definitely," Zach said.

Life didn't get much better than this, cruising through the heart of Manhattan, tucked against Zach Evans while both Zach and Mario agreed that her tuna was a good idea. She'd anticipated loving a lot of things in New York, but she'd never imagined a cab ride would be near the top of her list. Or that a kiss would rank higher than a view from the top of the Empire State Building.

"Here we are." Mario pulled up in front of the Pearson.

"I'll just see her to the door," Zach said.

Mario nodded. "I'll wait."

Hannah considered protesting, but she really did want Zach to walk her to the door. Even with Mario there, Zach might give her a quick kiss. He might not, but unless he walked her to the door, there was no chance.

"Thanks for a great evening," she said.

"It was fun. I just thought of something. Do you have an interview tomorrow morning?"

"No, fortunately. The first one's at two. I'll have time to get some different clothes."

"I'll only have about an hour at lunch, so—"

She met his gaze. "You don't have to do this. I can shop on my own."

"I want to. We can meet at a coffee stand run by a friend of mine." He pulled out another business card from his wallet and scribbled an address on the back of it. "I'll be there about noon."

"Then so will I." She took the card and smiled at him. "Thank you, Zach. For everything."

"I had a great time." He reached up and tucked a daisy more securely into her hair. "See you tomorrow."

"You bet. Bye, Zach." It looked like he wouldn't kiss

her, after all. Well, she could live with that. She turned toward the door.

"Hannah." He caught her by the shoulders and spun her around. His kiss was softer and sweeter than the first one, but because it was unexpected, it still took her breath away.

"Tomorrow," he said with a tiny smile. Then he walked back to the cab and got into the front seat with Mario.

Heart thudding, she watched the cab pull away and followed the zigzag path of its red taillights until she couldn't distinguish them from the others going down the street. Finally, taking a deep breath, she pulled the lapels of Zach's coat closer together and started toward the front door.

Zach's coat! She hadn't thought to give it back to him. And being the considerate guy he was, he hadn't asked. But that meant that he didn't have her cell phone number if he should need to cancel tomorrow's shopping trip.

Then Hannah smiled to herself. After that quick kiss, she didn't think he'd cancel. She thought he might be as eager to see her as she was to see him.

What a coincidence that Mario's networking contact had turned out to be a guy who seemed so right for her. That was amazing, considering the millions of people living here. Then again, what if it hadn't been pure coincidence? She remembered the pictures on Mario's dash. They'd all been couples. What if…no, that was too crazy, even for a place like New York City.

MARIO ARCHED BOTH EYEBROWS as he glanced over at Zach. "Dinner, huh?"

"Yeah, and I'd thank you not to gloat about it. This was a matchmaking deal from the beginning, wasn't it?"

Mario cut in front of a limo. "Maybe."

"Just as I thought. And you swore it wasn't." Considering how the evening had turned out, Zach couldn't get very upset.

"All's fair in love and war."

Zach sighed. "Yeah, you win. She's hot, and I'm…attracted to her. I won't deny it. But she's a dreamer. I don't see her lasting more than a few days in this town."

"Really? How come?"

"Here's a prime example. After dinner we ran into my boss, and just like that, she thinks I should quit my job."

"So you can get another one that pays better? Because so help me, if this is yet another woman after money, then I'm hanging up my—"

"No, she's not another Adrienne. She's the exact opposite of Adrienne, in fact. She wasn't the least bit worried about the consequences if I quit. She just thinks I should get far away from Drake Medford. Never mind that I could end up on a street corner selling pencils."

"You wouldn't do that, would you? Quit, I mean." Mario sounded worried.

"Not in a million years."

"That's good. Quitting your job is not a wise move."

"I know that, but she doesn't."

"Ah, she's new in town. She doesn't know how tough it is to make a living here. She'll wise up." Mario landed on the horn as someone dared to swing in front of him. "Were you able to help her get any interviews?"

"We'll see. The person with the best contact happens to be Ed."

"Ah. And you don't want to ask him for help."

"Come on, Mario, would you?"

"Probably not. Maybe she'll do fine without that contact. I take it you're going to see her again?"

"We're meeting at noon at Iris's coffee stand." Zach told Mario about the sage and the sprinkler incident. "I'm going to try to steer her toward more subdued stuff. I think she'll interview better if her clothes aren't so bright."

Mario smiled. "I kind of like that about her."

"Me, too. But I think she'll have a better chance if she looks more like a New Yorker." Zach pulled out money as they cruised to a stop in front of his apartment building.

"Nope." Mario held up his hand. "My treat."

"Hey, you have to stop doing this. You'll go broke."

Mario adjusted his Giants cap. "Don't worry about it. I could quit tomorrow and be fine."

"I suppose if you were careful, you could." The thought had never occurred to Zach. "I figured you drove a cab because you wanted a bigger nest egg for retirement."

"Nah. I love the job." His cell phone rang. "Gotta go. Keep me informed, okay?"

"Sure, Mario. And if I didn't, you'd probably find a way to tail me, knowing you." With a grin, he climbed out of the cab.

So Mario loved his job. Zach envied him. These days he dreaded going into the office, especially tomorrow, when he'd be moving into Ed's spot. Maybe he should take Hannah's advice and quit. Then he could follow Mario's example and drive a cab.

MARIO USED HIS HANDS-FREE device to answer his cell phone. He knew who it was. He'd called Iris on his way over to pick up Zach and Zach's mysterious companion. She was probably dying to know who it had been.

"So? Who was he with?" She spoke in her normal tone because she was using the phone in her apartment instead of her cell.

"It was Hannah, the woman I'm trying to set him up with."

"*Bueno!* But you don't sound very happy, *amigo.*"

"Well, I hope I didn't make a serious mistake this time. I wanted her to slow him down some, get him to smell the roses, but instead this woman's advising him to quit his job! I'd hoped he'd fall in love, not end up in the poorhouse."

"See what can happen when you go messing with people's lives?" There was no bite to her comment, though.

"Ah, it'll probably be okay. Zach's too sensible to do something so irresponsible." Mario heard a whistle and eased over to the curb.

"He is sensible, that one."

"You'll get a look at the two of them together tomorrow. They're coming by the coffee stand at noon."

"Will you be there?" Iris sounded as if she'd like that.

"Not right then. I have to sleep sometime. But I'll see you early, like usual."

"*Bueno.*"

Mario savored the wealth of enthusiasm in that two-syllable answer. One of these nights he should just take the evening off and ask her out. But he hadn't dated in a while. A long while. He was chicken. "Got a fare. See you later."

HANNAH HAD TAKEN THE TIME to wash out her yellow sundress and hang it to dry before going to bed. She'd originally liked the dress and it was collecting some amazing memories, but she was the kind of girl who enjoyed changing her look. She could hardly wait to get some new duds. At least the warm sunshine felt great on her bare arms and shoulders.

Carrying Zach's coat over her arm, she stepped off the bus within half a block from the address Zach had given her. The sound of Latina music made her homesick for Arizona as she walked over to the source of the music, the coffee stand where Zach had promised to meet her. The olive-skinned woman running it was doing a brisk business.

Whatever she was serving smelled delicious, and Hannah decided to buy something for both her and Zach, since she was a little early and he hadn't arrived yet. They wouldn't have time for a real meal, and she wanted to treat him to some food after all the help he'd been. She had another reward in mind for later on, if all went well. The hotel had decided to give her a suite, and she felt the urge to share it.

She stood in line and finally came face-to-face with the woman working there. "What smells so good?" she asked.

The woman smiled, revealing beautiful white teeth. Her colorful earrings jangled as she nodded enthusiastically. "Everything, *señorita*."

"Ah. *Habla español?*" Hannah felt more at home every minute. Some of her best friends in Phoenix were Hispanic and she'd soaked up the language.

"Sì!" The woman seemed delighted to discover another Spanish speaker, and before long they were chattering away.

Once names were exchanged, Iris became even friendlier, and in about thirty seconds Hannah figured out that she'd been expected at the coffee stand. Even more interesting, Mario had been the one to alert Iris. The two seemed to know Zach very well, and Hannah's suspicions grew. She tried to think of the Spanish word for what she wanted to ask, but couldn't.

Finally she decided to switch to English. "Iris, does Mario like to play matchmaker?"

Iris clapped her hand over her mouth and her cheeks got very pink.

Hannah stared at her. "He *does*." Suddenly all that had happened made perfect sense.

"Of course he does," Zach said, walking up to the coffee stand. "We're his latest project."

Hannah spun to face him. "You knew that?"

"Not immediately. He swore to me that he was trying to help out someone who was light on contacts in the city." Zach didn't seem too upset about being manipulated.

Hannah was busy processing how she felt about it. She'd liked the scenario better when she'd thought it was pure coincidence, a touch of kismet. Instead she'd been manipulated by a wily cab driver. And yet…could she say she was sorry she'd met Zach?

"So when did you figure it out?" she asked.

"When I saw you standing in the lobby yesterday morning."

"Because?"

He looked into her eyes. "Because you're beautiful."

Oh. A girl couldn't get too indignant after a response like that, could she?

"Mario, he means well," Iris said. "He only wants to see his friends happy."

"I'm sure he does." Conflicting emotions rolled

through her. "But…no offense, Zach…I've always liked the idea of choosing for myself."

"Me, too. But I decided not to let that keep me from spending a little time with you. And that's all I have in mind. Just because ninety percent of Mario's fix-ups turn into marriages doesn't mean—"

"Ninety percent?"

"Good instincts, that Mario," Iris said.

Hannah took a deep breath. Despite how much she liked Zach, she couldn't help feeling railroaded, almost like a mail-order bride. A guy with a ninety-percent ratio in matching couples had targeted her for Zach. Mario knew Zach fairly well, but he didn't know Hannah hardly at all. How could he guess what she wanted or needed at this stage in her life?

She gazed at Zach. "Look, I got to New York yesterday. I'm looking for a new job, a new life. One thing I'm not looking for is a husband."

Zach nodded. "Fair enough. I'm not looking for a wife, either."

"A steady girlfriend?" She wasn't sure that she wanted to fill that slot, either. If they'd met by accident, it would be different, but this had been plotted out. She wasn't a rat in somebody's science experiment, damn it.

"I'm not looking for a steady girlfriend, either," Zach said.

A hot, temporary lover? She thought of her plans for the suite tonight. What a shame if she turned out to be the only one using that king-size bed and Jacuzzi.

Zach sighed. "Hannah, I can see you're upset about this. We don't have to spend the lunch hour shopping together if you don't want to. We can go our separate ways, and in a city of this size, we'll probably never see each other again."

Now, that was an unpleasant thought. She'd had fun with Zach last night. More than fun. He kissed better than any guy in recent memory. She shouldn't let that ninety-percent thing scare her into giving up those kisses forever. Hot kisses did not a wedding make.

"I'd like to go shopping," she said. "I just want us to understand each other."

"I think we do."

She took a deep breath. "I think so, too." Maybe her big bed and hot tub wouldn't go to waste, after all.

CHAPTER SIX

ZACH WAS GLAD HE AND Hannah had cleared the air. He'd had a rough morning between moving into the corner office and watching Ed set up in the little space Medford was giving him. Spending some carefree time with Hannah during his lunch hour had been something he'd looked forward to. If she'd wanted to end their relationship, that would have made this a totally sucky day.

Instead they munched on Iris's *pastels de carne,* meat-filled pastries Hannah had insisted on buying for both of them, as they walked to the first resale shop a couple of blocks away. Iris had suggested Zach leave the suit jacket Hannah had returned at the coffee stand and pick it up on his way back. As she'd taken it from him, she'd murmured an apology for causing problems.

Zach had assured her that it was better to have everything out in the open. Before he'd left, Iris had whispered that she really liked Hannah. Well, so did he. That still didn't mean they'd end up on the ninety-percent side of Mario's record.

When they arrived at the first resale shop, Zach saw a women's black business suit in the window. "There you go." He pointed to it. "If that fits you, it would take you through all your interviews."

Hannah gazed at the suit and wrinkled her nose. "It's so *black*."

"Right. People tend to wear a lot of black in New York."

"If you'll excuse my saying so, I think that's boring." Hannah opened the door of the shop and walked in.

In fifteen minutes they walked out again. Hannah carried a bag that contained a blue-and-gold dress and she wore her other purchase, a bright green blouse paired with a skirt that included every color in the rainbow. Zach gave her credit for shopping speed, and he had to admit she looked great in the clothes, but she bore no resemblance to a typical New Yorker.

At least, thanks to his bargaining skills, she hadn't paid much for any of it. In the second shop, it was the same song, second verse. Zach tried in vain to suggest more subdued outfits, but Hannah fell in love with a bright purple suit with turquoise trim. She said she had a necklace from Arizona that would look great with it.

"Now this, I would buy in black." She reached for something on a rack of new clothes.

Zach stared at the flimsy negligee. Mostly it was transparent, except for little bits of fake fur here and there. The thought of Hannah wearing it threatened to provide him with an embarrassing erection.

He stepped behind a display table to conceal the evidence. "It's nice."

"I think so, too." She checked the size. "Perfect. I'm getting it."

With the negligee thrown into the mix, Zach was so distracted that he forgot to bargain. He didn't even realize it until Hannah spoke up as they were leaving the shop.

"I guess you thought those prices were better than the first place," she said.

He didn't dare admit that he'd been too busy thinking about her wearing that black number to think about prices. "Yeah, I think they were priced about right."

"Me, too. And you can't very well bargain on something new, like the nightie I bought."

He started to speak and only a croak came out. He cleared his throat. "True."

"Zach, you'll never guess what the hotel gave me as a replacement room."

"What's that?"

"A suite! Now, granted, a suite at the Pearson isn't exactly a suite at the Plaza, but I have this *huge* king-size bed and a big Jacuzzi in the bathroom. With a setup like that, I really need this nightie. All I have is a sleep shirt. This is not a sleep shirt kind of room."

"Doesn't sound like it." And he was a dead man. Now he'd be able to think of nothing else but Hannah prancing around that suite, red hair bouncing, as the transparent negligee floated around her body. "Um, would you like to have dinner again tonight at seven?" Surely she could see right through that and know what he was really after.

If she did, she didn't let on. "I think dinner sounds lovely. Then I can tell you all about my interviews." She glanced at her watch. "Yikes. It's late. Maybe I should splurge and take a cab over there."

"I'll get you one." He spotted a taxi half a block away. Amazingly, he was able to subdue his lust long enough to produce a decent whistle.

"See? That's what I want you to teach me how to do. You used your tongue and your teeth to make that sound, didn't you?"

"Um, yeah." And he was ready to deploy those resources tonight in her suite, if he got the opportunity.

"So you'll teach me tonight?"

"Absolutely." *Anything you want to learn.* He opened the cab door and helped her in. "Good luck with those interviews."

"Thanks! See you at seven!"

He stood there in a daze, knowing that he was at least a half hour past his normal lunch hour, knowing that Medford would notice and think he was slacking off, and yet he couldn't get himself to care. He had clients to call, business to transact. He had his new desk to organize.

And nothing mattered but seeing Hannah again in five and a half hours. A king-size bed, a black negligee and Hannah. What could be more important than that?

THE INTERVIEWS HADN'T BEEN particularly promising. Hannah had interviewed for and been hired for plenty of jobs in her life. At first she'd needed to earn enough money to keep the family together, and after that she'd worked her way through college. She could tell when a potential employer was interested and when they weren't. So far, she'd felt no positive signs that she had a chance at a job.

But she had a date with Zach, a new dress to wear with her favorite turquoise necklace and a nightie to put on later, if all went as she'd hoped. This time she met Zach in the lobby.

"You were right about the dress." He held out a single rose, an exotic violet color that blended perfectly with her outfit.

She broke off the stem and tucked the rose behind her ear. "Glad you like it."

"Very much." His gaze lingered on the spot where she'd tucked the rose in her hair.

"I hope you don't mind." She'd been playing pretty fast and loose with his flower gifts, and they couldn't be cheap. This rose looked pricier than your average red one. "Maybe I should have taken it upstairs and put it in some water."

"No." He took her hand and led her to the hotel's front door. "I pictured you tucking it into your hair. I've never known a woman who likes flowers in her hair before. I'm starting to see what a great idea it is."

"My mother used to." It was one of her fondest memories, her mother with flowers in her hair. Soon little Hannah had wanted flowers in her hair, too, and her mother had obliged, plucking them from their backyard garden. A couple of teachers' salaries didn't pay for many florist deliveries.

"It's a wonderful tradition." He squeezed her hand as they stepped out onto the busy streets of New York.

She couldn't believe how much difference twenty-four hours made. The night before she'd been eager to be part of the crowds, part of the excitement that was the city. Tonight she longed to be alone with Zach.

"Mario sends his apologies," Zach said.

"You invited him to dinner?" That startled her.

"No. I told him you were upset about being hand-picked to be my blushing bride. He apologized for meddling with your future. And he also thinks quitting my job would be crazy."

"Oh." She thought about that as she fell into step beside Zach. It didn't escape her notice that tonight they were walking hand in hand. "So is he sorry for meddling in my future, or sorry because I'm in favor of you quitting your job?"

Zach grinned. "A little of both. But I told him not to

worry about the job. I'm staying. The 'meddling in your life part,' though, deserves an apology."

"I accept it. Like Iris said, he means well." Hannah had taken some time to think about her recommendation that Zach should leave his job, especially after getting the cold shoulder during her interviews today. "I suppose I was meddling in *your* life, telling you to quit."

"You just got to town. You don't know how tough it is."

"I have a better idea after this afternoon."

Zach made a low sound of sympathy. "No nibbles?"

"I'm not sure there was fish in the river. I heard stories about the number of qualified applicants. And I don't think they were particularly impressed when I told them this was my first trip to New York."

"It's not easy." Zach rubbed his thumb over the back of her hand. "Have you called any of the people I gave you?"

"I did, after I came back to the hotel. Nobody's hiring right now. I could fill out an application, take an editing test, but they warned me it could be months before anything opens up."

"I'm sorry, Hannah. But don't give up."

"Are you kidding? It's only my first day of interviews. I'm not even close to giving up. Sure, I would have loved to get a job right away, but that's not the real world." She glanced at him. "I kept my eyes open, and you're right. Lots of people dress in black."

"Want to go back to the resale shop tomorrow and buy that little suit in the window?"

"Not yet. I like to think I might bring a new perspective, and if I dress like everyone else, they won't see that." She could feel his hesitation. "You don't agree with that, do you."

"I can't decide if I should encourage you to blend in, or if I should jump outside the box with you."

As the implication of that settled over her, she had serious reservations about her influence on him. Last night she'd blithely told him to quit his job if he didn't like it. What if he took her advice and ended up in financial trouble? She'd be responsible.

She waited until they were seated at the Italian restaurant he'd picked for tonight and each of them had a glass of Chianti. "Remember when I said that you shouldn't work for a guy like Medford anymore?"

"I remember, and I've been giving it more thought."

"Don't."

His eyebrows lifted. "Why not? He hasn't reformed in the past twenty-four hours. He might even be worse. Every time he walks past Ed's cubby in the outer office, he makes a sarcastic remark."

"Maybe Ed needs to take care of that. Hitting the pavement this afternoon gave me a dose of reality. I still expect to get hired, and I hope on my terms. But you have a job, and you should look around a little, put out some feelers, before you jump ship."

He gazed at her over the rim of his wineglass, a tender smile warming his expression. "I'll take that under advisement. But for now, let's drink to your success."

"I'd like that." As their glasses touched, she couldn't find it in her heart to be angry with Mario. Without his meddling, she'd have no one to share her job search...or her roomy suite.

She'd created quite a welcome for Zach—the radio tuned to a jazz station with the volume down low, dabs of perfume on the lightbulbs and sprinkled on the sheets, her black nightie laid across the foot of the bed and two condoms on the pillow. She could hardly wait for him to see it.

HE WOULDN'T SLEEP WITH HER. About the time the waiter brought the dessert tray and they each decided against having any, Zach made a similar decision about having sex with Hannah. And he'd even brought condoms because he'd thought he might get an invitation to her room tonight.

The truth was, he plain didn't deserve it. Here she was struggling to establish herself, and he wasn't man enough to talk with Ed and get her the contact that would make all the difference. He must have subconsciously hoped she'd find a job this afternoon on her own.

But she hadn't, and Zach had a bad feeling that she wouldn't find one easily. How long before her sunny outlook dimmed and she decided to head back to Arizona? Zach could change all that. Ed's client would be perfect—a vice president at a major company that edited a huge fiction list.

Zach even knew that Ed would be happy to help. He was that kind of guy. But Zach's conscience wouldn't allow him to ask for that help unless it included standing up to Medford on Ed's behalf, and that would cause a showdown. Most people didn't survive a showdown with Medford.

Then Zach might be the one pounding the pavement, and most likely without a glowing reference in his pocket. He thought about the years he'd spent getting a foothold here, the clients he'd have to leave and the very real possibility that he'd end up like his buddy, forced to go back to his old hometown.

Besides all that, what kind of relationship could he expect with Hannah if he was out of work? She might not be money-conscious like Adrienne, but he didn't relish the idea of trying to keep a romance going while he scrambled to make ends meet. He had some savings, but not enough to last very long.

So unless he was prepared to be her knight in shining armor, unless he was willing to leave his job and take the consequences of that, he had no right to climb into her bed. From the way she was looking at him, she expected to end the night that way. She wouldn't have bought the negligee and mentioned the amenities of her new room if she didn't expect that.

Oh, God, how he wanted to. All through the meal he'd watched her with lust burning in his veins. He longed to comb his hands through her hair and kiss that beautiful mouth until they were both panting. He'd tried not to spend too much time focusing on the way her delicate turquoise-and-silver necklace dipped into her cleavage.

Maybe she intended for him to focus his attention there. She'd toyed with the necklace a few times, and he thought that might be deliberate. She was definitely flirting with him in other ways, too. Her laughter bubbled like champagne, and she found reasons to reach across the table and lightly touch his hand. Then there were the coy looks and the veiled sexual references.

He'd loved every minute of it. And hated that the evening wouldn't go the way it should go. Mario had no idea what a pickle he'd put him in. Zach had no intention of telling him, either.

As they left the restaurant, Hannah took his hand. "Are you going to teach me how to whistle?"

"Sure." That much he could do. They were approaching a vacant bus-stop bench. "Come over here and sit down. I can't teach you while we're walking." And after he finished giving whistling instructions, he'd tell her, as gently as he could, that they wouldn't be spending the night together.

He wasn't sure yet how to say it so that she wouldn't feel rejected. Giving her the real reason wouldn't work. She'd already told him he should hang on to his job, so she'd refuse to let him jeopardize it for her. He didn't think she'd understand that he couldn't take her to bed without making that sacrifice. Women thought differently about such things.

They settled on the hard bench and he turned to face her so that their knees were touching. "To start with, you might have to use your fingers. That's how I learned."

"How old were you?"

"About ten."

"*Ten.*" She groaned. "What if I'm too old to learn?"

"Nah. As long as you have a mouth, teeth and a tongue, you can learn."

"I have all those things."

Did she ever. He wondered if he'd be able to do this without kissing her and putting those components to a different use. "Okay, stick a finger in each corner of your mouth like this."

She mimicked him.

It was so cute that he wanted to grab her right then and there. Somehow he restrained himself. "Then put your tongue behind your top teeth, like this."

Nodding, she followed his lead.

"Now blow out." He whistled softly through his

teeth. He didn't want either a cab or a passing woman to get the wrong idea.

She produced a little wheezing sound, but it wasn't a whistle. "Rats. I'll never catch a cab with that lame tootle."

He steeled himself against the urge to kiss that adorable, nonwhistling mouth. "No, but that's the idea. Just work with it. I had to practice quite a while before I made a real whistle."

She tried again, and a little tweet came out. "There!" She beamed at him. "Now, *that* has promise. Come on, let's go back to the hotel. I'll practice as we walk along."

He should follow through with his plan and tell her now that when they got to the hotel, he'd be saying good-night. But she looked so happy that he decided not to have that conversation yet. He wasn't sure exactly what he was going to say, anyway. Maybe he could think of something while she was practicing her whistle.

"All right." He stood and took her hand. "Let's go."

CHAPTER SEVEN

HANNAH PRACTICED HER whistle on the walk back to the Pearson, but she had trouble concentrating as they drew closer. Now that the moment was almost here, she was nervous. Something seemed to be going on with Zach, but she couldn't put her finger on what it was.

Partway through dinner his mood had changed. Until that moment she'd been sure that he was thinking the same way she was—that they should enjoy that suite together tonight. Now she wasn't so sure.

But if she didn't ask him to come up, she'd always wonder if they could have spent the night wrapped in each other's arms. She hadn't made it to New York by being a coward, so there was no point in starting to act like one now. She would ask him, and if he said no, she'd…well, she'd probably be devastated.

No, damn it, she wouldn't be devastated! She would take it with a smile, figuring he was the one losing out. But if he said yes…oh, the glory of that! They would set the night on fire.

She didn't want to have this scene right outside the front door of the hotel, so about half a block away she stopped walking and turned to him. Her heart was beating so fast that she was breathless. She paused to gulp some air. This was silly, being so nervous over such a simple thing. She wasn't a virgin, for heaven's sake.

Except this wasn't a simple thing. She couldn't shake the feeling that having sex with Zach would have vast repercussions. And although she wasn't a virgin, she didn't have a lot of experience with asking a man to share her bed. Usually the guy had been the one asking her.

Maybe Zach would still do that. She hesitated a moment to give him that chance. He must know she wanted him to.

He cleared his throat. "Hannah, I—"

"Of course. Of course you can come up."

He looked stricken. "It would be better if I didn't."

Icy disappointment and humiliation slid over her. She wanted to and he didn't. How awkward. "Of course. I…didn't mean to…" She had no clue how to smooth this over.

And she wanted to know why he was rejecting her. Was it something stupid, like she'd accidentally chewed with her mouth open at dinner, or something important, like he'd discovered he couldn't stand the sound of her voice?

"I know you must be confused," he said gently.

She swallowed and made herself look into his eyes. "A little."

He seemed miserable. "It's not that I don't want to."

"Then why not?" She sounded desperate, and she hated that, but the words were out.

"Because…because I can't be the man you need."

She stared at him. "Then I need an overhaul on my 'gaydar,' because I've felt heterosexual vibes coming from you from the very start."

"I'm not gay. Or impotent, or married, which might be the other conclusions you could draw from what I said.

I just—God, this is complicated." He blew out a breath and stared up at the lighted buildings surrounding them.

She launched into self-preservation mode. "Look, if there's something about me you don't like, that's okay. You don't have to explain. In fact, my ego would appreciate it if you'd keep that particular truth to yourself. I shouldn't have asked for reasons. We're not going to continue this little interlude, and that's fine. Good night, Zach. Dinner was great."

He caught her arm before she'd gone more than three feet. "Wait."

She glanced back at him. "Let's not make this any more awkward than it has to be, okay?"

"I don't want you to leave thinking it has something to do with you." He released his grip. "Hannah, you're terrific. You're gorgeous and sexy, and I would love to go to bed with you."

"Then what's the problem?" she said softly.

"It wouldn't be right."

"You have religious scruples?"

"No! I—you know what? You're right. I'm only making this more awkward. Just believe me when I say I'd love to, but I can't."

"Okay." She was still confused, but not quite so humiliated. She could see that he was tortured and thoroughly believed he wanted to come upstairs but couldn't for some mysterious reason. "Well, if you should change your mind…just whistle." Then she turned and headed for the Pearson's front entrance.

She shouldn't be surprised that she'd misread the situation with Zach. She'd landed in a new town, where there could be new rules, and she'd met the guy only yesterday. It seemed as if they'd known each other longer, but that was an illusion. Yes, they'd appeared to click, but something was gumming up the works.

Well, she'd enjoy that suite all by herself again tonight. She'd soak in the Jacuzzi and read one of the paperback thrillers she'd picked up on the way home from her interview. Then she'd get a good night's sleep with plenty of room to spread out in that big bed. She didn't need a guy to complete her, or make her happy, or any of that junk. In fact, she…hold on.

What was that noise? She strained to hear. Sure enough, interspersed with the sounds of traffic, came the unmistakable sound of a soft, low whistle.

She turned to find Zach walking toward her.

HALFWAY THERE, ZACH BROKE into a run. So did Hannah. They almost collided in their eagerness to reach each other without losing another second. Then they were laughing, hugging and kissing as if they hadn't seen each other for weeks.

"I'm an idiot!" he said between kisses. "Can we start over?"

"I don't know." Smiling, she wound her arms around his neck and gazed up at him. "I like where we are right now."

"Me, too, except it's way too public."

Her eyes sparkled. "I know somewhere a lot more private."

"Then let's go there."

"No obstacles?"

"Not a one." To think he'd almost let worry over a stupid job keep him from doing the right thing. Tomorrow he'd talk to Ed, and then to Medford. And he'd let the chips fall where they may. If he ended up jobless and that meant he and Hannah didn't work out, that would be the breaks. But in the meantime…

"Then come with me." Slipping her arm through his, she started toward the front door of the hotel.

Somehow they navigated the revolving door without losing touch. Silly things, revolving doors. He'd never liked them. The blessing of a small lobby was that it took no time at all to cross it. They were almost to the elevator when the desk clerk called Hannah's name.

She glanced at him and slipped her arm from his. "Excuse me a minute."

"I'll go with you." He followed her over to the desk.

"Miss Robertson," the desk clerk said. "I'm so glad I caught you. We have a small problem. We've had to switch your room again."

"Oh!" Hannah turned bright red. "Did you…um… move everything?"

"Absolutely. Certain…pest-control issues on the top floor came to light this evening, and they had to be dealt with. You wouldn't have wanted any of your belongings in that room while we handled that. The top floor will be sealed for the next twenty-four hours."

"But I do have a room, right?"

Zach touched her arm. "Listen, if not, it's no problem. You can stay with me." She could stay with him as long as she liked, or until his rent money ran out. Strange how that possibility didn't bother him as much as he'd expected it to.

"Oh, you definitely have a room!" The desk clerk reached for an envelope. "Here's the key." Then he glanced at Zach. "The room should work out fine, at least tempo- rarily. With the top floor out of commission, we had to do a little squeezing." He chuckled, as if that was a huge joke.

"All right." Hannah took the envelope, which had the room number written on it. "Twenty-five B? Where is that, exactly?"

"It's one of our few basement rooms. Quite charming, really. There may be some slight noise from the furnace units, but on the whole, it's very quiet. No hallway noise, which is such a bother in the rest of the hotel."

"Um…" Hannah looked over at Zach. "Are you okay with that?"

He was trying hard not to laugh, because he wasn't sure if she thought this was funny. Now that he'd decided to risk his whole future on one night with her, everything seemed funny. "I never liked hallway noise," he said, trying to keep a straight face.

"Then let's go take a look at it." She picked up the envelope with the key and started toward the elevator. "I am so embarrassed," she said once they were out of earshot of the desk clerk.

"Don't be." Zach put his arm around her shoulders. "Suite, schmeet. Who cares what kind of room it is?" But he had to admit he was curious about this basement deal.

"I'm not embarrassed about the room." She pushed the elevator button and the doors slid open. "I'm sorry we don't have the suite, but if they had pest issues, I'm just as glad we're not up there."

"Me, too." He stepped into the elevator with her. "I hate to think what would cause them to seal off an entire floor."

"I just wish I'd known in advance, that's all." She punched a button marked B.

"Yeah, I'm sure you don't want them manhandling your stuff."

"You don't know the half of it." Her cheeks had turned pink again.

"Oh?" As the elevator descended, he massaged the back of her neck. "Gonna tell me about it?"

"I don't think so."

"Then I might have to kiss it out of you." As he leaned down to try that technique, the elevator thumped to a stop and the doors opened.

"Greetings!" A short, stocky man in a gray maintenance uniform stood beside the elevator. "You folks lost?"

Hannah stepped out of the elevator and held up her envelope. "We're looking for 25B."

"With any luck we'll have to take a secret passageway and use pitch-soaked torches," Zach said.

The maintenance guy laughed. "Not quite. Go all the way to the end of that hallway. You'll find it." He got into the elevator and the doors closed.

"Alone at last." Zach reached for Hannah. Yes, he should probably use some restraint and wait until they were inside the room, but his lust had been building for two solid days. "I need to kiss you."

"Here?" Smiling, she dropped the key into her purse and wound both arms around his neck, letting her purse dangle over his shoulder.

"Right here." And he backed her up against the wall beside the elevator. "Right now."

"This place reminds me of a dungeon. It echoes."

"Yeah." He wanted her so much he could barely see straight. "Kinky, isn't it?" Then he kissed her with all the longing he'd kept bottled up, all the passion he'd tried to deny as he'd been making his rational decision not to do this.

But he was so doing this. He was going to taste, touch and enjoy all that was Hannah Robertson, starting with her incredible mouth. The dank scent of the basement made everything seem forbidden and exciting. From the way she moaned as he thrust his tongue deep, he thought she might be experiencing the same thrill of breaking some unspoken rule.

So much woman, so little time. He hadn't really meant to unzip her dress, but when she arched against him, he slipped his hand up her back. And darned if there wasn't a metal tab right there just asking to be pulled down.

As the zipper gave way, she wrenched her mouth from his. She was breathing hard. "Should you…do that?"

His voice was thick. "I have to."

"Okay." Then she went right back to kissing him, her mouth even more hot, more wet.

He managed to pull the top half of her dress down, but only after she dropped her purse with a loud clank to the cement floor. She'd had tuna in there, no doubt. But once he cupped the lace of her bra, he forgot all about the tuna.

With one flick of his wrist he opened the front catch and pushed the material aside. She quivered and gasped against his mouth. With a groan he filled both hands with her plump, silky breasts. To think he'd ever questioned whether she would be worth it.

Lifting his head, he gazed into her eyes as he ran his thumbs over her nipples.

She licked her lips and her eyes darkened until they were almost black. "This is crazy. We have…a room right…down the hall."

"It seems miles away."

"I know." She dragged in a breath, making her breasts shimmy in his hands.

"And I want…this." Crouching, he closed his mouth

over one turgid nipple. As he sucked, his erection pressed urgently against the restriction of his suddenly too-tight slacks.

She whimpered. "That feels so good."

That was all he needed to hear. Kissing his way back to her mouth, he tasted its sweetness one more time before sliding his lips close to her ear. "I'm taking your dress off."

She shivered against him. "Someone might come."

"Uh-huh. You."

She inhaled sharply. "I meant—"

"I know what you meant." He worked her dress over her hips and let it fall to the floor. "No one will." He peppered her face with kisses. "We've been banished to the basement."

"You're a wildman."

"If you don't want this, then tell me no." He cupped her face in one hand and slipped the other one inside her panties. Her very wet panties.

She looked into his eyes. "Yes," she whispered.

"I thought so." Threading his fingers slowly through the curls covering her secrets, he watched as languid surrender relaxed her features and brought a wanton glow to her eyes. He'd thought she was beautiful before, but now…now there were no words to describe how she affected him.

He wanted to give her everything, starting with a mind-shattering orgasm. As he found the right spot and caressed her there, she closed her eyes and leaned her head against the wall.

"I feel shameless," she murmured.

"Good." He slid his fingers in deep, exulting in how ready she was. He had condoms. They could do it up against the wall.

No. When that moment came, he wanted to be horizontal, braced to take his time and draw out the pleasure. This was about spontaneous combustion. The next time he would light the match slowly and tease the flame until he'd created a roaring fire.

He stroked her gently at first, loving the way her labored breathing made her breasts quiver. Leaning down, he kissed the point right below where her necklace nestled. Then he nibbled his way to one erect nipple, all the while coaxing her higher with the rhythm of his fingers and the insistent pressure of his thumb.

She moaned and thrust her hips forward. He nipped at her breast and increased the speed of his probing fingers. She was so wet, so very wet. He sensed that it wouldn't take much.... On an impulse he sucked hard on her nipple and pressed upward with his fingertips. She came in a rush, gasping and bucking against his hand.

Her cries were suddenly drowned out by a giant boom that bellowed around them, as if the basement had exploded right along with Hannah. Her eyes flew open and she struggled to speak. "What...?" She gulped.

"I don't know." With his fingers still buried in her moist heat, while he was still registering the contractions of her climax, he tried to get his bearings. Somewhere nearby a giant motor churned away, and at last his passion-fogged brain figured it out. "The furnace."

"The furnace?" She looked at him in dazed incomprehension.

He was only marginally more able to analyze the situation. Slowly he disengaged his fingers. He couldn't be expected to make any sense while he was touching her so intimately. With contact like that, his primitive brain took control.

"The furnace," he said again. "The desk clerk said something about furnace noise being a slight problem down here."

"A slight problem?" She looked indignant. "That sounds like a train hurtling through a subway tunnel!"

"There's a sexual image for you." He kind of liked it. She could be the tunnel and he could be the train. Maybe they could work with that later.

"Come on, Zach. We're expected to sleep with *that* going on?"

He couldn't help it. That made him laugh. "It won't be a problem."

"Why not?" She appeared ready to demand a different room.

"We're not going to sleep."

"Oh." She relaxed back against the cement wall. "I suppose you have a point there."

"And there's another advantage to that noisy furnace."

"There is?"

"We can make all the damn noise we want here in the basement. In a place like New York, where everyone is so packed together, that's a luxury."

She nodded and reached down to pick up her dress. "Okay, then. Let's you and me go make some noise."

He followed her down the hall, a song in his heart and tension in his groin. He was more than ready to make some noise.

CHAPTER EIGHT

No MATTER HOW THIS ALL turned out, Hannah would never forget having a climax in the basement of a New York City hotel. Or walking down the hall wearing only her panties and her necklace while she carried her dress and her bra over one arm. She wasn't sure why Zach had changed his mind about spending the night with her, but she was very happy that he had.

"Got a key?" he asked as they approached 25B.

"Somewhere." She had to search the depths of her purse until she finally found the envelope with the key card in it. Not long ago she'd been embarrassed because the hotel personnel had seen her seduction scene, complete with nightie and condoms. After her basement climax, being caught with a nightie and condoms seemed like small potatoes.

Still, she was curious as to how they'd transferred her belongings and whether they'd taken the trouble to put things back the way they'd found them. She opened the door, not sure what she'd find on the other side. For sure it wouldn't be a suite with a view, but as Zach had mentioned, there were advantages to being in the basement cohabitating with a large and noisy furnace.

As the door swung open, it almost hit the bed. Or,

more accurately, the twin-size daybed as illuminated by the light from the hall.

"It's a closet!" Zach said.

"Want to complain?"

"I'm too horny to complain. Don't tell me those are mints on the pillow."

"No. They're my condoms."

"Yours?" He turned to gaze at her. "You had condoms, too?"

"Laid out on the pillow, exactly as you see there. Only it was a pillow on a huge bed. We've been downsized." Now that she'd had a most wonderful orgasm, she was beginning to see the humor in the situation.

"I suppose it doesn't matter." Zach peered into the room. "I mean, when we have sex, either I'll be on top of you or vice versa."

"Maybe there's a trundle."

"We're not going there. One of us would end up falling through the crack. Or some significant body part could end up getting caught in the crack. Guys have nightmares about that kind of thing. Better one small but solid mattress, than one that could split at the most inopportune moment."

"It's pitch dark in there. Before we go in and close the door, we'd better turn on a light." She reached inside the doorway and found a switch on the wall. When she flicked it on, an overhead light revealed them both reflected in a giant mirror on the wall behind the daybed. "Yikes!" She looked so...*naked*.

"I like it."

"I'm not sure I do." She found it disconcerting, staring at herself wearing only a necklace and a pair of panties. "I guess the mirror is to make up for the lack of a window."

"I have a different theory." Zach continued to gaze appreciatively at Hannah's reflection.

"If you think it's a two-way mirror, I'm so outta here!" Hannah held her dress protectively in front of her.

"No, no, not a two-way. I think it's here to provide fun and games for any members of the staff who are so inclined."

"You think?"

"I do. And it beats the hell out of a break room."

Hannah peered around the edge of the door to make sure there was a bathroom included. There was, although it was about the size of one in an airplane. "So we stay?"

"Hell, yes, we stay. That mirror closes the deal for me." Zach pulled her inside and shut the door. Then he started unbuttoning his shirt. "We stay and we get naked."

"I pretty much am already."

"So I noticed. Naked looks great on you, by the way."

She reached for her nightie. "I'd planned to waltz around the suite wearing this." She'd hoped to make an entrance. Now that he'd seen most of what she had to offer, her entrance might be a little anticlimactic.

He paused in the act of taking off his shirt. "I remember that. When you picked it out at the resale shop I almost swallowed my tongue."

That decided her. Maybe she had one good entrance left. "I'm going into the bathroom to put it on. I want to see if I can make you do that again."

The bathroom scored low for maneuverability, but because she only had to take off her necklace and panties, she was dolled up in the nightie and matching thong in no time. She stood on tiptoe, trying to see the effect in the medicine cabinet mirror.

The skimpy black thong barely covered the subject, and the sheer black top was strictly for effect. It disguised nothing. Trimmed in soft black fur around the scooped neck and the hem, it hung to the tops of her thighs. Ties at the neck ended in black furry pom-poms that bounced as she walked. Wearing the outfit, she felt like a very bad girl, indeed.

When she walked back into the room, she discovered she'd paired up with a bad boy who was obviously eager for some action. He'd thrown back the covers and was propped up on the bed watching the bathroom doorway. She'd always thought he looked good in his clothes, but he looked way better out of them.

He'd taken off everything except a pair of skimpy navy briefs. From the sizable bulge there, she guessed that would be a package well worth unwrapping. She was so busy staring at his nicely sculpted pecs and impressive six-pack that she forgot about her planned entrance.

But he hadn't. He let out a low whistle. That prompted her to pose, just a little, and he responded with a playful growl.

She thought of the soft lighting she'd arranged in the suite and glanced up at the overhead light glaring down at them. "This place has about as much atmosphere as a hospital operating room."

His voice was low and husky. "So let's play doctor."

Suddenly the bright light, the mirrors and the tiny, soundproof room took on a whole new emphasis. She and Zach were starring in their own X-rated video. Excitement rolled through her, arousing her in ways she hadn't known she could be aroused. She wanted to do wild things, erotic things.

"Bring that good stuff on over," he murmured.

"That won't take long." In three strides she was beside the bed. "Here I am."

"Yeah. So you are." His hungry gaze raked over her as his hand closed on her arm and he urged her closer. "Come on down here, you."

She climbed on the bed, straddling his thighs and bracing her arms on either side of his shoulders as she leaned forward. "Like this?"

"That's good." He cupped her head and brought her closer until their lips almost touched. "How I want you," he whispered right before he kissed her.

The kiss was so hot that she wondered if she could come simply from the persuasive movement of his lips against hers. He made love to her mouth, telling her in no uncertain terms what he had in mind.

By doing that, he gave her ideas of her own. Breaking away from his mesmerizing kiss wasn't easy, but she had other uses for her mouth. Sliding it over his chin, she began a slow, deliberate journey. The furnace came on again, but she barely registered the noise blasting through the basement and hammering at their door.

He groaned and combed his fingers through her hair. "Hannah…"

"Enjoy." With the furnace rumbling just down the hall, she paid tribute to his muscled chest and felt his body tighten under the pressure of her lips and tongue. Heart racing, she kissed the hard planes of his stomach, inching her body lower on the bed. Then she caught the elastic of his briefs in her teeth, and he gasped.

She would have loved to pull the briefs off using only her teeth, but she ended up needing both hands to finish the job. By then Zach was breathing very fast, and once she'd uncovered him in all his glory, so was she. He was magnificent.

With her first taste, he began to quake. He gripped her head and tried to hold her back. "I can't... I might not be able to...control..."

"Sure you will."

"I don't know." But his grip relaxed.

"You will." She licked the underside of his penis. "Because you don't want me to stop."

The furnace grew quiet, but Zach groaned loudly, filling the silence. "No, I don't want you to stop. But I...oh...ooooh."

"Good?" She closed her mouth over the quivering tip.

"You have no idea."

She glanced up and saw that his eyes were squeezed shut. "Don't you want to watch in the mirror?" She would never have dared make that kind of suggestion before tonight, but tonight she was more daring, more ready for sexual adventure.

"Can't."

"Why not?"

"I'll come for sure."

"Chicken." Then she picked up one of the furry pom-poms dangling from her nightie and began to stroke his balls.

He yelled and nearly came off the bed. "Hannah! That's..."

"Nice?"

"Fantastic." He moaned. "I love it."

Music to her ears. She wanted him to remember this night for a very long time, because she certainly would. She continued her sweet torture until the ache inside her and the moisture gathering between her thighs were impossible to ignore. There was only one remedy, and she was looking at it.

Easing back to the head of the bed, she nibbled on Zach's ear. "Where did you put those packets?"

He reached behind the mound of pillows and silently produced one. "I can—"

"I know you can. But I want to." She ripped open the package and took out the condom. Her fingers shook, and he was trembling, too, but she got him suited up at last. Then she pulled her nightie over her head and threw it on the floor. Her black thong followed.

When she glanced back at him, his eyes were open and he was watching her, his chest heaving.

"I'm taking the top this time," she murmured.

"Take what you want." His voice sounded strangled. "I'm…desperate."

So was she. Swinging one leg over him, she braced both palms on his chest and looked into his eyes as she lowered herself, taking his penis deeper, and deeper yet. *Oh, yes.*

His eyes darkened as he grasped her hips, his fingers flexing. "So…good."

She nodded. Then slowly she turned her head, so she could see their reflected image. What a rush. She'd never have believed how beautiful the two of them would look, their bodies glowing with shared passion.

Zach turned his head, too, and their glances locked in the mirror.

Watching his eyes, she began to move. Being able to see the heat in his gaze and the rhythmic movement of their bodies hurtled her toward a climax faster than she could have imagined. The image blurred as she came, crying out with abandon, knowing no one could hear her.

But he didn't follow her down that path. His laugh was triumphant and very male as he urged her on, inserting one hand between them to massage her throbbing clit. "I want another one, louder than that!"

Faster and faster they bucked against the narrow mattress. Her hair flew out around her, and her breasts bobbed with every thrust.

The furnace kicked on again, as if to add to the energy swirling through the room, and she obliged him with another orgasm, this one noisier than the first.

"There!" he cried. "Ah, Hannah, now!" And he bellowed with satisfaction as his own climax surged through him.

At the force of it, they both nearly toppled off the bed. Hannah saved them both by making a grab for the headboard. Laughter and moans of pleasure mingled as they collapsed against each other and clung to the sides of the small bed.

Zach gulped for air. "This is the best damn hotel room I've ever been in."

"No kidding." Hannah snuggled against him. "Who needs a suite?"

"Not us." Zach held her tight. "We have all we need right here."

She did, that was for sure. "I can't believe you almost went home tonight."

"Me, neither." He stroked her back for several long, sensuous moments. Finally he spoke again. "Hannah, I want you to come down to the office tomorrow morning."

That startled her. Not exactly pillow talk. "Look, forget what I said about your boss. I'm sure he's terrific, and I should never have—"

"It's not about that. I want to introduce you to Ed. He…might have exactly the publishing contact you need."

How strange. Ed, the guy who'd been kicked out of the corner office. "Okay. That would be great." Something was going on here, but she wasn't sure exactly what.

She didn't have time to think about it, either, because it turned out Zach had a very short recovery time. And the furnace was rumbling again….

IN THE MORNING ZACH suggested they order room service, his treat, just to see if anybody could find them down in the basement. To his surprise, the service was speedier than usual, and he ended up giving them a sizable tip for being so prompt. The staff seemed to know exactly where 25B was, which validated his suspicion that it was a rendezvous point.

After breakfast he longed to hang around for more fun and games, but he needed to make sure he got to the office on time so he could talk with Ed. "You know where to go, right?" he asked for the fourth time as he finished dressing.

"I know exactly where to go." She'd taken a shower and washed her hair, so she sat on the bed with one towel wrapped around her wet hair and the other barely concealing her lush body.

He deserved a medal for keeping his hands off her. "I just want to make sure."

She smiled. "I'm new to town, but I'm reasonably intelligent."

So was he, but all his intelligence threatened to abandon him when she smiled like that. She was so incredibly beautiful, and spending the night with her had convinced him that he would never find anyone so special if he searched for a million years. But she wasn't in the market for a commitment, and he might soon be unworthy of making one.

"Zach, are you okay?" She stood and walked over to him, which only took two steps in the tiny room.

"Yeah." He gave in to temptation and pulled her close. Just a few moments, to carry him through. No telling when he'd ever be able to hold her again. Life could get complicated after today.

She put her arms around his neck and the towel came undone. "You spaced out there for a minute."

He saw the towel slip and deliberately raised his glance to her face. "You sitting there in a towel would make any man space out. And now the towel arrangement is getting dicey." He held her tight and gazed into those dancing brown eyes. He was in love with her, and he couldn't say a word. "Another few seconds and I can't be responsible for what happens."

"It's not my fault. The towels are skimpy."

He leaned down and brushed his lips over hers. So sweet. So very sweet. "I bribed the front desk to make sure they stocked the tiny ones in this room."

"You keep talking like that and I'll think you arranged to have me kicked out of the suite, just so we could end up here."

"I can't take credit." One more little taste of her mouth. Just one. "But it turned out to be a most excellent place to spend the night."

"Uh-huh." She nibbled on his lower lip.

"I have to go." That sounded very unconvincing.

"I know." She kissed his chin. "Mmm. My razor did a pretty decent job."

He forced himself to think about the conversation

with Ed, the one that could mean all the difference to her. A night of wild sex was all well and good, but an intro to the right people in the publishing business was what she really needed.

"I really am leaving." He cupped her face in both hands. "But before I go, I want you to know…last night was…" He couldn't find the words.

"For me, too." She reached up and brushed a lock of hair off his forehead. "Maybe we can do it again sometime." She grinned. "Like tonight."

"That would be great." He wasn't about to tell her how different his life could be by tonight.

She frowned. "You look uneasy, Zach. Don't worry. I'm not trying to tie you down. I don't picture us on the dash of Mario's cab, or anything like that."

And he did, he realized with a jolt. It wasn't fair to her, considering that she'd only just arrived, and he might not be a good candidate. But the idea of being added to Mario's rogue's gallery had become very appealing in the past twelve hours.

He couldn't say that. "I know you don't. I was thinking about the time. It's late, and I really have to leave." He kissed her hard and backed away.

Her towel fell, and she made no move to retrieve it. "See you in a couple of hours."

"Right." Swallowing, he managed to get out the door, but the image of her standing there, her face filled with something that looked suspiciously like love, was etched forever in his mind.

An hour later, after he'd changed into clean clothes at his apartment and downed another cup of coffee to compensate for his lack of sleep, he was still thinking about all that he'd shared with Hannah. But he had to put a lock on those thoughts. He didn't want to act like some lovesick fool when he went to Ed with his request. This needed to be a friendly and straightforward matter.

During the bus ride to the office, he rehearsed what he wanted to say. Talking to Ed had never been difficult, but that was before Zach had taken over Ed's corner office. He'd avoided Ed yesterday, and so he had no idea whether they were still on friendly terms or not. God, he hoped so.

When he walked through the door, Ed, coffee mug in hand, was over by the receptionist's desk kidding with her. He was a burly guy with a round, friendly face, the kind of guy you'd expect to find tending the barbecue grill in the backyard on a Saturday afternoon.

Ed and Shirley, the blond receptionist, were both laughing about something. Trust Ed to keep his sense of humor after being relegated to a little cubby in the outer office.

Ed turned when Zach appeared. "Hey, Zach." His tone was casual, but he wasn't smiling.

Zach didn't blame him. In Ed's place, he wouldn't smile at the guy who'd replaced him. "Could I talk to you for a minute?" he asked.

"Sure." Ed gestured toward the cubby with his coffee mug. "Step into my office."

"Thanks." Zach felt Shirley's gaze on him. Shirley had always liked Ed, which might mean that she wasn't too fond of Zach right now.

Ed's partitioned area was claustrophobic, barely enough room for the desk, Ed's chair and a chair in front of the desk for a visitor. Zach would be embarrassed to ask clients to meet him at a place like this. He noticed that Ed had mounted his framed industry awards on the temporary partitions, as though he was prepared to settle in.

They were impressive, although the most recent was ten years old. Other stuff was on the wall, too, including pictures of Ed with several Little League teams. One had been taken last year, with the team posed in front of a championship banner.

"We damned near went to nationals last year." Ed gazed at the picture. "Some of those kids are back again, and I think we might do 'er this time."

"That's quite a feat." Zach remembered his own Little League days in Illinois. One coach in particular had been his hero. Ed was probably a hero to these young boys, too.

"Yeah, well, it's what I love. Have a seat. I was wondering if you'd stopped talking to me for some reason."

"Sorry about that. I felt awkward yesterday." Zach sat down in the chair, which wasn't all that comfortable. "Look, I'm not happy with Medford's office switch."

Ed waved a beefy hand. "Forget about it. Medford has his game plan, and I'm just glad to have this. I know I'm not blazing any trails right now. I only need a couple more years, and I'll be able to retire. I can live with the situation."

Zach recognized a guy who understood his priorities. As someone who was still discovering his, Zach appreciated how difficult it could be to stick to those priorities when the pressure was on.

Ed set down his mug, which had COACH lettered on it in red. The entire surface of the mug was covered with childish signatures. "What can I do for you?"

"I need a favor. I can understand if you don't want to help me under the circumstances, but I—"

"Hey, of course I'll help you. It's not your fault I'm out here."

"I could have refused to take the corner office."

"And risk pissing off a guy like Medford? You could lose your job. That would be crazy."

Zach didn't think so. As he gazed at those signatures on Ed's mug, he knew that confronting Medford would be one of the sanest things he'd done in a while. Between that and making love to Hannah last night, he felt as if he was finally getting his priorities in order.

CHAPTER NINE

HANNAH COULDN'T BELIEVE IT. The vice president of one of the biggest publishers in New York had just offered her a job. And she'd accepted, controlling her glee as best she could while she was still in his office. But once she was standing on the sidewalk in front of the building, the building where she would be working starting tomorrow, she gave in to the urge to punch her fist in the air and do a victory dance. So what if people stared?

They didn't, though. They were used to street performers in this town, and they might figure she was another one. As a piece of performance art, she'd label this one *Jubilation*. She had a job! She could hardly wait to tell Zach and thank him for the contact. He'd come through for her, big-time.

She could call him on her cell, but they'd agreed that the news was too important to be delivered by phone. She was supposed to meet him at Iris's coffee stand when her interview was over. Hannah felt as if she could fly there, but because it was at least four miles away, she decided to splurge on a cab.

Mario wouldn't be on duty, and she didn't have a number to call him, anyway. But she could try out her whistle. She put her fingers in the corner of her mouth the way Zach had shown her, stuck her tongue behind her front teeth, and blew.

The little tweet that came out was beyond pathetic. She worked at it for another five minutes before finally giving it up as a bad job. Zach had said she'd need a lot of practice, and he was right. She resorted to standing in the street and waving her arms frantically until a cab finally swerved over and picked her up.

Neither the taxi nor the driver had Mario's charm, but they transported her to Iris's coffee stand in good order. Once there, she gave the driver a sizable tip, because she was feeling incredibly generous. Then she leaped out and ran over to the coffee stand. Zach wasn't there yet, so Iris would be the first to hear her big news.

ZACH HAD WORKED AT THIS investment firm for eight years, and yet it took him less than an hour to pack up his belongings. He'd managed to find a couple of boxes to put everything in, but now he had to figure out the logistics of this. He could load them into a cab, but he didn't have time to take a cab back to his apartment and then over to Iris's coffee stand. Hannah was probably already there by now.

Ed came in carrying a box of his stuff. "I still think you're crazy," he said. "You never should have had it out with Medford. You knew how he'd react."

"That's why I had to do it." Zach closed the flaps on the second box. "I confirmed what I pretty much knew already. I don't want to work for a guy like that."

Ed set the box down on the desk that would now be his again. Then he studied Zach for a long moment. "Yeah, okay. You're young enough to start over. That makes a difference."

"I'll be fine. No worries." Zach hoped to hell he'd be able to start over. But no matter how it turned out for him, he'd done the right thing.

"I appreciate getting your client list, buddy."

"I'm glad Medford didn't give me any crap about that. I was afraid he would, but he seemed to think it served me right, for you to get the office back and all my clients, too."

Ed nodded. "The reason he can be generous is that I've given him no reason to be vindictive. I'm afraid you have. He might try to screw with your professional reputation."

"And if he does, maybe I'll go into something else. Hell, I might decide to drive a cab like my friend Mario." He glanced at the boxes. "Hey, could I leave these here for an hour or two? I'm supposed to meet Hannah to find out about the job interview, so I don't have time to call a cab and take them home."

"You want them schlepped over to your apartment? I can do that on my way home from work. I have the truck, you know."

"That would be terrific. I'll make sure I'm home by then." Zach scribbled his address on a piece of paper and handed it to Ed. "I'd forgotten there were people who drive in from the suburbs. I haven't owned a car in eight years."

"Or driven one, either, I'll bet."

"Nope."

Ed laughed. "You might want to practice before you get into the taxi business."

"Yeah, I might. Well, I'd better go." He shook Ed's hand. "Thanks for taking the boxes."

"My pleasure. It's the least I can do."

In the outer office Zach said goodbye to Shirley, who was much friendlier than she had been early this morning. Then he rode the elevator down and walked out of the building, probably for the last time. With Ed taking care of his boxes, he'd have no reason to go back.

He'd expected to feel depressed, and instead he felt only relief. But he had to prepare himself to say goodbye to Hannah. She didn't need some jobless schmuck hanging around as she settled into her new life in the big city. If he'd given her some help, that was great, but he would never forgive himself if he dragged her down.

Although he should be conserving his cash for the possible money drought ahead, he whistled for a cab to take him over to the coffee stand. Whistling reminded him of trying to teach Hannah how to do it. When he thought of her earnest effort to learn, his heart gave a twinge of sorrow.

Face it, he'd miss the hell out of her. In a very short time she'd managed to become essential to him. Maybe, if he got on his feet again in a few months, he might call her.

Of course, by then she could easily have a new boyfriend. A woman like her would attract all kinds of interest. He'd been a lucky SOB to get the inside track, thanks to Mario.

But now the logical step was to let her go. She wasn't like Adrienne, who judged a man by his bank account, but she was a normal woman who needed a guy who was at least relatively solvent. An employed guy. Which he wasn't.

As the cab pulled up near the coffee stand, Zach found Hannah with no trouble. Her deep red hair glowed in the midday sun pouring down between the buildings. She'd worn the blue-and-gold-striped dress today, and the dress was like a banner announcing her presence.

He imagined he could tell by the animated way she

was talking to Iris that she'd nailed the job. Maybe not, though. She was such an optimist that she'd be animated whether it was win, lose or draw. He tipped the cab-driver well, figuring that he wanted to do that while he still had the money.

Iris must have said something to Hannah about him being there, because as he climbed out of the cab, she came running toward him. They met in the tight space between two parked cars.

"I got it!" She flung her arms around his neck and damned near threw him off balance. "I got the job! Thank you, oh, thank you, Zach!" Then she gave him an espresso-flavored kiss.

He kissed her back, unable to help himself. Later he could be strong, but when she was in his arms all he could think of was keeping her there.

At last she came up for air. "I start tomorrow." Her brown eyes shone with excitement. "They handle some really big authors, Zach. I won't get to work with *New York Times* bestsellers right away, but I'll be in the same building when they come in. I might be able to bring them coffee. And the authors I do work with could *become* bestsellers, because this is a really good house. Did you thank Ed again for me? I should call him."

"He might be at lunch." Zach didn't want her calling Ed just yet. He had some things to explain first.

"Even better!" She wiggled out of his arms and dug in her purse for her cell phone. "This is why I took his number while I was there, so I could let him know what happened." She found a pad of paper and flipped it open to where she'd written Ed's cell number.

"Listen, before you call, there's something—"

"It'll only take a minute. Then we can go celebrate!

Where can you go? I know you don't have much time, and I don't want to make you late for work again, so we could put it off until—" She paused and stuck her finger in her ear. "Hello? Ed? I can barely hear you."

"Reception's bad," Zach said. "You can call him back later."

Instead she stepped up on the sidewalk. "There, that's better. Ed, this is Hannah. I got the job!" Then she smiled. "Yeah, it is wonderful. Thanks for recommending me to your client. We really got along. What?" She glanced at Zach. "Just a sec." She put her finger over the speaker.

Zach would have liked more time. He'd wanted to give her a chance to bask in her glory before hearing his announcement. "Hannah, listen, there's something I need to tell you."

"I'm guessing so." She looked worried. "Ed says he forgot he has a Little League practice and wonders if he can drop your boxes off tomorrow morning at your apartment. What's that all about, Zach?"

"I quit."

"You *what?*"

"It just isn't the place for me, so I quit."

Hannah groaned. "This is my fault. I should never have said that! Is it final? Maybe you could go back this afternoon and say you'd reconsidered."

"No, I can't do that."

"Oh, Zach." Still gazing at him in concern, she brought the phone back to her ear. "Ed, are you still there? Listen, we'll call you back about the boxes. And thanks again for the recommendation. Bye." Then she snapped her phone shut and tucked it in her purse.

"First of all," Zach said, "it's not your fault that I quit.

I'm grateful to you for showing me that I didn't have to accept what Medford had laid out. I told him I didn't want the corner office, and he should give it back to Ed."

She sighed. "Not a good move."

"It was a perfect move. Medford got all purple in the face. You would have loved it. He totally lost his cool."

"Really? He turned purple?"

"Like an eggplant."

Hannah put both hands to her mouth. "I shouldn't laugh. This is serious. You just threw away a perfectly good job."

"It wasn't a perfectly good job. Not with Medford in charge."

She lowered her hands and cleared her voice. "Okay, maybe this isn't so terrible. But I still feel responsible. You wouldn't have done it if I hadn't come up with the idea."

"As I've told you, I want to thank you for that. I'll sleep much better tonight knowing I don't have to go back there."

She gazed up at him with a tiny smile. "Do you think you'll get to sleep tonight?"

Here came the hard part. "Yes. Because…because… I've decided we should stop seeing each other."

She looked as if she'd been slapped. "Why?"

"I'm out of a job, Hannah. You just got a really good one. You said yourself that this wasn't the time for you to make a commitment. That's doubly true, now. I refuse to be a stone around your neck right when you're ready to enjoy this great city."

"But—"

"Trust me, this is the right thing. For both of us. Goodbye, Hannah." Taking a deep breath, he turned and walked down the street. He wasn't sure where he was headed, but he wasn't going to stand around waiting for a bus or take the time to hail a taxi. He just needed... out of there.

As he was striding down the sidewalk, dodging everyone who got in his way, he heard a strange sound. It wasn't exactly like a whistle. It was more like somebody blowing a very loud raspberry. He paused to listen. And then he heard a whistle. An actual, taxi-worthy whistle. She'd done it.

Only a man with no heart would keep walking. He turned. Hannah was running toward him, her skirt caught up in both hands. It wasn't graceful, but it certainly was enthusiastic.

She plowed to a stop right in front of him. "You... can't!" She gasped for breath. "I want to be there for you! You helped me get a job, and now I'll help you!"

"That's a nice thought, but—"

"Don't you *but* me, Zachary Evans! I will be employed in a huge building with dozens of contacts. I'll be networking out the ying-yang. You want clients to start up your own investment counseling business, I'll get you clients."

She was magnificent. And irresistible. "What if I want to drive a taxi?"

"Then I'll get you fares! Publishing people need a *lot* of taxi rides. I will get you so much business you won't be able to handle it all. If you leave me, you're giving all that up!"

"What if I'm in love with you?" The words came out before he could stop them.

"That works." Her voice softened. "Because I'm in love with you, too."

His heart warmed with the first rays of hope. "It's too soon."

"Says who? Everything moves fast in New York. Everyone knows that."

"Look, I have no problem with making a commitment, but you—you just got here."

She stepped closer. "And I was lucky enough to meet the sexiest man in the whole city first time out of the box."

"You have no basis of comparison."

She made a face. "Zach, I'm offering myself to you on a silver platter. Are you going to be stupid enough to argue with me about it?"

That did it. "No." He gathered her close. "I'm going to be smart enough to ask you to marry me, contribute to the ninety-percent ratio and get our picture taped to Mario's dash."

She looked into his eyes. "The blue picture."

"Absolutely the blue picture." Then he kissed her, taking his own sweet time. He ignored the harried pedestrians eddying around them, treating them like an obstacle in the middle of a fast-moving stream. Some things, even in New York, were too wonderful to rush.

EPILOGUE

"MARIO, YOU REMEMBER WE'RE supposed to go slow, right?" Hannah climbed into the backseat of the taxi while clutching the skirt of her floor-length dress with one hand and holding a bridal bouquet of yellow roses and daisies in the other.

Meanwhile Zach was trying to deal with the dress's long train. "I think it's either me or the dress," he said. "There's not room enough in this taxi for both of us."

"Then maybe I should ditch the dress." Hannah grinned at him.

"There will be no disrobing in my taxi!" Mario hollered from the driver's seat. "Especially not when we have a man of the cloth riding shotgun."

Hannah laughed. "Okay, okay. I'll keep my clothes on. Zach, hand me the end of the train. I'll fold it over my lap."

"Tell me again why we have this train." Zach managed to find the end of it and pass it over to her. "We're getting married in the taxi. The guests are all following in their cars. It's not like you'll be walking down the aisle."

"But it will look fantastic when we make our entrance at the reception." She accordion-folded the train as she pulled it into the taxi.

"It's Central Park. We'll be on grass, so you'll get

grass stains on it. Maybe you should just take it off. Mario can put it in the trunk."

She blew out a breath. As gorgeous as he looked in his dove-gray tux, a color that matched his eyes perfectly, he was getting on her nerves. "Zach, a wedding dress train is a must-have for me. I love the idea of getting married in Mario's taxi, but I'm not giving up the train, and that's final."

"But—"

"Get in, Zach. It's time to start. Our guests are growing impatient. Everybody's honking their horns, plus we're causing a traffic jam."

"Okay, but I think you'd be a lot happier without that train." He scooted in next to her.

"That's how much you know." She glared at him.

He glared back for about a second. Then he started to laugh. "It's about time!"

"For what?"

"Our first fight! Now we have to kiss and make up." He reached for her.

"You can kiss later!" Mario put the taxi in gear. "After the minister says so!"

But it was too late. Zach had already settled his mouth over Hannah's, and she was lost to the world. Vaguely she realized the taxi had started to move.

Dearly beloved, we are gathered here today... The minister's words spilled out of the speaker mounted on the roof of the taxi, but Hannah didn't want to stop kissing Zach, the man she loved more than life itself. That didn't mean she'd let him win all the arguments, but making up was turning out to be excellent.

Zach was right about the fighting. There hadn't been any. They'd been too busy loving each other and settling into their new lives and new jobs—Hannah with her new position as assistant editor and Zach with the investment counseling business he'd started on his own.

Suddenly Mario swerved, throwing Hannah off balance and ending the kiss.

"Hey, Mario, watch it!" Zach said. "We could break a tooth!"

"Had to do something," Mario said. "We're getting to the part where you have to say stuff. Now, pay attention, kids. This is important."

And so they did pay attention. Holding hands, they repeated the vows into the microphone the minister handed back to them, vows that floated out over the streets of New York. Traffic was light this early on a Sunday morning, but the few drivers and pedestrians they encountered shouted and whistled their approval of the ceremony.

You may kiss the bride, the minister said into the microphone. *Again.*

As horns blared from the procession of cars following the taxi, Zach gazed into Hannah's eyes. "I love you so much."

Her throat felt tight as her heart filled with enough joy to make her cry. "I love you, too."

As they kissed, Mario pulled over to the curb beside the grassy area set up for the reception. Zach and Hannah seemed in no hurry to stop kissing, but Mario didn't mind. He had a little chore to take care of before he locked up the cab, anyway.

He turned to the minister. "Could you open the glove compartment for me? I need to get something out of there."

"Sure." The minister popped it open.

"If you'll hand me that picture right on top and the tape next to it, I'd be much obliged."

"Ah." The minister looked at the picture. "It's them. The picture's really blue, though."

"I thought so, too, but this is the one they want, so I'm going with it." Mario pulled off some tape and positioned the picture in a prime location on his dash.

"So you brought all these couples together?" the minister asked.

"Yep." Mario finished taping Zach and Hannah to the dash. "And I'm proud to say that my percentage just went up!"

DRIVEN TO DISTRACTION

Julie Elizabeth Leto

CHAPTER ONE

ORDINARILY, RACHEL MARLOWE wouldn't have minded a little vibrating action while naked in her bed, luxuriating beneath her silk sheets, sated from the second explosive orgasm of the night. Ordinarily, she would have snuggled deeper beneath her comforter and allowed sweet exhaustion to lure her into dreamless sleep.

Ordinarily.

But damn it, over the past four months, making love to Roman Brach had elevated her ordinary, everyday, work-for-a-living existence into an intriguing, captivating adventure. To achieve this level of excitement, she usually had to stuff her duffel with a week's worth of whatever and catch the next cheap flight to another continent. Her whirlwind, spontaneous one-woman excursions had, not too long ago, been her only means of finding balance in her life—excitement to offset the boring; magnificence to alleviate the mundane.

Until Roman, who thanks to his vibrating pager, was now rolling out of bed. He opened his mouth to speak, but Rachel silenced him with a soft palm over his generous lips.

"If you say 'duty calls' I might have to kill you," she jokingly warned.

His grin, warm beneath her touch, pooled her insides

into melted goo. She yanked her hand away. Despite her threat, the only lethal one in the room was Roman.

"If you kill me," he warned, "I won't be able to return to you tonight."

She rolled her eyes, determined not to show her emotional hand. What fun would that be? "I'll live."

"Yes," he agreed, running a strong, callused finger from her lips, down her neck, to the slightly moist crevice between her breasts. "But without me, what quality of life would you enjoy?"

Despite her ire, she laughed at his unstoppable ego and swatted his hand away. He chuckled and started rummaging through the clothes scattered about the room for his pants, shirt, tie and jacket. He'd find them all. And they'd be impeccably unwrinkled when he did. She wasn't sure how he managed that feat, but it annoyed the hell out of her.

Lots of stuff about Roman annoyed the hell out of her, even while concurrently thrilling her right down to her curled toes. With his choice television-consulting job that took him to the four corners of the world on a regular rotation, Rachel never knew when he'd show up on her doorstep, his blue eyes rich with desire, the hard muscles in his arms and chest tense with need, his perfect Armani suit and custom-made Dege & Skinner shirts practically begging to be ripped free from his body. That's how he'd shown up tonight just after midnight—and similarly every night this week. Such regularity was downright weird, but who was she to complain? The sex was great. The conversation witty and quick. Yet now, at nearly five o'clock on a Thursday morning, she found herself once again in the unenviable position of either pretending his inevitable departure didn't bother her in the least…or confessing that she wished he'd stay and risk looking needy and clingy.

She frowned. She'd keep her mouth shut. As always. God forbid that she exhibit vulnerability. She'd learned long ago that putting her heart on the line might make her feel empowered in the short run, but in the long run, she'd end up just like all the women in her life—her mother, her sisters, her roommate, Jeannette…hell, all the chicks she knew from the gym and the various offices she worked in—lonely and bitching about all the men who'd broken their hearts.

Not Rachel. She'd come to New York City from Miami with one thing and one thing only on her mind. Her career. Okay, two things. She also wanted to travel. Come to think of it, math was not her strong suit. Her third most important goal revolved around having lots of hot sex with all the intriguing, international and successful men she'd inevitably meet in the famed Big Apple or wherever her passport took her in between freelance gigs as a graphic designer. And yet, for the past four months, she'd only been having sex with Roman. She wasn't complaining, of course. Not, at least, until his annoying pager went off.

"Any idea when you'll be back?"

She delivered the question with the right combination of vague interest and cool boredom. Or at least she hoped so. She practiced hard enough every time Roman prepared to disappear.

He turned, his ice-blue eyes warmed by a simmering desire that never seemed to cool when they were together. From the first moment her attention had flashed on his hypnotic gaze, she'd been snagged. Caught, like the tarpon her stepfather used to fish for off his yacht. And just like the mighty silver game fish, she'd fought and flailed against the hook.

Well, she'd struggled at least until she'd found a way to justify that flirting with a consultant was not the same as coming on to a boss. Technically, for the duration of his contract at the network—and hers, since she free-lanced—he'd been her superior. He'd supervised her work, but he didn't sign her paychecks. He didn't even write her performance reviews. Armed with those facts, she'd thrown caution to the wind and succumbed to a potentially destructive affair with a colleague.

She'd been working for A&E at the time. Or maybe Bravo. Encore? She couldn't remember the cable network exactly, but her project had reeked of high-brow entertainment—that much she remembered. As a specialist in opening credits and flashy promo pieces, she went where the jobs took her, and generally, she switched focus every six weeks at the most. She worked hard enough in a short period of time to save money, and then she took off for parts unknown. Indonesia. Pakistan. Brazil. She'd been on the verge of heading out on another unplanned, unrestricted trip to Costa Rica when Roman had strolled into her life and made leaving the last thing on her mind.

As he dressed, she thought back to the first time she'd seen him. She'd been in the studio, working on the final edits for a documentary promo. On mating. Of apes, of flamingos, of New York City drag queens? That detail blurred. Unforgettable, however, was the glance over her shoulder when she caught sight of Roman Brach conferring with some uppity-up in the company.

She'd stared. Brazenly. And after a few long moments, he'd looked up. Locking gazes with Roman, even for just a split second, filled her thoughts with enough sensual possibilities to script several rather lurid short films of her own.

He'd been wearing gray. Dusky coal gray. And a silver tie flecked with slate blue that matched his steely eyes. He'd tried to blend. To remain unnoticed. That in and of itself was enough to arrest her attention since her experience told her that here in New York, just like back home in Miami, men as handsome as Roman usually wanted nothing more than to catch the attention of every female within a ten-mile radius.

But not this guy. Oh, no. He'd wanted to move stealthlike in the television graphic arts room, glancing over shoulders and lingering at workstations just a few seconds too long to be an ordinary executive only interested in increasing ratings. When she'd asked around and discovered he was actually a consultant, she'd made the first move.

One well-timed quip later, and she'd received a charming invitation to dinner. One elevator ride down from the restaurant and she'd started a hot, lusty, unstoppable affair that she knew, soon, would be all too…over.

"Sorry, love." He secured the buttons on the cuffs of his sleeves. "Don't have a clue when I'll be back. But I know it will be soon."

She loved how he didn't sound like Hugh Grant when he called her *love*. She wouldn't have minded Colin Firth, but Roman's accent wasn't as easy to peg as British or Aussie or South African or even Scottish. He'd claimed to be American by birth, but a resident of the world. It was one of the few things about him she believed.

She shrugged one shoulder. "Your loss."

He quirked half a grin, bringing one devastating dimple into sharp relief against his stubble-roughened cheek. "You have no idea."

She expected his kiss to be brief, yet he surprised her again by making it long and lingering. Rachel's libido stirred just before he flashed out of the bedroom, and ten steps later, out of her small apartment in the SoHo section of Manhattan.

Her roommate, Jeannette, was in California on business and would be gone for at least another week. Rachel had the entire apartment to herself, and the loneliness suddenly echoed like shouts in a cave.

She relaxed against her pillows, closed her eyes and imagined how Roman would skip the elevator for the stairs, slip onto the lonely, nearly deserted sidewalk and hail a cab within moments, having some special magic when it came to summoning the often-impossible-to-find taxis that roamed the city.

She doused the light and for all of fifteen minutes, tried to sleep. The day before, she'd finished her assignment with the local news station, designing the new graphics for their eleven o'clock broadcast. She had a couple of new freelance projects to work on and a long-running assignment with an independent filmmaker to fiddle with, but otherwise, the next few days were hers to sleep late and explore the city since, because of Roman, she'd decided to stick around rather than head to the Costa Rican cloud forest. Her duffel bag had been calling to her for weeks, but she'd ignored her wanderlust. Somehow, trekking around Central America didn't quite measure up to making love to Roman on a semi-regular basis.

After twenty minutes of tossing and turning, she roused herself out of bed and took a hot shower, hoping to wash the alluring smell of Roman's cologne off her skin. If she didn't, he'd haunt her all day. She was already obsessed enough.

Once dressed in her favorite sweats and Miami Hurricane T-shirt, Rachel grabbed her hip pack and keys. She wasn't sure if she'd actually make it to the gym to do a round of circuit training and an hour on the treadmill, but she'd at least make it as far as Iris's coffee stand.

Rachel jogged down the steps of her building just in time to see Iris flick on the little rotating disco ball that told the neighborhood that her street-corner stand was open for business. The smell of fresh *pastelitos* and strong Cuban espresso assailed Rachel's nostrils, making her stomach rumble. She was going to work out, right? One pastry wouldn't kill her.

"You're up early, *mija*," Iris said, her thick Puerto Rican accent not hiding her surprise.

"I haven't really gone to sleep."

Iris arched a perfectly painted, black eyebrow. "Mr. Roman come to visit? Is that the third time this week?"

Rachel dug her hands into the pockets of her sweats and shrugged. "Fourth, but who's counting? I'm sure I won't see him again for a few days."

"Why are you so sure?"

Iris handed Rachel a large foam cup steaming with frothy milk, espresso and the four sugars Rachel preferred.

She blew on the hot drink, then took a tentative sip. The sweetened warmth slid down her throat, then pooled in her belly, chasing away the last chill of Roman's quick departure.

"The last two mornings, he left late, without the pager going off. But today, the pager summoned. He's probably on his way to the airport as we speak."

"Nah, just Uptown."

Rachel nearly jumped with fright at the gravelly voice—how Mario Capelli could consistently walk up behind her with such stealth, never mind park his cab on the sidewalk only a few car lengths away, continued to amaze her—and Iris, who'd clearly seen him coming, now blushed a healthy pink on her cocoa skin.

"You dropped Roman off?"

Mario nodded, and then gave Iris his signature greeting with a touch to the brim of his battered Giants cap. "Had some meeting. Looked pretty happy for a guy on his way to work," Mario said, wiggling his eyebrows.

Rachel slapped him playfully on the arm. She hadn't been in the city very long when she'd been lured from the backseat of Mario's cab to this street corner by the scent of authentic Cuban coffee. Rachel's mother, a Cuban immigrant, had twice married men who didn't share her Latin blood, but though her name no longer ended with a *Z*, Mireya Diaz Marlowe had refused to leave Miami and the rhythms of her roots. She'd never managed to teach her daughters to speak Spanish or get them interested in Castro's politics, but they did all have a weakness for Caribbean food and music. Because of Iris's stand, which now hummed with the music of Celia Cruz on a battered CD player Iris hung from the cart handle with a locked bicycle chain, Rachel had shelled out more than her budget allowed for the one bedroom walk-up just so she could get a little taste of home every day. Luckily, her roommate, when she was in town—which wasn't often—didn't mind the Murphy bed in the living room.

Rachel asked Iris for one of the *pastelitos* before turning back to Mario. "The man should look happy," she said confidently. "He was with me."

"I figured," Mario said with a smirk, nodding his thanks when Iris handed him his single-shot espresso in a tiny porcelain cup that she kept just for him.

Rachel took a bite of the warm pastry, humming

when the sweet, flaky crust opened to reveal the mildly spiced meat inside. She'd have to do two hours of tread-mill to make up for all these carbs, but she didn't care.

"God, Iris. This is delicious. I swear, you need to teach me how to make them."

"Then you won't come down every morning and buy one."

"If I promise to buy a dozen every Friday, will you teach me?"

The banter lasted until a few other customers showed up, leaving Mario and Rachel to shuffle over to a nearby mailbox, where they perched their coffees and enjoyed their familiar early-morning conversation as the city that never slept fully embraced being awake. Honking horns, blaring sirens and the rumble of a million commuters provided the background music Rachel dearly loved. Mario worked the night shift, but on his way home, he nearly always stopped by to see Iris as she was opening and would oftentimes pick up one last fare from in front of Rachel's building on his way back to Brooklyn. More often than not lately, that fare was Roman. And chatty as Mario was, Rachel realized that he might have some elusive information about her mysterious lover.

Question was, would he share?

"So, Mario. Where did Roman go this morning?"

He eyed her suspiciously. "Some meeting Uptown."

She knew that already. "Where Uptown?"

"You want the specific address?"

She shrugged indecisively.

"He had me drop him off just north of Central Park."

Mario's voice dipped a bit. They weren't best buddies or anything, but Rachel knew a dodge when she heard one. "Dropped him off? Not at a specific building?"

Mario pursed his lips. His eyes narrowed and he

scrunched his bushy, salt-and-pepper eyebrows over his kind, but shrewd, brown eyes. "Why you asking so many questions all of a sudden?"

She expelled a breath, not realizing she was holding the air so tight in her chest. "Roman and I have been seeing each other for almost four months, Mario, but I don't know a thing about him. He's so secretive. Guarded."

"This didn't bother you before," he said, grabbing his coffee cup again and downing the last of the potent brew.

Rachel took another ravenous bite of her breakfast. "It bothers me now," she replied, her mouth overstuffed.

Mario grinned. "Things getting serious?"

Rachel nearly choked. "No!"

Liar. Liar, liar, liar! Truth was, Roman had been around *too* much lately. Before, he'd come and go with such irregularity, Rachel hadn't invested much in him or their interactions. Naturally free-spirited, she hadn't craved commitment and consistency from the men in her life. Not, at least, until Roman started showing up more often. Now she couldn't seem to take her mind off him.

Mario's doubtful gaze forced her to amend her denial. "How can things get serious if I don't know anything about him?"

"Did you ask him?"

She rolled her eyes. Of course she'd asked. Roman simply had very persuasive means of turning her attention to other matters. Like sex.

"He's elusive," she replied.

"Elusive? The last thing you need is a guy with something to hide. Dump him," Mario offered.

"Just like that?" Rachel couldn't believe she was objecting. She'd kicked other guys out of her life for lesser crimes than keeping their personal information close to the vest. "What do you know that you're not telling me?"

"Nothing. I just think you should cut your losses before you get hurt if this Roman ain't being straight. There are a lot of great guys out there, Rachel. Maybe you need a little help finding one."

Rachel frowned. Mario had a reputation for matchmaking, but so far, he hadn't attempted to work his magic on her.

"I've never had trouble finding men, Mario, but thanks for the offer." She finished up her pastry, her mood dampened. "I can't believe you think I should dump a perfectly amazing guy just because he won't tell me details about where he grew up or where his parents live now or what company he's currently working for as a media consultant."

Mario shook his head. "Guys who are so secretive usually have something big to hide. Maybe he's married."

Rachel swallowed and the light and flaky meat *pastelito* thunked to the pit of her stomach. "He's not."

"You know that for sure?"

"It's one of the few questions he's given me a straight answer to. I don't think Roman lies. I think he avoids telling me more than he thinks I need to know."

"And that's not good enough anymore?"

Rachel's gaze drifted over her shoulder, back to her building, back to the stoop at the top of the stairs where she and Roman often groped and grabbed each other while she searched desperately for her keys so they could make love halfway up the stairwell inside or perhaps, if they were lucky, just after falling through her front door onto the living room carpet. Their lust had been a constant, insatiable part of her life for the past four months, but suddenly, this morning, she realized sexual desire simply wasn't enough.

Or, more likely, the suspicion had been brewing for weeks.

"Tell me where you took him, Mario. Please."

Mario's gaze darted to Iris, who was now tending to a line four or five deep. The morning rush had started and both he and Rachel knew he wouldn't be able to exchange a private word with his favorite coffee-stand owner for at least another two hours, maybe three. He flipped off his hat, ran his hand through his graying dark, curly hair, and then rubbed a bit at the rather thick stubble on his leathery cheeks.

"I'll do you one better," he said with a grin. "I'll show you."

CHAPTER TWO

"HE DIDN'T GO INSIDE?"

Rachel leaned forward on the dash, straining her neck to look up at the tall residential building where Mario had dropped Roman off. The place was swank. Two doormen. And a security guard. Did he live there?

"Nope. Got into a dark sedan parked at the curb," Mario replied.

Rachel sat back, bouncing against the worn leather seat. "Did he talk to anyone? Wave at the doorman?"

Mario shook his head. "Paid his fare, left me a generous tip and got straight into the other car."

"Does he always do that?"

Mario scrunched his nose as he thought deeply. "Nah, but sometimes. I kinda noticed this morning that I usually don't see him go inside. So out of curiosity, mind you, I waited."

Rachel turned and eyed Mario with new suspicion. "Did he know you were watching him?"

Mario glanced aside, and then pretended to adjust his side mirror through his open car window. "I wouldn't know."

Rachel eyed her friend suspiciously. Mario had a reputation for being a bit of a busybody. And he wasn't telling her the whole truth.

"After you dropped him off, did he wait for you to leave before heading toward the other car?"

Mario's expression displayed exaggerated thought. "Guys like him don't like to be watched, that much I can tell."

"So you…"

Mario sighed and gave up trying to be cool about what he'd done. "I made a U-turn and double-parked at the corner while he crossed. There were cabs all over. He probably didn't know it was me."

Rachel swallowed a chuckle. She'd known Mario for nearly three years and she'd pegged him long ago as the curious sort. He'd caught more than one guy casing Iris's corner with the intention of robbing her, and he'd averted several muggings of fares he'd dropped off in questionable parts of town.

"What made you stop and watch?"

Mario adjusted his cap. "Can't say."

"Can't or won't?"

He eyed her boldly. "Can't. It's just gut instinct."

Rachel grabbed the seat belt and strapped it across her body, which keyed Mario to put the car in gear and start the return ride back to her apartment. "We didn't learn much."

"No, but we could learn more," Mario suggested. "I mean, if you want to."

Rachel's heart skipped a beat. "How?"

He arched a brow.

She knew how. Next time Roman left her apartment, she and Mario would follow him.

Did she really want to go behind Roman's back? Spy on him? Part of her abhorred the inherent childishness of the prospect, but the other part—the part that didn't like to be taken for a fool—was interested.

"What would I have to do?" she asked.

"A little detective work," Mario said, as if the idea were as natural as breathing. "Nothing complicated or illegal."

She eyed him skeptically. "Stalking someone isn't illegal?"

"Hey, can you help it if he leaves and you just happen to be going in the same direction?"

"You'll need more than one cab," Rachel pointed out. "Our job would be easier if he gets into a car that knows we're tailing him."

Mario smiled broadly. Clearly, he liked the way she thought, which surprised her. Rachel really wasn't one for cloak-and-dagger stuff. But she had been around the block, and well, if a good thriller was on television, she usually tuned in.

"I can call in a favor," Mario said.

Rachel remained silent for the rest of the trip. After Mario pulled up in front of her building, he handed her a business card with his cell phone number inked at the bottom. "You call me next time he's at your place."

After an instant of hesitation, Rachel snatched the card. She offered Mario money for taking her Uptown, which he refused, then promised to call him unless her common sense got the better of her, which she didn't figure had much chance of happening.

Determined not to waste the entire day thinking about Roman or what she might discover if she followed him on one of those mysterious mornings when he left her at the summons of his pager, she headed toward the gym. On the short walk over, she couldn't help thinking about her mother, her sisters—the poster women for trust issues.

She supposed the fact that their father had left them high and dry when Rachel was only ten should have explained the plethora of neuroses shared by the Marlowe women, but Rachel hated to think that she was such a textbook case of deep-seated issues. Wasn't like every relationship she'd ever had imploded because she didn't trust her man. Okay, maybe a few. But not...oh, what was his name? Sean? Yeah, Sean. She'd dumped him because she didn't like football. And the man had been entirely obsessed with the game. Of course, he had played right guard for the Hurricanes at the time they'd been dating—hence the shirt she was wearing today— but that was no excuse for him to spend from ESPN's College Game Day on Saturday morning until the last whistle on Monday Night Football in front of the tube.

Yeah, that one hadn't been about trust.

Unfortunately, she decided as she yanked on the door to her gym, he'd been the only one.

Rachel exchanged greetings with the receptionist in the too-tight sports bra, waved her ID card under the barcode reader, and, after scoring a bottled water from the vending machine, jumped on the first empty tread-mill she saw, the one with the broken distance meter. She groaned, but opted to use the clock on the opposite wall as her gauge. Not that she had anything pressing to do today. In fact, her life seemed incredibly up in the air—and she suspected it would remain that way until she figured out just what Roman was hiding from her.

And Lord knew when that would be.

A WEEK. ROMAN SNUGGLED closer to Rachel and la-mented the fact that he'd only managed to stay away from her for a measly seven days. In his younger years, he would have cursed his lack of willpower. Now that he was older and wiser, he knew he was playing with fire, `auburn-haired, green-eyed fire. Recklessness hadn't gotten him to where he was in business. But taking chances with Rachel had invigorated his life to a level he hadn't experienced in years.

"Was that your pager?"

Roman glanced at the bedside table. The annoying cube of technology was completely still and silent.

He rolled over and caught a momentary glimpse of panic in Rachel's dark-green eyes.

Odd.

"Duty's not calling just yet. Why?" he said, slipping his hands over her bare belly and inhaling the musky, sweaty scent of recent, delicious sex. "Anxious for me to go?"

She forced a smile. Forced. What was that about?

"Of course not. I guess you've been here a little longer than usual. Call me Pavlov's dog, but the longer you're here, the more I expect you to leave."

He chuckled, but her instincts weren't far off. He knew the pager would likely go off at any moment. His operation had been at a virtual standstill until last week, when new data had started to filter through. The Agency, the code name for the covert group of the highest level agents from various organizations under Homeland Security had sent word that a contact from a separate, even more secret division would soon provide needed information for his case. In all honesty, he'd had no business visiting Rachel on the eve of something so crucial to his mission. He should have been at the office, monitoring the situation firsthand rather than leaving the task to a subordinate or waiting for the contact to make himself known. But once this assignment was over, he knew the Agency would shuttle him out of New York at the speed of light.

His obligations to the mission kept him from revealing the true nature of his job to Rachel, so he couldn't utter anything close to a goodbye. And for all he knew, this was their last night together—his last chance to imprint her silky skin, sweet scent and warm touch into his consciousness. He didn't want to waste time anticipating the moment he'd have to leave—this time, perhaps, for good.

"You look nothing like anyone's dog," he said, his voice rough with renewed lust as his fingers inched over her breasts, eliciting a soft, seductive whimper from the back of her throat. God, the woman was like a drug.

"You always say the right things," she whispered.

"And do the right things?"

He scooted the sheet out of his way and encircled one taut, brown nipple with his tongue. The heady saltiness of her flesh danced in his mouth like the bite of fine caviar.

She threaded her fingers into his hair, massaging his temples as he plied his mouth against her oh-so-sensitive breasts. He could make her come like this. He'd done it before, stirring her to madness when his own body wasn't quite ready yet for another orgasm, but hers was primed and pliant.

Her breath came in shallow pants and he could hear her accelerated heartbeat in her chest. She writhed on the bed and he knew if he dipped a hand lower, he'd find her sex wet with readiness. If he timed his ministrations just right, one flick of her clit would send her over the edge. Then he could kiss her hard and swallow the sounds of her release.

With Rachel, he was no less than a hungry carnivore and no more than a man ensnared by an attraction more powerful than any other he'd ever encountered.

Unfortunately, just before he could slide his hand to that precise spot that would drive her wild, the bedside table buzzed with the sound of his pager. He should

finish what he started, ignore the device and his respon-
sibilities and obligations and give this woman what she
so richly deserved, but on the second, longer vibration,
Rachel stiffened.

The moment was lost.

Damn.

He curled away from her, grabbed the pager and
pressed the button that lit the LCD.

The number he expected flashed across the screen,
along with the code that told him he had no time to lose.

Rachel sat up, the sheet yanked tight across her chest.

"Looks like our fun is over," she said.

He nodded. If she only knew.

CHAPTER THREE

"YOU'RE OUT EARLY."

Mario looked up guiltily, his mind grasping for an explanation for Iris, who'd caught him in the act of working out the pain in his sacroiliac. Rachel had called him just after midnight and for whatever insane reason, he'd decided to forgo his comfortable bed and instead spent his night off in the backseat of his cab, parked around the corner from his usual spot near Iris's coffee stand. He'd paid a night's wages to his pal Sam to meet him before sunrise and wait outside Rachel's building. This Roman Brach person had piqued his curiosity. He didn't want to see Rachel hurt.

Unfortunately, pulling all-nighters in the backseat of a cramped vehicle wasn't as kind to his old body as it used to be when he was on the force. Stakeouts had been his specialty back then. Now, they were literally a pain in the ass. And the back. And the neck.

"Morning," he said by way of greeting, trying to look as nonchalant as any man who was hanging out on the sidewalk long before the sun came up over Manhattan. "How you doing?"

"I've been up since three baking, that's how I'm doing."

Even when she was grousing, Iris's melodious, accented voice caused a thrill in the center of Mario's belly. Suddenly, sleeping in his cramped backseat didn't seem so bad.

"You smell great," he said, inhaling the sugary scent of the fresh baked goods clinging to her worn pink sweater, the one she wore every morning until the sun came up, when she'd toss it over the back of the stool she kept near the cash register.

"I smell like lard." She smoothed a hand over her thick, bunned black hair as she moved in the direction of her stand.

"More like fresh-baked dough sizzling with creamy butter and a dusting of cinnamon."

She stopped, the rolling cooler she tugged behind her knocking against her heels.

"That was almost...*poético*."

He knew little Spanish, but he got her point. Besides, he was fluent in Italian and the languages weren't so different. Just like the cultures. Just like the people.

"I can wax with the best of them when it comes to food. Can I help you set up?"

She resumed her walk, and like the dog he was, he followed. The minute they reached the front of Rachel's building, she immediately started unlocking the door with the impressive collection of keys she extracted from inside her blouse.

Oh, to be those keys.

Stop it, Mario! Have you lost all your respect for women?

He cleared his throat and looked away, suddenly feeling more like sixteen than sixty. He glanced up at what he thought was Rachel's window. The lights were off. Or perhaps, on in the adjacent room only.

"Where's your cab?" she asked, once she had the

coffee brewing and had tossed him a roll of paper towels and some Windex to clean the front of her display case.

"Around the corner. I didn't want any fares this morning."

"You still on the clock?"

"Nah, it was my night off."

She eyed him suspiciously but didn't ask any more questions until she had her stand nearly ready for operation. He'd helped her set up once before, about three months ago when she'd sprained her wrist. She hadn't accepted assistance easily, but Mario could be fairly stubborn when he wanted to be.

He could remember the first day he saw Iris again, the fateful morning three years ago when he'd picked Rachel Marlowe up outside a real estate agent's office. She'd promised him a big tip if he drove her around so she could find a new place, but the twenty she'd slipped him that day in addition to her fare had been nothing compared to what she'd really started. The first question out of her mouth had been, "Where can a girl get a decent cup of real Cuban coffee around here?"

The answer had brought him to Iris, a woman he hadn't seen in years.

The whole scenario—his attraction to Iris, his friendship with Rachel, his inability to keep his half-crooked Italian nose out of other people's business—had led him right here after getting little sleep the night before, his adrenaline buzz spawned by an attraction he didn't know if he could ignore much longer. And then there was his cockamamie plan to find out if Roman Brach was who he said he was.

Which Mario doubted. His cop instincts wailed that Brach wasn't just some liar leading on his latest squeeze, or a married dude who wanted Rachel on the side. He'd had a friend at the precinct run the plates on the car that had picked Roman up yesterday and got nothing but one of the million car services available throughout town. And a quick search of the guy's name scored nothing by way of priors. What little he'd told Rachel checked out.

Still, Mario had a strong feeling that this guy wasn't on the up-and-up. And if the man turned out to be the worst kind of con, Mario would be there. He owed Rachel, since she'd been entirely responsible for Iris coming back into his life.

"If you're off duty, why are you here?" Iris finally asked.

He put on his best, most appealing grin. "My morning's shot if I don't see your smiling face first thing."

She rolled her eyes, but her tiny grin revealed the effectiveness of his compliment. "You're full of it, Mario Capelli."

"Full of what? Infatuation for you? Full of an irresistible need to maybe—" he took a deep breath "—sometime soon, see you somewhere other than on this street corner?"

He waited a full minute, watching Iris's dark eyes narrow as she considered what he'd said. Out of the corner of his eye, he caught sight of someone coming out of Rachel's building. On instinct, he grabbed Iris's elbow and tugged her down so they were both concealed by the cart.

"What are you doing?"

He glanced around the side of the cart. Roman quickly surveyed the street, probably looking for Mario's perennially parked-at-the-end-of-the-block cab, then took off toward Avenue of the Americas, right to the corner where he'd positioned his co-conspirator, Sam.

Mario leaned forward and without giving himself a moment to think, kissed Iris soundly. Knowing he had only a few moments before Rachel came down looking for him, he forced himself to break the lip-lock and ignore the fire surging through his veins. "I'm asking you to dinner."

She stuttered. "W-when?"

"Tonight. Five o'clock?"

Good enough time as any, especially since he knew that Iris went to bed early so she could open her stand before dawn.

"Where?"

Mario stood and, as gentlemanly as he could, helped Iris back to her feet. "You pick!"

He started down the block to his cab. With traffic light, he'd be able to spin around the nearby side street and reach Rachel before they lost sight of Roman's ride.

RACHEL SLID INTO MARIO'S waiting cab, out of breath and unable to speak. Luckily, she didn't have to say "follow that car." Mario had torn away from the curb before she could grab the door handle and yank it shut.

"You're flushed," Mario said.

She gulped in air, forcing the oxygen into her lungs. "I ran down the backstairs and out through the alley. I didn't want to run into him in the lobby."

Closing her eyes, Rachel counted backward from one hundred, her heartbeat slowly calming to as close to normal as she was going to get until this was over. For a split second, she wondered why she had come up with such a sneaky plan. Why couldn't she just ask the man what, if anything, he was hiding? *Because he won't answer.* She could always give him an ultimatum. *Yeah, right.* Somehow, she couldn't see a man like Roman reacting well to her laying down the law. He'd walk out. And damn it, if anyone ended things, it was going to be her.

"There!" Mario shouted, his finger jabbing his windshield. "There's Sam."

"Wasn't it dark when Roman went out? Are you sure he got in with your friend?"

Mario glanced at her sideways. He picked up his radio and, after contacting the dispatcher, was patched in to Sam's car. He asked some questions in Italian. Rachel understood, and she'd bet big bucks Roman would, too. But the conversation was innocuous enough that unless he was suspicious of his driver, he'd never realize he'd been scammed.

"Satisfied?"

Rachel smirked. "You're awfully good at all this covert stuff. Why is that?"

Mario turned his attention back on driving. "Natural talent."

They headed toward the Upper East Side, where Mario had dropped Roman off before. Did he have a home there? A wife or lover or family she knew nothing about? His nomadic lifestyle appealed to her own sense of wanderlust so much at the beginning, she'd never questioned how a man could go from place to place with no real home. In fact, she'd envied him. He seemed to feed on the spontaneity of his job, just the way he seemed to revel in the unpredictability of their so-called relationship.

Hadn't she been attracted to the same life? Her spontaneous trips fulfilled her desire to travel and her career as a freelance artist paid the bills. In Roman, she'd seen a kindred spirit—a career-focused professional at one moment; a free-wheeling vagabond at another. Maybe that's why she couldn't just let him go. He was too perfect for her. He understood her like no other man ever could.

And yet, she was practicing the ultimate deception to find out more about him. Would he forgive her if he found out?

"Maybe this isn't such a good idea," she suggested as Mario followed the other yellow cab onto a quiet street with tall, thick elms in decorative iron planters embedded in the sidewalk.

Mario kept his expression blank. "Tell me now, Rachel. You don't want to know what the man is hiding, we go home."

She pressed her eyelids shut. She was so close. Would it really hurt to finish what she'd started? "I need to know," she said, her voice nearly a whisper. What if he *was* married? What if everything between them had been a lie? Okay, she had to admit that in the trust department, she and Roman had a huge deficit. But until one of them broke the casual pattern of their relationship, things would never change, right?

"Here's your chance," Mario said.

The yellow cab pulled up to the curb in front of a clearly upscale condo building, only this one had no doormen—at least, none out at the early hour of the morning. After a moment where Rachel assumed he was paying the driver, Roman got out. Almost instantaneously, a tall, slim brunette emerged from the shadows.

And made a beeline for Roman.

Rachel sat forward, watching out of the corner of her eye as the cab Roman had ridden in pulled away. He didn't seem to notice. His attention was one hundred and ten percent on the leggy brunette.

"Now, who is she?" Mario asked.

Rachel opened her mouth to ask the same question, but before she could, the brunette with the waist-length, glossy black hair grabbed Roman by the lapels and tugged him into a hot, hard kiss.

"Holy shit."

They'd cursed in unison.

Rachel reached for the door handle. Mario grabbed her by the elbow.

"You have your answer. Rachel, let it be," he said, his dark eyes glossy with warning.

Rachel looked at his hand with disdain, but then quickly realized he just wanted to protect her. She appreciated the sentiment, but she could slay her own dragons. She'd sliced a few open in her lifetime. She could again.

"Yes, I do. Mario, trust me on this." Her gaze flicked to Roman, who was still swapping spit with the Cher-on-a-stick look-alike in skintight leather jeans. "I will not let that man, or any man, walk all over me. Never have, never will."

Mario released her arm, and before she lost one ounce of indignation, Rachel pushed out of the cab. Sure, she and Roman had never pretended to be exclusive. Hell, they'd never even talked the matter over. But while Rachel Marlowe may have grown up with three sisters, she'd never learned to share. Especially not her lovers.

As soon as she was close enough, she tapped the chick in the boob-hugging turtleneck on the shoulder and said a polite excuse me. Once. Twice.

The exotic brunette turned slowly, her eyes a dreamy onyx mix of shadows and mystery. "May I help you?"

Rachel grinned. "Actually, yes. Could you step aside?"

The woman complied, giving Rachel a perfect shot with her fist on Roman's jaw. "You son of a bitch!"

Roman barely flinched, but his eyes widened and his face, so healthy and tanned less than half an hour ago, lost all color. He grabbed Rachel by the arm and yanked her behind him so quickly, she lost her footing on the dew-slippery sidewalk.

He turned and shot a finger out at her. "Stay there."

With a spin, he faced the woman in black, who'd gone into an odd fighting pose. He raised his hands in front of him, as if she was going to attack. "Dom, don't get crazy."

The woman's stare was ice. "I don't get crazy, Brach. But if you don't keep that—"

Her threat was cut off by the squeal of tires. Rachel half expected Mario to come riding to her rescue, but instead she saw a dark sports car approaching, headlights off. She narrowed her gaze, and at the same moment that she noticed something protruding from the passenger-side window, Roman dove over her, shielding her body as gunfire rent the air.

Rachel screamed. Bullets shot from the car and pinged nearby. Then return fire exploded near her ears.

From the barrel of Roman's own gun.

CHAPTER FOUR

THE INCIDENT LASTED LESS than three seconds, but Roman could have sworn a painful, torturous hour had passed before the bullets stopped piercing the sidewalk. The attacker in the sports car sped away, tires screeching. Domino darted into the street, firing her weapon until the distance made her shots wasteful. The agent dashed back to him just as he was rolling off of Rachel. Leave it to his superiors to send his former lover, Domino Black, as his contact.

"Rachel, are you hit?" he asked, desperately searching her for signs of blood.

Except for a scrape on her cheek, she was clean. Her amazing jade-green eyes were glossy from shock. He leaned forward to check her breathing when tires squealed again.

Roman turned and aimed, concurrently with Domino, who still had her weapon at the ready. But this time, the offending car was a taxi and Mario Capelli swung open his driver-side door. He remained behind the door, a large, unfriendly-looking .357 Magnum clutched confidently in his hands.

"Let her up," he ordered, jerking his head toward Rachel.

Domino made a slight move to the right. Through clenched teeth, Roman ordered her to stand down. The woman was the most accomplished marksman in the Agency—and a trained assassin. She could take Mario out without batting an eyelash.

"He's a friend," Roman explained.

Domino lowered her weapon. She was deadly but not cruel.

Beneath him, Rachel groaned. The sound tore through him with the same velocity as a jacketed hollow-point bullet fired at close range. She'd almost died. On account of his job, his enemies. His lies.

"She's fine, Mario," Roman called out. "Just a little groggy."

The wily taxi driver stepped around to the front of his car with strong, bold steps that belied his advanced age. He kept his weapon out, but he'd lowered the barrel. "Who are you?"

Roman checked Rachel for signs of any other injury. He found nothing, but her eyes were dilated. Unprepared for his jumping on top of her, she'd likely banged her head hard against the ground. "I'm not one of the bad guys, Mario."

"And why should I believe you?"

Sirens wailed in the distance. Damn. The police would descend any minute. He didn't have to look up to know that Domino had blended back into the shadows, disappearing into the morning as if she'd never been there. He should have shot her in the back for the trouble she'd caused, kissing him like that. He'd only allowed the kiss to linger because he'd figured Domino had a good reason for creating a scene where they were lovers once again. Now he knew she'd only entrapped him because she knew Rachel had been watching.

Typical.

Rachel pulled herself up onto shaky knees.

"Who was that?"

He didn't know if she was talking about Domino or the shooters in the car, but he decided going with the latter as a safer topic.

"I've never seen that car before," Roman said, not lying, but of course not telling her the truth, either.

Unfortunately for him, Rachel wasn't stupid, but she was angry. She pushed up on to her feet, and when she wobbled, Mario buoyed her by the elbows. Roman reached forward to help, but both of their poisonous stares made him retract his hands.

"Rachel, I can explain."

"Of course you can," she said, her tone venomous. "Lies spill easily from your lips, don't they?"

"You have no idea," he replied, regretfully.

The sirens grew louder.

"Mario, get her out of here."

She grabbed his arm, but the move cost her as she wavered and nearly toppled.

"Tell me who you are," she begged.

In that moment, Roman's heart cracked. God knew, he wanted to tell her everything, but there was no time. And if he let her in on his secrets, what dangers would she face?

"Rachel, go, now. I'll find you. I'll tell you everything."

"Tell me now."

All around them, faces peered from the windows and doors nearby. A few people in the park across the street pointed and stared. He had to get Rachel out. He'd already involved her more than he had a right to.

"Rachel, you have to understand—"

She pulled herself up to her full height, this tiny auburn-haired sprite of a woman he'd come to care deeply for. "Never mind. I understand completely," she said, her voice shaky but curt. Her eyes darkened with his betrayal, and as she looked at him one last time, Roman's chest felt as if someone had just riveted a steel plate between his ribs.

Mario whisked Rachel away. Roman pressed his lips tightly together, for the first time wanting to shout his secrets to the world. He'd broken nearly every other regulation set down by his superiors. Why get all obedient now?

Because lives were at stake. Millions of lives. Not just his and Rachel's. Not anymore.

The curious had spilled from nearby buildings. Witnesses. He'd have to call in big favors to keep this drive-by contained. Domino he didn't worry about. She operated on a security level far above his own. But Mario and Rachel? They'd driven into this mess simply because Roman hadn't been able to tell Rachel goodbye after his investigation of her had been complete.

He knew everything about her now. Every friend she'd ever had. Every country she'd ever visited. Every political view she'd ever possessed. Every erogenous zone that could cause her to cry out in unabashed pleasure if he applied just the right combination of moisture, pressure and suction. He knew everything the Agency had sent him to find out—and more.

The only thing he didn't know was how to let her go.

IRIS EMERGED FROM RACHEL'S bedroom and quietly shut the door. She padded over and sat beside Mario on the couch, eyeing his Scotch and water, on the rocks, with trepidation.

"I know it's early," Mario said, lifting the drink with shaking hands and taking a welcome sip. "But these are unusual circumstances."

"I have an ex-husband who thinks every moment he's awake is an unusual circumstance."

Mario put the drink down. He'd figured a woman Iris's age, somewhere in her fifties, had been married before, but he knew little about her personal life except that she'd accepted his date for tonight—an event that might not go off after what happened less than an hour ago.

"I'm not an alcoholic, if that's what you're asking."

"I am asking. *Pero,* would you admit it if you were?"

Mario grinned. "Yeah, to you, I would."

She matched his smile with a shy curve of lips. The expression melted away the worry that had creased her brow since he'd skidded to a stop just behind her stand with a shaken Rachel curled into a fetal ball in his backseat. Iris had quickly and unceremoniously shut down her coffee stand and helped him lead Rachel upstairs.

The poor kid had hardly said a word except for mumbled phrases that sounded a lot like "How could I be so stupid?" and "What kind of man is he?"

Mario and Iris had soothed Rachel with a combination of mild recriminations on Roman Brach and a Xanax from the stash Iris kept in her purse for her anxiety disorder—another new thing Mario had learned about the object of his affection. Soon, they'd washed the grit from Rachel's hands, feet and face and had tucked her into her bed for a well-deserved nap. Maybe sleep would give her more perspective. More calm. She'd gone through a hell of a shock in the past hour— first, witnessing the man who'd sworn up and down that he wasn't involved with anyone other than her sucking face with an exotic, black-haired beauty, then rushing to confront him in order to regain an ounce of her self-respect only to be shot at in a drive-by and, lastly, watching her lover, a self-proclaimed television consultant, brandish a handgun and return fire with confidence and ease.

"Want to tell me what happened?" Iris asked.

Mario recounted the situation point by point. With each revelation, Iris reacted with increased shock.

"*Dios mio!* She could have been killed. You both—"

"I was okay. By the time I realized what was happening, it was over. I got a description of the car. Called it in to my dispatcher. I need to make sure he called the cops."

Iris tilted her head, her eyes questioning.

"I'm retired NYPD," he explained. "Thirty-five years."

Her dark eyes widened. "I didn't know."

"You thought I drove a hack all my life?"

She shrugged shyly. "I guess we don't talk as much as we think we do, in between customers, I mean."

He nodded. "That's why I wanted to do the dinner thing tonight. You know, find out about each other."

Iris glanced regretfully at Rachel's bedroom door. "I don't think we should leave, you know?"

Yeah, Mario knew. He didn't want to leave Rachel, either. Funny how the kid had grown on him. Like Iris, Mario had been married before, but he'd never had kids. His wife, God rest her soul, hadn't been able to conceive. Yet, he'd always looked at the circumstance as a blessing. He'd walked beats in everywhere from Flatbush to Harlem. By the time he'd made detective, he'd seen more than his fair share of cruelty and crime and death. Bringing kids into the world had seemed a bad decision. After his wife died, he hadn't been so sure.

But with his job driving cabs, he met lots of young adults who seemed to fill the void. He liked getting to know them, meddling in their lives a bit, using his personal experiences with life and love to push them in the right direction.

With Rachel, however, he'd screwed up, big time. He would have bet his best night's tips that Roman Brach hadn't been up to anything sinister, that her fears about his secretive nature had been nothing more than imagination and supposition—and maybe, he was getting a little on the side. Yeah, he'd pegged Brach for the quiet, untrustworthy type, but he'd never, even with all his old cop's instincts primed, have imagined the guy had been wrapped up in the criminal world.

Despite Brach's claims, Mario had no idea which side Brach was on, but he was going to stick around Rachel's place long enough to find out.

"You gonna reopen the stand?"

Iris pressed her lips tightly together. "I didn't lock up properly in the rush. I should go back downstairs and make sure I haven't been robbed blind. But I'll close for the rest of the day and help watch after our *mijita*."

Mario shifted in his seat. "We could take turns running the register, if you want to stay open." That way, he could watch the street for any sign of Roman Brach, or the car and drivers that had tried to gun him down.

"You'd do that?" she asked.

He knew Iris struggled financially. Most working-class people in New York did. He had a fairly nice nest egg and pension, so he worked more as a way to keep out of trouble, stay active. If he didn't drive the cab for a few days, no one but his dispatcher would give a damn.

"We'll do what we have to," he replied. "Rachel shouldn't be alone. I have a strong feeling that the scene on the sidewalk won't be the last between Rachel and Roman, and one of us should be here to make sure she doesn't get hurt."

RACHEL BACKED AWAY from her bedroom door.

Too late, Mario.

Despite the drugs, she'd been too wound up to really sleep, though the medication had soothed her racing heart to a nice, even beat. She was now calm enough to realize that everything Roman Brach had told her, shown her, implied to her, had likely been a lie. From his profession to his interest in her…hell, probably even to his name.

And worst of all, his deceptions tore at the very core of who she was. She'd always considered herself smart, savvy, brave. She'd traveled the world with little more than a backpack and passport, even venturing into countries where government rule was as insubstantial as feathers on the wind. She'd studied graphic arts at the best school in Florida, interned with the hottest graphic arts company in Miami, and then hopped on the next plane to New York City to work with the best in the business, bar none. She had no unfulfilled dreams. No unreachable goals. No regrets.

Until now.

A broken heart was nothing new. Hers had been cracked and had healed many times. But this time, when she'd least expected the trauma, when she'd told herself over and over that her dalliance with Roman was just an exciting, once-in-a-lifetime affair, she'd been ripped apart at the seams.

Roman had lied to her in so many ways, her mind was still spinning. She staggered to her bed and clambered back beneath the sheets. Yes, he'd hurt her. But that didn't mean she wouldn't survive. She just had to figure out how.

CHAPTER FIVE

"WHAT DO YOU MEAN YOU HAVE no report of a shooting at Seventy-eighth and Madison? It happened this morning! I was there. I saw it. I heard sirens."

"Ma'am, if you were a witness, why didn't you call earlier?"

Rachel pressed her lips together tightly. This certainly was a question she'd rather not answer. "I was terrified, okay? Bullets were flying."

"Was anyone shot?"

"Not that I know of. Look, I just want to find out what happened."

"So far as my computer shows, ma'am, nothing. Not even a record of a call."

Rachel half listened to the desk sergeant as he ran through a list of possibilities for the glitch, her body still numb from the medication Iris had given her, her mind still trapped in the violence she'd witnessed on the street just twelve hours ago—a shooting the NYPD now declared had never happened.

"You're sure?" she asked again. "There is no official record? Maybe the investigating officers are still looking into the matter? Haven't filed the right paperwork yet?"

Mario had schooled her on the process, but he'd also guessed that by six o'clock in the evening, the computers at the police department would have some reference to the shooting on the sidewalk. When he returned from helping Iris pack up and move the last of her wares back to her apartment, he was going to be shocked by what Rachel had learned.

Which was, essentially, nothing.

She thanked the officer and mindlessly hung up the phone.

The soft knock on the door drew her attention away from the mess with the cops. She'd expected Mario and Iris back any moment and hadn't thought to give them a key.

"Just a minute," she shouted automatically, but recoiled when she touched the dead bolt. What if it wasn't Mario or Iris?

"Who is it?" she asked, her voice trembling.

"Rachel, it's me."

Roman.

"Go away," she ordered.

"Are you okay?"

"If I wasn't, I'd be at the hospital. Or at the morgue."

"I'm sorry, Rachel. Please, let me in so I can explain."

She laughed. Okay, the situation really wasn't funny, but that didn't mean she couldn't enjoy the absurdity. Explain? Roman? The king of secrets and lies?

"I don't want to hear anything you have to say. You're a liar and maybe even a criminal. Forget you ever met me, Roman. Forget you know where I live. Forget that I'm alive. We'll both be better off."

Though her chest felt as if a heavyweight wrestler had wrapped his arms around her to begin a slow and eventually fatal squeeze, Rachel propelled herself away from the door and waited. She paced the living room, watching the trifecta of locks—a dead bolt, a chain and the key—for any motion. She listened for footsteps in the hallway to announce the arrival of Mario and Iris. She shouldn't have let them go—but then, she'd encouraged them, hadn't she? She was a big girl and didn't need chaperones. What she needed was space—away from Roman, away from the city, away from the memories.

Infuriated with herself, Rachel slammed into her bedroom. He'd leave. He'd have no choice. God! Why couldn't Roman's secret have been just about the sexy woman in the skintight leather pants? Why couldn't he have been just a liar and a cheat? Why did he have to be the kind of man people shot at?

This wasn't the life she'd designed for herself. She didn't have enemies. The most controversial thing she'd ever done was work on the opening credits for a documentary on birth control. Sure, she'd gotten a few nasty e-mails, but so had everyone else whose name had been listed in the credits. No one had targeted her for death.

But what of the other woman? Maybe Ms. Sleek-and-Sensual was an international drug dealer. Maybe she seduced big government officials and then sold their secrets to the highest bidder? Maybe she had been the target. Not Roman.

"Who was she?" she muttered.

"I can answer that."

She spun around, her heart slamming up into her throat at the combined surprise and anger at seeing Roman standing in her bedroom doorway.

"How did you get in?"

"I had to see you."

"You didn't answer my question! But then, you never do, do you? You just turn the focus on to something else. Get out!"

She stepped forward, questioning whether or not the ire swimming through her veins was hot enough yet for her to throw him out. No matter what she'd witnessed this morning on the sidewalk, even considering the gun he'd pulled out of nowhere and fired into the street, she wasn't afraid of him. Her judgment was clearly off, though, so she kept her distance.

He must have read the fear in her eyes. "I wouldn't hurt you, Rachel. Ever. I swear."

"I have no reason to believe anything you say, Roman."

He released a pent-up breath. "I know."

"Then why come? Why bother?"

"I had to see for myself that you weren't hurt."

She spun around in a circle, her arms spread wide. She even managed to cover up the tiny half stumble her dizziness caused when she came to a halt. "I'm perfect. Now, get out."

"I wasn't just worried about you physically, Rachel."

She raised her eyebrows high, wanting to make sure he understood his audacity.

"You're worried about my feelings? If maybe my heart was broken after seeing you snogging with some sexy chick with no color palette in her fashion decisions? I don't give a rat's ass who you screw around with, Roman."

"You cared yesterday."

"That's because I was the one you were screwing. So not the case anymore."

Emboldened by the fact that she'd sparred with him for a good ten minutes without either dissolving into tears or falling victim to his practiced charm, Rachel took a step closer. Yeah, it hurt like hell to have him here, right in front of her, forcing her to confront the stupidity of her choices over the past four months, but she could take it.

"Tell me something, Roman."

"Anything."

She laughed, even as her heart wept, knowing he couldn't answer the question she was about to pose, even though she was still compelled to ask. "Is anything I know about you true?"

"What do you know?"

She cursed. He never could answer a straight question. She'd start simple.

"Your name?"

His mouth tightened.

"Are you a television consultant?"

Again, nothing.

"Is that woman your lover?"

"No."

"Never? She's never been your lover?"

He glanced aside.

"An ex. Nice."

"I didn't expect to ever see her again. She only kissed me because she knew you were watching."

Rachel staggered a step backward, her knees folding until she sat on the bed. "You knew I followed you?"

He shook his head. "No, I didn't know. She knew."

"How?"

"Apparently, she's been following me for the past week."

"Hopeful of a romantic reunion?"

"She and I slept together, Rachel. Nothing more."

She leaned back on her hands. "That's your modus operandi, so I shouldn't be surprised."

"She's involved in my business."

"Which isn't television consultation."

"No."

She sat up straighter. "Holy shit. I think you just answered a question."

"That's all I can say, Rachel. I'm not really a television consultant. Everything I've told you about myself from the first moment we met has been a lie, first as a way to get to know you, then as a way to protect you."

"From what?"

He stared at her and she could see the conflict in his eyes. Truth? Lie? So many choices for a clearly complicated man.

"From people like the shooter in the car. People who don't care about collateral damage. That's only one reason why I should have stopped seeing you months ago."

"Why didn't you?" she challenged.

He stepped forward and his voice, for the briefest moment, sounded strangled from the tightness in his throat. "How could I?"

She glanced aside. "It was just sex."

"Now who's the liar?"

For a moment, she sat there, chastised, knowing that if she could stop pretending for just a second, she'd realize she'd come to care about the man. But how could that caring mean anything when the man she'd thought she was getting to know was nothing more than an illusion? A cover?

"Look, Roman, or whatever your name is, the sex was great and the affair was fun, all full of spontaneity and mystery and all the things that are biting us in the ass right now. Fact is, you're probably on your way out of town—you and that gun of yours—so why are we wasting our breaths talking about nothing?"

Silence reigned. God, she wanted him to reply with "It's not nothing. We connected, Rachel. We were something to each other. You matter to me." But his mouth remained closed. She supposed she should have celebrated when he turned and started to exit the room, but instead, a sob caught in her throat.

Luckily, Mario and Iris swept in before Roman could change direction.

"What the hell is he doing here?" Mario asked.

Iris muttered in Spanish, something Rachel was pretty damned sure was a curse. Not the cussword type, either. The "may your penis turn purple and fall off" type.

"He was just leaving," she replied.

Roman cast a glance over his shoulder. The regret and self-recrimination in his steel-blue eyes nearly caused her insides to buckle, but she pressed her hand against her belly and silently ordered herself to remain still.

He opened his mouth to speak, but she narrowed her eyes and speared him with a glare that told him any excuse, beyond the honest-to-God truth, would be too little, too late.

With a polite "excuse me," he moved out of the apartment and consequently, out of her life.

Forever. For good.

Iris rushed past Mario and caught Rachel by the arms before she could sink onto the bed and dissolve. Into tears. Into a puddle. Into a pathetic mess.

"*Mija,* you're better off."

Rachel forced strength into her legs, willed herself to remain standing. "I know that, Iris. I swear, I know that with every fiber of my being. But why, then, why do I feel like I'm about to fall apart?"

CHAPTER SIX

"JUST HOLD ON THERE, SON."

Roman turned, not entirely surprised to see Mario Capelli stalking after him in the hallway outside Rachel's apartment. The wizened cabdriver shut the door behind him firmly, then marched down the hall. Roman waited. He supposed he shouldn't deny the man his opportunity to ream him out.

"Mario," he said by way of greeting.

The old man arched an eyebrow. "That's it?"

"I can't explain to you any more than I could explain to Rachel."

"She has a lot of questions."

"None that I can answer."

He'd wanted to answer them. He'd fully intended to come here and offer complete disclosure. But on the way over, using all his skills as a covert agent to make sure that the enemies who had fired on him this morning didn't get a second chance to fill him full of holes, he'd realized that the truth would be too selfish and dangerous. What she didn't know couldn't hurt her. Right?

Mario shifted his hands into the pockets of his baggy khakis. "Maybe she doesn't know the right questions to ask, her heart being broken and all."

"We were never serious that way," Roman insisted,

knowing the statement was only true from her perspective, not his.

"Maybe not in words, but when you jump into a woman's bed, you jump into her heart, too, whether she likes it or not."

Roman blew out a frustrated breath. "That's a fairly old-fashioned viewpoint."

Mario shrugged. "I'm a fairly old-fashioned guy. But unlike Rachel, I do know what questions to ask. You a crook?"

Roman chuckled. He was a lot of dastardly and despicable things, but a thief wasn't one of them. "No, sir."

"Drug dealer?"

He shook his head.

"Assassin? Gunrunner? Bank robber?"

"None of the above."

"So you're legit?"

"Not exactly."

"That can mean only one thing—you're government issue."

Roman arched a brow. He supposed he'd led the man to his conclusion by replying with honesty to his questions, but the cabbie had had the forethought to ask. "You in the biz?"

"Just a cop. Detective. Thirty-five years for the NYPD."

"And now you drive a cab."

"Beats withering away. I know the city. And I know people. And you're one who can turn a conversation on a dime so he doesn't have to talk about himself."

Roman grinned, not wanting to take the compliment, but what choice did he have? His talent for lying and twisting conversations had brought him to this very place—on the brink of losing a woman he'd risked everything for, simply because he couldn't tell the truth.

"Rachel is better off without me," he said, accepting that if he said the mantra often enough, he might, eventually, start to believe it.

Mario clucked his tongue. "That's obvious. But I've got to know that what happened this morning isn't going to come back to haunt her. You haven't marked her for a hit, have you?"

Roman opened his mouth to protest, but stopped and thought he'd better think long and hard about his answer first. Clearly, his mission had been compromised, which was probably why the Agency had sent Domino to intercept him this morning. Not to kill him—if that had been her mission, he'd be dead by now. To warn him. He'd yet to be debriefed, but instead he'd spent his day backtracking and thinking about Rachel, ensuring that he could pay her one last visit without endangering her life. But while he had strong suspicions about who the shooters were and that their attack had simply been a way to send the Agency a message, he couldn't be sure that they wouldn't try to use Rachel against him if given the chance.

"Can you stay with her tonight?" he asked.

Mario nodded. "But I can't stay every night."

For an instant, Roman thought Mario might be implying that he should be the one to make sure Rachel was safe, but both men knew that his hanging around one minute longer wasn't good for either Rachel or him. He'd screwed up large.

He never should have dallied with her in the first place, but the attraction had been so powerful, so tempting. Once he'd cleared her of suspicion of providing information through her graphic designs to the terrorist group he'd been tracking, he'd justified their affair by promising himself it would be brief. One night, maybe two. Enough to sate both of them. But the more he tasted, the more he craved. Everything about her entranced him. She was so fresh, so bright-eyed and in love with the city, with her job, with her friends, with the world. Rachel Marlowe was completely and totally unlike the women he dealt with at the Agency, who were all slightly jaded by what they'd been trained to recognize and prevent. Or like Domino, jaded to her core so deeply, she could kill without regret.

He'd been weak. He knew that now. And his inability to fight his desires had resulted in Rachel getting hurt. Under different circumstances, he might have fallen in love with her. He had to make things right—in the only way he knew how.

"I'm checking in with my superiors next. They don't want any collateral damage, so I'm sure they'll take care of Rachel until the heat is off. I'll contact you, let you know when Rachel is safe. She's probably not in any danger, but—"

"Better safe than sorry."

Roman turned to the stairwell, but Mario stopped him with a halting hand. "Hold on, cowboy."

The older man ambled back to Rachel's apartment, knocked on the door, then whispered through the chain to Iris that he'd be back in less than an hour. He gave her strict instructions not to open the door for anyone but him.

Mario then gestured gallantly toward the exit.

Roman frowned. "Where do you think you're going?"

Mario smiled, smug and confident that whatever he had planned, Roman would comply. Which he would, since the man had promised to take care of Rachel—a task Roman should have been able to do for himself, but couldn't.

"I'm going to give you a lift."

"That's not necessary."

Mario caught him by the elbow. "Sorry, but it is."

"I CAN'T BELIEVE YOU LET HIM drive you here."

Domino Black, or so she was called by their superiors, emerged from the shadows of the stairwell in the Agency safe house, her keen almond-shaped eyes gleaming with disgust. Fortunately, Roman had seen her eyes gleam with other basic, elemental emotions before—lust, mostly—so the effect, while disconcerting, didn't penetrate his already guilt-ridden body.

"We'll be out of here in an hour," he said, sliding his hand along the doorjamb to find the hidden-key compartment. "Once we're gone, there will be no trace of either one of us. What's he going to do? Call the cops? Clearly, the Agency has them under control."

"I don't buy it," she snapped, perennially suspicious.

"The guy just wanted to read me the riot act about hurting Rachel. She's like a daughter to him. You can't blame him."

"I could kill him."

Roman clucked his disbelief. "Even you aren't that cold."

He checked the doorjamb on the opposite side, then cursed. He was just about to ask Domino if she knew where the key was when the metal piece materialized in her black-leather-gloved hands. When he moved to take the key, she snatched it away with a childlike grin.

Well, with what she wanted him to think was a childlike grin. So far as he knew, Domino Black had never been a child.

The second time she brandished the key, he took it quickly into his possession. "I've had enough games today."

He opened the door and let them inside. The room in the boardinghouse was sparse, but relatively clean. The furniture, consisting of a couch, a twin bed, a coffee table, a small refrigerator and safe, would provide all he'd need for the next hour or so until he made contact with the Agency again. First, he'd need some time to gather his thoughts.

Roman locked the door securely behind him and pressed a button on the wall, activating a mechanism that rendered all listening devises useless. Anyone trying to eavesdrop on their conversation electronically would hear nothing but a buzz.

"Isn't pulling contact duty a step down for you?" he asked.

She sneered. "I was in the city. They called me in. We caught the shooters. They're in custody. Well, one of them is in the morgue."

He caught the sly grin on her face. She had returned fire that morning. That the driver hadn't been taken out, too, remained a miracle of sorts.

"How did you catch the driver so fast?"

Domino removed her gloves but was careful to touch nothing. "The cabbie provided a dead-on description of the car to his dispatcher before he rescued that girlfriend of yours. We intercepted the car just four blocks away."

"You had agents in the area?"

"We had credible information that the sleeper cell had identified you as the one trying to stop them from intercepting the final message, which was probably why the Agency sent me since I knew you on sight. You may not be any closer to figuring out who the cell members are, but you're clearly pissing them off."

"So I suppose I have a price on my head now?"

Domino clucked her tongue. "Wouldn't be the first time. Oh, and I'm supposed to give you this," she said, handing him a small silver disk. "These are communication intercepts from the cell in Madrid. We think you'll see a similarity in the rhetoric."

"We have a solid connection to the larger network?"

"Looks like. If you can stay alive long enough, we might be able to save the world."

Roman smirked, running his hand through his hair as Domino chuckled at her dark joke. The situation couldn't get any worse. Not that he gave two shits about a death warrant from a bunch of terrorists—the Agency would ensure his safety. But during the ride over, he'd assured Mario that Rachel wouldn't be in any danger. Now he wasn't so sure.

"Did the shooters make Rachel?"

Domino waved her hand dismissively. "Can't be sure."

"I want agents watching her."

"Already done. The Agency wants to avoid any messy civilian interference."

Roman couldn't believe how a mission that had started out so relatively simple could have spun so wildly out of control. The technical side had been rather complex, but he'd never dreamed Rachel's life would be endangered.

Intercepted cell phone conversations between a Middle Eastern terrorist organization and a sleeper cell in New York tipped off the U.S. government that the opening credits of various documentaries were being used to deliver messages between terrorists in Europe and their American counterparts. The Agency, an off-shoot organization comprised of operatives from the CIA, the FBI and a task force from Homeland Security, had identified two such messages—and one had been designed by Rachel.

Naturally, she'd been the first focus of the investigation. She'd traveled around the world extensively and could have easily had contact with terrorists outside of the United States. Roman had been brought in because of his ability to make everyone believe he was a television consultant, when in truth, he knew very little about the industry before he'd been briefed. But he had a natural, chameleon-like quality and a photographic memory. His mission had been to find out if Rachel had terrorist sympathies or if she might have been coerced into planting the images in the graphics she'd designed.

She hadn't. They'd found no proof whatsoever. Neither he nor the Agency suspected her any longer. Intelligence sources suggested that a third party was inserting the images after the designers turned their work over for post-design production. The minute Rachel had been cleared, Roman should have dropped all contact with her. But he hadn't.

Sleeping with her, knowing her, caring about her, had simply been too wonderful to stop.

He'd made mistakes in judgment before. All agents did. But none of his had ever put a civilian in danger. And he had nothing to blame but his own selfishness and insatiable libido.

If Rachel got hurt now—physically, permanently—because he hadn't had the strength and self-discipline to stay out of her life, he'd never forgive himself.

"What are my orders?"

Domino gestured to the safe.

Roman crossed the room, knelt down, then keyed in a series of universal Agency codes. Once the door popped open, he extracted a digital recorder and pressed a second series of numbers. Only then did the device play and let him know what the Agency expected him to do next.

The orders, essentially, came down to one word.

Disappear.

CHAPTER SEVEN

"WHAT DO YOU MEAN HE disappeared?" Rachel asked, incredulous.

She hadn't had a chance to talk to Mario after he'd taken off the night before. By the time he'd come back to her apartment, Iris had forced a second Xanax down her throat and she'd been out for the count. She'd woken up alone but downstairs, had found both Mario and Iris running the coffee stand. Since it was nearly nine-thirty on a Sunday morning, there were few people around.

Mario pulled a note out of his pocket and handed it to Rachel. There, in black and white, in Roman's even handwriting, was a message that made her clutch at her throat.

The shooters have been apprehended. Rachel is safe. Tell her I'm sorry. Roman

"What about *his* safety? Are they hunting him?"

Mario didn't reply.

Rachel stormed away from her friends and wondered how the hell she'd gotten to this point in her life. She'd been in New York a few years, but her circle of friends wasn't very big. Jeannette was still on the West Coast. Her workout friends and poker buddies weren't the type you trusted with such outlandish tales. She was grateful to both Iris and Mario, but they were older. She couldn't keep putting them in the middle of a dangerous situation.

But she needed them. Mario had proved more than

capable of holding his own. And Iris was probably the strongest woman Rachel had ever met. They'd want to help her, just as she'd want to help them if they were in trouble.

She swung back, trusting she could rely on them one more time. They already knew the story. Besides, her needs focused more on Roman the man than Roman the criminal or cop or whatever the hell he was.

"He can't just be gone," she insisted.

Mario looked at her with eyes that bespoke a lifetime of experience and just as much caring. "You're better off, Rachel. You said it yourself. You don't know what the man is mixed up in—and you don't want to know."

"I didn't yesterday. But I was scared and angry and dizzy as hell from being tossed to the ground while bullets whizzed by. Now I'm thinking more clearly and I want to know. I want to know the truth about Roman. He would have told me the truth yesterday, I think. But I was too angry to listen."

Mario and Iris exchanged glances that told her they didn't want her to pursue this further. Rachel sighed and for the first time since she moved to the city, felt lost and unsure.

She'd walked down this street a million times. She was home, in the part of New York City she knew best of all—and yet, this afternoon, nothing looked familiar. Not the coffee stand, not the nearby falafel booth, not the facade of her building. In all her travels, Rachel rarely took more than a few hours to acclimate to her surroundings and feel as if she'd lived in Jakarta or Tokyo or Sydney all her life.

But losing Roman had left her more damaged than she expected. The hurt ran deep—too deep for her to simply let go.

"I'm going to find him," Rachel decided.

"*¿Qué?*" Iris asked, her eyes wide.

Mario stepped around to her. "Why do you want to put yourself through that?"

Rachel shoved her thumbs into the pockets of her jeans. "I want the whole story."

Mario's mouth curved down hard. "He's mixed up in something bigger than you want to get involved in."

"I don't want to get involved!" she insisted. "I just want to know why he picked me. If he couldn't be with me, if he couldn't stay, then why come into my life at all?"

Iris wiped her hands on her apron. "Why wouldn't he pick you, *mijita?* You're beautiful and smart and everything a man could want."

Rachel grinned at Iris's compliment, and honestly, she couldn't argue. She was an attractive woman and she was, except for situations that required picking out the spies from the television consultants, pretty darned smart. She was sexy, interesting and kindhearted to boot. All those good qualities may have inspired Roman to stay with her longer than he'd planned, but she doubted they were the reasons he was drawn to her in the first place.

She'd seen his ex. Rachel couldn't think of any woman she was less like. Rachel was adventurous and fun, but the woman who'd kissed Roman on the sidewalk exuded a combination of lethal danger and exotic sensuality. Rachel usually didn't wonder why a man was attracted to her, but she'd had all morning to recap her interactions with Roman, and something about that first meeting suddenly seemed staged. Arranged. Planned.

She wanted—no, she deserved—all the details.

"I was part of something, I can feel it. Something dangerous. What if his leaving doesn't take away the risk?"

"He said you'd be safe," Mario said.

"He also said he was a television consultant. His word hasn't been entirely reliable. You said he was some sort of agent. Maybe he plans to have me watched for the rest of my life. I can't live that way."

At this, Mario made excuses to Iris and shuttled Rachel up the stoop of her apartment, his gaze darting from side to side to make sure they weren't overheard. "He wouldn't verify anything, but yeah, I think maybe he's FBI or CIA. Something covert. Either way, you've got to let this go."

Certain Mario knew more than he was letting on, Rachel decided to push. "I can't, Mario. I won't. I need answers. I deserve them, especially if my life is in danger."

Mario's lips pressed tightly together, a thin but pronounced line, not too different from the kind kids drew in the sand in the schoolyard.

"You'll never find him," he concluded.

"I could go back to the network where we first met, start asking questions. A *lot* of questions."

"That's an invitation to unwanted attention."

She bounced excitedly on the balls of her feet. "If someone comes looking who can lead me to Roman, then I win."

"What if the people who tried to kill him get to you first?"

She hadn't really thought the plan through, but Mario definitely had a point. Still, he didn't have to know that she shared his concern. Not yet.

"It's a risk I'm willing to take," she claimed.

Mario cursed, first in good, old Brooklyn English, then threw in a few Italian words for good measure. "You're pigheaded."

"I like to think of myself as single-minded."

"You're reckless," he added.

"That point has already been proved."

He grabbed her by the hand and pulled her up to the entrance to her apartment complex. "Then you'll need someone with a better plan."

RACHEL NEVER IMAGINED that tracking down an undercover secret agent on the lam would prove her particular talent. Luckily, Mario was an ex-cop and an excellent partner in crime. He knew how to work the system, and despite his long and decorated devotion to the law, he'd been willing to bend a few New York statutes in order to get her to where she was now—in a dark, dingy apartment where just forty-eight hours ago, Roman had made his last known appearance in the city.

The process hadn't been easy. First, Rachel had had to return to the network where she'd first met Roman to do some snooping. She'd kissed up to the top executive's secretary and, as a result, now had Roman's pager number in her possession. She wasn't sure the number was still valid or even if it was the pager that Roman had used to receive the messages that had sent him running out on her every morning after lovemaking, but it was her best shot. She'd dialed the number—with a prophetic 911 at the end—and in the coded message, she'd left the address of the last place Mario had seen Roman.

Well, Mario had remembered the building. She'd had to guess on the rest. Luckily for her, all the other apartments were occupied and this one, from the looks of it, had government stash house written all over it. She was also quite fortunate that a fifty-dollar bill slipped to the super had gotten her inside. Clearly, if the secret agency that Roman was working for used this place, they weren't anymore.

Comfort hadn't been a consideration in the decor, but Rachel made do on the faded, dusty couch sitting dead center in the room. She waited just over two hours, finally dozing off with her cheek pressed against the arm and her legs folded safely beneath her. She woke to a light knock, but she didn't rise. She waited. Seconds later, the locks surrendered to keys.

She should have been shocked to see him, surprised that he'd followed her breadcrumbs, but instead, relief washed over her the minute her eyes connected with Roman's steely-blue gaze. The possibility that she'd be greeted by an austere government agent ordering her to keep her nose out of serious spy business had definitely occurred to her—and to Mario, who insisted on waiting at the curb. If he hadn't heard from Rachel by sundown, he was coming up to get her.

But now she concerned herself only with Roman as he slid inside and locked the door behind him. His face held no emotion, except, perhaps, a tiny glimmer of sadness.

"You came," she said, her voice deep and raspy after her unplanned nap. She sat up, stretched, cleared her throat.

"I shouldn't have," Roman replied.

"Then why did you?"

"Because you asked."

Volume wasn't needed in the enclosed space of the apartment. His words echoed off the bare walls. Roman then turned and revealed a panel near the door, then cursed when he found the compartment empty.

"What's missing?"

"Jamming device. In case anyone is listening. This safe house isn't used anymore. They released it yesterday."

Rachel nodded. "That's why I had no trouble getting in."

"We can't talk here."

He held his hand out to her and Rachel's fingers itched to touch his. But what price would she pay for feeling his warmth against her skin, even for an instant? She'd come here only to hear his explanation, to understand why he'd chosen her and what pawn's part she played in this intriguing chess game. Because perhaps she'd played no role at all. Maybe she'd just been a woman he couldn't resist. Maybe she'd just been a decoy. Or worse, a distraction.

She stood on her own and ignored his proffered hand.

"Where can we go?"

Without warning, he snatched her hand, which she immediately tried to yank away.

"Let go of me."

"We need to get out of here quickly."

She tugged harder as he turned to undo the locks. "Mario is waiting for me. He'll call the police if he thinks for one minute that I'm in danger."

"Mario knows I'm here."

For a long, intense moment, he stared into her eyes.

"He trusts you?"

"I had him move his car to the alley around back, just in case. I'm sure he'll take us somewhere we can talk, unheard."

She stopped struggling. No way would Mario succumb to Roman's charm. She seemed to be the only one who had trouble resisting that particular weapon. If Mario trusted Roman, she could, too. For the moment, at least.

They exited through a back door, cutting through a stinking alley, and after Roman picked the padlock on an iron gate, he directed her onto a side street lined with old, sagging oaks. Mario had pulled up to the curb only a few steps away, so soon they were inside and speeding down the street. Roman leaned forward and murmured instructions into Mario's ear. The older man nodded, then headed downtown.

"Where are we going?" she asked.

"Somewhere busy. Somewhere we can blend in and not draw attention to ourselves."

She nearly growled in frustration. "Who are you?"

"I'll explain everything once we arrive."

She crossed her arms tightly over her chest. She'd come looking for him to hear what he had to say for himself. Doubts about his veracity niggled at her, but when Roman turned to her, his gaze intense, his mouth moist, as if he'd just softened his lips with his tongue, as if he wanted nothing more than to kiss away the tension she knew emanated in fractious waves off her body, she knew he'd tell her the truth.

And that frightened her most of all.

CHAPTER EIGHT

"NICE PLACE," MARIO SAID, his tone tight and uncomfortable as he slowed his cab in front of the famed Sherry-Netherland hotel.

Roman nodded but didn't speak. He handed Mario a few bills, making some sort of gesture of male-to-male understanding and exited the cab.

On her way out, Rachel placed her hand on the back of Mario's seat. He stopped her.

"You're all right with this?" he asked.

Rachel watched Roman just outside the taxi, scanning the street methodically as he waited.

"He won't let anything happen to me," she said, completely convinced of that truth, if nothing else.

Mario harrumphed. "Damn straight he won't. Before I agreed to play a part in this, I told him there was no place on God's green earth he could hide if you got even a scratch on your pinkie."

Rachel wiggled her littlest finger at him. "Me and my pinkie will be fine. I have your cell phone number in my pocket. I'll call you if I need anything, I promise."

Mario didn't seem happy about letting her go, but he didn't interfere. Rachel knew she needed to do this and she couldn't deny the way her heart lightened at knowing that Roman wanted to talk, too. Hadn't he come when she called? Hadn't he taken the care to move them to a location where they could speak freely? Clearly, he wanted to explain. Or at the very least, he believed she deserved his time.

She hadn't forced him to come back for her, and from what she could tell by the hurried way they dashed through a side entrance to the hotel's back stairwell, Roman was still concerned that he might be recognized. After they'd climbed several flights of stairs, he immediately slid a card key into the nearest guest-room door on the sixth floor, and in seconds they were inside.

Safe.

Alone.

He reached into the closet, pulled out a mechanical device she didn't recognize, attached it to the door and flicked a switch that activated a blinking red light.

"What's that?"

"Combination alarm and jamming device. No one will come in without us hearing and no one will be able to listen from the other side to what we say."

Or do.

Rachel cursed at herself for allowing such a libidinous thought into her brain. This wasn't going to be about sex. She'd arranged to meet Roman so that she could understand why and how they'd ended up together—and if anything beyond the lust had been real.

Or especially if lust had been all they shared.

Luxury hotel rooms weren't exactly an everyday occurrence to Rachel, so she couldn't help but be swept away by the plush carpets, antique furniture and glistening chandeliers. Except for a stack of barely touched magazines on the coffee table—*Vogue, Cosmo* and *Elle* among them—the room looked unoccupied. Even the bathroom seemed bereft of a toothbrush or a discarded towel.

"Whose suite is this?"

"A friend's," Roman replied. "We have until morning."

Spying a flash of material under the bed, she leaned down and gingerly retrieved a tiny pair of black thong underwear.

"A female friend? Good God, not the woman who kissed you."

"She only kissed me to piss you off," Roman explained.

Rachel dropped the panties as if they were a dead bug and rushed into the bathroom to wash her hands, tossing a spiteful, "She succeeded" over her shoulder as she flew by him.

Roman was close on her heels. "She'd had me under surveillance and knew you'd followed me from your apartment. She was trying to discourage you."

Rachel wiped her hands on a clean towel. "She could have just told me to back off if she wanted you so bad."

The burst of laughter erupted from Roman's gut before he could call it back. He certainly didn't want to go into the dynamics of his interactions—couldn't call it a relationship by any stretch of the imagination— with Domino, but the thought of the woman playing possessive with him was hilariously funny.

"She's been through with me for a long time, Rachel. And vice versa."

"But you were lovers once."

"Yes, we were. So were we. And it wasn't so long ago, either."

"Don't change the subject," she snapped.

"I'm not. I'm actually getting to the subject. I came here to talk about you and me, not about my past."

Rachel took a step closer to him, her gaze darting between the walls on either side of her, as if they might close in at any moment. He sidestepped and she squeezed past him with such haste, he felt a cold wave of wind.

"Do you have a past?" she asked rapidly.

"A varied one," he replied, knowing he'd be breaking contracts, agreements and regulations up to his ears if he told her one single detail. And yet, he was willing to share some of what led him here—what led him to Rachel.

"Can you tell me about any of it?"

Her arms were crossed tightly over her chest and her lips were frozen in a lethal line.

"Does it matter?" He winced. His reply had been automatic, practiced, grilled and ingrained into him. Could he ever revert to the man he used to be? Honest? Forthright? Real?

"Stop it!" she said, stamping her foot in such a way that she didn't look the least like a petulant child, but a woman on the edge of losing control. "Answer the question! Stop hiding behind the persona some phantom agency cooked up for you. They're not here now. It's just me. Me and, please, for the love of God, the truth. I want to know who you are, Roman. But if you can't tell me that, I at least deserve to know who you were, once, before you turned your life over to people who probably don't give a damn if you live or die. I made love to you, Roman. Not once, not twice, but more times than I can count. So many times that my body still reacts to the air you breathe."

He could hear her voice shaking, could see the force of need in her eyes, and he wondered how he'd gotten in so deep, so fast. And yet, his own passions matched Rachel's point for point. What had started as sex, somehow, despite all the lies and omissions, had turned into something more.

He gestured toward the love seat in the center of the

room. She sat, her hands tense on her knees, her shoulders tight. He dug into his pockets and decided not to sit beside her. He couldn't possibly be that close and not take her into his arms.

"I work for a division of Homeland Security."

Her eyes widened. "The terrorist people?"

With a nod, he started to pace. "Smoking out terrorist threats is our main directive. I was recruited to a joint FBI and CIA task force specifically investigating reports that a certain, deadly terrorist network has been using televised images in order to send messages to sleeper cells here in the States."

Rachel sat back in the love seat, her stare disengaged from his. He knew this was a lot for her to process, but he'd decided to go for broke. Since he'd been shot at, he knew his position on the task force had been severely compromised. His cover had been blown. He suspected that the next time he reported to headquarters, he'd be taken off the case he'd worked since the first report came to his desk. But right now, there was no real harm in him letting an average citizen know that the government was actively pursuing potential killers.

Too bad Rachel wasn't the least bit average or he wouldn't be in this mess.

"What kind of messages?"

He stepped forward. This part, she'd understand. "Messages imbedded in the graphics."

The whites of her eyes suddenly contrasted starkly with the dark, hypnotic green. "Graphics…where?"

"In the opening credits of certain productions."

"Like documentaries? Like the one I was working on when we met?"

He nodded.

She took a few moments to process what he'd said,

then skewered him with a quizzical glare. "But there are hundreds if not thousands of graphic designers working in television in this city. Why'd you pick me?"

"I didn't pick you, the Agency did."

She drew a quivering hand to her stomach. "Why? How did I come to the attention of the government?"

He closed his eyes, then rattled off the name of the documentary that had aired on Animal Planet, the one the task force had intercepted.

"I designed the opening and closing credits."

"Yes, you did."

"Tell me there wasn't a hidden message in there."

He pressed his lips together tightly.

She jumped to her feet. "Oh, God! Roman, please, I swear, I didn't put any message for anyone in my graphics. I would never—"

With no reason not to, Roman reached out and took her by the elbows of her outstretched arms. "We know, Rachel. Someone else imbedded the message after you turned in your work. We found your original files, untouched. But those that aired were a different story. We're still checking into who had access to your work, but first we had to investigate you. It was the first logical step."

Despite how soft her skin felt against his palms, when she tugged to be free, he let her go.

"So that's why you were at the network. Ours wasn't a chance meeting."

"No."

"Were you sent to seduce me? To find out the truth over pillow talk?"

He closed his eyes and shook his head. The scenario sounded like something out of a spy flick or romantic suspense novel, but the truth wasn't anything so dark and glamorous. He and all the other male operatives at the Agency only dreamed of such choice assignments.

"We don't work that way, Rachel. I was only supposed to get to know you, check out your apartment, your friends, your computer. How I accomplished that task was entirely up to me."

She jammed her fists on her hips. "You could have pretended to be anyone. A friend. A gay friend," she offered, her voice lilting upward as if the idea sounded promising. "You didn't have to sneak into my bed."

Roman's lips quirked into a grin. "Our first time wasn't in a bed and, Rachel, I didn't have to sneak."

Yes, he'd been dishonest with her about who he was and why he'd sought her out—but he'd never uttered one mistruth about wanting her so much that his skin seared with need when she so much as glanced in his direction. The desire he'd felt for her had been instantaneous, incendiary and instinctive. The choices he'd made had been based on the primal part of him that had never been awakened—not to that degree—before Rachel.

He figured at first it was intense chemistry. Pheromones gone wild. But the more time he spent with her, the more times he heard her laughter pealing through her apartment or watched her chew her bottom lip as she furiously manipulated the graphic images on her computer screen, the deeper he fell. Every word out of his mouth had been a lie—except when he told her how much he wanted her— just as powerfully then as he wanted her right now.

And the sheepishly sexy grin on her face didn't deter him one bit. "I guess I was pretty hot for you."

He allowed a smile to lighten the mood even further, and he couldn't help but tug at the insides of his pockets to lessen the tightening of material across his groin. "The feeling was mutual."

"Is that why you stuck around, kept in touch with me, even after I left that job?"

He nodded. "I've been at two networks since then, investigating various design departments and independent contractors. My attention should have been one hundred percent on the case, but I couldn't seem to get you out of my head."

She stepped aside, clearly uncomfortable with the turn in their conversation.

"You checked out my friends?"

"Mario, Iris, your ever-absent roommate, your mother, your sisters and all the men they've dated, which is a rather impressive list."

She smirked. "They'll be thrilled to know you approve."

"They can't know anything, Rachel. Everything I've told you has to be in complete confidence. My job is already on the line because my cover has been blown. That shooting the other morning was the work of the terrorist group who wants to make sure the cell they've implanted in the U.S. gets the messages they're sending."

A chill of icy fear must have sliced through her bloodstream from the way she visibly shivered. Good. She needed to be afraid. Fear would keep her safe—and away from him.

"What will happen if you don't stop this cell?"

He looked away, unwilling to impart on Rachel just how dire the circumstances were. The information he possessed could cause a national panic, or even worse, national paralysis. He wanted her safe, but he didn't want her holing up in some desert bunker, afraid to walk outside. Afraid to breathe. Afraid to live.

"You don't want to know. The bottom line is that the Agency has known for months that your work is legit.

You're free and clear of this whole mess. I can't make the same mistake twice and keep you involved. After tonight, we can't see each other again."

She barely blinked. "Any idea yet who tampered with my graphics?"

The way her eyes narrowed, Roman knew she was ignoring the emotional fallout of what he'd said by focusing on the threat at hand. His respect for her rose a notch. Even if he had been at liberty to share a suspect's name with her, which he didn't even have, he would not have answered her question. He'd learned over the last seventy-two hours that Rachel Marlowe was not only beautiful, creative, interesting and sexy, but she was also determined, clever and stubborn as hell. He could imagine her taking serious umbrage to the fact that some terrorist sympathizer had used her work to spread a potentially lethal message—and judging by how she'd contacted him, he imagined she might do something reckless like pursuing the matter on her own.

"The investigation hasn't turned up that information yet."

Her chin dipped in a lost, little nod. She was processing what he was saying, but the brutal truth wasn't going down easily.

"And the fact that you continued to be with me, intimately, all this time, that had nothing to do with your orders from this Agency of yours?"

He pressed his lips together and shook his head. "I caught all kinds of shit when they found out," he confessed. "And you know what? It was worth it. *You* were worth it."

Their gazes locked, and he hoped like hell she could read the truth in his eyes, because as unaccustomed as he was to spilling information to an unauthorized source, he wasn't sure he could say out loud what he felt so strongly in his body—and possibly, even his heart.

She slammed to her feet, her hands slapping decisively against her thighs. "All right, then!" she announced before she rounded the coffee table, looked him straight in the eye and reached out with her hand.

He didn't touch her, but flicking his gaze between her hand and her eyes did the job of telling her he didn't know what she intended for him to do with that hand if he took it. Give her a platonic shake, thank her for cooperating with the United States government and then send her on her merry way?

Her hand dropped a little. "Thank you for telling me the whole truth."

He arched a brow. "You didn't get the whole truth."

She stared at him quizzically. "What part did you leave out?"

At this point, he knew what to do with her hand. He grabbed it and used her arm to reel her in as close as two people possibly could be with their clothes still on—a detail he hoped to rectify momentarily. With his chest flush against hers and her suddenly accelerated heartbeat egging him on, he pressed his lips just beside hers and whispered, "The part where I tell you I can't live without you."

CHAPTER NINE

HE KISSED HER WITH SUCH a rough, desperate intensity that all questions, protests and logical reasons why she should deny herself another taste of him disappeared. He'd confessed all to her, including the fact that although he'd initiated his pursuit of her for his case, he'd actually jeopardized his investigation by staying with her. He'd admitted how he'd been drawn to her with the same force that had kept her enthralled, a man she'd known so little about—and most of what she had known had been a lie.

But clearly, she no longer cared. She wanted him. Here. Now. Because possibly, this was all they'd ever have.

Clothes melted away with the fire burning between them. The dimming sunlight against the sheer curtained window marked the dwindling time that they had to say goodbye, spurring him to lift her fully and completely against him, pressing her skin as tightly against his as he possibly could. She needed his heat to brand her, mark her, imprint her with the indelible passion that belonged to them alone. After tonight, she'd likely never see him again. There would be no more sneaking, no more bucking the rules. His job injected inescapable danger into his life, risk that had spilled into hers that morning on the sidewalk. She knew the thought of her paying the price for his choices sickened him. He was that kind of man.

So he'd say goodbye. But he'd make it count.

Roman lured her to the bedroom, her hand cupped softly in his, and watched her eyes turn glossy with the kind of anticipation and fear and need that he'd never seen in her before. Then again, he'd never much stopped to look, had he? They'd been too enraptured, too enslaved to lust and sexual pleasure to truly know each other.

Of course, there was the matter that if she'd known who he was then, she would have kicked him to the curb. Or at least, out her door.

But now she knew. And she'd stayed.

Roman couldn't waste another moment. His first taste, taken with his lips across her neck, jacked his adrenaline to dangerous levels. His heart pounded, his blood surged, his muscles tightened, all from a simple kiss. She kissed him back, hard, lacing her tongue with his, spearing her hands into his hair and tugging gently, oh-so-subtly urging him to their usual frenetic and ravenous pace.

He smiled as he trailed his kisses higher—behind her ear, along her chin, to the tip of her nose, his hands solid on the sides of her cheeks.

With a frustrated sigh, she pushed him away, her eyes blazing.

"You act as if we have forever," she complained.

"No," he corrected her, "but we do have all night."

She glanced toward the door, as if someone might rush in at any moment and interrupt. "You don't know that for sure," she said, her voice cracking with uncertainty.

There wasn't a lot Roman seemed to know anymore, but he did know they would not be interrupted. Domino had not only agreed to lend him her suite, but she'd promised to keep an eye out until morning when she had to leave on another assignment. He wasn't sure he trusted the covert operative, but oddly, his ex-lover hadn't objected to his proposal that they buck the system and raise a finger at the rules so he could have one more night with Rachel. He'd even caught a glimmer of rebellion in her blue eyes—the source unknown. But he'd had no trouble using her newfound defiance to his advantage. She owed him.

"Trust me, Rachel."

She licked her lips. Her tiny movement caused a painful tightening in his groin. His sex, thick and straining for her touch, ached as blood rushed downward. Her fingers danced across the bare skin of his hips, taunting him, zapping his brain so that he wondered, momentarily, why he wasn't inside her yet.

"You've never asked me to trust you before, Roman."

He skimmed his hands across her shoulders and down her back, yearning to clutch her buttocks and press her tight to him, but knowing he had to wait, draw this out, make this last.

"How could I?"

"Because you weren't who you were pretending to be."

He succumbed to temptation and laid his hands possessively over her backside. "I was when we made love."

Her eyes turned pleading. "Prove it."

He dropped to his knees. She gasped and her balance wavered at his unexpected attack, but he held her steady as he delved between her feminine lips with his tongue, easily finding the tiny tip of her sex. A sweet cream slipped onto his lips, amplifying his hunger, electrifying his need. He tugged her forward and she boldly wrapped one leg over his shoulder, increasing his access, surrendering completely to him in ways he knew she never had before.

A quivering announced how close to the precipice she was, so he eased back, kissing her thighs, her knee, before sweeping her into his arms and onto the bed. With only the tiniest grasp left of his self-control, he grabbed her hands and held them tight above her head while he kissed her until her passion ebbed to a manageable rhythm.

Her eyes flashed open. She'd regained a semblance of control and, in a quick move, flipped him over onto his back. He couldn't help but laugh in surprise.

"Where did you learn that?"

She grinned down at him, her eyes alight with naughty intentions. He could feel her warm heat hovering just above him and the sensation nearly stole his breath.

"From you," she admitted. "Don't you remember?"

She arched a brow, but for the life of him, he couldn't recall ever employing such a move on her. Of course, in the acrobatics of their usual lusty sex, instincts often took over. What he could remember of their lovemaking from before wasn't details, just general impressions. Immediate, hot, animalistic impressions.

"I hope I didn't hurt you."

Her grin was pure sin. "Not like I'm going to hurt you. Torture you is more like it. I mean, I suppose I should have tortured you weeks ago in order to make you talk, but now that you've spilled all—"

He relaxed completely against the cool cotton sheets, forcing his muscles to surrender to her wicked intentions. "Feel free to have your way with me. I'll try not to complain."

The smile that bloomed on Rachel's face came from

deep within in, from a center that had never felt so balanced until tonight. Despite the lies, mistruths and danger, she and Roman still possessed an easy banter and intimate trust she'd never shared with any other man. Nor could she deny the intimate need she had to join with him, be one with him, as many times tonight as they could physically manage. She reached between his legs and, after stroking him with her palm and fingers, guided him inside her—partway. Enough to drive them both mad with wanting, but not far enough to topple them over the edge.

Balanced on her knees, she leaned forward and suckled his taut male nipples. She speared her tongue through the light smattering of hair on his chest, reveling in the flavors of his skin, in the sensations of his heart-beat against his chest. He upped the ante when he cupped her breasts, his thumbs dancing over her nipples until she could barely think or breathe.

She sat up, bringing them together completely. The sensation of his sex sliding deeply into her filled her with a warmth that spread like wildfire, growing hotter and hotter with each second. Through heavy-lidded eyes, she watched sheer wonder play over his features as he plucked and pinched her breasts with the exact amount of pressure that drove her wild, his hips shifting beneath her with subtle, powerful results. She grabbed his hands, desperate to stop his pleasurable assault, but lacing her fingers with his ignited a new kind of heat. The held on to each other with desperate tightness as passion and need commandeered their bodies, pushing them in a menagerie of sensation from which neither could escape.

And why, Rachel wondered just before she collapsed onto his chest, would she want to?

RACHEL WAITED, CONCENTRATED, regulating her breathing to a steady pace. The ability to fake sleep had come in handy many times in her life, from childhood antics to avoiding morning sex with her ex. To him, she'd been the soundest sleeper in the world. Not that she had anything against morning sex, but morning breath was another thing entirely. She'd already gotten up an hour ago, but Roman didn't know that. While he'd showered, she'd dressed from the waist down, shoes included. She had a strong suspicion he was going to sneak out on her and, well, it simply wasn't going to happen.

Lie for lie, she was still way behind—and still unsatisfied with letting him go. Now that she knew the depth of what he'd done to stay with her before, she realized that traditional strategies for keeping tabs on him were not going to work. He had her personal safety at the forefront of his mind, not to mention his job, which he clearly loved. When he left the hotel room this time, she'd never see him again. Unless she acted.

The shower had stopped minutes ago and now the bathroom door opened. She heard his light footsteps approaching and braced herself, willing her muscles to remain relaxed, which wasn't all that hard after a night of delicious, bone-melting sex. He kissed her softly on the forehead, gently combed her hair away from her face, murmured something, and then left the hotel room.

The soft click was like a starter's pistol. Rachel bolted out of the bed, flipped her arms into her bra and threw on a shirt. She leaned against the door for a moment and, hearing nothing, exited the room.

She didn't know everything about him, but she did know he hated elevators. Six flights of stairs would take him a few minutes. If she hurried, she could beat him to the lobby.

She dashed down the hall and jabbed the elevator button, squelching a triumphant squeal when the mechanism dinged almost immediately. Luck was on her side this time.

She was going to follow Roman. She didn't know what she was going to do once he reached his destination, but maybe if she knew more about his life, more about how to contact him if the need arose, she wouldn't have such a hard time letting go. At least, that was the logic that had driven her this far. She'd always been spontaneous in her travels, so applying that instinct now wasn't such a stretch.

The elevator swallowed up the space between the sixth floor and the lobby in seconds. Gingerly, Rachel leaned out of the doors, watching for any sign of Roman. Seeing no one except a housekeeper running a vacuum cleaner and a pair of uniformed clerks behind the desk, she walked out briskly, making her way toward the staircase exit. If she could just get behind the potted ficus before Roman emerged, she'd have a clear shot at following him.

She dashed behind the thick, glossy green leaves—right into Roman's chest.

CHAPTER TEN

"ROMAN!"

He quirked an eyebrow. "Rachel." His tone held a lilt of amusement. "What do you think you're doing?"

She stamped her foot in frustration. Okay, maybe watching episodes of *Alias* and *Veronica Mars* did not qualify her to be either a spy or a private investigator, but she'd given it the college try. She just hadn't expected to get caught so easily.

"Duh, I'm following you," she said.

"Why?"

She skewed her face, trying to come up with a reasonable explanation. She hadn't really had much time to think. "I didn't want you to leave."

He slipped his hands around her waist. "I didn't want to leave."

"But you did."

"Rachel, I have a job to do. Maybe once…"

His voice trailed away. Just like him not to make any promises he couldn't keep. She opened her mouth to assure him that he didn't have to placate her when he clamped his hand over her lips and pulled her flush against the wall.

Her heart slammed against her chest when she saw fear skitter across his face. Not fear for himself. Fear for her.

Seconds later, a man in dark clothing with the collar

of his jacket pulled up high against cold that didn't exist in New York in June disappeared into the stairwell.

After a long, torturous moment, Roman released her, but he ensured her continued quiet with a barely audible shush.

He pressed her tight against the wall, told her with his intense eyes to stay put, then stepped out from their cover to see if the coast was clear. The move ended up unwise. A shout from the other end of the lobby spurred Roman to grab her by the wrist and yank her out of hiding as they made a mad dash for the back exit.

They stumbled into the alley, dark and rank and glossy with the kind of dew that only steamed up from the dank New York City streets. Rachel felt her boots slip beneath her, but Roman counterbalanced her and kept her from falling.

"Run!"

She complied, wishing as her lungs began to burn that she'd been a little more regular with the workouts. As they approached the end of the alley, a bullet pinged on the building just to their right. Roman gave her another push, propelling her out onto the sidewalk.

Which wasn't any safer. A dark sedan peeled away from the curb in front of the hotel, revving up to intercept. Roman grabbed Rachel by the elbow, and just as the car cut off their escape, he dragged her behind a parked delivery van. Shots rent the air and Roman pulled his gun.

"We're sitting ducks here," he said.

"The park," Rachel said, panting.

Roman nodded. He headed around the back of the van and upon emerging, picked off the gunman.

Rachel didn't have time to scream. She ignored the splash and splatter of the gunman's blood against the white, dirt-encrusted van and instead concentrated on dashing into Central Park, where they would have the thick cover of trees to shield them. They ran past the gilded bronze statue of Sherman on his horse, past the manicured and sculpted shrubbery, into the winding paths that might give them the edge to escape the second gunman and his possible accomplices.

They stopped just inside the darkness so Roman could get his bearings.

"This way," he directed.

They'd taken a few steps out from their cover when shots pricked at the concrete, sending shards chasing after their ankles. Roman spun and fired, ordering Rachel to dive into the trees. Just as she landed with a thud, she heard the distinctive grunt of a slug to the chest. Behind them.

Roman joined her in the trees.

"Who's trying to kill you this time?" she asked.

With a grunt, Roman led Rachel to an opening on the other side of the foliage. They rounded a large planter blooming with fragrant flowers and stopped long enough to catch their breaths. There were no footsteps behind them. No shouts in what Rachel suddenly processed had been a foreign language. For now, they were safe.

"Domino warned me that a second sleeper group had been ordered to eliminate me," he explained.

"To stop you from figuring out how they are getting their messages into my graphics?"

"Yours and that of other artists. I don't think they believe we'll ever figure out their pattern, but they want to kill me for trying. Send a message to the Agency not to fuck with them."

Rachel rolled her eyes. "Yeah, like that's going to deter the U.S. government."

"Exactly."

Once they'd regained their ability to breathe, they doubled back. Roman estimated they'd have better luck escaping if they caught a cab near the plaza across from the hotel, since authorities would already have been alerted to the shooting. They approached with caution and stayed in the square. They saw no one lingering, no one in pursuit. Chances were high, Roman explained, that the gunmen had given up quickly rather than risk detection.

But they'd strike again at another time and place.

Remaining cautious, he ducked with her behind a semipermanent structure at the far corner of the plaza. Clearly erected for some upcoming event, the booth looked like it wouldn't do much to keep bullets from slicing through them, but maybe if they could hold out a few minutes until the police arrived, they'd be free and clear.

"Now what?" Rachel asked.

"I'm getting you out of here."

"Like I'm going to leave you to fend for yourself?"

Roman stared down at her, his eyebrows nearly touching, thanks to his vexed expression. "What exactly are you going to do to help me, Rachel?"

She smirked. "I don't know, slowing you down and screaming like a girl every time a bullet whizzes past my ear can be helpful in some situations, right?"

Despite the direness of their situation, Roman chuckled as he checked his weapon. "That's why I have to let you go, Rachel. I can't drag you into my lifestyle."

"More like death-style if you ask me," she muttered.

"Exactly."

She glanced over her shoulder and, certain they were

still alone, whispered at him harshly. "These guys with the guns, they've seen me with you twice now, yes?"

Roman squeezed his eyes shut for a split second.

That's all he needed to change his mind, apparently. "You win. You're coming with me to headquarters."

As ROMAN PREDICTED, the attackers had flown the coop soon after Roman and Rachel had disappeared into the park. Sirens wailed shortly after the shooting had begun and roadblocks nearly kept them from making their escape. Luckily, Roman used his cell phone to dial in help from the Agency, and moments before a police dragnet searching the park for the shooter of the man near the delivery van stumbled upon them, a trio of dark-suited agents shuttled them into a waiting car.

Rachel rested her cheek against Roman's chest during the silent drive. She didn't bother looking outside or trying to gauge where they were or where they were going. She didn't care. She was with Roman, safe and warm, and after ten minutes or so, the chill of nearly being killed surrendered to the residual heat of their lovemaking. Roman cared about her. She knew that now. He may have sought her out because of his case, but he'd stayed longer than he should have because they'd connected in ways neither one of them had experienced before—in ways neither of them wanted to give up.

The car pitched downward as the driver pulled into an underground parking garage. Rachel held tight to Roman's hand as they got out of the backseat and went straight into a dark, mirrored elevator. Sensing a gentle vibration in his touch, she squeezed harder. He didn't like elevators. She'd known that fact for a while. She'd never thought to ask why, figuring he just preferred the exercise of jaunting up and down the stairs. There was so much about this man she didn't know—could he tell her? Was his fear born of some innocuous childhood mishap or was this phobia rooted in international secrets?

She had no time to ask since the moment the doors swooshed open, they were led into an office with clear glass walls that darkened to an opaque blue the moment the door closed. Flat plasma screens dominated the room, each playing opening credits from a half-dozen documentaries in a successive loop. Rachel recognized the two that were hers and was drawn to the images. They were so familiar and yet…

Roman cleared his throat, trying to divert Rachel's attention to the smartly dressed woman at the other end of the conference table.

"Agent Brach, report."

To an outsider his boss, Amelie Tremayne, likely appeared less than intimidating. Physically, she was average height and weight. Her hair was shock white but softly styled, and he couldn't remember ever seeing her without dangling pearl earrings. She dressed conservatively, but usually wore a brooch or scarf to lend a dash of color to her somber navy or charcoal-gray suits. He wasn't good at guessing ages, so he'd never try with Tremayne, who had earned the respect of her minions with a cool, ageless wisdom. She didn't amuse easily, so Rachel's curious presence didn't so much as inspire a crack of a smile.

Roman ran down the facts of what had occurred at the hotel, leaving out the most interesting parts, naturally. Tremayne didn't need to know—and clearly wasn't interested—in the sexual and emotional precipices that he and Rachel had climbed tonight. She wanted only the details that mattered regarding the terrorists.

"We identified the man in the street," Tremayne said. "He's confirmed as a member of the second cell. We know now that their orders are simply to provide support to the first cell, the one receiving their instruction from the graphics."

Roman's eyes widened. He didn't anticipate his boss speaking so freely in front of Rachel. She was, after all, a civilian. Though in all honesty, she didn't appear to be listening to a word they said. From the moment they stepped inside the conference room, Rachel hadn't stopped watching the looping opening images and credits to the documentaries. He knew she'd found the message, because she'd also found the remote control. She'd stopped each screen at the precise moment the message flashed on the screen.

"Find anything interesting, Ms. Marlowe?" Tremayne asked, her tone barely interested. She clearly gave little credence to Rachel's presence, which made Roman tense with worry. Tremayne had the power to make Rachel disappear. She'd come to no harm, but if Tremayne made a case that Rachel's presence in New York could jeopardize an ongoing investigation, she could be shipped off and tucked away where even Roman might not ever find her.

Roman stepped forward and, despite Rachel's narrow, concentrated stare, removed the remote control from her hands.

"She didn't see anything she hasn't seen before."

Rachel started to shake her head, but Roman stopped her by clutching her arm tighter.

She responded by punching him hard in the shoulder.

Twice. Three times. She'd keep pounding until he released her, so he did.

"Manhandling me in the park was acceptable since you were trying to save my life. But back off here, Roman. I'm perfectly safe."

Tremayne sat forward, her manicured nails tapping lightly together.

Not a good sign.

"No," he said, through tightly clenched teeth, "you're not."

"Mr. Brach is quite correct, Ms. Marlowe. Your presence here is ill advised. But since Mr. Brach's judgment has proved questionable so far where you are concerned, I'm afraid I'll have to take your future under advisement myself."

No one but him heard Rachel's sharp intake of breath, but she quickly covered it with a sly grin. "Then take this under advisement, Ms. Spy Boss. I know who designed those graphics. And with a little negotiation, I may let you in on the secret."

CHAPTER ELEVEN

"Ms. Spy Boss may be accurate and mildly clever, but silly nonetheless." The elegant woman stood and extended her hand. "Amelie Tremayne."

Rachel arched a brow. "Is that your real name?"

"For the moment."

With a nod, Rachel accepted her hand. "Fair enough."

"Roman," Ms. Tremayne said, her eyes barely flicking toward her operative as she gestured for Rachel to sit. "Would you excuse us? I think Ms. Marlowe and I have a few things to discuss."

Ice rippled over Rachel's spine at the sound of her lover's cool dismissal. She could only imagine how he bristled. Well, she didn't have to imagine for long. Roman stood his ground.

"I don't see the logic in that, Amelie. This is my project. I'm still the lead field operative, unless something has changed?"

A miniscule degree of regret glazed Tremayne's sharp blue eyes. "Quite a bit has changed. You jeopardized the mission by your continued involvement with Ms. Marlowe. Your status on this case is pending at best."

Rachel didn't turn and look at Roman. She didn't have to. She figured humiliation looked the same on proud men as it did on women, and right now, her entire expression radiated beet-red with anger.

She crossed her arms over her chest, tucking her hands tightly under her armpits to keep from jumping up and slapping this rude, vindictive woman. So what if she held the safety of innocents in her hands? She didn't have to be so holier than thou about it.

"His status better change quickly or what I do know will remain just that—what *I* know and you don't."

Tremayne arched a pencil-drawn brow. "You're feisty."

Rachel grinned, pushing away the creepiness of having another woman call her that. "Must be what Roman loves about me."

She swallowed her wince and forced her expression to remain confident. Love. She'd used the word *love*. Well, that was presumptuous.

"How do you know he *loves* anything about you at all? You have too much faith in men, Ms. Marlowe."

"Actually, until I met Roman, I had none whatsoever."

Amelie Tremayne took her seat, sliding closer to the table with casual grace. "So you've changed your views based on a man who has done nothing but lie to you from the beginning?"

"Ultimately, what he lied to me about was unimportant. When push came to shove, I got the truth. I'm here, aren't I? And I have information you need. So unless you're going to try to beat it out of me, I suggest you drop your attitude toward Roman and let's get down to business."

A long moment thickened in the air. Rachel had to admit she had no idea if Tremayne *would* order the information beaten out of her, but she had to trust that she could bluff her way just a little further.

Tremayne's gaze flicked to Roman and then, after a brief clash with Rachel's unwavering glare, to the chair beside hers. He sat, a handsomely smug grin on his face. He'd probably pay for it later, but Rachel guessed he didn't care much. Like her, Roman was a live-for-the-moment kind of guy.

"You win, Ms. Marlowe. So tell me, what do you know about the images you saw?"

"Graphic art is just that—art. There are styles, signatures, sometimes very subtle since the images go by so quickly."

"We've broken down each image frame by frame," Roman insisted.

"I'm sure you did. Even if you've studied every aspect of graphic design, you might not pick up something so insignificant. In fact, I might not have seen it myself if I wasn't such a geek. I love studying the work of other designers. That's how I learn and improve. Most working artists don't really bother."

"What can you tell us about this person?"

Rachel took a deep breath. "He's not in New York."

"It's a man?"

Rachel nodded.

"Where's he located?"

She shrugged. "I can give you his name, that's it. His work is fairly popular. He's in high demand. Though come to think of it, he's dropped off the circuit a bit lately. Being really choosy about what he does, from what I hear from production people who wanted to hire him and then got me instead. Our styles are fairly similar."

Amelie Tremayne's stare narrowed. "This is a rather convenient coincidence, don't you think?"

Rachel had considered that, but the truth was the truth. "Perhaps. Or maybe just one hell of a lucky break."

WHAT HAPPENED NEXT HELD no resemblance whatsoever to what Rachel expected. Even before she'd stopped talking, Roman had dashed out of the room, stopping only to kiss her thoroughly and deeply so that her knees nearly buckled from the overload of pleasure.

Then he was gone.

Tremayne remained for a few minutes more, extending the interrogation until another operative came in and took over. Rachel was given a computer with secure Internet access, and through a portal she was sure wasn't legal, she was able to tap into her home computer. She pulled up as much information as she could about those old studies, but she didn't have much more than what she'd told Tremayne and Roman initially. She admired the man's work.

Then she'd waited. The Agency had put her up in a fairly comfortable room within the same building, provided her with hearty meals and endless entertainment in terms of television, satellite radio and video games. But she hadn't been interested in anything but the computers.

Surprisingly, she was allowed to continue to study the images she'd seen in the conference room, and after nearly twenty-four hours of trying, she'd perfectly mimicked the messages she'd seen—just to prove she could. Only moments after she'd popped open a can of Diet Dr Pepper to celebrate her success, Director Tremayne knocked on her door.

"You've been a busy bee," she said, walking inside the apartment with a dark-haired, dark-skinned male lackey behind her.

"I'm not good at relaxing," Rachel said.

"Clearly not. You've succeeded at copying the style of the graphic in question. Very clever. We should have asked you initially instead of wasting our own team's time."

Rachel took a sip from the soda. "Yes, you should have."

"Do you think you can replicate the graphic again?"

With a snort, Rachel set the cola can beside the laptop. Every move she'd made had been watched. She wasn't surprised, but that didn't mean she wasn't creeped out.

"With my eyes closed."

Tremayne's eyes narrowed, her expression serious to the point that Rachel felt her stomach roil with dread.

"We've intercepted the artist you directed us to. According to the agents on the scene, he was preparing to send a final message to the sleeper cell."

"But you stopped him?"

Tremayne shook her head slightly, but enough for Rachel to understand that this was not a victory. "If the cell expects a message and receives none, they may take that as an order to attack."

"What kind of attack?"

Tremayne frowned. "We're not sure. We haven't been able to locate the cell, Ms. Marlowe. And at this point, the only way we can find them is by sending another message in the style of their initial contact. They've likely been trained to recognize the signature— a signature you've succeeded in re-creating."

Rachel shivered. It was one thing to mess around on the computer, something else to have the safety of the free world on her shoulders. She expected the weight of what Tremayne was asking her to do to stop her dead in her tracks. Instead, a rush of adrenaline shot through her body like a precise line of newly lit gunpowder.

"I'm a civilian," she said.

"That can be changed," Tremayne replied. "The communication between terrorist cells through various media forms is becoming more and more common. You're a freelancer, yes? We're simply asking you to work for us now."

Rachel knew Tremayne was one of the good guys—technically. But something in Tremayne's tone, an underlying sharpness along the edge of her voice, caused Rachel's skin to prickle in warning.

"Where's Roman?" she asked.

Poised to help his investigation, the least Rachel could demand was a one-on-one with the lead field operative, or whatever he'd called himself. Besides, she missed him. Deeply. Even now, with a prospect of being able to help avert a tragedy sizzling in her blood, she wanted to share this with him. He'd understand, right? He'd appreciate the importance of what she was about to attempt in order to fight the terrorists.

"Roman Brach is no longer your concern. Concentrate on your new assignment. Once you are done, we've arranged for you to leave the country."

Rachel's heart slammed against her chest. "What?"

Tremayne laughed lightly, as if she enjoyed toying with Rachel. The woman had a sick streak, nearly making Rachel refuse her offer.

"We're talking a brief vacation from the city—just until we round up all the men who might have recognized you from your association with Roman."

Rachel frowned but remained silent. She didn't want to be sent away, separated from her apartment and friends. She loved to travel—but on her terms and under her own direction. But there was world safety to think of—and the fact that the whole idea of using her skills to help stop terrorists from communicating worked for her in ways she never imagined they would. Even as a dreamy teen, she'd never fantasized about being a spy. She always thought James Bond was sexy, yeah, but the idea of joining up with any suave super-agent gave her hives. She loved to travel and set off for distant lands, but avoided guns and thieves and con artists at all costs. Now she was thinking about becoming all of the above?

Unless, of course, the suave, sexy agent was Roman Brach. That might change her mind a bit.

"Don't be alarmed," Tremayne instructed. "I'm simply suggesting a nice vacation once your work is complete, and you can consider then whether you'd like to remain on our payroll. We understand that two friends of yours, Mario Capelli and Iris Rivera, are planning a trip to Puerto Rico. It's reportedly a romantic getaway, but we thought, perhaps, you'd like to tag along. I doubt they'd mind."

"You've spoken to them?"

Tremayne shrugged one shoulder. No, she wouldn't have any way to speak to them. Mario wouldn't trust this woman if she paid her full fare with a fifty-percent tip, cash up front. But Roman, he'd trust. With a hard swallow, she tamped down her hopes for a rendezvous with Roman. For now, she had a job to do.

"How much time do I have?"

"From the notes we retrieved, the scheduled broadcast is only a few days away."

"What language will the message be in?"

Rachel had copied the signature but not the images. She had never seen them before.

"That's where this agent comes in," she said, gesturing to the man who'd entered behind her. "He's an expert linguist and has studied the text of all the previous messages for nuance and syntax. He'll tell you what to write."

"How do the terrorists know when to look for the graphics?"

The pattern, Tremayne explained, hadn't been so difficult for them to figure out, once they realized exactly what they were looking for. Rachel had a little over three days to work with Tremayne's Arabic-speaking assistant and create the graphic that could possibly stop some unnamed and unexplained attack.

For now, Rachel would concentrate only on that goal. Only once she was successful would she allow herself to contemplate if she'd ever see Roman again—and if she did, what then?

YOU WOULD THINK AFTER saving the world, the CIA or the FBI or whatever agency she'd really been working for could have sprung for tickets on a plane that actually departed on time.

Realizing in her exhaustion that her wrist had slipped from holding up her head and ended her nap, Rachel shook consciousness into her body and reached for the caffeine-laden diet soda she'd balanced on her backpack. The warm, fizzy bubbles scraped down her throat, and once her vision cleared, she glanced down at her watch. The plane was now more than two hours late. A quick look around told her that Mario and Iris had once again left her for a stroll around the terminal. She couldn't blame them. She wasn't exactly delightful company, especially since the two of them had stars in their eyes only for each other.

In spite of her own foul mood, she grinned a little at the way Iris and Mario's romance had developed. Mario had a reputation as a matchmaker. This time, however, her ill-fated affair with Roman had actually spurred Mario to make a move on Iris. About time, too, since he'd been sniffing after her for as long as Rachel could remember. She was happy for them.

And miserable for herself.

After yawning unattractively—something she realized only when a blond guy in a baseball cap leaning against a nearby wall chuckled and made brief eye contact—Rachel shifted in her seat. She rubbed her make-up-free face, combed her fingers through her hair and hoped she didn't look as exhausted and cranky as she felt.

Once she'd turned over the new graphics to the Agency, she'd expected to hear from Roman. Perhaps even see him. How hard would it be to run into him in the Agency's headquarters? But he'd not only made himself scarce, she'd also had no further dealings with Amelie Tremayne. None of the other agents seemed to know how to contact Roman, and this time Rachel didn't feel like chasing him.

She'd done her bit as the hunter. Might be nice to be the prey again. Maybe she'd find someone new in Puerto Rico. Someone whose career didn't interfere with pursuing a real life with real lovers and real relationships. Someone who would tell her his real name the first time they met. Someone who would be honest that their affair would last only a few hours or a few days, instead of playing her by her heartstrings. Not that Roman was guilty of all that, but the longer they remained separated, the worse his crimes and misdemeanors would become. It was the law of ex-lovers.

"Ms. Marlowe?"

Rachel looked up into the serious gaze of a rather official-looking airline employee. A woman. At least, Rachel was almost sure she was female. The gruff tone and boxy suit made it hard to tell.

"Yes?"

"Could you come with me, please?"

The *please,* while tacked on, definitely held no graciousness.

"Why?"

The employee curled a strand of her short hair around her ear, revealing a small earpiece like the ones worn by the agents Rachel had been working for all week.

"The delay will be minimal, I assure you. Please." The woman gestured toward the hallway, and from the wide-eyed stares of her fellow passengers, Rachel was fairly certain her travel mates had pegged her as some sort of terrorist moll. Did terrorists even have molls?

She grabbed her backpack and laptop, glancing around for Mario and Iris, who were nowhere to be found. She hadn't been around these Agency types much, but she figured the disappearance of her friends had been no accident. She had no idea why the Agency wanted her again—their business had been concluded. But this imposing woman's attitude unnerved her and she had to fight the instinct to flee.

The people around her murmured and stared, but no one said anything. The blond guy in the baseball cap made a motion toward her, but then stopped before she could make eye contact again. Even as she walked away, she spun around to glance back at him, experiencing a vibe that denoted more than idle curiosity. But he had his back to her, with his cell phone glued to his ear.

False rescue alarm, she supposed. Probably best for both of them.

After a short walk down the terminal, the so-called airline official led her to an unmarked door. She slid a card key through the lock and pushed it open. Rachel walked through and the door was shut soundly behind her. The hallway was narrow and dark, with only weak fluorescent lighting lining the path to another door at the end. That revealed a staircase that conveniently only went down. Rachel ventured into what she imagined were the bowels of the airport. When she emerged, she saw only one door to the left. She took a deep breath and walked through, not entirely surprised to see Amelie Tremayne sitting comfortably in a well-appointed luxury suite sporting a full bar, several plush couches, a small conference table and fine art on the walls.

Rachel always wondered where celebrities hung out when they flew commercial. She figured this was it.

"Please, come in, Ms. Marlowe."

Rachel paused with her hand on the doorknob.

"Do I have a choice?"

Tremayne smiled, and the effect was as sharp as steel. "Not if you plan on leaving the country in half an hour, no."

"Technically," Rachel said, closing the door behind her, "Puerto Rico is part of the United States. You'd think someone in your high-ranking position would know that."

Tremayne toasted her with a highball glass filled with an amber liquid Rachel would bet big bucks was ginger ale. "I should be more specific. If you wish to leave the mainland, then I'll need a few moments of your time."

Rachel tossed her backpack on the nearest table. She really didn't have much choice. But she'd already told the Agency where to shove their long-term job offer. She just wanted to get away.

"You've got five minutes," Rachel said.

"What makes you think I'll let you go in five minutes?"

Rachel sighed wearily. "Oh, you can keep me here as long you want. But any offer you make me after five minutes won't be listened to with an open mind, so I suggest you start talking."

"You've gotten much bolder than when Roman first reported on you."

She crossed her arms tightly across her chest, hating

the idea that he'd reported back to this woman about their interactions, but knowing that until very recently, their personal relationship had been a well-kept secret, even from this super-spy. Besides, the bitch was probably just jealous, anyway.

"You're wasting my time and yours."

"As you know, your graphics did the trick," Tremayne said. "We were able to direct the leader of the sleeper cell to a rendezvous point. We identified him, and we're in the midst of an operation that we're certain will result in not only his arrest, but the capture of his cohorts."

Rachel yawned. It had been a long day. "Good for you."

"Good for you, as well. The higher-ups in the Agency believe that your expertise is needed to continue the success of this mission."

"I taught your tech how to do what I do."

"Yes, but for whatever reason that completely eludes me, they want you."

Rachel grabbed the strap on her backpack. "Not interested."

"We're willing to increase your level of both compensation and security clearance."

Rachel glanced at her watch. "You know what I want."

"Agent Brach is currently on assignment elsewhere. And besides, we can't negotiate with the love lives of our operatives."

Rachel laughed. Loudly.

Tremayne placed her iced drink on a coaster, then stood, straightening her slim, tailored slacks. "Perhaps you'll be more amenable after your vacation."

Rachel leaned her weight on one hip. "Unless you plan on making Roman Brach materialize on a sun-drenched Puerto Rican beach, I doubt it."

"Did it ever occur to you that perhaps Roman doesn't want you?"

Did it ever occur to her? Who was this woman kidding?

She snapped up her backpack and swung it jauntily over her shoulder. "Nope, never crossed my mind."

She was inches from the door when it swung open, a somber operative attached to the knob. Rachel sashayed past him and made her way back through the maze until she emerged in the terminal again. Her flight, not surprisingly, had already begun to board. She had to sprint to make it to the gate, just in time for the attendant to glare at her. After waving her boarding pass beneath the scanner, the guy forced a smile and waved her through. The doors were pulled shut behind her before she'd even taken ten steps inside.

By the time she made it to the aircraft, nearly everyone was seated. She spotted Mario and Iris canoodling in the bulkhead row. She expected a seat beside them, but glancing down at her boarding pass, she realized she wasn't seated in Coach, but First Class.

Let the Agency suck up. She wouldn't change her mind.

"Excuse me, ma'am," a handsome flight attendant said from behind her. "You need to find your seat."

She turned, ready to aim a sharpened barb at the guy for stating the obvious, but decided he wasn't worth her ire. He was just doing his job. Instead, she smiled, apologized for her tardy arrival and headed into the front of the plane. There was an empty window seat beside, of course, the blond guy in the baseball cap. An empty seat that corresponded with the number and letter on her boarding pass.

He stood up, allowing her to pass, though the spacious seats made his gesture unnecessary. As she skimmed by him, his cologne caught her attention. Warmed by his skin, the subtle citrus scent teased her with a hint of mint. Completely unlike the haunting, smoky musk tinged with patchouli and sandalwood that Roman wore, the aroma aroused her curiosity. She fought the urge to glance at his face, explore the depths of his eyes, assess whether or not the man fate had deemed worthy of sitting beside her might not make an interesting way to wash the missing Roman out of her hair.

Not that she really wanted him washed out, but what choice did she have? She'd denied Tremayne's suggestion that Roman hadn't returned from his assignment because he was avoiding reconciling with her, but most of that had been bravado and good, old-fashioned pride. Didn't mean the heart-crushing thought hadn't occurred to her more than once.

She busied herself with stuffing her backpack under her seat, fastening her seat belt and accepting a hot, wet hand towel from the flight attendant to wipe the grime of the long wait off her hands, arms and neckline, dipping deep into her V-necked blouse to remove the collected sweat.

"You're killing me, you know that, right?"

The voice was unmistakable. A chill breezed over her freshly moistened skin, and in a daze, she dropped the towel on the flight attendant's proffered tray and turned slowly to the man beside her.

His hair was blond. His eyes were…green? She leaned in closer, determined to see the telltale rim of colored contacts. The scar dipping into his top lip threw her off for a moment, and the new, thinner shape and lighter color of his eyebrows nearly changed her mind, but the rugged shape of his chin, the texture of his skin, the curve of his smile finally gave him away.

"You son of a bitch," she whispered.

She moved, but Roman caught her hand and held it fast to the armrest. Smart man. She had the incredible need to slap the smug smile off his face.

"Not exactly the greeting I expected," he said.

She tugged her hand away, gluing her gaze to the seat in front of her as the plane roared down the runway. "I don't know why you expected anything more. Or less. You left."

"I was deployed to complete the mission. I couldn't have succeeded without you."

She rolled her eyes. "Clearly. My life would have been a hell of a lot easier over the past few days if you just would have been honest with me and asked for my help rather than playing all these games, including the ones that nearly got me shot."

His fingers tap-danced on the armrest, and she couldn't help but give them a cursory glance. If he touched her, she'd kill him. Then she'd kiss him. But killing definitely came first.

"That sounds very fair and self-righteous, but you know as well as I do that things couldn't work that way. As romantic and grand a gesture it would have been if I'd stayed behind to hold your hand at the Agency, that's not who I am. And it's not who you need me to be."

Had he spoken those words a few weeks ago, Rachel wouldn't have been so sure of the honest truth in his assessment. Wrapped up in her own life and career, Rachel hadn't given two thoughts to how much she might need a man until Roman's continual abandonment drove her to secretly follow him and enlist her friends in carefully planned schemes to trap him and force him to tell her…what? That he loved her? That he couldn't live without her?

But now she'd gotten her life back, her strength.

She'd wanted him back, yes, but she hadn't been willing to pay any price. She'd helped her country, that was a perk, but most important, she'd returned to her original groove of an independent woman open to the possibility of love, but not bound to it.

She turned in her spacious seat, giving a little yawn she covered daintily with her hand. Her ears popped as the plane ascended to cruising altitude. "So why are you here?"

He looked down into his lap, his expression sheepish. "What can I say? I can't resist you."

"You'll lose your job," she pointed out. "I don't think Tremayne likes the idea of you and me together, especially if I keep turning down her job offers."

"Tremayne likes to think of herself as all-powerful, but now that I've completed this mission, my clout within the Agency is assured. With the right spin, which I've already set in motion, I may just have her job by the end of our vacation."

Rachel sat back, trying to hide the thrill that sparked through her body. "Our vacation? You sure you didn't just stowaway aboard in order to seduce me and leave when your pager goes off?"

He leaned forward and dug into the duffel he'd shoved under the seat. He retrieved a small gift-wrapped box and placed it softly in her hands.

"Open it," he instructed when she seemed more interested in the shiny bronze box rather than the contents of his offering.

She pulled off the top. Inside was his old pager…or at least, what was left of it.

"Anger issues?" she asked, a smile teasing the corners of her mouth.

He shook his head and extended his palm. She placed

the box in the middle of his hand and grinned at the mess inside. "I had to show my credentials just to get it through Security. I like to think of this more like frustration. And determination. How long do you plan to stay in Puerto Rico?"

"Well," she said, retrieving the box and capping it with the bowed top, "I was going to decide after I found out who I met poolside. What's your schedule like?"

He leaned in, twisting so they faced each other, then took off his hat and stuffed it in the pocket in front of him so he could close in even more. Rachel couldn't help but run her fingers through his newly dyed hair, which also seemed longer, thanks to what she suspected were extensions. The picture of Roman sitting still for the procedure in some frou-frou salon made her giggle, but when his newly green gaze glittered with curiosity, she tamped down her mirth and instead concentrated on the sudden, overwhelming awareness sparking between them. He obviously would do whatever it took to be an effective agent. And by boarding this plane, he'd proved that he was also willing to do whatever it took to bring her back into his life.

"I'm completely in vacation mode for the foreseeable future. Things are going to shake up at the Agency, and until then, I'm all yours."

"And what if they call you back?"

"First they have to find me."

She licked her lips, trying to sate her incredible need to lick his instead. "They are Homeland Security."

"Are they?"

She arched a brow. "Are you keeping secrets from me, Roman Brach, if that really is your name?"

YOUR PARTICIPATION IS REQUESTED!

Dear Reader,

Since you are a lover of fiction – we would like to get to know you!

Inside you will find a short Reader's Survey. Sharing your answers with us will help our editorial staff understand who you are and what activities you enjoy.

To thank you for your participation, we would like to send you 2 books and a gift – **ABSOLUTELY FREE!**

Enjoy your gifts with our appreciation,

Pam Powers

SEE INSIDE FOR READER'S SURVEY

What's Your Reading Pleasure...
ROMANCE? _OR_ SUSPENSE?

Do you prefer spine-tingling page turners OR heart-stirring stories about love and relationships? Tell us which books you enjoy – and you'll get 2 FREE "ROMANCE" BOOKS or 2 FREE "SUSPENSE" BOOKS with no obligation to purchase anything.

Choose **"ROMANCE"** and get **2 FREE BOOKS** that will fuel your imagination with intensely moving stories about life, love and relationships.

FREE!

Choose **"SUSPENSE"** and you'll get **2 FREE BOOKS** that will thrill you with a spine-tingling blend of suspense and mystery.

FREE!

Whichever category you select, your 2 free books have a combined cover price of $11.98 or more in the U.S. and $13.98 or more in Canada.

And remember. . . just for accepting the Editor's Free Gift Offer, we'll send you 2 books and a gift, ABSOLUTELY FREE!

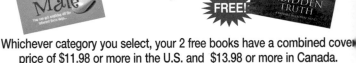

YOUR READER'S SURVEY
"THANK YOU" FREE GIFTS INCLUDE:

▶ 2 Romance OR 2 Suspense books

▶ A lovely surprise gift

PLEASE FILL IN THE CIRCLES COMPLETELY TO RESPOND

1) What type of fiction books do you enjoy reading? (Check all that apply)
- ○ Suspense/Thrillers
- ○ Action/Adventure
- ○ Modern-day Romances
- ○ Historical Romance
- ○ Humour
- ○ Science fiction

2) What attracted you most to the last fiction book you purchased on impulse?
- ○ The Title ○ The Cover ○ The Author ○ The Story

3) What is usually the greatest influencer when you <u>plan</u> to buy a book?
- ○ Advertising ○ Referral from a friend
- ○ Book Review ○ Like the author

4) Approximately how many fiction books do you read in a year?
- ○ 1 to 6 ○ 7 to 19 ○ 20 or more

5) How often do you access the internet?
- ○ Daily ○ Weekly ○ Monthly ○ Rarely or never

6) To which of the following age groups do you belong?
- ○ Under 18 ○ 18 to 34 ○ 35 to 64 ○ over 65

YES! I have completed the Reader's Survey. Please send me the 2 FREE books and gift for which I qualify. I understand that I am under no obligation to purchase any books, as explained on the back.

Check one:

	ROMANCE
	193 MDL EE3V 393 MDL EE37

	SUSPENSE
	192 MDL EE4K 392 MDL EE4V

FIRST NAME | LAST NAME

ADDRESS

APT.# | CITY

STATE/PROV. | ZIP/POSTAL CODE

◀ DETACH AND MAIL CARD TODAY! ▶

(SUR-SS-06) © 1998 MIRA BOOKS

The Reader Service — Here's How It Works:

Accepting your 2 free books and gift places you under no obligation to buy anything. You may keep the books and gift and return the shipping statement marked "cancel." If you do not cancel, about a month later we'll send you 3 additional books and bill you just $5.24 each in the U.S., or $5.74 each in Canada, plus 25¢ shipping & handling per book and applicable taxes if any.* That's the complete price and — compared to cover prices starting from $5.99 each in the U.S. and $6.99 each in Canada — it's quite a bargain! You may cancel at any time, but if you choose to continue, every month we'll send you 3 more books, which you may either purchase at the discount price or return to us and cancel your subscription.

*Terms and prices subject to change without notice. Sales tax applicable in N.Y. Canadian residents will be charged applicable provincial taxes and GST.

He leaned sideways so that his smooth, recently shaven cheek brushed lightly against hers. "It is really my name," he whispered.

Her flesh rippled with goose bumps. "Really? And what other secrets are you willing to share with me?"

"Whatever you need to know to love me again, I'll tell you."

"How do you know I ever loved you to begin with?"

"Because you did. No more games, Rachel. No more distractions. Being away from you made me realize I'd lost a shot at something amazing. I love you. I probably have since the moment I spotted you in that television studio, but more than likely since the first time we made love. And I loved you even more when you put up with Tremayne in order to save my project."

"You love me because I saved your ass?"

"It's not the only reason, no, but it damned well doesn't hurt. In this business, saving someone's ass is serious business."

"Like us?"

"Like us."

Rachel closed her eyes in anticipation of Roman's lips descending on hers to detonate all other thoughts from her brain. They had a lot to talk about, a lot to explore, a lot to admit and a lot to learn. But so long as Roman was willing to lay his heart on the line, so was she. The payoff could be more than she ever imagined that fateful morning when she'd stepped into Mario's cab and followed Roman into a life she never thought she'd have the fortitude to deal with—until she had.

Luckily, she didn't have to wait long for the feel of his mouth on hers and the mind-exploding sensation of the kiss she'd longed for. With his hands around her waist and his tongue coaxing her into sweet delirium, Rachel cherished his ability to drive her to distraction, en route to delivering her to love.

* * * * *

Look for Domino Black
to return with a vengeance in
THE DOMINO EFFECT,
an August "Extreme" Blaze!

TAKEN FOR A RIDE

Kate Hoffmann

CHAPTER ONE

THE TINY BRASS BELL above the shop door jangled wildly as Sabina stumbled through, her iced latte clutched in one hand. She kicked the door shut, the click of the latch echoing in the silence. Outside, the temperature was already rising, the weatherman promising at least an eighty-degree day. Hot weather in Manhattan was always good for business, Sabina mused.

Her grandmother said that the spirit world felt closer when the air was thick with heat and humidity. Sabina believed that the stress of summer in the city brought more people into the shop for psychic relief, the same as it did around the holidays. Either way, more business was good business.

She wandered through the familiar interior of the shop, exotic scents mingling in the still air. The tourist guides had called Ruta's "disarmingly peculiar" and "an odd little establishment" and "a relic of the Village's colorful past." For Sabina, it was more than that. It was home.

She'd taken her first steps on the thick Turkish rugs and she'd done her schoolwork on the round table with the crystal ball. Her friends used to play with the stuffed marmot that sat on a shelf above the ornate cash register and she'd learned to add and multiply with well-worn decks of tarot cards.

Sabina had never really thought of her grandmother as unusual, at least not when she was younger. Ruta was like so many other immigrants living in New York. It wasn't until later that she learned how different her grandmother really was. Descended from Gypsy kings and queens, Sabina's ancestors had once roamed eastern Europe in wagon caravans, peddling potions and amulets and even curses.

Ruta had come to America as a child over seventy years ago, escaping Hungary months after the war broke out. A stranger in a strange land, Ruta's widowed mother had told fortunes in Times Square while Ruta sat by her side, learning her secrets.

And so it had been, the secrets of the Gypsies passed from Ruta to Sabina's mother, Katja, to Sabina. Unfortunately, Sabina had never developed her own powers. She couldn't see into the future, she couldn't decipher a person's life from the lines on their palm, and she'd never made a potion or a charm that worked. Still, that didn't stop her from plying the only trade she knew.

Both her grandmother and mother had assured her that her gift may arrive late, but it would indeed come. In truth, Sabina knew she had no professional future in the fortune-telling business. She was lucky to have skated by for this long. When Ruta finally retired, the shop would pass to Sabina. And she'd already begun to make a few changes that reflected her own talents and interests.

She closed her eyes and imagined what her shop might look like. Instead of the dark, mysterious interior, she would throw open the heavy drapes and tear down the tapestries. Sabina's shop would be bright, with glass shelves and warm wood cabinets. She'd sell lingerie, beautiful, sexy creations of her own designs. And she'd sell scented lotions and fine soaps, luxurious robes and pretty sleepwear. There would be candles and bath oils, anything to please the senses. Her customers wouldn't need a psychic reading to feel good.

Sabina glanced over at the far corner of the shop. She had already convinced her grandmother to try an aromatherapy counter, and she'd recently ordered a new line of herbal candles. Ruta was stubborn and Sabina had to make her changes gradually.

"Bina, I've been looking for you."

Sabina turned to watch her grandmother emerge from behind a bead curtain. As always, Ruta was dressed in her traditional Gypsy costume, a flowing skirt with an embroidered peasant blouse. Her wrists were adorned with gold bangles and a bead necklace hung from her neck. She'd twisted a colorful scarf through her long gray hair.

"Morning, Nana. Did you sleep well?" She circled the counter and pressed a kiss to Ruta's cheek.

"No," she said, a heavy Hungarian accent coloring every word. "I was up all night. Look what I have for you." She reached into the pocket of her skirt and placed a photo on the counter in front of Sabina. "Mrs. Nussbaum's nephew. She gave it to me last night at her reading. He is a doctor. A proctologist. And he is very handsome, don't you think?"

Sabina groaned inwardly. "Nana, please. No more matchmaking. I can find men to meet on my own."

"Then why don't you do it, Bina? You have not had a boyfriend in many months. You spend every spare minute upstairs in your apartment, drawing your designs and sewing them up. I am starting to worry about you. Your whole life has become underwear. If you do not let someone else see your underwear, you will grow old a spinster."

Sabina shuddered. That word was so awful. *Spinster.* It ranked right up there with troll and gargoyle. But she was willing to die a spinster before she let Ruta fix her up again. Her grandmother's matchmaking efforts up to this point had been nothing short of disastrous. "I don't need your help."

"Maybe just a little bit?" She reached in her pocket again and withdrew a red string with a clay amulet dangling from it. "Here, put this on. It is a love charm."

"Nana, this won't work."

"You will never know unless you try it," Ruta said. "I have been open-minded about your smelly oils and silly candles, so you could do the same about my charms. Your destiny is out there waiting for you if you would just open your eyes to it." She brushed Sabina's hands away as she lowered the charm over her head. "There," she murmured, fussing with a series of knots in the string. "You have made your grandmother very happy now. Tonight, I will sleep well."

Sabina fingered the amulet. "This is silly. How could this possibly help me find a man?"

"Give it a chance to work, Bina." Ruta sighed softly. "I only want what is best for you. Now that your mama and papa are living in that horrid place, we must stick together, yes?"

Sabina laughed softly as her grandmother walked back through the bead curtain. She'd been to Branson, Missouri, and it wasn't all that bad. Between the tourists and the retirees, her mother's new shop had more customers than Katja could handle.

Sabina plucked at the charm, holding it up to examine it. "Sometimes it's just better to pacify her than to argue," she murmured to herself.

"I heard that!" Ruta shouted. She reappeared at the bead curtain, poking her head through to give Sabina a disapproving look. "If you spent half the time talking to eligible men as you spend talking to yourself, you would be in the midst of a grand romance now."

What was she supposed to do? Everyone else in her family spent their time communicating with the spirit world. And since she didn't possess the power, Sabina had always chosen to discuss her problems with herself. "I'm going to buy some bagels." She tucked the amulet beneath her blouse, then grabbed her iced latte. "I plan to meet at least six or seven men along the way. In fact, by the time I get back, I'll be married and pregnant."

"It is good to think positively," her grandmother replied. "But no talking to yourself. The men will think you are crazy."

Sabina walked out the front door and headed toward the corner. Crazy? Sabina was the only normal person in her family. She glanced down at the charm swinging from her neck. Well, almost normal. She'd agreed to wear the amulet, hadn't she? Sabina wondered just what was mixed with the clay. Her grandmother had shelves and drawers and boxes full of strange ingredients— dried beetles and cats' whiskers and boars' teeth.

Sabina dodged an old woman walking her Peking-ese, her attention still focused on the amulet. She didn't see the man approaching until she ran squarely into his chest. Her iced latte exploded in front of her. Sabina jumped back, but her legs tangled in the leash of the Pekingese and she fell forward again, the drink splash-ing into the man's face. He cursed as they both tumbled to the sidewalk in a flurry of arms and legs.

For a moment, Sabina was afraid to move. The old woman scolded her as she extracted the leash from around Sabina's ankles, but when she tried to apologize, she realized that the breath had been knocked out of her.

The man beneath her groaned, and slowly she placed her hands on either side of his broad shoulders and pushed up. "I—I'm so sorry. I wasn't looking and I didn't—" Her gaze met his and the apology died in her throat as she stared into impossibly blue eyes.

Even with her latte dripping off his face, she could see she was lying on top of the most gorgeous man in all of Manhattan. Her eyes drifted to dark lashes, a per-fectly straight nose and a sculpted mouth. As the heat of his body began to seep through her thin cotton dress, a wave of giddiness washed over her.

He reached up and softly brushed the hair away from her eyes. "Are you all right?" he asked, concern etched across his brow. His voice was so deep and smooth that it sent a tiny shiver down her spine.

He wasn't a dream. He was real, all hard muscle and long limbs. The scent of his cologne teased at her nose and she drew a deep breath, closing her eyes and turning into his touch. Could the amulet have worked so quickly?

"Hey," he murmured. "Open your eyes. Talk to me."

Sabina did as she was told. "What would you like me to say?" she replied.

"Are you all right?"

Sabina blinked. "I—I'm not sure. How about you?"

He slowly pushed up, bracing his hands behind him. Sabina rose with him, her knees resting on either side of his hips. "I don't think I'm bleeding." He moved his arms, then his legs. "And all my limbs seem to be functioning." He frowned. "Why am I wet?"

"That would be my Hazelnut iced latte," Sabina said apologetically. She reached out and brushed the sticky drink from his face, her fingers skimming across his smoothly shaven skin.

He grinned crookedly. "Well, that's fine. I haven't had my morning coffee yet. I guess wearing it would probably help me cut down on the caffeine, but it's going to be hell on the dry cleaning bill."

Sabina smiled, pleased that he found their situation amusing rather than irritating. They'd only just met, but she already knew this man. He was sweet and charming and sexy. He smelled good, he dressed well and she loved the sound of his voice.

"I'd love to sit here and chat," he said, straightening his tie. "But I'm in a hurry."

Sabina felt her cheeks warm with embarrassment, then quickly scrambled off him. "I'm sorry," she said, getting to her feet. "It was my fault. I—I was distracted."

"No, it was my fault," he countered.

Sabina offered him a hand. When he stood beside her, she realized how tall he was—well over six feet. His suit was impeccably tailored to his lean body. Her eyes rested on the messy brown stain seeping through his tie and white shirt.

"Oh, look what I've done. I've ruined your shirt and tie. You can't go to work like that."

This was perfect! She could offer to take his shirt to the cleaners and they'd have to see each other again. Or maybe he'd be willing to stop by her apartment while she soaked it in cold water. Her mind flashed to an image of him, shirtless, standing in her kitchen.

He gave her a shrug, then waved his newspaper between them.

"Really, I'm fine. That will teach me to read the baseball scores on the way to the subway."

"At least let me pay to have your clothes cleaned," Sabina offered.

He shook his head as he brushed stray droplets of her latte off his suit. "I just live a few blocks from here. I'll run home and change." He reached out and touched her shoulder. "You're sure you're all right? No broken bones, no internal injuries?"

Sabina nodded, desperately searching for something more to say to him…anything that would keep him standing on the sidewalk just a few moments longer. Couldn't he feel the attraction between them? Her heart fell. Maybe he wasn't interested. And just because he was the most gorgeous man she'd ever met didn't mean he was available. He could be involved, maybe even engaged or married. It would be just her luck to meet the only perfect man in New York, then find out he was already taken.

"All the good ones are," she muttered, raking her dark hair out of her eyes.

"What?"

Sabina swallowed hard. "Nothing."

"Well, it was nice running into you," he said, giving her a nod. "Maybe we can do it again sometime." He glanced at his watch. "I really am going to be late. So, take care." He gave her a quick wave and started down the sidewalk.

Sabina watched him walk away, certain that she'd just blown any chance she had with him. But at the last minute, he turned around. "When?" he shouted.

Confused, Sabina shook her head. "When what?"

"When can we run into each other again?"

A giggle bubbled up inside of her at the sudden turn of events. "How about right here? Tomorrow morning? We can go for coffee."

"Same time, same place." He waved, then ran across the street and disappeared into a stream of pedestrians.

Sabina reached down and took the amulet between her thumb and forefinger. "I guess it does work," she murmured.

"RUTA'S. IT'S ON Christopher Street. I know just where it is," the cabbie said.

Alec Harnett glanced at his watch, then surveyed the gridlocked traffic on Sixth Avenue through the cab window. He reached into his briefcase and picked out the file folder labeled LUPESCU. The corners were dog-eared and the label was yellowed owing to the age of the file. Inside, he found a detailed listing of yearly visits to Ruta Lupescu's shop by his father, Simon Harnett, written offers that had remained unsigned, and a stack of property appraisals that increased in value with every year that passed. In addition, there were copies of reports by the building inspectors, claiming that, despite his father's insistence, Ruta Lupescu was in compliance with all New York city building codes.

The old Gypsy woman had been a thorn in his father's side for nearly thirty years, ever since his father took over Harnett Property Development from Alec's grandfather, George Harnett. And now that Alec had been named president of the company, the problem of Ruta Lupescu had fallen onto his desk.

He'd been headed to Ruta's earlier that morning when he'd been knocked to the sidewalk. Alec smiled as he recalled the beauty who had caused the accident. He'd known more than his share of women in Manhattan, one more beautiful than the next. But this woman was different from all of them.

Alec had always been drawn to willowy blondes, the all-American beauty, cool and aloof, except in bed. The woman he'd met that morning was the opposite. She had an exotic beauty, every feature magnified just enough to make it extraordinary. Her mouth was wide, her lips lush, her skin like silk. Her violet eyes were ringed with dark lashes, and her raven hair tumbled around her face, creating a perfect frame for her beauty.

"You payin' a visit to Ruta's?"

Alec glanced up and the cabbie grinned, watching him in the rearview mirror.

"Do you know her?" Alec asked.

"Oh, yeah. Ruta is the best in the city. I met her back when I was working with NYPD. Now I see her whenever my luck goes south at the track." He chuckled. "If she devoted herself to the ponies and lottery numbers, she'd probably be a millionaire. That woman has some scary psychic powers."

"Interesting," Alec said. His eyes came to rest on the cabby's photo. Mario Capelli. He wondered if Mario knew that Ruta Lupescu was sitting on a multimillion-dollar lottery ticket. She owned a piece of property that every developer in Manhattan would trade his mother to own.

In the past twenty years, real estate values in the Village had skyrocketed. Most of the undeveloped property had been scooped up long ago in a mad race to provide housing and retail space to a growing population of very affluent New Yorkers. But Ruta Lupescu had acquired her building fifty years ago, before Greenwich Village became one of the city's most attractive neighborhoods.

Now her building sat smack in the middle of a row of six properties owned by Harnett Property Development. With all seven in hand, they could build something special—a new hotel, luxury condominiums, or maybe a shopping complex with a movie theatre. But without Ruta's property, plans for anything big were put on hold—unless Alec could convince her to sell.

His father had always considered the property to be his to begin with and had never made a reasonable offer, preferring instead to badger the old Gypsy into selling. But Alec took a more pragmatic approach to the problem. Everyone had their price, even Ruta Lupescu. It was his job to find it.

"What can you tell me about her?" he asked.

"Ah, she's a sweetheart. Always willing to help a person in need. Why, most of those folks who live in her building are on fixed incomes. She barely asks for rent."

"Seems a bit silly in this day and age," Alec commented.

Mario shrugged, glancing over his shoulder. "I suppose it does. But Ruta came from nothing. She and her mother were refugees back in the late thirties. They came with only the clothes on their back. Just a few years after they arrived, her mother died. Ruta was a teenager. She told fortunes on the street and lived in the basement of an old building until she saved up enough to rent her shop. The story goes that one night, her landlord stopped in and she told him his fortune. And when it came true, he gave her the building, free and clear. A whole building for one fortune. Like winning the lottery, don't you think?"

"Yeah," Alec murmured. He'd heard the story a million times, but told with much less awe and reverence. His grandfather, George Harnett, had been the man. And Ruta's fortune had predicted good health and a long life for Alec's grandmother Judith, who had been seriously ill for nearly a year. The very next day, Alec's grandmother had miraculously gotten out of bed, and within a week, she was her normal cheery self.

"Back then, the Village wasn't the best place to live," Mario commented. "But things have changed." He laughed, shaking his head. "That Ruta could live like a queen, but she's still telling fortunes for ten dollars a pop."

"What about her family? You'd think they'd want her to be comfortable."

"Her daughter moved to Missouri with her husband a few years ago. She wanted Ruta to come with them, but the old lady was determined to stay. I don't blame her. She loves that place. And everyone in the neighborhood loves her."

Alec sat back, glancing around the cab. The interior was decorated with photos. At first, he assumed they were of Mario's children, but upon closer examination, Alec found smiling couples, many of them dressed in wedding wear. "What are all these pictures?" he asked.

"Ah, most of them are fares. At least, that's how they started. Once in a while, I make a few introductions and one thing leads to another and before you know it, they're walking down the aisle."

"You're a matchmaker?"

"I guess you could call me that. Are you looking for a wife?"

Alec chuckled. "No, not at the moment." But he couldn't ignore the image of the violet-eyed beauty that drifted through his mind. He imagined she was a woman who could keep him interested for a long time. He'd find out tomorrow morning, but for now, Alec had to concentrate on the job at hand.

Mario pulled the cab over to the curb, then pointed to a brick five-story. "That's Ruta's. Say hello for me and tell her I'll see her tomorrow afternoon. I take her out to Brooklyn every Thursday. She tells fortunes for free at a retirement center there."

Alec paid the cabbie, then hopped out. He walked along the sidewalk, back and forth in front of the shop, as he collected his thoughts. His father had always come away frustrated from his meetings, unnerved by the yearly curse she had put on him. She'd even become a legend around the office. Whenever the photocopy machine broke or important paperwork got lost, it was blamed on the Gypsy's wrath.

Alec took off his jacket and draped it over his arm,

then loosened his tie and unbuttoned the top button of his shirt. All he had to do was keep his cool, listen to her concerns and then address them, logically and calmly. His father had never tried that approach, so it might just work the first time out.

A tiny bell rang above his head as he entered the shop. The interior was a hodgepodge of old wooden display cases, thick tapestries and threadbare furniture, just another in the mix of odd establishments scattered throughout the Village. He wandered over to the counter and bent down to examine Ruta's merchandise, if it could be called that.

There were birds' nests and the jaw from some sharp-toothed animal, a small bowl of amber crystals and a bottle of dark green liquid. Everywhere he looked, there was something more bizarre—feathers and pickled eggs and dried roots and berries. His gaze halted on a stuffed weasel that sat above the cash register. The place was downright creepy—and empty. "Hello?" he called.

An instant later a slender figure popped up from behind one of the counters. Her long black hair tumbled around her face, and when she brushed it back, he met familiar eyes of a strange violet color. For a long moment, they didn't speak, a tiny frown marring her smooth brow.

"It's you," he finally said. "From the sidewalk this morning."

"Yes," she murmured. Her fingered fluttered up to her necklace and she rubbed the pendant nervously. "How are you? How did you find me?"

"You work here?"

She nodded. "I do. My grandmother owns this place. Ruta Lupescu."

"Your grandmother," Alec said very slowly. "Ruta is your grandmother." He fought the urge to step back out to the sidewalk and regroup. Either this was incredible luck or terrible irony. He'd been thinking about this woman all day and now here she was, as if destiny had put her in front of him.

Was there any way to separate business from pleasure now? Ruta had made her feelings about the Harnett family well known. What were the odds that her grand-daughter would feel differently? Given time, perhaps he could enlist her help to convince Ruta.

For now, that's what he needed—time. He could play it cool, collect a bit more information and revise his strategy. "I understand you tell fortunes here." He swallowed hard, suddenly finding it difficult to speak. Out on the street, he felt safe, in control. But this was her environment. His mind drifted back to the old woman's curse. Perhaps her granddaughter was even more powerful than she was.

"My grandmother usually does the readings," she said. "She's not in right now, but she'll be back in about a half hour." A tiny smile twitched at the corners of her mouth. "Funny, I wouldn't have pegged you for the type to come into this shop."

"I've always been curious," Alec admitted, returning her smile. "And some power must have made me walk through that door." He leaned in closer, bracing his elbows on the counter. "Maybe you would do my reading?"

She paused, then shook her head. "I'm really not that—"

"I won't hold you to anything you tell me. I just have a few simple questions." At first, it looked as if she might refuse and he'd be forced to leave without learning anything more.

"All right," she finally said. "Why don't you have a seat and I'll go get the cards."

"Cards? Aren't you going to look into a crystal ball or read my palm? Or maybe you could do the tea-leaf thing?"

"There are many ways to do a reading," she explained. "I prefer tarot cards, but if you'd like me to read your palm, I can do that."

Alec sat down across the table from her and held out his hand. Right now, all he wanted was to touch her, to see if her fingers elicited the same intense reaction they had that morning. "Let's try this first, and if I don't get the answers I want, we'll give the cards a shot."

She reached out and took his hand in hers. The moment she did, Alec felt his blood warm and his pulse leap. Slowly, she drew her fingers over his palm, stroking it gently. He tried to concentrate on the task at hand, but Alec found himself fascinated by the sensations her touch evoked.

As she stared at his palm, he took the chance to examine her more closely. She was even more beautiful than he remembered. His eyes fixed on her mouth, and he imagined kissing her. She'd taste like some sweet, exotic fruit, strangely addictive, yet unfamiliar to him.

"What would you like to know?" she murmured, glancing up.

"Let's start with your name," Alec said. The words came out before he realized what he was saying. In truth, that was the only question he wanted answered at the moment.

Another smile curled the corners of her mouth and Alec's regret evaporated. "It's Sabina."

"Like the Audrey Hepburn movie?"

"But without the *R*. Sabina, not Sabrina. Sabina Amanar."

"Sabina," he repeated.

"What's your name?"

"You're the psychic. Why don't you tell me?"

She stared down at his palm and continued to run her fingertips over his skin. "Your name makes no difference. It won't change your future."

Alec winced inwardly. If she knew his last name was Harnett, it would definitely change his prospects for dinner with the lovely Sabina. "What do you see there?"

"You work very hard. Even now, your thoughts are occupied with matters of money and power. But there is one problem that weighs heavily on your mind. There is something you want, something you…" She paused as if to carefully choose her words. "Covet, but it will not come easily. You are tempted to use trickery to obtain this thing, but that will not bring it to you."

Alec shifted uneasily. She could be talking about anything from the new Jag he'd been looking at to his next real estate deal to her grandmother's building. But then again, she might actually be talking about his desire to yank her into his arms and kiss her. Either way, he didn't like that she was able to see through him so easily. "Can you be more specific?"

She frowned, then drew in a sharp breath, as if what she saw surprised her. "There—there is family involved.

And a decision made many years ago." Sabina placed his hand on the table, then drew back. "That's all I see," she said softly. "You should come back when Ruta is here. She's much better than I am."

"I think you're doing a fine job. So what do you advise I do?" He reached out and took her hand, turning his palm up again. "Tell me."

"Be honest," she said, not bothering to look down. "Say what you mean and mean what you say."

"Have dinner with me," he countered.

Sabina gasped. "What?"

"You told me to be honest. We were going to have coffee tomorrow morning. Let's have dinner tonight instead."

"I hardly know you," Sabina said with a coy smile.

Alec knew she'd accept the invitation. The attraction between them was obviously mutual. "You're psychic." He grabbed her hand and placed her fingertips on his temple. "Just read my mind and you'll know everything you need to know. I'm a good guy, right?"

"Yes, I suspect you are. But I still don't know anything about you."

Alec stood. "My name is Alec. Alec Har—" He paused, then cleared his throat. Now was not the time to reveal all. "Harper. I'll pick you up this evening in front of the shop. Seven, if that's all right."

"I really think we should start with—"

"You read my palm, Sabina. You must know that I don't take no for an answer." Alec pushed back from the table and walked to the door. "See you this evening."

When he reached the street, he turned back and looked through the glass-paned door to find Sabina staring at him, an odd frown on her face. Alec gave her a little wave, then stepped to the curb to hail a cab. But when the cab pulled up, he hesitated, then pulled open the passenger-side door. "Can you wait a few seconds?"

The cabbie nodded and Alec strode back inside the shop. She was standing where he'd left her, toying with her necklace as she had earlier. Without hesitation, Alec reached around her waist and drew her up against his body. A moment later, he lost himself in the taste of her mouth. A tiny cry of surprise slipped from her throat, but then she softened in his arms and returned the kiss, her tongue gently teasing at his.

Alec could have stood there for the rest of the day, kissing her, letting the waves of desire wash over him. But there would be time for that later. He drew away and smiled. "I'm not sure why I did that," he whispered. "But if you figure it out, let me know."

With that, he turned and walked out of the shop. As he hopped into the cab, Alec chuckled to himself. So maybe it wasn't such a bad idea to mix business with pleasure. Besides, from the very moment had Sabina touched him, all thoughts of business had disappeared from his head. Right now, he had one task at hand—romancing Sabina Amanar. And that would be nothing but pleasure.

CHAPTER TWO

"HOW DO I LOOK?"

Sabina stood in the center of the shop and twirled around once. Chloe Kincaid watched her from behind the counter, a lollipop stuck in her mouth. Asking Chloe was probably not the best choice considering that the twenty-two-year-old graduate student preferred to dress like a vampire. Her lips were painted a bright red and her pink-streaked black hair stuck up in unruly shocks.

"What are you going for?" Chloe asked.

She smoothed her hands over the embroidered blue silk. "Sexy, but not too sexy. Interesting. Maybe a little aloof, but approachable. Mysterious?"

Chloe stared at her a long moment, her head tipped to the side. "I'm not sure a dress can do all that. Maybe you ought to try therapy."

Sabina was well used to Chloe's arid sense of humor. "Well, do I at least look pretty?"

She shrugged. "Yeah."

Sabina's spirits lifted. She'd designed the dress herself out of a piece of vintage silk she'd found in a store in SoHo. Body-skimming and sleeveless, with a fitted waist and skirt, the dress was Asian in influence, with a bit of Village bohemian tossed in. And the deep sapphire color was perfect. "Maybe I should wear something a bit more conservative. I have a little black cocktail dress that—"

"You are a goddess," Chloe replied flatly, turning back to the magazine she was reading. "I do like the necklace."

Sabina reached up, surprised to find that she still wore the love charm her grandmother had given her. She carefully tucked it beneath the mandarin collar of the dress.

"I've got one of those, too," Chloe said, holding up a clay amulet nearly identical to Sabina's. "Your grandmother gave it to me for Christmas last year, and since then my sex life has been fantastic."

"Really?" Sabina asked. "Then you think it works?"

Chloe nodded as she blew a bubble with her gum. The bubble popped and she smiled. "Oh, yeah. Ruta knows what she's doing. I've had more boys than I can handle."

Sabina admired her grandmother's abilities, but she had never placed much faith in the magic that Ruta practiced. Sabina had learned that telling someone's fortune was more about reading their behaviors and attitudes, about drawing conclusions from carefully asked questions, than actually seeing into the future. As for charms, how could a simple clay disk wield any mystical power over a man?

But since she'd put the necklace on that morning, her social life had improved by leaps and bounds. She had a date with a devastatingly handsome man. "I'd settle for just one. A really good one."

"It may not be the amulet that's getting me the men," Chloe said, bracing her chin on her hand. "I suppose it could be the potion."

"Ruta gave you a potion?" Sabina groaned. "She knows she's not supposed to give out potions. I've told her again and again. Someone could have an allergic reaction and die."

"It's all herbal," Chloe said. "I watched her make it. It doesn't taste great, but it works." She grabbed her bag from beneath the counter and rummaged through it. A few seconds later, she pulled out a small brown bottle and handed it to Sabina. "You should try it. He won't be able to resist you."

With a quiet curse, Sabina shoved the bottle into her purse and snapped it shut. "I'm going to have to talk to her about this. If we sell potions, we have to have a license and insurance and inspections. This isn't like the old days."

The bell on the door rang and Sabina spun around, her stomach fluttering with nerves. She held her breath as Alec closed the door behind him, then let it out slowly when he faced her. "Good evening, Sabina," he said with a devilish grin.

"Good evening, Alec." Her eyes lingered on his face for a moment, then slowly drifted down his body. He wore a navy linen jacket that hugged his wide shoulders and a crisply starched blue oxford, which set off the color of his eyes. Faded jeans made him look just boyish enough to set her heart racing. Her sapphire silk had been the perfect choice.

"You look beautiful," he said. "That color suits you."

Sabina felt her face grow warm and she dropped her gaze. She'd hoped for aloof and mysterious, but any second now, she'd begin drooling and then he'd know exactly how she felt. She glanced over at Chloe, who was watching them both, a bemused smile curling her painted lips.

"Chloe, don't forget to drop that mail in the mailbox on your way home," Sabina said.

Chloe leaned forward. "Don't worry about the dress," she whispered. "The way that guy is looking at you, you won't be wearing it long."

Sabina sent her a warning glare, then pasted a smile on her face. "Don't tell Nana I had a date. She'll wait up until I get home and then I'll have to tell her all about it. Just say I went to a gallery opening."

"Sure thing, boss," Chloe said.

When Sabina reached Alec's side, he took her hand and wrapped it in his, then pulled the door open in front of her. "So, are we going to have a good time tonight?"

"What?"

"I just thought you might have a sense of how this is all going to go. Maybe you can give me a few pointers, warn me off before I make any big blunders. You're the psychic."

"Why don't we let the evening just develop on its own," Sabina suggested. "I'm going to switch off my powers now. No mind reading, no soothsaying."

"All right." He tucked her hand into the crook of his arm. "Would you like to catch a cab or should we walk?"

"Where are we going?"

Alec shrugged. "We can go Uptown or we can stay in the neighborhood. Or if you like, we can stop by Balducci's and pick up something from the deli. I make a really good sandwich. And I'm good with frozen pizza. That's the extent of my cooking expertise."

Though she would have loved to see Alec in the kitchen,

for now, Sabina wanted to stay on neutral turf. "Why don't we just walk until we find a place we both like?"

They strolled in silence for a few blocks, heading in the direction of SoHo. Sabina didn't feel as if she needed to make conversation. It was enough just to be with him, to know that he wanted to be with her. "Do you live in the Village?" she asked.

"I have a house over on St. Luke's and a place up in Vermont. Where do you live?"

"Above the shop. There are eight apartments. My grandmother has one, I have one, and we rent the rest out. She owns the building, so I get a break on the rent."

"So you live comfortably on the income you make telling fortunes?" he asked.

"I do. We do." She smiled.

"And where does one study to become a psychic?"

"I never studied for that. That sort of thing comes naturally. I actually studied fashion design at Parsons."

"Really. And why didn't you pursue it?"

"I am. I've been gradually making some changes at the shop, and when my grandmother retires, I hope to turn it into my own boutique. Now, tell me what you do."

"It's not nearly as interesting," Alec said. "I buy and sell things—apartments, buildings mostly, sometimes just land."

She frowned. "You sound like a real estate agent."

"That's part of my job," he replied.

"My grandmother and I don't like real estate agents," Sabina said, the suspicion thick in her voice. "They're always trying to get us to sell her building. You wouldn't believe what they've tried. They call every day and send letter after letter. Some of them even give us gifts. They bring over these elaborate plans, photos of homes in Florida and Arizona. It's ridiculous. And the worst of them, Simon Harnett, reports us to the building inspectors every month. Are you one of them?"

"For you, I'll be anything you want me to be."

"The perfect gentleman," Sabina said. "That's what I want you to be."

He stopped dead on the sidewalk, dragging her to a halt. His hand came up to her face and he smoothed his palm over her cheek. "I'm not sure I can do that."

"And why not?"

In what seemed like nothing more than a heartbeat, Alec wrapped his arm around her waist and pulled Sabina into the shadow of a doorway. His mouth came down on her hers, so quickly that it took her breath away. What began as a desperate kiss soon turned soft and gentle, and Sabina surrendered to it willingly.

His hands skimmed over her torso, smoothing across her back. Sabina's skin tingled beneath the thin silk of her dress and she shivered in reaction. At first, she was barely able to think. But then her mind began to focus on the feel of his lips, the taste of his tongue, the wonderful way he held her face between his hands.

It wasn't a proper kiss from a proper gentleman. This was kiss that invited further seduction, a kiss that made promises about what they might share together once they were completely alone—and naked.

The longer it lasted, the more light-headed she became. Maybe it was the heat. It was awfully warm tonight, so humid it was hard to catch her breath. When he finally drew back, Sabina gulped in fresh air, but that only seemed to make her more dizzy.

"I—I'm not feeling very well," she murmured, pressing her palm to her forehead. "I haven't eaten all day and I feel like I could—" Sabina's knees suddenly gave out beneath her.

Alec caught her around the waist and held her up. "My place is just around the block. Why don't we go there and get you something cool to drink?"

Sabina hesitated, then nodded. A drink of water. What harm could that do? Just because they were alone together didn't mean that they were going to lose control.

He was right when he said he lived just around the block. They crossed the street and a few minutes later climbed the steps to a beautiful row house across from Walker Park. "You must sell a lot of buildings," Sabina said, impressed by his address.

He chuckled, then held the door open. The interior was cool and dark, a relief from the heat outside. She glanced around as they walked back to the kitchen, admiring the simple yet traditional decor. "This is nice," Sabina commented.

"The house?" Alec shrugged. "Thank the decorator. I didn't have time to do it myself, so she did it all."

The kitchen was sleek and modern, cherry cabinets mixed with granite countertops and stainless-steel appliances. Compared to the vintage kitchens in Sabina's building, this was positively luxurious. Her grandmother hadn't done much to the building since she'd acquired it beyond simple repairs. "This is nice, too. It looks like something out of *Architectural Digest*."

He pulled out a stool tucked beneath the edge of the

island, then crossed to the refrigerator. "We'll get you a drink, then I'll get my car and drive you home. We can go out some other time."

"I'm sure I'll be fine," Sabina said.

He opened a bottle of water, then grabbed a glass from the cabinet above the sink. Alec placed both in front of her. She wanted to tell him that it wasn't the heat, or dehydration, that had caused her knees to buckle. It was the experience of kissing him. Even now, staring into his eyes, Sabina felt off balance. She took a long sip of the water.

He reached out and captured her hand, toying with her fingers as she continued to drink. "Better?" he asked.

Sabina nodded, ignoring the tingle that skittered up her arm at his touch. She needed time to think, time to compose herself. Maybe she could hide out in the bathroom until she regained her senses. "Much." She rubbed her forehead, feigning a headache. "I could use an aspirin, though." A temporary headache should buy her a little more time. "I'm just going to go—"

"You could use dinner," he interrupted. "But we'll start with aspirin."

He stepped over to her and gently brushed her hair out of her eyes. "I don't think you have any idea just how beautiful you are," he whispered, dropping a kiss on her lips. "I think you've bewitched me."

One kiss wasn't enough for him. With a low moan, he furrowed his hands through her hair and molded her mouth to his. Everything about the kiss challenged her to give more, to surrender to his taste and his touch.

With trembling fingers, Sabina skimmed her palms over his chest, brushing aside his jacket. Without breaking contact with her mouth, he pulled his arms out of the sleeves and tossed it on the floor.

The simple act of removing his jacket seemed to break some invisible barrier. Sabina reached up and nervously worked at the buttons of his shirt. His breath quickened at her touch and Alec tugged his shirttails out of his jeans, his mouth trailing kisses along her shoulder.

Sabina knew where they were headed, but she was powerless to stop it. Touching him…kissing him… needing him seemed like the most natural thing in the world.

When she'd undone the last button, Alec shrugged out of the shirt. His skin was warm to the touch, his chest smooth and finely muscled. Sabina pressed her lips to the skin at the base of his neck and breathed his scent in deeply.

He tipped his head back and she dropped lower, nuzzling his skin until she reached his nipple. Sabina suddenly felt bold, uninhibited and very powerful. But when her tongue touched his nipple, Alec drew a sharp breath and stepped back.

He smiled crookedly, then ran his thumb along her lip. "I think I'll get you that aspirin," he said.

As he walked out, Sabina sighed softly. What had happened? Why had he stopped so suddenly? At the rate they were going, they would have ended up in bed within the hour, a prospect that didn't seem distasteful to Sabina.

She grabbed her purse and pulled out her mirror. "Oh, God," she murmured, pinching her cheeks to restore some of her color. "Breathe. Everything will be fine."

As she put the mirror back into her purse, she noticed the little brown bottle—Chloe's love potion. Sabina pulled it out and untwisted the cap, then dumped a small measure into her glass. She wasn't sure of the dosage, but right now, she needed any help she could get. Closing her eyes, she drank the remainder of her water.

Almost immediately, she felt an odd imbalance descend on her. Though she was perfectly calm, every nerve in her body was suddenly alive and aware. Sabina ran her hands up and down her arms, the sensation of her fingertips raising goose bumps along the way. She felt an overwhelming need to touch him again, to taste his kisses and to press her body against his. No man had ever affected her as strongly as Alec had, awakening desires that she never knew she had.

Sabina felt as if she'd stepped onto a carnival ride and was waiting for it to begin. The anticipation was almost too much to bear, every thought focused on the wild and thrilling and slightly dangerous ride ahead. It was scary, but she wasn't about to get off now.

ALEC STARED AT HIS reflection in the bathroom mirror, a frown creasing his brow. Everything was moving way too fast. Never mind that he felt like a first-class cad lying to her about who he was. But now there was absolutely no way he was going to give her up. And how the hell could he even think of seducing her as long as she didn't know who he really was?

A curse slipped from his lips and he shook his head. This had to stop right now. If he hoped for anything to happen between them, it couldn't begin this way. Alec drew a deep breath. He'd known her a day, less than twenty-four hours, and already he was planning their future together.

"What is going on in your head?" he said, raking his hands through his hair. If he didn't know any better, he'd suspect she'd used one of those crazy Gypsy spells or curses and rendered him completely defenseless to her beauty.

Hell, maybe she knew exactly who he was. After all, she was psychic. And that fortune she'd told in the shop hit pretty close to home. This could all be a plan for revenge, cooked up between her and her grandmother. She'd lure him into bed, make him all hot and crazy, and dump cold water on him.

He stared at his reflection for a moment longer, then opened the medicine cabinet and grabbed the aspirin. "You're not bewitched," he muttered. "You're temporarily insane." On the way back to the kitchen, Alec stopped and grabbed a T-shirt from his bedroom. He found Sabina waiting where he'd left her.

"Aspirin," he said, popping the cap off the top of the bottle. He shook two into her palm, then refilled her empty water glass.

Sabina watched him with a curious gaze before she tossed the aspirin into her mouth. Tilting her head back, she took a sip of the water, then smiled. "There," she said.

Alec could see that she waiting for him to step closer and kiss her. His eyes were fixed on her lips, still damp from the water and slightly parted. She clenched and unclenched her fingers, but Alec stayed glued to his spot. "I should take you home. We'll do this some other time."

"I'm fine," Sabina insisted, sending him a sultry smile. "My headache is gone."

"You still look a little pale. You really should go home and rest. I'll go get my car."

She opened her mouth, as if to protest, but thought better of it. A tiny frown worried her brow. "You're probably right. I still do feel a bit dizzy." She quickly stood up and grabbed her purse. "You don't have to drive me. I can get a cab."

"Don't be silly," Alec said. "I'm parked just a few blocks from here. It will only take me a minute to go get my car."

Sabina shook her head. "I'm perfectly capable of getting myself home."

Alec sensed the anger in her voice and decided to let the argument go. "All right." He grabbed her hand before she had a chance to leave and gave it a squeeze. "I'll call you."

"Fine," she said.

With that, she turned and walked out. At the last minute, Alec decided to stop her, but then he heard the front door slam and he thought better of it. If she stayed any longer, he'd forget that he was a nice guy deep inside. He'd forget that there was a reason he couldn't spend the rest of his evening kissing her and undressing her and making love to her.

He strolled into the foyer and watched through the beveled glass of the door as she descended the front steps. If he looked at the situation objectively, she was just a woman. A beautiful woman, but a woman all the same. Hell, Manhattan was full of them—models, actresses, socialites, heiresses. Up until now, he'd had his choice.

But suddenly he didn't want his choice. Only one woman interested him and that was Sabina Amanar. Maybe that was the Gypsy curse, to want something that you knew you could never have.

Alec wandered back to the kitchen. His briefcase sat on the counter where he'd dropped it that afternoon. He opened it and pulled out the Lupescu file, then spread the papers out on the granite-covered island.

Acquisition of the Lupescu property had been a crusade of sorts for his father. Simon Harnett didn't like to lose. For him, business was like war. There were those who agreed with him, his troops, as he liked to call them. And then there were those who opposed him...the enemy.

If Alec opposed him now, then his tenure as president and chief operating officer of Harnett Property Development would come to a quick end. And why was he even contemplating that move? He'd only just met Sabina. He was acting as if he'd fallen in love with her at first sight.

Alec stared down at the papers scattered in front of him. It had been so easy when the building was just a building and not the people who inhabited it. But the five-story on Christopher Street was Sabina's childhood home, not just a mass of bricks and mortar. She pinned her future on the shop.

If he bought the building, all that would be gone. At the least, they'd gut the interior, and at most, they'd tear the building down and build a new one. "This is why my father said you never get personally involved."

That's how Simon Harnett had turned the business from property management into development. His grandfather had begun his company before the war with two apartment buildings. He'd gradually purchased more, using an uncanny knack for buying buildings a few years before the neighborhood experienced a renaissance.

If his grandfather were still alive, Alec knew he

wouldn't approve of this move. Ruta was given the building as a gift, and to take that gift back would somehow break a promise between the Gypsy and George Harnett. And if his father was still running the business, he'd say there was no room for sentimentality.

Alec and his father had shared a fractious relationship. In truth, Alec never expected to work in the family business. His sister, Cassie, was much better suited for the job. But Cassie had married five years ago and was more interested in her growing family than the cutthroat business of Manhattan property development.

So a temporary job had become permanent. And after his father's heart attack last year, Alec had become the man in charge. Though Simon still spent most days in the office, he'd given up the stressful job of property acquisition to concentrate on project management, the job Alec had done since he'd graduated from NYU ten years before.

Hell, what twist of fate had brought Sabina into his life? If he'd left just a few minutes earlier or a few minutes later that morning, he never would have run into her. And he never would have touched her face or run his fingers along her arm. And that current would have never passed between them. And then he could have ruthlessly done his job.

"Yeah," he muttered. Turning from the counter, Alec retrieved a bottle of Scotch from the cabinet above the sink and poured a healthy measure into a glass. "You're ruthless, all right. You take one look into those violet eyes and turn into a freaking marshmallow."

He tossed down the Scotch in one quick gulp, then poured himself another. A new plan was in order. A strategy to deal with unexpected feelings. He grabbed the bottle and headed upstairs to the den. The Yankees were playing. He'd watch the game, get a little drunk and try to convince himself that he had absolutely no attraction whatsoever to Sabina Amanar.

And if that didn't work, he'd resign from his job and go sell houses in Brooklyn.

"HE WAS IN MY CAB. I'm sure it was him," Mario said. "I picked him up a few months ago in SoHo and he was talking on his cell phone. I remember him because I thought he might be a good match for Mrs. Methune's youngest daughter, Lydia. It was definitely Alec Harnett."

Ruta leaned forward and braced her arms on the back of the cab's front seat. She peered through the small Plexiglas window. "And you dropped him off in front of my shop?"

Mario nodded. "That's where he wanted to go—Ruta's. I drove around the block and I saw him go inside."

Ruta shook her head. "Simon Harnett hasn't had any luck with me and now he sends his son to do his dirty work? I'm sure Bina told him exactly what I would have said. No! Her first loyalty is to her family."

"Maybe she's too loyal?" Mario asked, his brow arching. He met Ruta's gaze in the rearview mirror.

"And what are you trying to tell me now? Do not speak in riddles. We have been friends for far too long."

Mario pulled the cab over to the curb in front of Ruta's shop, then twisted around in his seat. For a woman who claimed to be psychic, she wasn't very good at reading her own granddaughter. "What life is this for a pretty young lady?" Mario asked. "This city is made for romance, and Sabina spends her weekends working on your accounts and sewing pretty dresses that she never gets to wear."

"I have introduced her to many young men. What more can I do? In the old country, she would have been married years ago, with babies at her feet. I have made charms, I have given her potions. Nothing seems to work."

"Romance is a bit more difficult these days," Mario said.

Ruta pointed to the photos on the dash of the cab. "Your pictures say differently. Do you think you can do better for Sabina? If you can, then I give you permission to try."

Mario chuckled. "And what if you don't approve of this young man I choose?"

"You are my friend, Mario. I trust you to drive me around this city safely. I will trust that you can find a good man for my Bina."

"I already have a good man in mind."

Ruta reached into her pocketbook and withdrew a ten dollar bill. "Then you do your magic. And I will begin to save for the wedding, yes?"

"Yes," Mario said. He flipped off the light on the top of the cab, then jumped out and circled around to Ruta's door. "But I want one promise from you," he said as he helped Ruta out. "You will not interfere with Sabina's romantic life. No predictions, no warnings, no visions. And no curses."

"It is against my natural instincts. I must look out for the girl now that her parents are gone." She sighed. "But I suppose I can make that promise."

Mario gave Ruta a quick peck on the check. "Why don't you and I have a cup of tea at that nice little coffee shop around the corner? And when I'm done, you can read the leaves. I'm thinking of making a...change in my life."

"A change?" Ruta slipped her arm through his and walked with him down the sidewalk. "I sense this has to do with Iris. I had a vision of Iris last night while I was watching Letterman. I saw her in a beautiful white gown with a lovely diamond ring on her finger."

"You did, did you?" Mario chuckled softly. "You always see my future much more clearly than I do, Ruta. And did you happen to see how and when I proposed to Iris?"

"No," Ruta replied. "But I am sure if we put our heads together we can figure that out on our own. The important thing is that she will say yes."

"And you're sure of that?"

"As sure as I can be. But I can always mix up a little potion to dispense with any reservations she might have. And you can do your part by finding a ring with a very large diamond."

Mario gave Ruta's hand a squeeze. If only it were so simple. Now that he'd made the decision to propose to Iris, all he could think about were the reasons she might refuse him. Maybe a potion was the answer. After all, what could it hurt?

CHAPTER THREE

"IT DIDN'T WORK," Sabina muttered as she walked through the bead curtain into the shop. She set the small brown bottle on the counter in front of Chloe.

Chloe took a sip of her quadruple espresso and stared at the bottle. Sometime between last night and this morning her hair had gone from pink to blue and she'd pierced her other nostril. Sabina shook her head in bewilderment. Chloe was strange, but she was the best employee they'd ever had.

"How much did you give him?" she asked, holding the bottle up to the light.

"I didn't give him anything. I drank it," Sabina replied.

"That's not how it works. You give it to him and then he'll find you irresistible. If you take it, then you'll find him irresistible. And you already do, don't you?"

"It worked!" Chloe and Sabina turned to see Mrs. Nussbaum hurry through the front door, the bell announcing her arrival.

"Are you all right?" Sabina asked as the old woman stumbled to the counter.

"I'm much better than all right," she replied. "I'm…" She bent closer and whispered in Sabina's ear. "Satisfied." Mrs. Nussbaum drew back, her eyes twinkling. "I'm sure you know what I mean."

Sabina frowned. "I'm not sure I do, Mrs. Nussbaum."

The old woman fanned herself with her hand. "Your grandmother is a treasure. A worker of miracles. A gift from God. My husband, Irving, was having issues...." She lowered her voice again. "In the bedroom. Well, we tried everything. Those little blue pills, racy movies, I even performed a little striptease for him."

"Did you try bondage?" Chloe asked. "I hear older guys like that a lot."

Sabina shushed Chloe, then turned back to Mrs. Nussbaum. "What did she give you?"

"She gave me a potion. I have no idea what was in it, but it worked. I poured a bit on top of his apple cobbler and we had a night of passion that you wouldn't believe. I just came to get more. I have big plans for tonight. I'm making a custard pie. Mr. Nussbaum loves custard pie."

Sabina cleared her throat. "I'm afraid my grand-mother is busy at the moment. But I'll have her call you when she gets back." She gently grabbed Mrs. Nuss-baum's elbow and steered her toward the door. "Good day, Mrs. Nussbaum."

The elderly woman turned and smiled. "It is a very good day, isn't it?"

Sabina watched the older woman exit, then turned and stalked to the back of the store, cursing beneath her breath. "One day, that stubborn old woman is going to get us both in trouble," she muttered. "Nana! Nana, come out here right now."

A moment later, Ruta emerged, dressed in her Gypsy costume. "I hear you had a date last night, Bina," she said.

"That's not what I want to talk about."

"The charm is working." She gave Chloe a wink. "You said he was handsome. Where did you meet him, darling?"

"I met the man on my way to get bagels. It had nothing to do with the charm. But we do have to discuss the potions you gave Chloe and Mrs. Nussbaum."

"I have to get ready for Mrs. Marston's reading. We are going to summon the spirits of her three dead ex-husbands today. Something about missing stock certificates."

"Nana, what did I tell you about potions?"

Ruta blinked, then sent her granddaughter a nervous smile. "I don't know, Bina," she said, waving her hand distractedly. "Did you tell me something about potions?" She gave Sabina a blank look, but Sabina wasn't about to fall for that old trick. Ruta was an expert at using her advancing age to manipulate any situation. She conveniently forgot conversations whenever it suited her, yet managed to remember the vital statistics of every single professional man who walked in the door of the shop.

Sabina raked her hair out of her eyes. "Do not play the old woman with me. We've discussed this at length and still you won't listen." She reached out and grabbed her grandmother's hand, turning it palm up. "Let me tell you your fortune, Nana. If you want to lose this shop, then you keep right on mixing those potions."

"What is wrong with my potions? They have been handed down for generations. Tested by time. I may be an old woman, but you worry like an old woman."

"And if one of our customers has an allergic reaction or doesn't follow your directions or heaven forbid, dies, what then? We will be sued and you will lose this shop and everything you own. And Simon Harnett will be waiting on the sidewalk to snatch it all up and turn it into condominiums or a huge hardware store or some silly shops that no one really needs. And then where will we live? Where will all our tenants live?"

Ruta waved her hand. "Don't be so dramatic, Bina. No one is going to die. Neither Simon Harnett, nor his son, Alec, can force us to sell if we don't want to."

A sick feeling settled in Sabina's stomach. "Alec Harnett?"

"Hey, wasn't that the name of the guy who was in here last night?" Chloe asked.

"He came again last night?" Ruta asked. "Mario told me was here yesterday around noon. He dropped him off out front and saw him go into the shop. Did you talk to him, Bina, or did you kick him out? You should have called me. I would have given him a piece of my mind."

Sabina swallowed hard. Her mind spun with confusion. They'd had no other customers over the lunch hour except for Alec Harper, the man she'd met on the sidewalk that morning. A whirl of emotions surged inside of her as the truth became more apparent.

Sabina drew a shaky breath. "No, Nana," she lied. "We didn't have any customers. Mario must have been mistaken. Besides, we're not talking about the Harnetts, we're talking about potions. No more. Agreed?" She reached up and tugged the charm over her head, then pressed it into her grandmother's palm. "And—and no more charms. They give people false hope."

"No more potions." Ruta muttered something else in Hungarian before she spun on her heel and walked back through the bead curtain, her jewelry jingling as she moved.

She glanced over at Chloe. "Why are you smiling?" Sabina asked.

"This is the most interesting thing that's happened in this shop since your grandmother summoned the spirit of Marilyn Monroe by mistake." Chloe paused. "She was supposed to be looking for Caroline Monroe." She tucked her hands under her chin and braced her elbows on the counter. "So, what are you going to do? You could always put a curse on him. Maybe make all his hair fall out. You know how men are about their hair. Or you could make him impotent. Not forever, because that would be cruel, but for a year or two."

Sabina glanced up at the clock, then grabbed the phone book from behind the counter. "Find out where Alec Harnett's office is. Harnett Property Development. I'll be back in a few minutes."

"Where are you going?" Chloe asked.

Sabina didn't bother with an answer. She and Alec had made a date yesterday to meet for coffee. "Same place, same time." It was nearly nine. If he was waiting out on the sidewalk, then she wasn't going to miss the opportunity to tell him exactly what she thought of his deception.

As she walked down the sidewalk, she recalled their encounter in his kitchen. Things had been going so well and then everything had come to a dead halt. He'd probably begun to feel guilty. No, Sabina thought. That would mean he had a conscience, something that didn't run in the Harnett family line.

Sabina held her breath as she rounded the corner. She froze when she saw him leaning against a mailbox. In truth, she hadn't expected him to be waiting. And now that he was, she wasn't sure where to begin.

He straightened as she approached, his gaze fixed on her face. "I was hoping you'd come," he said, smiling weakly.

Sabina stopped a few feet away. It wouldn't do to get too close. "Alec Harnett," she said.

His smile faded into a grimace. "So you know. Was it the mailbox? I just realized that my name was on the mailbox. When you left the house yesterday."

"No, it wasn't the mailbox," she replied. "Never mind what it was. What difference does it make? You lied to me. You led me on. You tried to seduce me so that you could convince me to convince my grandmother to sell her building."

He held up his hand. "That's not true. I tried to seduce you because you're beautiful and sexy and irresistible. It had nothing to do with real estate, believe me."

"You are a snake. A—a sleazeball. Slime." She turned to walk away, but Alec reached out and caught her hand.

"When I came into the shop, I did have business on my mind. But then you were her—the woman I'd met on the sidewalk earlier—and business didn't seem to matter."

"So then you don't want to buy my grandmother's building?"

"I didn't say that. But my interest in your grandmother's building has nothing at all to do with my interest in you—at least not anymore."

"I'm supposed to believe that? Your father has been waiting like a vulture to swoop down and snatch that place out from under her. He's filed lawsuits and bribed city officials and worried my grandmother needlessly. She cares about the people in that building. They're her friends and there is no way she'll ever leave them to your mercy."

"I'm not the bad guy here," Alec said, holding tight to her hand. "We're not going to turn them out on the street. We'll find them new apartments, and we're even prepared to offer them a generous settlement for agreeing to move. Believe me, they won't be homeless."

"Because they all have a home. In my grandmother's building."

"Your grandmother got that building when my grandfather wasn't of sound mind. He was distraught over my grandmother's illness and he would have done anything to make her well. Including letting himself be taken in by a charlatan."

Sabina gasped at his accusation. Sure, she didn't have much faith in her grandmother's power, but that didn't give him any right to insult the family honor. "As I recall, that was the basis of the lawsuit your father brought seven years ago. And the judge threw it out. Your grandfather gave my grandmother a run-down storefront with eight shabby apartments above it. It wasn't any great gift. It's only now, when the building is worth millions, you've decided you want it back."

"We've wanted it back for years. This is nothing new." He paused, drawing a deep breath. "Arguing about this isn't going to get us anywhere, Sabina. Let's find a place where we can talk and I'll explain my offer."

"Why? So you can take advantage of me again?"

"Hold on there. Now you're rewriting history. I may have kissed you first, but you were a willing participant after that. You enjoyed it as much as I did."

"I was confused," Sabina said. "And misinformed."

"Really?" Alec reached out and slipped his arm around her waist. He leaned closer, so close she couldn't twist away. "You know who I am, so you're no longer misinformed. And you know what I want, so there should be no confusion. Now, what are you going to do, Sabina?"

His eyes dropped to her mouth and Sabina felt a thrill of desire race through her body. The attraction between them was undeniable. Even now, in the midst of her anger and indignation, she still wanted him. The air seemed to vibrate around them and she could hear her pulse pounding in her head.

He reached out and ran his fingertip over her lower lip. Sabina shivered. She wanted him to kiss her, to prove to her that none of this made any difference. But she'd already misjudged him so completely. How could she trust that he wouldn't fool her again?

"This doesn't have to be the end of us," he said. "Let me make my offer to your grandmother. If she refuses, then that will be fine with me. I won't push. Except to convince you to have dinner with me again tonight."

He leaned forward, but Sabina stiffened in response. "I won't kiss you," she said, twisting in his embrace.

"Yes, you will," he murmured. "Maybe not now, but you will kiss me again."

His arrogance pricked her temper. "I won't kiss you. I'll—I'll curse you." Sabina twisted out of his arms. "I, Sabina Amanar, granddaughter of Ruta Lupescu, curse you. May all your luck be bad. May—may all your dreams be nightmares. And—and may you fall in a hole and break your leg!"

At first he looked a bit shocked. But then a smile broke across his face and he laughed out loud. "That's it?" Alec said. "That's all you have?" He crossed his arms over his chest. "I didn't hear a lot of conviction in your voice."

She sent him a murderous glare before walking away. For the first time in her life, she wished she actually possessed some special powers. Whether her curse took or not didn't really make a difference. She'd made her feelings about Alec Harnett perfectly clear. He was to stay away from her and her grandmother.

"SHE CURSED ME."

Simon Harnett leaned back in his chair and linked his hands behind his head. "The old woman?" he asked.

"No, her granddaughter. It seems that Sabina is even more powerful than Ruta." Alec maneuvered over to one of the guest chairs, his crutches slipping on the hardwood floors.

"Did you break your leg after the curse or before?"

"It's not broken, just badly sprained. And it happened after the curse. I was playing basketball with some friends day before yesterday and I stepped in a hole."

"On the court?" Simon asked.

"No, on the sidewalk on the way to my car." He lowered himself into the chair, groaning at the ache in his ankle. The pain was exacerbated by exhaustion, which was probably due to lack of sleep. He hadn't had a decent night's rest since she'd issued the curse a week ago. And he'd lost two deals in as many days.

Alec was ready to cry uncle. Sabina Amanar was obviously more powerful then he could have ever imagined. "I've been thinking we might want to make alternative plans. I mean, why sit on those properties when we don't know if the old lady is going to sell?"

"Are you giving up already?" Simon asked, disdain dripping from his voice. "One little curse and you get scared off. I was cursed every year and I never let it bother me." He shook his head. "When I put you in charge, I thought I could trust you to get the job done."

"You said it. You've been after Ruta for years and she's never wavered. Unless she gets into some financial trouble, she's there to stay. And her granddaughter has plans to stay long after she's gone. I think we better consider doing the condo project. We don't need Ruta's building for that."

"Have you even made an offer?" Simon asked.

In truth, whenever he'd been around Sabina, the last thing he thought about was business. His mind became consumed with touching her and kissing her, testing the limits of their attraction to each other. "Well, not formally. But I've already been turned down."

Simon stood up, bracing his hands on his desk. "Don't come whining to me until you've tried for at least five years. Then we'll talk."

Sensing the meeting was over, Alec got to his feet and tucked the crutches under his arms. But there were still things that needed saying. "You gave me this job because you wanted me to make the big decisions. If I decide to do the condo project, then that will be my decision. And if you don't like it, then you're going to have to find someone else to run this company."

Simon slowly sat down, a scowl on his face. His father was stubborn. But he'd also gotten used to the lifestyle of a semiretired real estate mogul. Weekends in the Hamptons, golf with his buddies and winters down south. "Are you going to make an offer?"

"I'm going over there now. But first I'm going to get her to remove this curse."

Alec hobbled out of the office and grabbed his

briefcase from the receptionist's desk. "Did you call a cab?" he asked.

Karen nodded. "Security said he's waiting out front."

Alec turned for the elevator. But it was impossible to hang on to his briefcase and the crutches. Karen hurried out from behind the reception desk and took it from him, then rode the elevator down.

"So she cursed you," Karen mused, staring up at the lights above the door. "My grandmother has this neighbor who goes to a psychic healer and she'd probably be able to break the curse. Would you like me to call her?"

Alec smiled politely. "I think I can take care of this myself."

Getting into a cab was tricky, but after a few stumbles, he was comfortably seated. Only then did he realize he was sitting in a familiar backseat. Photographs lined the interior of the cab and Mario Capelli's face stared back at him from the rearview mirror. "Ruta's?" he asked.

Alec didn't even want to consider the sheer luck it took for him to get inside Capelli's cab for a second time. He could only take comfort in the fact that he was relatively safe considering Capelli and Ruta were friends. "Yeah, Ruta's," Alec replied.

"She's not home. I took her to New Jersey this morning. She's doing a brunch for a family reunion. She's very popular as party entertainment."

"I'm not interested in seeing Ruta. I have business with her granddaughter, Sabina."

Mario's grin grew wider. "Now, there's a beautiful girl."

"Beautiful, but dangerous," Alec muttered. "Very, very dangerous."

"Ah, but what woman isn't? When they have the ability to steal your heart away, it's a frightening thing. But once it happens, you realize that it's better off in their keeping."

"That's a pretty sappy sentiment," Alec said.

"I believe in romance. I believe that for every single guy, there's a gal out there waiting to be needed. And for every gal, there's a guy waiting to be saved. Look around you. I know what I'm talking about."

Alec scanned the photos, the smiling faces of at least a hundred couples, young and old. "And you think Sabina and I are one of those couples?" He chuckled as he held up his hand in protest. "She cursed me. In the past week, my life has gone straight to hell and she's the cause."

"I never said it was going to be easy," Mario replied.

As the cab headed downtown, Alec leaned back and closed his eyes. No, it wasn't easy. The entire thing had been confusing and frustrating. But it had also been exhilarating and crazy. It had been seven days since he'd last seen Sabina, and he'd spent almost every waking hour thinking about her, wondering what she was doing and where she was going. He'd looked for her face on the street every morning on his way to work. He'd visited her favorite coffee shop, hoping that they might run into each other.

Hell, their relationship had begun and ended in a twenty-four-hour span, yet Alec felt as if he'd known her so much longer. In the past, women had come and gone without much fanfare or fuss. He'd preferred to keep his social life uncomplicated. But Sabina had been nothing but trouble.

Maybe that's what he found so intriguing. With any other woman, he would have walked way. But there was something undeniable about his attraction to her. She was worth the trouble—or at least she had been until she'd cursed him.

Alec lost himself in a lazy replay of the time they'd spent together, rewinding their encounter in his kitchen over and over again. If he hadn't decided to suddenly grow a conscience, they may have ended up in bed. Even now, the thought of losing himself in that beautiful body sent a wave of heat pulsing through his veins. Whatever relationship he had with Sabina Amanar might be over. But he preferred to believe that it was just beginning.

"Here we are," Mario said.

Alec was surprised at how quickly the cab ride passed. Either Capelli was a terrific cabbie or Alec had been caught in a long daydream. He grabbed a twenty out of his wallet and handed it to the cabbie. "This may be over pretty quick. Wait ten minutes and if I don't come out, you can leave."

"Sure thing," Mario said.

Alec grabbed his briefcase and crawled out of the cab, but without Karen's help there was no way to carry it. Instead, he kicked it along in front of him, the rough sidewalk scratching the Italian leather.

The bell jangled as he stumbled inside, the briefcase making an entrance before he did. But he didn't find Sabina behind the counter. Instead, he found the same salesgirl, her hair now streaked with blue. Alec drew a deep breath and balanced himself on the crutches. "Where is she?"

Chloe pointed up. "Second floor, apartment 2B. You can use the stairs. They're right through that bead curtain."

"Stairs," Alec muttered as he moved to the back of the shop. It took him nearly five minutes to navigate the doors and stairs up to the second floor, throwing his briefcase from landing to landing, the air stuffy and warm. By the time he got to 2B, he was exhausted.

Alec reached up and banged on her apartment door, but the sudden motion caused him to sway on the crutches. He tried to catch himself, but there was nothing to grab on to, and a few seconds later, he was sprawled on the floor. The door opened and he looked up to find Sabina staring at him, wide-eyed.

"I want you to remove the curse," he said, attempting to keep calm. "I'm willing to pay whatever you want. Just reverse it. Make it go away."

"What happened to you?"

"Do you really need to ask?" Alec shook his head. "Per your orders to the spirit world, I fell in a hole and broke my leg." His gaze fixed on hers and he couldn't deny the joy he felt in seeing her again. She really was extraordinarily beautiful, even with her brow furrowed in concern.

"It's broken?" Sabina asked.

"Severely sprained," he admitted. "On top of that, two of my biggest deals went south this week and last night I had a dream that I married my eighth-grade science teacher…who happened to be a fifty-year-old man." He shuddered. "So just do whatever it is you Gypsies do and get rid of the curse."

Sabina bent down and helped him to his feet, but the moment Alec tried to straighten a dagger of pain shot through his lower back. He sucked in a deep breath and

winced. "I—I don't think I can move. My back is out."
He tossed the crutches aside. "I just need to lie down
for a moment."

Sabina wrapped his arm around her shoulders and
helped him inside. He expected her to lead him to the
sofa, but instead she took him to her bedroom. "Lie
down," she said.

"Here?"

"No, underneath the bed," Sabina said. "I'll go get
you something for the pain. I think I have some arsenic
around here somewhere."

"I'm not taking anything that isn't in a clearly labeled
bottle," Alec called. "I don't trust you." He leaned back
into the pillows and surveyed his surroundings.

Sabina's apartment had all the charm of a turn-of-the-
century building, coved ceilings and built-in cabinets.
She even had a fireplace in the living room. Compared
to his overdecorated house, her place seemed homey
and comfortable…lived-in. Everywhere he looked he
saw bits and pieces of the woman she was—a pretty
pillow embroidered with a bunch of violets, a jeweled
egg, an old photo of a beautiful woman surrounded by
an antique frame.

These were her things, yet he had no idea what they
meant to her. He wanted to find out. Alec wanted to
know every little detail of her life before him, the
dreams she'd had and the disappointments she'd
suffered. He'd never be completely satisfied until he
knew it all.

Groaning softly, he stretched his hands over his head,
trying to work the kinks out of his back. There had to

be a way to parlay a momentary twinge into a full night of spasms. Alec was exactly where he'd always hoped to be—in her bedroom. And he had no intention of leaving anytime soon.

CHAPTER FOUR

SABINA STOOD IN THE hallway outside her grandmother's apartment, wringing her hands and glancing over her shoulder. "I—I don't know what to do," she whispered. "This was my first curse. I never thought it would work."

"Well, I am glad it did," Ruta said, her voice defiant. "You should have wished that his manhood would have shriveled up and fallen off. A broken leg can heal."

"Nana! I never meant to hurt him. I was just angry. I said the first thing that came to my mind."

"And I say a fine time for your powers to show themselves." Ruta walked out in the hall and peered into the open doorway of Sabina's apartment. "Where is he?"

"I put him in my bedroom," Sabina explained.

A horrified expression suffused Ruta's face. "The son of my enemy is in your bed." With a long string of Hungarian expletives, Ruta stormed into Sabina's apartment and headed directly for the bedroom.

Sabina chased after her, pleading with her to stop, but it was no use. She caught up to her beside the bed, where Ruta was standing over Alec, her hands braced on her hips, her mouth pressed into a tight line. "So you have a little problem with a curse?"

Alec glanced over at Sabina and she smiled weakly.

"You must be Mrs. Lupescu." He held out his hand to her grandmother. "It's a pleasure to meet you."

Ruta looked at his hand as if he'd just offered her a rotten fish. "There is no pleasure in it. Just this warning. As long as you are in Bina's apartment, you will behave like a gentleman. If you do not, you will suffer the wrath of one of *my* curses. And I do not trifle with broken bones."

She turned on her heel and stormed out, leaving a dumbfounded Alec in her wake. He drew a shaky breath. "Well, I think she likes me. What do you think?"

"Is your back really hurt or are you just malingering to get into my bed?"

Alec feigned shock and disappointment. "How could you think that?"

Sabina arched her brow. "You know, one of the benefits of being psychic is that I can spot a liar a mile away." She tipped his chin up with her finger and stared intently into his blue eyes.

"Are you trying to read my mind again?" Alec asked.

"Yes," Sabina lied, an uneasy feeling growing in the pit of her stomach. She couldn't even figure out what was going on in her head, much less his. Her only thought was to kiss him, to lean forward and press her lips to his and see where it all led. Over the past week she relived every single second they'd spent together and it just hadn't seemed like enough.

She wasn't psychic, but she sensed that they were far from through with each other. There was more to be said, more to learn and much, much more to experience.

Alec grinned. "Good. Now, concentrate hard. Do you know what I'm thinking?"

"I do," Sabina replied. But this time it wasn't a lie.

She saw the flicker of desire in his eyes and knew he was thinking exactly what she was thinking. How long would it take to get out of their clothes?

An instant later, his mouth covered hers. The warmth of his lips ignited her desire and heat raced through her like fire in her veins. It had been nearly a week since she'd been kissed by him, but she hadn't remembered it being so wonderful.

She parted her lips so that he might taste more deeply. Alec pulled her down on top of him, his fingers furrowing through her hair. Wild sensations coursed through her body, tingling at every nerve and heightening every caress. Sabina drew back slightly, her dark hair a curtain around them.

Their gazes met and she realized there was no need for words. The two of them knew exactly what they wanted—each other. Sabina didn't care about tomorrow or next week or next month, for that matter. All she needed was now, this moment in his arms and complete surrender.

She slowly bent to kiss him again, running her tongue along his lower lip, then biting gently. He growled, then captured her mouth, this time more softly.

The light cotton dress was a meager defense against his touch. He ran his hands along her back and grabbed her waist, pressing her body against his. She felt his desire, hard and hot, between them, as his hips cradled hers. Suddenly, Sabina wanted to strip away every last barrier between them, to feel his naked body against hers.

As if he could read her mind, he sat up, pulling her along with him. Without breaking their kiss, he twisted out of his suit jacket and started yanking on his tie. But

Sabina brushed his hands aside and worked at the knot herself, her fingers trembling slightly.

She knew she ought to be more hesitant. Sleeping with a man on the first date was something she'd never, ever done. Even worse, this wasn't a date. They hadn't had a first date—not a complete first date! Oh, hell, what difference did it make whether it happened now or later? They both knew it was going to happen, right?

Sabrina finally loosened his tie enough to pull it over his head, then began to fumble with the buttons of his shirt. He began from the bottom, and by the time their hands met, she was desperate to touch him. A moment later, he reached for the zipper at the back of her dress, then pulled it down until she could slip her arms out of the bodice.

He pulled her into another embrace and rolled her beneath him on the bed. His palm softly caressed her belly, then moved up to her breast, teasing at the nipple through the silk and lace of her bra.

It felt so right to have him touch her. She'd never experienced such desperate need for a man. Every nerve cried out for his touch. When his lips trailed kisses down her neck to her breast, Sabina held her breath, knowing what was about to come would shatter the very last ounce of resistance she possessed.

But before he could go any further, a sharp rap sounded on the door of Sabina's apartment. She froze at the same time he did. Slowly, he pushed up and looked into her eyes. "Did you invite someone else over?"

Sabina shook her head. "I didn't lock the door." With a soft curse she slipped her arms back into the sleeves of her dress. But her fingers weren't working properly and she couldn't reach the zipper. "Do it, do it," she cried, turning her back to Alec.

"Bina?"

"Oh, no," Sabina muttered as she scrambled off the bed. She picked up his suit jacket and tossed it at him. "Get dressed."

Alec stared at her for a long moment. "I'm not exactly naked. Not yet, anyway."

"Stop it!" Sabina hissed. She quickly ran her fingers through her tousled hair, then smoothed her dress. "I'm in here, Nana." She cleared her throat, hoping to clear away the nervousness in her voice. "Taking care of the patient."

Ruta swept into the bedroom, a tray in her hands. She looked at Sabina, then studied Alec, who'd managed to button the bottom half of his shirt. Ruta's eyebrow shot up. "You have taken off some of your clothes," she said.

"I was just trying to get more comfortable," Alec replied. "And it was getting a little warm in here."

Sabina shot him a glare as Ruta set the tray down on the bedside table. She poured a cup and handed it to Alec. "Just make sure there is no more undressing. I will not warn you twice." She nodded at the teacup. "Drink. It will help relax your muscles. Then maybe you can get out of my granddaughter's bed and go home."

Alec sniffed at the tea. "Just how relaxed are we talking here? If I relax too much, I'll be dead."

"I will not kill you," Ruta said as if he'd insulted her. "It would be too much trouble to get rid of the body. Go ahead, there is nothing in it but herbs."

Alec glanced over at Sabina and she shrugged. Her grandmother might not like him, but she'd never deliberately harm another human being. "You know, Nana, Alec may be the son of your enemy, but he is also the grandson of your friend George Harnett. And you know how protective grandparents are of their grandchildren. If there is anything in that tea, I'm not sure George would look kindly on it."

"There is nothing in the tea," Ruta insisted impatiently. "Nothing harmful at all. Now, drink."

Sabina nodded at Alec and he took a sip, then set the cup down in the saucer. "I feel better already."

"Good, then you can leave," Ruta said.

"Not that good." A grin quirked at the corners of his mouth. "But I'm sure Sabina will do everything she can to make me comfortable."

She shot him another glare, then stepped up to her grandmother and took Ruta's elbow. "Why don't we leave Alec to relax? I'll walk you back to your apartment."

When they reached the front door, Sabina pulled it open, then followed her grandmother out into the hall. "You don't have to worry about me, Nana. I'm perfectly capable of handling myself around him. He doesn't frighten me at all."

Maybe that was the problem, Sabina mused. She wasn't afraid of anything that might happen between her and Alec. In fact, she was eager to plunge into a fullscale seduction the very moment she went back inside her apartment.

ALEC SWUNG HIS LEGS over the edge of the bed, then rubbed his lower back. Oddly enough, he did feel a bit more relaxed. He kicked off his shoes, then tugged his shirt over his head, tossing it on top of his jacket. The air conditioner purred softly from the bedroom window, cooling the midday heat.

Sabina returned a few moments later and stood in the doorway. Alec watched her, wondering what was going through her mind. This attraction between them was beyond all explanation. He'd taken women to bed before, but it had always been about satisfying a need. With Sabina, there was more to it. It wasn't about him, it was about the two of them, becoming closer, knowing the most intimate details about each other.

He wanted to give her pleasure, to hear her murmur his name in the midst of her passion. Alec smiled as he rubbed the back of his neck. He was in unfamiliar territory here and the trip had been at the speed of light. But he didn't want to slow down. If he slowed down, he might start thinking about all the reasons it couldn't work.

"How does your back feel?"

He held out his hand and she came to him, sitting down beside him on the edge of the bed. "I could probably get up and go home," he said. He reached up and smoothed his palm along her cheek. "Would you like me to do that?"

She hesitated for a moment and Alec cursed himself for giving her the choice. He should have just pulled her back into bed and continued where they'd left off. He leaned forward and brushed a kiss across her lips. "Ask me to stay," he whispered.

She didn't reply. Instead, she stood up in front of him and slowly unzipped her dress. As she brought her arms together, the wide neck gaped and then slid down to her hips. Sabina stepped out of it.

Alec's eyes drifted over her body, so perfect, exactly

what a woman's body ought to be. He reached out and ran a hand over her hip, then gently drew her forward. His lips found a spot in the center of her belly and he kissed her, nuzzling the soft skin.

Sabina pulled him to his feet and helped him slip out of his shirt, then worked at his belt. When he stood in only his boxers, she stepped into his arms and kissed him, her soft body molding to his.

He pulled her leg up alongside his hip, then tumbled back onto the bed. He forgot all about the ache in his ankle. It had been replaced with an ache deep inside him, a need that couldn't be satisfied by her kisses or her touch. Alec reached between them and undid the front clasp of her bra, then hooked his thumbs on her panties and slid them down along her legs.

His shaft pressed against the silk of his boxers, hard and ready. He felt like a kid, fighting for control, ready to explode at the slightest provocation. They tumbled back onto the bed and Sabina shifted above him, her hips sliding against his erection. Alec's breath caught in his throat and he held it until the sensation passed.

Gently, she stroked him through the silk, and then suddenly she dipped below the waistband and encircled him with her fingers. Alec groaned, pinching his eyes shut and fighting against the need to come.

He rolled to his side and wiggled out of his boxers, then pulled her back on top of him. Her long hair fell in soft waves around her face and he reached up and tucked it behind her ear. It was a simple gesture, but it felt so intimate, as if he sensed that she were about to do the same herself.

"Do you want me?" he whispered, his fingers trailing across her face.

Sabina nodded. She twisted around to reach for the nightstand and a few seconds later produced a condom. "Do you want me?" she asked.

"From the moment you knocked me over on the sidewalk," Alec replied.

"That long ago?" she teased. "I don't know how you've managed to wait all that time."

Was it too soon? He worried that he might be putting everything at risk for this one night of pleasure. Maybe they should get to know each other better. Maybe they should take it slower. "It's been hard."

"Yes, I can feel that." Sabina ran her fingers along the ridge of his shaft. "I'd better do something about that." She tore the package open and sheathed him. Alec closed his eyes and enjoyed the feel of her hands. A moment later, when she sank down on top of him, every rational thought left his mind.

Sabina moved above him, slowly at first, and he responded instinctively, arching against her. He held her hips, controlling her rhythm when he drew close. His eyes fixed on her face, and he watched as her expression changed from languid pleasure to intense concentration. He reached between them and touched her, teasing her with his fingers.

Sabina opened her eyes and looked at him, and a current raced through his body. Her breathing quickened and she bit at her lower lip and Alec knew she was close. And when she froze, he waited for the spasms to hit. They did in a powerful wave of pleasure, for both him and her. He surrendered to the moment, erupting inside of her.

Slowly, the spasms subsided and she fell forward across his chest. Her silken hair tickled his face and he brushed it aside, letting his fingers slip through the strands.

"It's strange, isn't it?" Sabina asked.

"That's not what a guy wants to hear right after he's made love to a woman. You're supposed to say, it's amazing. It's huge. It's better than I've ever had before."

Sabina nuzzled his chest, laughing softly. "We've probably passed each other on the street, maybe even sat in the same subway car or stood in line at the grocery store together. And we may have gone our entire lives without ever meeting. But that morning on the sidewalk, it was as if there were outside forces at work."

"Maybe there were," Alec said.

"Or maybe everything does happen by chance." Sabina looked down into his eyes. Alec pressed a kiss to her forehead. "Why do you want my grandmother's building?" she asked. "Why is it so important to you?"

"We don't need to talk about this now," Alec said.

"It's like the elephant in the room," she replied.

"It's business." He ran a fingertip along her shoulder to her breast, then slowly circled her nipple. "This was pleasure."

"Was it? Or are you hoping that if you spend enough time with me, you'll convince me to help you out with your plan? That won't happen, you know." Her words contained only a trace of teasing humor. She was looking for assurances.

"Is that want you think?" Alec murmured. He pushed up on his elbows. "Do you regret what just happened?"

"No. I wanted it as much as you did. I'm just wondering if we wanted it for the same reasons," Sabina said. "I've lived here my entire life. This isn't just some building to me, this is my home. And I don't plan to leave it anytime soon."

"You feel safe here," Alec said.

"I do. These people are like my family. The Wilburns have lived here thirty-five years. They were both teachers in the public schools. And Mr. Harcourt had a little shoe repair place just around the corner. He's lived here for almost forty years. And Mrs. O'Keefe was a nurse. Her husband died last year. They moved in here on the day they were married in 1963." Sabina paused. "They helped raise me."

"Sometimes it's good to make a break with the past, to start a life of your own."

Sabina rolled her eyes. "Pot, I'd like to introduce kettle. You're not the one to make that point, Alec. You work for your father."

"Technically, he works for me now. And if I had to, I could make a living anywhere."

"This is where I chose to make my life," Sabina said. "Near my grandmother, and our friends."

"And what if you had a reason to leave?"

"What possible reason would I have to leave?" Sabina asked. "Money? I have all I need for now."

"What if you got married?" Alex challenged. "Moved to a new city, a new state?"

"And why would I have to move? Why couldn't my husband live here with me?"

Alec glanced around. "It's a little small for a family, don't you think?" The moment the words left his lips, Alec regretted saying them. He wasn't planning their future together, he was merely posing a hypothetical question. Still, he was desperate to know where he stood with her.

Did Sabina consider this just a simple one-night stand? Or did she imagine them in a relationship, falling in love and then getting married? For so long, he'd avoided even the thought of commitment. But now Alec understood the allure. To spend every night in bed with a woman like Sabina would be like a little slice of heaven on earth.

He pulled her closer, tucking her backside into the curve of his body. "I like your apartment," he said, his lips pressed against her shoulder. "It feels like a home."

Sabina sighed as if willing to give up the argument for now. Alec closed his eyes and let his thoughts drift. It did feel like home, lying in her bed with his arms wrapped around her naked body. This was all a man really needed out of life, he mused. He could be satisfied with this and nothing more.

But Alec knew from experience that sooner or later reality would creep back in. For him, it had always been sooner. But this time, he'd found something special, something he was willing to protect at all costs.

Sabina wriggled in his embrace. "Why are we talking about this?" She tossed the covers back and crawled out of bed. "I'm getting dressed and then I'm going to go fetch us dinner. You can relax."

"I'll come with you," Alec said.

"No," Sabina said. "You'll just slow me down with those crutches. And I'm starving. Thai or pizza?"

"Thai," he said. "Noodles with peanut sauce."

"To drink?"

"Beer. Always drink beer with Thai food."

She grabbed a light cotton dress from her closet and pulled it over her, then slipped into a pair of sandals. Bending over the bed, she gave him a quick kiss. But Alec slipped his hand around her nape and held her close, lingering over her lips for a long moment.

"I'll be back in a few minutes," she said.

As he listened to her leave, he realized just what had happened in Sabina's bedroom. He'd crossed a line, stepped into something that he'd never experienced before. He didn't want to spend a single minute away from her. Already, the world seemed empty without her near.

Alec rolled over and stared at the ceiling. Was this what love felt like? He threw his arm over his eyes and cursed softly. He thought when it finally happened to him it would come slowly, giving him time to be certain of his feelings. But this had hit him like the express train to Brooklyn, knocking him flat on his ass and jumbling his senses.

CHAPTER FIVE

ALEC STOOD IN THE HALLWAY outside Sabina's apartment. She'd left the apartment an hour earlier to tend the shop, telling him she'd bring coffee and bagels back once Chloe arrived for work. He'd spent the past four nights in her bed, falling asleep with her in his arms, then rushed back to his house the next morning to shower and change before work.

But today was Saturday, and he'd decided that now would be a good time to settle things once and for all. It was time to shoot the elephant in the room, or at least move it to other quarters. Alec reached up to rap on Ruta's apartment door, but it swung open in front of him before he could touch it.

She stood in the doorway, dressed not in her Gypsy costume, but in a simple pair of trousers and a teal polo shirt. She looked so young, her gray hair drawn back into a ponytail and her feet bare. Alec was drawn to her eyes, the same pretty violet that Sabina's were.

"You have come to talk to me," Ruta said. "I have been expecting you."

Alec observed her dubiously. "How did you know I was here?"

"I felt your presence," Ruta said.

"Or you were watching out the peephole?" Alec asked.

Ruta gave him a grudging smile. "Not much goes on in this building that I do not know about." Her blunt words made her meaning perfectly clear. She knew he was sleeping with Sabina and she wasn't pleased. Still, she hadn't cursed him, that was a positive sign.

"We need to talk," Alec said. "We need to sit down and discuss an offer for this building. I'm not going to badger you like my father did. I ask that you listen and then give me an answer one way or another. I promise I'll make a fair offer if you'll give me a fair hearing. May I come in?"

Ruta nodded. "I think you are a gentleman like your grandfather. It is good you do not take after your father. He is a jackass."

Alec chuckled. "I'd tend to agree with that opinion."

He followed Ruta into her apartment. Though the layout was a mirror image of Sabina's place, this apartment was decorated like the interior of a Gypsy wagon.

Rich fabrics draped the walls and windows and an assortment of bizarre items cluttered all available surfaces. A stuffed raven perched on the mantel and a jar full of black pebbles sat on a table near the door. He crossed the room and stood by an ornate Victorian sideboard, examining an intricately carved box, inlaid with ivory.

"This is beautiful," he said, running his fingers over the top.

"It belonged to my mother," Ruta explained. "She carried it from the old country. It was filled with all her charms and potions." She crossed the room and opened the box. She held up a necklace with a small clay pendant on the end. He'd seen Sabina wear one much like it. "This is the charm my mother used to catch my father." She pulled out another necklace. "And here is the charm that I used to catch my own dear husband. And I gave it to my daughter when she met a man she wanted."

"And they worked?" Alec asked.

Ruta nodded. "We fall in love fast in our family. I expect Bina will be the same, once she finds the right man. It will happen like a thunderbolt."

The old woman was very wise. It was no wonder so many came to her to help them solve their problems. She charged far less than a Manhattan psychologist, but she seemed to know human nature just as well. "I didn't know my grandfather well," Alec said. "But I can understand why he gave you this building."

Ruta reached out and took Alec's hand, giving it a pat. "He was a fine man. A man who loved his wife as much as any man I have ever met."

"He died when I was nine," Alec explained. "My grandmother died five years later. I always remembered how happy they were together. You were part of that."

Ruta shrugged. "Your grandmother would have gotten well whether I told that fortune or not. Her fate was not in my hands." She pointed to the sofa. "Let us sit down and you will tell about this deal of yours. I will listen and then I will politely refuse you. Or perhaps, this time, I will change my mind."

"Would you really consider that?" Alec asked, stunned by her admission.

"If the terms are right. But I have terms of my own. I would expect you to take good care of all of my tenants."

She sat down on the sofa and he sat next to her. "We'd be prepared to find them new places to live, together if they'd like. And they would get a generous settlement that would make them all very comfortable."

"And if they wanted to stay?"

"I think I could arrange that," Alec said. He leaned forward, catching her gaze. "Why sell now? What changed your mind?"

"It was something my friend Mario said," Ruta explained. "As long as I am here, Sabina will feel tied to this place. It is time she set out on her own path in life and stopped following mine. She is a very talented designer, but she is stuck here watching after me and the people in this building. This is not the life I want for her. If I sell, I can give her the money to start her own company. I can give her a future."

"Maybe this is the life she wants," Alec said.

Ruta reached out and took his hand again. But this time, she turned his palm up. She traced the lines with her fingertips. "I think you are falling in love with my granddaughter," she said. "Or are you in love with her already?"

"You can see that there?"

Ruta laughed softly. "No, I see it in your eyes when you look at her. In the way you stand beside her as if you are ready to protect her from anything that might hurt her. You watch out for her the way my husband did for me."

"It's crazy, I know," Alec said. "We've known each other just over a week. The moment we met, she had me. For a while, I thought she might have put a spell on me, but now I realize that she's just the most wonderful woman I've ever met."

"Perhaps it was your destiny that you meet." She frowned. "I must speak to your grandfather about this.

I am certain he would approve." She turned his hand over and gave it a pat. "So, Alec, what do you plan to do about this?"

Alec braced his elbows on his knees and studied the lines in his palms. "I don't know how she feels. I don't think she really trusts me completely."

"Do you blame her?" Ruta asked.

He shook his head. "I guess not. But I'm happy to wait until she does."

"Good. Then, let us talk terms. Tell me your offer."

They talked for a long time, Alec outlining his proposal and Ruta countering with her own ideas. She was a tough negotiator, but she was also fair, understanding his point of view on each matter, though not necessarily agreeing. He sketched out each of the conditions of the sale on the back of a manila envelope, and when he was done, he handed it to her.

Ruta slowly read the outline, then nodded. "This will do." She took the pen from his hand and scrawled her signature on the bottom. "I am satisfied that you have dealt fairly with me. You are a good man and George would be proud."

Alec took her hand, but instead of shaking it, he pressed a kiss to her wrist. "And you are a beautiful woman, Mrs. Lupescu."

"Alec!"

They both turned at the sound of Sabina's voice. A moment later, she appeared in the door. "Alec?"

"I'm in here," he said, rising from the sofa.

Sabina walked inside, frowning. She glanced back and forth between Alex and her grandmother. "What are you doing in here?"

"Mr. Harnett and I have been discussing his offer to buy my building. We've agreed on terms."

Sabina gasped. "What?"

"Do not worry. You will not be homeless, Bina. In fact, you will be a millionaire several times over. I plan to give you enough to start your own company and to settle you in a new apartment. You can sell all those pretty things that you make. And maybe you will be famous."

"No!" Sabina cried. "How could you do this? This is our home."

"And I am getting too old to care for it. It weighs on my mind, Bina. And it is time to let it go. Besides, your Alec is offering me a very fair price."

"*My* Alec!" Sabina shouted. She turned to him. "Is that what you told her? Is that why she's selling to you, because she believes there's something between us?" She turned to her grandmother. "Don't do this."

"The decision is already made, Sabina."

She stared long and hard at Alec, a look of utter betrayal on her face. She spun on her heel and walked across the hall, slamming her apartment door shut behind her.

Alec sighed deeply, then turned to Ruta. "Maybe this isn't such a good idea."

"No, it is. Time to push this chick out of the nest. She has gotten far too comfortable with her life here."

Alec folded the manila envelope in half. "I'll have the papers drawn up. But first, I'm going to go explain this all to Sabina."

Ruta touched his arm. "Leave her alone for now. She has many things to think about. I am sure she will see the wisdom in this."

At first, Alec didn't want to heed Ruta's advice. But she knew Sabina far better than he did. And if he'd learned anything from the Gypsy woman over the past few days it was that she had a good sense of people's emotions. "I'll call her tonight."

"Wait until tomorrow, or even the next day," Ruta said. "Make her wonder if you'll ever call again. And then when you do, she will realize how much she has missed you."

Alec nodded, then walked to the door. Though it went against every instinct he had, he passed by Sabina's apartment door and took the stairs to the lobby. When he reached the street, he paused, wondering if he ought to tear up the agreement and toss it in the nearest garbage bin.

But if Ruta didn't sell to him, then sooner or later she'd sell to someone, someone who might not treat her tenants as kindly as he would. No, this deal was for the best. And if Sabina never came to realize that, then he would be sorry for it.

But he had to trust that her feelings for him were as strong as his for her. If not, then there was really nothing to lose at all.

"I DON'T UNDERSTAND HOW YOU could do this," Sabina said.

She sat on the floor of the shop, a box of candles in front of her. Unpacking them seemed like a silly waste of time. Why was she even worried about sales when the shop would be just a faint memory by next year?

"You do not think I have a right to live the rest of my life in comfort, knowing that I have enough money to make you happy?"

"How could you think this would make me happy?"

"It gives you your freedom, Bina. You can do what you want with your life. You can open your own store or you can travel or you can sit in a room and sulk while your money earns interest at the bank. I do not care. Just find whatever it is that makes you happy and grab for it."

Sabina picked up a ylang-ylang candle and sniffed at it, letting the scent slowly seep into her. Mixed with myrrh, the resulting blend was meant to put a person in touch with their sensual side. She didn't want anything to do with that side of her personality. That's what had gotten her into this mess in the first place.

She snatched up a lavender candle and inhaled the soothing scent, then closed her eyes. Images of Alec swirled in her mind and she cursed softly, then dropped the candle back in the box. She couldn't ignore the fact that she missed him. Every night she went to bed determined not to dream of him, and every morning she woke with a strange, empty feeling inside her.

"When is this all going to be final?" she asked.

"He sent the papers over yesterday," Ruta said. "I had my lawyer read them and he says they are all in order. No tricks or fine print." Ruta held up the envelope. "I was hoping you might deliver them for me."

"No." Sabina shook her head. "I don't ever want to see that man again. He used me and then he betrayed me. If I hadn't let him into our lives, this never would have happened."

"What? I never would have sold the building? Believe me, Bina, I have been thinking about that for a very long time. Or perhaps you are talking about something different. If you wouldn't have invited him in, you wouldn't have fallen in love with him. Is that it?"

"Don't be ridiculous. I don't love him."

"But he loves you," Ruta said. "I made sure of that."

"What are you talking about?" she asked, getting to her feet and dusting off her hands.

"The charm I gave you," Ruta explained. "It worked. And then I gave him the potion that night when he was lying in your bed. It was in the tea."

Sabina's jaw fell and she stared at her grandmother. "You put a potion in his tea? Damn it, Nana, I told you, no more potions!"

Ruta shrugged. "It was just a little potion. But it did the job."

"And you think I'm happy about that? Why would I want to trick a man into loving me?"

"It is no trick, it is just a bit of encouragement. It gave him time to realize that you are the woman for him. Believe me, some men would never get there on their own."

Sabina grabbed the envelope. "This whole thing has been a nightmare and I just want to put an end to it once and for all. I'll take the papers over there and that will be it. I'll never have to set eyes on Alec Harnett again."

But as Sabina walked to the door, she knew that she'd still see him every night in her dreams. It would be years before she'd put this mistake behind her and move on. Maybe her grandmother was right. She needed a fresh start, perhaps in a new city where she wouldn't have to worry about running into Alec on the street.

She glanced down at the envelope. Fifty-ninth Street between Park and Lexington. She could catch the

F train and be outside his building in a matter of minutes. But as she walked to the subway stop near Washington Park, Sabina began to worry.

What if her grandmother was right? What if he did love her? And what if she refused to see those same feelings in herself just to prove a silly point? So he'd accomplished his goal—he'd bought her grandmother's building. Did that really negate everything they'd shared?

He'd made such a point of separating business from pleasure. But could he make that disconnect, or was that just a smoke screen to lure her in?

The subway was stifling, the air humid and close. Sabina found a seat and closed her eyes, the rocking of the car relaxing her. If she had anything to say to Alec, then perhaps it was best to get it done and get on with her life.

Sabina counted the stops—Fourteenth, Twenty-third, Thirty-fourth, Forty-second. By the time the train reached Rockefeller Center she was certain she'd simply turn around and go back home. But she'd regained her resolve when the train made the turn toward Queens. She got out at the Lexington Avenue stop and slowly walked up the stairs to the street level.

It was only a short walk to the spot where the building stood. Sabina stood across the street and stared at the sign above the door. "Harnett Property Development," she murmured.

She glanced both ways, then cut across the street midblock. A security guard opened the door for her and she gave him a tight smile. Sabina cleared her throat. "I'm looking for Alec Harnett."

"Fifth floor, the receptionist there will take your name."

"Fifth floor," Sabina muttered as she hurried to the

elevator. The doors opened immediately and she stepped inside. But as the elevator rose, she felt her uneasiness rise as well. Could she handle seeing him again? Or would she be consumed with thoughts of kissing him or touching him?

The doors opened onto an airy reception area. A pretty young woman sat behind the desk—Karen Donnelly, her nameplate read. She smiled as Sabina approached.

"I'm here to see Alec Harnett. Just let him know that Ruta's granddaughter, Sabina, is here."

The receptionist's eyes went wide. "Ruta, the Gypsy lady?"

"Yes," Sabina said.

The receptionist quickly punched in a number on her phone, an whispered into her headset. Then she glanced up at Sabina. "He'll be right with you. Would you like a beverage?"

Sabina shook her head. "I won't be staying."

A moment later, Alec appeared from behind a set of double doors. Sabina stared at him for a long moment. Emotions welled up inside of her—anger, humiliation, frustration and, above all, desire. But she pushed them all back and composed herself.

"Sabina."

His eyes caught hers and locked, penetrating to the very depths of her soul. Her heart beat fast and she tried to draw a deep breath, but she felt paralyzed. "I brought the papers," she finally said. She held out the envelope, but he didn't take it from her.

After another long silence, Sabina spoke. "This is what you wanted. Take them."

It was difficult to stand near Alec without losing the

capacity to think or speak. When she looked at him, her mind filled with images of them kissing, his mouth on hers, his hands furrowed in her hair, his naked body lying beneath hers. She'd never experienced feelings so intense for a man, and even with time apart they hadn't faded.

She felt the words forming on her lips. Just two words would be all it took and everything would be all right. *Kiss me. Kiss me.* "Kiss me."

"What?"

Sabina sucked in a sharp breath. Had she said that out loud? "What?"

"Did you say something?" Alec asked.

"No," Sabina replied.

"Oh, I must be imagining things."

"What did you think I said?" Sabina asked.

"I thought you said 'Kiss me.'" He frowned, deep lines creasing his brow. "Is that what you said, Sabina?"

She swallowed hard. What could the truth hurt? At this very moment, she felt as if he could read her mind. But he didn't wait for her answer. Instead, he took her hand and pulled her along with him through the double doors.

Sabina resisted, but only just a bit. It felt so wonderful to have him touch her again. They turned a corner and walked into a huge office. Alec shut the door behind them, then steered her toward the desk.

"Say it once more. Go ahead. Don't be afraid."

"I didn't say anything," Sabina lied. She stepped back, anxious to avoid the warmth and touch of his body. But she ran up against the edge of his desk. "And I'm not afraid of you."

Alec reached out and cupped her cheek in his palm. "That's funny," he said softly, his breath warm against her lips. "Because I'm afraid of you. You scare the hell out of me, Sabina. I'm afraid that I'll never see you again, or touch you again. I'm afraid that I'll wake up every morning and wonder why you're not lying beside me. I'm afraid that I'm going to go through life regretting that I didn't tell you exactly how I felt."

He opened his mouth to continue, but Sabina reached up and pressed her fingers to his lips. She knew if he said it she'd be compelled to return the sentiment. But Sabina wasn't sure how she felt, or even if she could trust Alec's feelings for her.

"Don't. Don't make this more difficult than it has to be. Don't you see, Alec? This was doomed from the start. It all happened too fast. We were caught up in the passion and didn't bother to see the reality."

"And what is the reality, Sabina? I love you and I think you love me. It doesn't matter how long we've known each other. Hell, maybe we knew each other in a past life. Or maybe this was love at first sight. If you don't believe in the possibility that this might just work, then we're going to miss out on the best thing to happen to either one of us."

She stared down at their hands, hers clasped in his. "My grandmother gave me a love charm the morning we met. And that first night you spent at my apartment, she put a potion in your tea. She's probably been casting spells on you as well, although she hasn't admitted it."

"So? What difference does that make? I don't believe in any of that stuff." He stepped toward her. "This is what I believe." He slipped his hand around her nape and pulled her into a kiss. Sabina felt the hum of desire racing through her body. She was acutely aware of every detail:

the warmth of his lips, the taste of his mouth, the way his tongue slowly teased until she surrendered to the kiss.

The moment she did surrender, the only thing she really thought about was making it all last—a minute, a day, a month. It didn't matter. She wanted to kiss Alec until she couldn't possibly kiss him anymore. She wanted to wash away all her doubts and insecurities, to forget everything that had happened in the past and turn her eyes to the future.

He gently pushed her back against the edge of his desk and then lifted her up to sit in front of him. Sabina parted her knees and he stepped closer, their mouths still caught in an endless kiss. His hands drifted from her face to her thighs and he bunched the gauzy fabric of her skirt in his fists.

When he finally drew back, his eyes were cloudy with desire. "That is what I believe in," he said in a husky voice. "That feeling. That's all that matters, Sabina. And I hope you'll realize that someday."

With that, he grabbed Sabina's elbow and escorted her to the door. He opened it, then pushed her through, before shutting it behind her. She stood outside, dazed and bewildered, the envelope still clutched in her hand.

"Well," she said. "At least I know how he feels. I guess I just need to figure out how I feel."

CHAPTER SIX

THOUSANDS OF TINY LIGHTS illuminated the rooftop garden of Ruta's building. A small crowd had gathered there for an engagement party for Mario and Iris. Sabina's grandmother was taking full credit for giving Mario the courage to propose, so she'd felt compelled to throw the party. Yet another one of her prophecies had come true.

Sabina grabbed a bottle of champagne and filled her flute, then gulped it down in a few quick swallows. She refilled the glass before wandering over to the hors d'oeuvres table. It was wonderful, she had to admit. Mario was head over heels in love and it was clear that Iris shared the sentiment.

"Don't they make a lovely couple?" Ruta stepped up from behind her and slipped her arm around Sabina's waist.

"They do. They seem very happy."

"You know, I have been considering what I might do with all my money once the sale goes through. I thought I might take a trip back to the old country. And I would like you to come with me. I think you need to know where your ancestors come from."

"I don't know, Nana. I've got so many things to

decide. I've got to find a new place to live, and if I'm going to open a boutique, I'm going to need to find retail space."

"Have you talked to Alec?"

Sabina watched the bubbles rise in her champagne glass, then took a long sip. "No. I've been trying to decide how I feel. I do love him, Nana, but after all that happened, I'm not really sure that he loves me. What if he did fall in love with me because of the amulet and the potion?"

"Bina, you needn't worry. The amulet is just clay with a few scratches in it, held by a piece of red yarn. And the potion was nothing more than honey and a bit of brandy."

Sabina gasped. "Really? But I thought—"

"It is all…how do they say…smoke and mirrors. The man loves you and that much is true. Now, what are you going to do about it?"

Sabina felt emotion clog her throat. "Oh, Nana, I've been so stupid."

"Yes, you have, Bina. Why don't you be smart and go talk to that man of yours." She nodded to her right. "He's over there."

"He's here?" Sabina whirled around and immediately saw Alec, perched on the edge of the rooftop wall. He was dressed in a casual shirt and khakis, and even in the heat, he managed to look cool and composed.

"Dance with that young man of yours, Bina. He looks lonely sitting over there."

"What is he doing here?" Sabina asked.

"Mario invited him. He tried a little matchmaking between the two of you and it didn't work out. He thought he'd give it one last shot. This is his party, Bina. Make him happy and dance with Alec."

Sabina straightened her spine and pasted a smile on her face, then slowly crossed the roof deck. Alec saw her and stood, taking a few steps toward her. They met in the vicinity of the dance floor, but Sabina found herself frozen in place, unable to move.

"How's the ankle?" she asked.

"Great," Alec replied. "And I've been sleeping well. No more bad dreams. And business has been good. Thanks for lifting the curse."

A blush warmed her cheeks. "Alec, there was no curse. I have no powers. Absolutely no talent for anything that has to do with the psychic arts. In fact, until I met you, I wasn't much of a believer."

"What changed your mind?"

"I guess I couldn't really believe that a man like you would fall for a woman like me. At least not in any natural way. I thought it had to be the charm I wore or the potion."

Alec chuckled and shook his head. "Sabina, you are a very foolish woman. And you're lucky I'm a patient man. I've waited my whole life to find you, and now that I have, I'm willing to wait as long as it takes for you to believe in my feelings for you."

"I do believe," Sabina said, tears flooding her eyes. "I do. I love you, Alec. And I don't care what has happened in the past. All I care about is my future with you."

He drew her into his embrace, then kissed her so softly and so exquisitely that it took her breath away. When she looked up at him, she saw the emotion in his eyes and knew that she wasn't wrong. He loved her and he wanted her, for today and forever.

"I have something for you," Alec said. He grabbed an envelope from his back pocket and handed it to her.

"What is this?" She opened the envelope and unfolded the papers. She recognized them immediately. It was the signed offer he'd made on her grandmother's building.

"It's yours. I'm going to buy the building from your grandmother and give it back to you. In return for the fortune you told me that first day in the shop. You said there was something I wanted. I think you used the word *covet*. You said I'd be tempted to use trickery, but that wouldn't bring it to me. That only honesty would."

"My grandmother's building. See?" Sabina said. "I was right."

"But that wasn't what I wanted." Alec paused, his gaze searching her face. "It was you. I wanted you."

Sabina felt tears press at the corners of her eyes. She stared down at the papers, then slowly put them back into the envelope. "We've come full circle," she said. "Your grandfather and my grandmother. You and me. And this building. Maybe this was meant to be all along."

"I think it was," Alec said, tipping her chin up until their eyes met again. Slowly, he bent forward and placed a gentle kiss on her lips. "I love you, Sabina. And I don't care what it took to get here, but we are here. This is the beginning of our future together."

"It feels right," she said, a smile teasing at the corners of her mouth. "Do you really love me?"

"I do," Alec said. He pulled her into his arms and kissed her long and hard.

"And I really love you," Sabina replied breathlessly.

Alec glanced over his shoulder. "Do you think your grandmother would miss us if we skipped out early? My ankle has been feeling sore today and I really should get off my feet. And you do have that very comfortable bed downstairs."

Sabina tipped her head back and laughed. "My grandmother would be deliriously happy to see us leave together. And I would hate to disappoint her. But then, she's psychic. She probably knew this was going to happen all along." Sabina wrapped her arms around his neck and kissed the spot below his ear. "Why don't we mess with her a little bit? Let's stay for a few dances."

"Whatever you say, sweetheart." Alec took her hand and drew her along to the small dance floor set up in front of the band. Sabina stepped into his arms as if she'd been dancing with him her whole life. As they swayed to the music, she stared up into the night sky and thanked the fates that had brought them together. She was glad she wasn't psychic, glad that she didn't see him coming. It made the surprise of falling in love all that much sweeter.

RUTA SAT AT A SMALL TABLE, a glass of champagne in front of her. She watched the couple dance to the small combo she'd hired for the party. A smile broke across her face and joy welled up inside her.

"They make a beautiful couple," Mario said. "I was right. They belonged together."

"You were right? But I was the one who saw it first. It was my amulet, my potion. You just drove the man around the city a few times."

"I thought you told Sabina there was nothing to the potion and amulet," Mario said.

"So I told a tiny white lie. What harm can it do?

She's never really believed. And I would rather see her happy with a good man than alone and confident in my talents. The charm and the potion worked. I am satisfied. This afternoon I saw a wedding in my crystal ball."

"Maybe it was my matchmaking that got the job done."

"We make good partners," Ruta said, patting his hand. "Maybe after I close my shop, we can go into business together. There are plenty of single people in New York looking for spouses."

"I don't know. I have a fiancée now to think about. Do you think we could make any money at it?"

"You know, it was all my work that got you and Iris together. And you haven't even thanked me."

"How is it your work?"

"Remember that key chain I gave you for Christmas last year?" Ruta asked.

Mario reached into his pocket and pulled it out. Ruta held up the charm and Mario gasped. He'd seen the very same charm dangling from Sabina's neck. "You gave me a love charm?"

"What harm could it do? Now look at yourself. You have a lovely fiancée and beautiful life ahead of you. You should thank me."

Mario chuckled, then gave Ruta a hug. "Thank you," he said.

Ruta blushed, then waved him off. "Go. Dance with your beautiful Iris. And remember, it isn't how we come to love, it is that we recognize it when we find it."

Everything you love about romance...
and more!

Please turn the page for Signature Select™
Bonus Features.

A FARE TO REMEMBER

BONUS FEATURES INSIDE

Adventures in Cab Riding
by Julie Elizabeth Leto

Because of my husband's job, we travel a lot. Lately, thanks to my job, I've been heading to New York with more frequency, as well as other cities. My experiences with taxicabs have been varied, but in keeping with the theme of this collection, I thought I'd share a few tips and experiences based on the cities I've visited.

First, the tips (mostly apply to New York, but other cities, as well):

- It's easy to tell if a cab is available to pick you up. When the numbers on the top of the cab are illuminated, it is empty. When the numbers are off, the cab is either occupied or on its way back to base.
- To hail a cab, stand at the curb with your arm held straight up and out. Someone called this the Statue of Liberty imitation. Yeah, that fits!
- When you enter cab, speak loud and clear to the driver of your destination. Not only are many of

them foreign-born, but the city is noisy and it's hard to hear through the Plexiglas partition.

- Taxi drivers can try to rip you off by taking a longer route if you don't seem to know where you're going. Study your map *before* you get into the cab and if you can, ask a hotel concierge or doorman what the quickest route is and then tell the driver. Be specific about cross streets. Let them think you know what you're talking about!
- Wear your seat belt.
- Don't smoke. It's against the law and you can be ticketed if stopped by the police.
- Always get a receipt! In New York, at least, the receipts are generated through the meter and have all the information you'll need to lodge a complaint, send a compliment (those are appreciated, I'm sure) or if you left something in the cab you need to retrieve.
- Always exit the cab on the curbside so you don't get hit by traffic.
- Tipping isn't necessary, but it is nice if the driver did his job exceptionally well. And in New York traffic, getting you to your destination in one piece is exceptional in my estimation!
- Remember that New York streets often run one way. Be aware of which direction you are heading in before you decide where to pick up

the cab. This can save you both time and money.

- Cabdrivers in New York will wave you off if they don't want to go where you are headed—even though it is against the rules—especially at the end of their shifts. Keep that in mind when planning travel time.

- Fares to and from the airports in New York have fixed rates. You can check the airport Web site to find out the going rate.

- "Gypsy cabs" are illegal in New York, but they are still everywhere. If it's not yellow, it's not an official, regulated cab. It's best to avoid these cabs if you can as they are often not the safest way to travel since they are not marked nor are they regulated.

- Consider not only regular rush-hour traffic when planning travel through the city, but also location. If you're in the Theater District, pay attention to showtimes. Getting a cab at four o'clock on a Wednesday afternoon can be tough because of the Broadway matinees!

- Passenger rights are usually posted in the back of a cab, but even if they are not, don't be afraid to insist that the driver turn the radio down or off, turn the heater or air conditioner on or off, close the windows, stop talking on their cell phone, etc. If they don't comply, report them, but most will do as you ask.

My personal taxi reviews by city:

New York

New York City cabs are pretty much everything you expect. The drivers are often foreign-speaking, but I have to say that only last trip there, I rode in at least ten taxis and while all my drivers had accents, all but one conversed easily in English and most had been in our country for a very long time. One reminded me a lot of Mario, as a matter of fact, and he told me stories on our short trip that were fascinating. I was careful not to distract him with chatter, though. I did want to arrive alive and New York traffic can be frightening!

Interesting New York Taxi Facts:
- The first female taxi driver in New York got behind the wheel in 1925.
- The last Checker cab in New York City was retired July 26, 1999.
- In 2003, 238 million people rode in New York taxicabs.

Chicago

This is my favorite city to ride in a cab. I don't know what it is about Chicago, but all the cabdrivers I've ridden with (and I go to Chicago about once a year—twice, if I can) have been super friendly, helpful and hardworking. I've never once been waved off by a Chicago cabdriver and on my last trip, my cabdriver asked if he could pick up an extra fare on the way to my destination and he'd give me a discount if I agreed. He had two fares, two travelers got a ride and I got a break on the fare and everyone was happy. Chicago cabs are not exclusively yellow as they are in New York, but I only ride in the ones with clear markings.

Fun Chicago Taxi Facts:
- Yellow Cab of Chicago was founded in 1915 by John Hertz, the same man who later started Hertz Rent-A-Car. He was the first taxi company owner to pick yellow as the taxi color of choice and his idea clearly spread to other cities, including New York, like wildfire!
- Chicago has a famous singing cabdriver named Ray St. Ray who croons love ballads and pop songs with his own social commentary to his fares.

Las Vegas

Like all of Las Vegas, the cabdrivers here are efficient and friendly. Las Vegas is not a big place, so getting from point A to point B is more a matter of traffic than it is distance. The driveways into the resort hotels are sometimes longer and more congested than the main thoroughfares.

The taxi drivers here do know what's going on where. They were always helpful if I had any questions. I've never tried to catch a cab in Las Vegas during the daytime in July, but I guess it wouldn't be an easy task unless you're at the entrance to one of the hotels. I can't imagine catching one in the street would be easy, so keep that in mind when you go out for a walk.

- Clark County taxicabs are fitted with surveillance cameras that have helped them catch people who have committed crimes in cabs, including stealing the cab from the driver.
- Cabs in Nevada base their fares on both time and distance—if the cab is moving at less than eight-to-twelve miles per hour, it calculates by time—over that speed, and it calculates by distance.

Reno

I have to mention the little town of Reno because on my most recent trip, I noticed that Reno had the most colorful cabdrivers I've ever encountered anywhere. One might have been partying a little hard before picking me up, if you know what I mean. But we arrived safely at our destination and he was super friendly. Another had fingernails much longer and prettier than mine—and he wasn't a she. In fact, he had formerly been a truck driver. I had a blast listening to the explanation regarding his manicure (due in

part to an industrial accident), but thought when
I did my taxi guide, I had to include this story.
Be prepared to wait for a taxi in Reno; they don't
just hang around outside of all the casinos
and often have to be called. Also, Reno cabs
sometimes won't take more than four passengers
in one cab, so if you're a large party, even if a van
approaches, you'll need more than one cab. It's
at the driver's discretion, but five is the max.

Here's a sneak peek...

The Mighty
Quinns: Marcus
by
Kate Hoffmann

In bookstores October 2006

CHAPTER ONE

"'Tis a fine thing, Friday nights at Finnerty's Pub. Cold beer and warm women. What more could we want?" Declan Quinn took a long sip of his Guinness, then set the pint glass down on the table in front of him.

The pub was dark and smoky, and a neon beer light on the wall illuminated the table where the three Quinn brothers sat. Over the bar, a television played a Red Sox game, now well into extra innings. The seven pubs in Bonnet Harbor, Rhode Island, could be divided into two types, those that rooted for the Yankees and those that cheered on the Sox. But Finnerty's was the only true Irish pub, with corned-beef sandwiches on command, an endless supply of Guinness on tap and a live Irish band on Friday and Saturday nights. It had become the pub of choice for Marcus and his brothers.

The pub drew a working-class crowd from the surrounding areas—fishermen, factory workers, shopkeepers and people that worked for the people who worked in the big houses in nearby Newport. It made for a rowdy mix of longtime residents and newcomers, nearly all of them claiming a drop or two of Irish blood.

Bonnet Harbor lay on the western shore of Narragansett Bay directly across the water from Jamestown and Newport, and was still relatively unspoiled by tourism, although that was slowly changing. New shops and restaurants opened every few months and even now, Marcus could pick out the tourists among those enjoying a drink at the bar.

Though Bonnet Harbor was technically his hometown, Marcus had always felt like an outsider. He'd spent most of his childhood in Ireland, and when he thought of home, he thought of the stone manor house where his maternal grandmother lived and the old stable where he used to play. Bonnet Harbor was where his parents had settled after leaving Boston and this is where the family business, Quinn's Boat Works, was located. Marcus's own business, Q Yacht Design, operated from a building tucked in the corner of the boatyard and he lived in a small apartment above his workroom.

"If I recall, Dec, you said that exact same thing last week," Ian commented. "We were sitting right over there and—" At the loud shout of a drunken darts player, Ian twisted in his chair. He'd changed out of his work attire, shedding the uniform in favor of a faded polo shirt and a well-worn pair of jeans. But he still watched the crowd with a careful eye, ready to step in if a simple argument turned physical.

Ian was police chief of Bonnet Harbor. Declan owned his own security firm headquartered in Providence. And though Dec kept an apartment in the city, he rolled into Bonnet Harbor nearly every weekend, camping out with either Ian or Marcus. They had been close as boys and now, as adults, they were even closer, enjoying a bond that could never be broken.

"It's true," Marcus said. "You did. Those very same words."

Declan frowned. He looked oddly out of place, dressed in a tux and pleated shirt, his bow tie hanging loose around his neck. He'd come from another of his high-society parties. But Dec exuded a steely confidence that silently warned against any comment about his highbrow appearance.

"We were sitting right over there at that table by the window," Marcus added.

Ian and Declan both looked at him, as if surprised by his entrance into the conversation. Marcus had always been known as the quiet Quinn, the only one in a family of seven children who didn't engage in the boisterous family arguments that took place over Sunday supper at their parents' house. If there was ever a disagreement, Marcus could be counted on to remain neutral. Declan was usually the one to start the argument, then sit back and watch as Ian did everything he could to win the argument.

Marcus just didn't see the point in arguing unless the subject was important to him. And there was very little he found to arouse either his ire or his passion. He reached out for his own beer and took a long drink. "Do you ever wonder if we're maybe in a wee bit of rut?"

"Jaysus, maybe we are," Ian said, allowing his Irish accent to tinge his words. "We've done this same bloody thing so many times, we've begun to repeat ourselves, like those old men down at the docks who tell the same stories over and over again."

"At least we still have our own teeth," Marcus commented.

"We go out, we look for women, we drink a little too much and then we go home," Ian added. "If we get lucky, we hook up with a pretty girl. If not, we wake up alone the next morning with a blazing headache."

"Predictable," Marcus murmured. As much as he wanted to deny it, it was true. He loved hanging with his brothers. But lately, he was beginning to feel restless, as if there were something better he ought to be doing with his time, some elusive goal he ought to pursue.

"Most of the guys our age are married," Ian said. "Our older brothers, the Quinn cousins, nearly all my friends done it. I haven't dated one woman that I'd consider marrying."

"What happened to Caroline?" Declan asked, reaching for the bowl of pretzels. "I thought you two were in love."

"She went back to her old boyfriend," Ian said morosely. "Said I was a great guy, but he was ready to make a commitment." Ian shuddered. "God, I hate that word."

"Well, there's your problem," Marcus muttered.

"I'm not interested in getting married, either," Dec offered. "And I make that very clear from the start. It's all about the sex. Most women appreciate my honesty."

"Yeah, right," Ian said. "Most women think they can change your mind. It's only after they realize they can't, they move on."

Dec groaned. "Can we talk about something else?"

"Why? Women spend most of their time talking about us," Marcus said.

Ian nodded in agreement, popping a pretzel into his mouth. "If we spent more time trying to figure women out, we'd probably have better luck. I'll wager I could have a five-minute conversation with any woman in this bar and she'd have me figured out, head to toe."

"You're just about as deep a mud puddle," Dec said. "It doesn't take a major intellect to figure you out." He glanced over at Marcus. "Now our baby brother, he's a different story. The girls like him because he has an air of mystery about him. He never speaks, so they don't know where he stands. And he's not all that interested in figuring them out, so they're even more intrigued."

"He's quiet because he can't think of anything intelligent to say," Ian teased.

"I know what your problem is," Marcus said after a long silence. "Instant gratification."

"What?" Dec and Ian said in tandem.

"That's all you look for. You find a girl, hook up and never call her again. The next weekend, you're right back out there looking for someone new."

"I'm not looking for a wife," Dec insisted.

"Neither was Conor or Dylan or Brendan," Marcus said. "Or Brian or Sean or Liam. They didn't want to get married until they found a woman they wanted to marry. And then they got married."

Dec took a moment to digest his brother's words then shook his head. "Wonky reasoning, that is," he said.

"I think finding a woman is a lot like fishing," Ian declared, leaning back in his chair and linking his hands behind his head. "You just keep hauling 'em into the boat until you get a keeper."

"And then you stuff it and hang it on the wall," Dec said with a chuckle.

Ian sighed. "Maybe we've been fishing with the wrong bait. Or maybe we're fishing in the wrong waters."

"And what fishing spots would you suggest?" Marcus asked.

"I don't know. Pubs haven't been working for us. So…" Ian drew a deep breath and shook his head. "I don't know. I hear the Internet works pretty well."

"We're smart guys," Dec said. "I don't think we need to resort to electronic means. We can certainly figure this out."

"I say we stop picking up random women," Marcus said. "Full stop. We try to get to know them before we sleep with them. We haul all kinds of fish into the boat, then take some time to decide which fish to throw back."

"I think I date some pretty decent women," Declan said.

"Ha!" Ian leaned back in his chair. "What about Danielle? She ties you to the bed during sex, then goes out to get breakfast for the two of you. On the way back, she gets distracted by…"

"A sale at Bloomingdales," Dec said. "It was Bloomingdales. Purses, I think. The girl really liked purses. More than sex." He turned to Marcus. "What about that woman you dated who couldn't get excited unless you spanked her."

"It was exciting the first few times, but when she pulled out a whip, I had to draw the line," Marcus murmured, shaking his head.

"Remember Giselle, that dancer from my building?" Dec asked. "What happened to her?"

"Exhibitionist," Ian said. "She liked to do it in front of the windows of her apartment, with the curtains open. I guess she's known in the neighborhood for her…performances. There were guys across the street with binoculars and video cameras."

"I've seen those guys," Dec said to Marcus. "I always thought they were watching birds."

"So we've all had our share of strange sexual encounters. If we want things to change, Marcus is right. We need to make a plan," Ian said. "I say we go out there and look for keepers. No bleach blondes or fake boobs or overbaked bodies."

"No aspiring Playboy models or ex–beauty queens or former professional cheerleaders, either," Dec added. "And no strippers."

"They prefer *exotic dancers,*" Ian corrected.

Marcus shook his head. There was a benefit to being reserved around women. He'd never had the courage to dip a toe into those dating pools.

"Just regular girls. I say, the three of us make a pact to meet one normal woman this week," Ian suggested. "We report back here and compare notes."

Marcus smiled inwardly. Ian had always been the competitive one. If an activity could be turned into a game, he found a way to do it. And he rarely lost. "I'm going to have to pass on this," he said. "I'm stuck out in Newport on a boat for the rest of the summer. Alone."

"Just you and your precious tools?" Ian asked.

"You took that job with Trevor Ross." Declan nodded. "I hope he's paying you well. He certainly can afford it."

Dec had provided security at a number of Ross's parties and also advised his corporate security office on a variety of matters. He had referred Marcus to the wealthy tycoon. "I figure if I impress him, I might be able to talk him into investing in my business," Marcus said. "More capital means bigger yachts."

"What's his boat like?" Ian asked.

A grin curled the corners of Marcus's mouth. "You should see her. She's a beauty. Built in 1923. Schooner-rigged. Ninety-foot wood hull. He had the cabin completely refurbished and it's sweet. But he wants more detailing so I'm adding some vintage carvings and a new figurehead. The crew is on vacation. I'm living on the boat while I work. He's got it anchored off his place on Price's Neck."

"So you're out of the game for now," Ian said. "You can get in later. But you still have to pay up every week."

"You're turning this into some kind of pool?" Marcus asked.

"Every week we throw a twenty into the pot," Ian explained. "First guy find a keeper—and keep her—wins it."

"Fifty-two weeks, twenty dollars a week times three, that's over three thousand in a year," Dec said. "Not bad incentive to start fishing. But who's to judge."

"We all have to like her and agree that she's worth marrying," Ian said.

"But we don't have to marry her, right?" Dec asked.

"Nope." Ian held out a clenched fist. "Deal?"

Dec bumped his fist against Ian's. "Deal."

Marcus had never liked being left out of his older brothers' games. Though he didn't have a lot of extra cash, he could afford to play. And considering the track records of the two guys sitting at the table, he probably had a decent shot, even if he did join the game late.

"Deal," Marcus finally said. "I'm in."

A SHAFT OF SUNLIGHT filtered through the porthole and warmed Marcus Quinn's face. He slowly opened his eyes and for a moment, he was transported back to his childhood, to those days spent playing in the stable at Porter Hall.

He rolled over in the narrow berth and grabbed his wristwatch from the small shelf above his head.

Wiping at his bleary eyes, Marcus tried to focus on the time, ignoring the dull ache in his head. "Eight-thirty," he murmured, sinking back into the pillows.

The schooner rocked gently in the water as the waves slapped against the hull. He closed his eyes and let his thoughts drift, the movement of the boat lulling him back toward sleep. He'd stayed out with his brothers until well after one, playing pool and shooting darts at Finnerty's.

He sat up and raked his hands through his rumpled hair, then swung his legs over the edge of the berth. When he'd come on board a week ago, he'd claimed an empty berth in the crew quarters next door to the captain's cabin. But now that the crew had left, Marcus had the boat all to himself, luxurious accommodations for a guy who was used to a three-room apartment above an old boathouse.

He dug through his clothes scattered over the opposite berth, searching for something clean to wear, then gave up. It was about time to check out the small laundry room aft of the engine room—right after he started a pot of coffee. Marcus wandered sleepily down the narrow companionway, past the two spacious guest cabins.

From the time he could stand on a deck, Marcus had loved being on the water. His earliest memories were of his father, standing in the wheelhouse of the *Mighty Quinn,* the family sword-fishing boat. Paddy

Quinn had been forced to sell his interest to Marcus's uncle Seamus to help pay for his wife's medical bills. The family moved to Rhode Island and Paddy worked for a boat repair business on the eastern shore of Narragansett Bay, a business he later bought from the elderly owner.

Before they were sent to Ireland, Marcus remembered one glorious summer spent racing little Sunfish sailboats on the bay, skimming across the water in hastily planned regattas. When they weren't sailing, they were fishing from a small skiff their father had restored.

The ensuing years took them away from the water and their older brothers, Rory and Eddie, but the moment Marcus returned at age fifteen, he began to build his own sailboat in his father's workshop. From that moment on, he knew he wanted to design boats— beautiful sleek sailboats that could cut through the water like a razor.

Four years of college at MIT followed by another two years working at IYRS—International Yacht Restoration School—set him on the path to opening his own business. He'd built his first boat while still at IYRS. The twenty-three-foot wooden day-sailer took three months, and by that time Marcus had three more commissions and enough money to hire two employees. And now with the job from Trevor Ross, things were really beginning to look up.

Marcus glanced around the spacious lounge of the *Victorious* as he passed through, his feet brushing against the cool teak sole of the boat. The ninety-foot schooner was a designer's dream, an inspiration for Marcus's future projects. He enjoyed discovering all the interesting nooks and crannies of the vintage yacht, examining the expensive restoration work that Trevor Ross so easily paid for.

As he turned the corner into the galley, Marcus stopped short, the breath leaving his chest. A woman, dressed only in lacy black panties, was bent over the refrigerator, her underwear riding up on the curves of her backside. She was dripping wet, water puddling around her feet, her long hair plastered to her back.

Marcus glanced over his shoulder, deciding if he ought to step out and throw on some clothes or stand his ground. He didn't want to give the stowaway a chance to escape. Brushing aside his modesty, Marcus braced his hands on either side of the door, then cleared his throat. She straightened, then turned and faced him, her face registering mild surprise. Her gaze slowly raked the length of his body, resting a long moment in the area of his crotch. "Good morning," she murmured, a smile twitching at her lips.

She didn't seem to be concerned about his lack of clothing—or hers, for that matter. He tried to avoid looking at her breasts, but he couldn't help himself. Her body was perfect, long-limbed and slender, with a tiny waist that flared out to lovely hips. His eyes drifted back to her breasts and he lingered there for just a moment, wondering how it might feel to touch her, to cup each perfect breast in the palm of his hand.

"Are you finished?" she asked. "Or would you like to take a closer look?" She held up her arms and slowly turned in front of him, offering him yet another glimpse of her backside.

Marcus's gaze darted back to her face, taking in the wide green eyes, high cheekbones and lush mouth now curved in a wry smile. Hell, this was every man's dream, the stuff of fantasies, stumbling on a nearly naked woman. Marcus swallowed hard. If he didn't find something to cover his crotch, she was going to see exactly what kind of effect she was having on him.

"Excuse me," he murmured. "I'll be right back." He turned and hurried toward his cabin.

"Is there coffee?" she shouted, poking her head out of the galley.

Marcus cursed softly as he dug through his clothes looking for a clean pair of boxer briefs. In the end, he tugged on baggy surfer shorts and made a quick stop at the head to brush his teeth. When he returned to the galley, she was still rummaging through the cabinets in the same state of undress. He cursed to himself, wondering why she hadn't taken the chance to put on some clothes.

"May I ask what you're doing?" he said.

"Coffee," she muttered impatiently. "Is it too much to ask that you start a pot of coffee in the morning?"

He stepped inside, moving past her. Her body brushed his, her breasts soft against his chest. He focused on the coffee, determined not to let her rattle him. The bag of beans was tucked behind a canister of sugar. Marcus pulled it out and dumped a healthy measure of the beans into the grinder. As the grinder whined, he glanced over his shoulder to find her perched on the counter, her hands braced at her sides, her long legs crossed at the ankle. He groaned inwardly, fighting back an impulse to reach out and touch her, just to see if this was all just a very vivid dream.

He dumped the ground coffee into a filter, then popped it into the coffeemaker, grateful for any distraction. Grabbing the pot, Marcus passed it over to her and she filled it with water from the tap. They both watched until a stream of coffee began to drip into the pot. Then she reached around her back and found a coffee mug.

"I can't wait," she murmured, nudging his shoulder with the cup.

He filled her mug and handed it back to her, keeping his attention firmly fixed on the coffee. "How did you get on board?" he asked.

"I swam," she said. "I left my clothes and my bags on the dock. Maybe you could take the dinghy over later and get them for me?"

"Yeah," Marcus muttered. "Maybe." He'd put that little task off for as long as possible. It wasn't every day he got to enjoy the company of a naked woman, especially a woman who seemed more comfortable out of her clothes than in them.

"You're new," she said. "You're a bit older than the boys Daddy usually hires. Are you here to take over for that old barnacle Captain Davis? Please tell me he's finally retired to the Crusty Old Sailor's Home. Or was he swallowed by some accommodating white whale on his last cruise?"

Marcus bit back a curse. Daddy? Bloody hell. The only person she could be talking about was Trevor Ross, which meant that the naked woman sitting behind him—the one he'd been drooling over—was his boss's daughter, Ariel Ross.

Pictures of her as a little girl hung in the master cabin. But the rest of the world knew her from her tabloid exploits. She looked different in person, without the clothes and makeup and celebrity hair. Her skin was smooth and flawless, with a tiny sprinkling of freckles across her upturned nose, and her hair was a much darker blond when it was wet. She looked almost…virginal. No, this was not the girl who jetted around Europe, dated princes and attended fashion shows.

"You're Ariel," he said flatly.

"And you are?"

He turned and faced her, leaning back against the edge of the counter. "The new barnacle."

She giggled at the answer and to Marcus's surprise, the sound sent a rush of heat through his bloodstream. "So do you prefer Barney?" she asked, holding out her hand.

He wanted to touch her. At that moment, it seemed like the most important thing in the world. He took the offered greeting, grasping her fingers in his, and Marcus instantly wondered how those delicate fingers would feel wrapped around him.

"Marcus. Marcus Quinn. I'm…" He scrambled for the words. *Fighting off a serious case of lust…fantasizing about dragging you to my bed…wanting to know if you taste as good as you look.* "Working for your dad," he finished, quickly dropping her hand.

He took a quick sip of his coffee, watching her over the rim of his cup. Was he expected to carry on a conversation with her? She didn't seem to be at all interested in getting dressed. The polite thing to do was keep his gaze fixed on her face. He risked another glance at her breasts. Easier said than done.

"Doing what?" she asked.

"Your father hired me to do some wood carvings

for the boat. I'm working on a figurehead for the bowsprit and piece for the wall in the dining area. And I'm carving some corbels for the lounge area and adding some ornamentation to the cabinets in the master suite."

"Well, well," she said, jumping down from the counter, "Sounds like you have your work cut out for you." She stepped toward him and lightly skimmed her palm down his chest, stopping when she reached his belly. Marcus held his breath and she sent him a provocative grin. "I'll try to stay out of your way. It'll be nice to have some company on board. Don't work too hard, Barney."

"It's Marcus. And you can't stay," he protested. How the hell was he supposed to concentrate on work with Ariel Ross prancing around the deck naked? There was just so much a normal guy could take and in a short ten minutes, he'd already reached his limit. All he could think about was finding a way to ease his sexual frustration. "Your father said I'd have the boat to myself. I can't work if you're here."

"Why is that?"

Was she that dense or was she simply toying with him? He'd already managed to lapse into a few brief and inappropriate fantasies. Given more time, Marcus knew what his imagination would provide—full-blown, erotic daydreams that would only be erased by prolonged physical contact with a beautiful

BONUS FEATURE

woman—like Ariel Ross. From the moment he stumbled upon her, all he'd been able to think about was how long he'd have to wait to touch her. No, there was no way she could stay! "You just can't," he murmured.

"I'm sorry, but I don't care what you want. This is my father's boat and I'll stay as long as I like. If you have a problem with that, you can take it up with your boss." With that, she turned on her heel and disappeared down the companionway to the master suite.

Marcus stuck his head out of the galley just in time to see her slam the door. "Oh, hell." This was trouble just waiting to happen. Ariel Ross had a reputation that was known worldwide—she was a man-eater, about as far from a "keeper" as he could get. And if she started nibbling on him, he wasn't sure he'd be able to defend himself.

A month didn't go by without a scandalous photo or article in the tabloids or a report on one of those Hollywood news shows. Ariel went through men as if they were trendy fashion accessories, something pretty to keep on her arm and enjoy for the moment, then to toss aside once she found another boy who pleased her more.

Marcus shook his head and headed back to his cabin. So she'd hang around for the weekend. A woman like Ariel would grow bored with the solitude and be off to more exciting places before she could even unpack. "Two days," he said. "I'll give her two days and then she's got to go. If she doesn't, I just toss her overboard."

Marcus chuckled softly. He wouldn't get a whole lot of work done in the next forty-eight hours, but that really didn't matter. If entertaining the boss's daughter was part of the job, then he'd do his best— just short of sleeping with her.

But in such close quarters, there was no telling what might transpire. If his desire did eventually overwhelm his common sense, at least he'd have a decent tale to tell his brothers about the sexy little socialite he'd reeled in, then tossed back.

BONUS FEATURE

...NOT THE END...

Look for THE MIGHTY QUINNS: MARCUS *in bookstores October 2006 from Harlequin Blaze.*

Drive Me Crazy
by Vicki Lewis Thompson

Even though Josh Gregory had told her he wasn't ready to get married until he built up his limousine company, Pris Adams thought she could change his mind. After all, they had a great relationship and even better sex! With her biological clock ticking, Pris gave Josh an ultimatum: Marry me or lose me! Josh chose option B.

Now, determined to get on with her life, Pris is engaged to marry someone else—and has hired Josh to drive the limo on her wedding day so that he'll see what he's lost! But then a funny thing happens on the way down the aisle...

CHAPTER ONE

A LIMO FULL OF BEAUTIFUL, twentysomething women. Ordinarily that would have thrilled Josh Gregory from the brim of his chauffeur's cap all the way down to his spit-shined dress shoes. Not today.

Priscilla Adams, a gorgeous blonde he used to date—a woman he used to have fantastic sex with, to be truthful—sat in the back of the limo with her bridesmaids. Within the hour, she and her luscious body would be lost to Josh forever. He told himself it was for the best.

After all, why would he want someone who'd smeared his nose in the fact that she was getting married, just because six months ago he'd said he wasn't ready for that march down the aisle? Talk about vindictive. According to Josh's boss, Pris had specifically requested him for this limo gig.

All the way to the church, he kept glancing in the rearview mirror to see if he could catch her gloating. Funny, she didn't seem to be gloating. He thought brides were supposed to look blissfully happy, considering they were about to get exactly what they wanted.

Apparently he wasn't the only one who'd noticed Pris's frown. Her maid of honor reached over and squeezed her hand. "Smile, there, babes! Don't worry. You've thought of everything. This shindig will go off without a hitch."

"Oh, you know me," Pris said. "I'm probably the only bride who spends her last twenty minutes of singlehood worrying about whether she remembered to tell the caterer to provide sparkling water as a beverage option."

Josh had to bite the inside of his cheek to keep from laughing. That was Pris, all right. Efficient and thorough. She hated the idea of making a mistake, especially a public mistake.

Yeah, he was well out of that relationship. She'd been very clear that she wanted the husband, the kids, the white picket fence, and if Josh wasn't inclined to give her that, she'd look elsewhere. Yes, she'd enjoyed the sex, but if Josh was more interested in saving for his own limo business than getting married, she'd regretfully move on.

Josh thought she'd moved on at warp speed, even for an efficiency expert like her. When they'd broken up, the Celtics had just started the season. Now it was play-off time. Without Pris, he'd watched a hell of a lot more basketball.

Come to think of it, he might watch a game on the limo's TV while he waited for Pris to come out of the church with her lucky groom. A good game might take his mind off the fact that Pris would be spending her wedding night with Brad somebody-or-other. But then, it probably wasn't the first time she'd had sex with Brad-baby. Pris wasn't the type to hold a guy off if she liked him.

PRIS HAD NEVER FELT so sexually frustrated in her life. And here she was in the same limo with the man who knew exactly how to please her. Her own fault. She'd wanted to show Josh Gregory what he was missing. He'd rejected the idea of marriage to her, and she was petty enough to crave a little revenge.

She tried to think about the lovely ceremony ahead of her and the house she and Brad were closing on in a month. True, they wouldn't have much of a honeymoon. She had to admit being disappointed that Brad had decided to buy her a life policy on himself instead of taking her to the Bahamas.

But that was small change compared to Brad's decision that they shouldn't have sex until the wedding night. Thanks to an ex-girlfriend of Brad's who'd called this morning, Pris now questioned that decision. The ex-girlfriend could be a jealous spoiler, or she could be telling the truth. Before Pris said *I do* to Bradley Davidson this afternoon, she was going to find out.

BONUS FEATURE

CHAPTER TWO

JOSH PULLED UP in front of one of the prettiest little churches in Connecticut. Stained-glass windows were set like jewels against the freshly painted white clapboard, and the bell tower and gray shingles made it look like something out of a New England travel brochure.

He'd driven other bridal parties here, and he'd always thought that when he'd built his business and was ready to get married, this would be the place. As of today, he was crossing it off his list. No way would he get married in the same church where Pris had married Brad-baby.

Parking out front so the bride and groom could run down the sidewalk and into the limo after the ceremony, he climbed out quickly and went around the car to open the door for the women, including the bride. He'd helped Pris into the limo without getting sweaty palms, so he'd somehow manage to help her out again.

The bridesmaids came first. Under different circumstances, Josh would have made sure he remembered their names. At least two of them were single and extremely date-worthy. He should really hit on them a little, to get back at Pris for hiring him. But his heart wasn't in it.

Then Pris started out of the limo, helped by her maid of honor, who fussed with the skirt, the veil and the train. Josh hadn't said much to Pris when he'd handed her into the limo. He figured that common decency required him to say something now.

He offered his hand so that she could use him to steady herself as she tried to maneuver all that white satin.

She grasped his hand and glanced into his eyes. "Thank you. I, um, apologize for…for—"

"It's okay." He gave her cold hand a squeeze and knew she was nervous. As he looked into her gray eyes, he felt a familiar tug on his heart. "This gives me a chance to wish you the best."

PRIS FELT about two inches high. She heartily regretted the impulse that had made her hire Red Carpet Limousine and specifically request Josh as her driver. She'd behaved like a spoiled brat, and now he was making her feel even worse by wishing her the best.

"Th-thank you," she said, stumbling over her words of gratitude. "That means a lot to me."

"I hope your fiancé knows what he's getting," Josh murmured so that only she could hear.

Pris knew he was talking about sex. "He does," she said, although it wasn't exactly true. Unfortunately, Pris didn't know what *she* was getting, either. That wouldn't have been the case with Josh, who hadn't been afraid to show her he was a fantastic lover. But Josh hadn't wanted to put a ring on her finger, and she would be thirty-one her next birthday, which was way past her timetable.

She wished Josh didn't look so good standing there by the limo. She'd always been a sucker for a guy in uniform, and Josh filled out the shoulders of his gray jacket to perfection. His dark hair peeked out from under the chauffeur's cap, curly and untamed as ever. She remembered how springy it felt, remembered how his dark eyes used to smolder whenever she touched him…anywhere. He was one hot guy.

And she was due to be married in ten minutes to a man who might be sexually dysfunctional. Sometimes life seemed totally unfair.

CHAPTER THREE

PRIS AND HER BRIDESMAIDS walked around to the side door of the church, and on the way she noticed that her parents' car was in the parking lot. She'd invited them to ride in the limo with her and her friends, but her mother had wanted to go on ahead and make sure everything was in order at the church.

Her mom and dad were the best, the very best, and they'd put out a bundle to make today special. If only she didn't have this gnawing feeling in her stomach about Brad, life would be perfect.

Kristin, a tall brunette she'd known forever, started to open the door that led to the small room where they'd wait for the ceremony to start.

"Hold on a minute, Kristin," Pris said. "Listen, does anybody have a piece of paper and a pen?"

They all looked at her as if she'd gone insane.

"Why?" said Jenna, the fiery redhead and long-time friend she'd asked to be her maid of honor.

"I, uh, I need to write a note to Brad."

Her attendants looked at each other in confusion.

"Okay, I know it sounds peculiar, but I—"

"You're allowed to be peculiar on your wedding day," said Jenna. "I'm sure we can come up with a piece of paper and a pen, but let's do it inside."

"No, out here. I don't want my folks getting wind of this. I need one of you to deliver the note to him right away and wait for him to write the answer and give it back to you. This is important."

"Did you guys have a fight?" asked Julie, a short blonde who was Pris's former college roommate.

"No. I just need to ask him something. And it can't wait until after the ceremony."

40

Jenna sighed and started rummaging through her purse. "Okay. All I have is a receipt from the grocery store."

"That'll work." Pris took the slip of paper and pen Jenna handed her and scribbled her question on it. Then she folded it four times.

"I'll take it to Brad," Kristin said.

"Thanks." Pris handed her the tiny note. "You can't read it. It's very personal."

"Oh, for heaven's sake, I won't read it," Kristin said.

Julie began to laugh. "I'm getting the picture. This is one of those questions like *Honey, did you pack extra condoms?* Am I right?"

"Sort of." Pris couldn't tell them. If it turned out the ex-girlfriend was making things up, Pris didn't want her friends getting the wrong idea about Brad.

"*Now* can we go in?" Jenna asked.

"Yes, now we can go in." Pris glanced back at the limo one more time. *Josh* was leaning against it, arms folded as he gazed in her direction. The next time she saw Josh, she'd be a married woman.

Once she walked into the small room, life became a blur of last-minute preparations, but through it all, Pris thought of little else but the note she'd given to Kristin.

At last Kristin came through the door and hurried over to her. "He kept the note. He looked a little embarrassed, but he said for you not to worry, that you and he would work it out."

Pris stood in stunned silence. So it was true.

CHAPTER FOUR

JOSH CLIMBED into the back of the limo, turned on the TV and tried to concentrate on the basketball game. But all he could see was Pris as she'd walked toward the church. She'd looked like a woman going to her doom.

42

When she'd glanced at him right before going through the door, he'd had the feeling she wanted to be rescued. Oh, hell, that probably wasn't what she'd been thinking. More than likely she pitied him for being such a stubborn SOB when he could have had a woman like her.

Admittedly, seeing her in that white dress had shaken him up. Most women looked good on their wedding day, but Pris was spectacular, with her blond curls done up in that arrangement on top of her head and a dress that emphasized her tiny waist and generous cleavage.

His stomach was in knots, and he couldn't sit still another minute. Snapping off the power on the TV, he got out of the limo and started pacing, pausing every few seconds to glance at his watch.

It could have been him in there standing at the altar with Pris. She hadn't cared whether he'd achieved his financial goals. But he cared. His father might have died broke, but that wasn't happening to him. He clenched his jaw and vowed to get through the next half hour with some kind of grace.

PRIS MOVED LIKE A ROBOT, barely hearing her mother's lavish compliments or her father's gruffly spoken words about how beautiful she looked. What a disaster. These moments were supposed to be so precious. And Pris was furious.

"I have to take my seat." Her mother gave her a tight hug.

"Thanks, Mom. Thanks for everything." *I don't want to do this.*

Was the whole mess partly her fault? She'd agreed with Brad that they should wait until the wedding night, maybe out of guilt because she'd had such terrific sex with Josh. Six months had seemed like a decent period of abstinence to make sure all her body memories of Josh were gone. Brad's plan had sounded old-fashioned and sweet.

Instead, it had been at best cowardly and at worst deceitful. According to his ex-girlfriend, Brad was a thirty-second wonder. Zero staying power, that Bradley. Pris was as sympathetic as the next girl when

BONUS FEATURE

given the chance to be. Brad hadn't been man enough to give her that chance.

She didn't want to marry him today. She might not want to marry him at all, but definitely not today. And yet…the small church was jammed with people, some of whom had known her since she was a baby. The wedding had cost a sizable amount of money. Her mother's eyes were filled with tears of happiness, and her father looked proud and nervous as he held out his arm.

"It's time, sweetheart," he said.

Pris slipped her arm through his and they walked into the church vestibule. Through the archway she could see the altar, with Brad looking handsome, but a trifle uneasy. As well he should, pulling the wool over her eyes like that. The ex-girlfriend had said she'd tried all sorts of remedies and nothing had worked. She'd thought Pris should know.

The Wedding March began. Pris gripped her father's arm and walked next to him the way they'd practiced. The aisle seemed a million miles long, but at last they reached the altar and her father withdrew, leaving her with Brad. The minister cleared his throat and smiled.

In an agony of indecision, Pris held up a hand, silently asking him to wait. Then she beckoned for Brad to lean down. Placing her lips next to his ear, she whispered, "Why didn't you tell me before?"

He turned red. "I didn't think it was important," he murmured.

"Not important?" Pris couldn't believe he'd said that. She backed away from him, no longer worried about being discreet. "Well, it damned sure is to me!"

CHAPTER FIVE

THE CEREMONY HAD STARTED. Josh faced the front of the church, as if he could somehow see through those white double doors. He needed to accept this, needed to make sure his heart had been properly notified that Pris now belonged to someone else. He hadn't thought it would hurt this much.

Before long, those double doors would open and Pris would come out. If she and Brad-baby were like most newlyweds, they'd be laughing in relief and joy as they hurried down the sidewalk to the waiting limo. Josh had left the passenger door open in preparation for them to plunge inside.

After that, he'd be forced to listen to their breathless words of love on the drive to the reception. And he'd know that within hours they'd be naked together.

As he was torturing himself with that final thought, the church doors flew open, and he gulped. Wow, that was quick. Wait a minute. Pris was running out, her skirts hoisted so she could move faster, but where was the groom?

"Start the car!" Pris yelled, her veil flying, her train dragging on the ground. "I'm outta here!"

Josh stared at her. "Are you serious?"

"Move it, Josh! We're leaving!"

He didn't have time to think of consequences. All he knew was that the woman of his dreams wanted to be rescued, and he was just the guy to carry her off on his sleek white horse...or limo. Whatever.

He ran around the front of the car, jerked open the driver's door and turned the key he'd left dangling in the ignition. "You in?" he called over his shoulder as he slammed his door.

"I'm in!" The back door shut with a solid thump. "Go!"

Josh glanced toward the church, where Brad, followed by a churchful of folks, was hotfooting it toward the limo. Josh checked for traffic, saw there was none, and shoved his foot to the floor. The limo leaped forward right before Brad reached it.

"Where do you want to go?" Josh asked as he fought the urge to speed away. The narrow streets of this tiny town had more cops per square block than New York City.

"I don't know. Take the turnpike north. Just drive. I don't...I don't want anybody to find me. Not until I figure this out."

The walkie-talkie on the dash crackled. "Base to Aladdin One. Come in Aladdin One."

BONUS FEATURE

Josh picked up the mike. Oh, yeah. He worked for a limo company. They might not be thrilled that he was taking this gas-guzzler on some yet-to-be-determined journey without prior arrangements being made. "This is Aladdin One. What's up?" A quick glance in the rearview mirror told him Pris was pulling off her veil, scattering bobby pins everywhere.

"Hi, Josh," said Rachel, the new dispatcher. "We have a request for a limo at seven tonight, and yours is the only one we have potentially available. I have you scheduled to return at six. Can you take this other assignment at seven?"

"Let me check." Josh switched off the mike. "Pris? How long do you need me to drive you around?"

She greeted the question with silence.

"Pris? The dispatcher has another gig for me at seven." Josh guided the big car onto the ramp leading to the turnpike. "Do you figure we'll be back by then?"

Finally Pris's voice drifted up from the back of the limo. "Look, I don't have anything with me, no cash, no credit card, nothing, but…"

"What?" His heart hammered. "What is it you want?"

"I want the limo for the whole night."

48

CHAPTER SIX

FINALLY FREE OF HER VEIL, Pris leaned back against the leather upholstery and gazed up at the quilted headliner above her. In her entire thirty years, she had never done anything remotely like this. But when Brad had told her that he didn't think his sexual problem was important, she'd panicked.

Now all she wanted was to stay in the comfort and seclusion of this limo for as long as possible, until everyone had a chance to cool down and think logically, including her. It was worth the hundreds of dollars it would cost her.

"Can I pay you when we get back?" she asked Josh.

"Uh, sure, I guess." He sounded reluctant.

"I don't want you to get in trouble. I'll bet my Visa's on file at Red Carpet, because I'm the one who made the arrangements." Her mother had tried to talk her out of it. They'd had their only wedding fight over hiring Josh to drive the limo, so Pris had decided to handle that expense by herself.

BONUS FEATURE

"I won't get in trouble. I just hope you know what you're doing."

"Well, I don't, okay? Listen, if this won't work, just drop me at the next exit. Find a convenience store. I'll call…somebody." She had no idea who. Everyone who cared about her was still at the church and would want to haul her back there for an explanation.

Josh laughed. "I'm not dropping you off at some convenience store, Pris. If you really want to hire the limo for the night, you've got it." He spoke into his mike again, telling a woman named Rachel that he'd need the limo for the entire evening, and the charge would be handled by Ms. Adams.

50 Pris decided Rachel must have been hired by Red Carpet in the past six months, because she didn't recognize the name. She wondered if Rachel was single, and if Josh had dated her. Not that it was any of her business who Josh dated. She'd lost that right when she'd broken up with him.

Damn, but she had a lot of white satin to deal with. She sat up and fumbled behind her for the buttons on her detachable train. They were small and difficult to reach. She swore softly as she tried to unfasten the loops.

"You wrestling with somebody back there?" Josh asked.

"I'm trying to get my train off. Shoot, I just broke a fingernail."

"There's a rest stop up ahead. If you want, I can pull off and help you."

"That would be terrific. I wouldn't mind having a chance to use the facilities, either." Then she had an image of walking into the rest-stop bathroom in her wedding dress and laughed. It felt good to laugh, and she realized that the weight that had settled on her heart since the ex-girlfriend's phone call was gradually lifting.

Or maybe the weight had been there before that phone call. Even without the information about Brad's little problem, she'd been wondering if the marriage was a mistake. She'd put her uneasiness down to pre-wedding jitters. All her married friends had said it was common to have doubts.

Josh took the exit, cruised into the rest-stop parking lot and pulled alongside the curb. He stopped the car. "Don't try to get out. I'll come back there. After we get the train off, I'll park in a truck lane until you come out of the bathroom."

"Sounds good."

Josh set the brake and went around to the passenger door. When he stepped into the back of the limo, his expression was all business. "Okay, turn around so I can get at those buttons." There was nothing sexual in his tone at all.

Then why, Pris thought, was she suddenly picturing the two of them naked on the leather upholstery?

CHAPTER SEVEN

THE MINUTE JOSH climbed into the back of the limo with Pris, he realized he'd made a huge mistake. The lust he'd assumed was under control…wasn't. Her perfume, her cleavage, her upswept hairdo and the look in those gray eyes took him right back to the days when he hadn't been able to keep his hands off her.

But those days were over, and in the meantime she'd become engaged to another man. She'd been ready to marry the guy until something had spooked her. Josh couldn't assume that the old flame burned for her, as well.

So he did his best to treat her as a professional chauffeur would treat a client. Unfortunately, having the client stoop over in the back of the limo and present her backside to him so he could unfasten her bridal train hadn't been covered during Red Carpet's orientation. As he worked with the tiny buttons and loops, he remembered the times he'd had sex with her in this position.

"Are you getting it?" she asked.

He was getting hot and bothered, if that's what she meant. "Almost," he said. She had such a sweet little backside. Even through the layers of satin, he could see the outlines of the tush he used to love to cup in both hands while he— Oh, damn. He didn't dare think about that.

"I'll bet you're wondering what happened to put me in this position."

"You mean braced backside out against the seat of my limo?"

"Very funny. No, I meant the Great Wedding Escape."

He'd come to the last button, so he stalled, pretending to have trouble with it. "I'll admit to being curious."

"Once I'm rid of this blasted train and I've made a trip to the bathroom, I'll tell you all about it. You'll probably laugh yourself silly."

"I wouldn't count on it. Running out on your wedding is serious stuff."

She sighed. "I know, and I feel terrible about it. My poor parents—all that time and money wasted."

He found it interesting that she'd thought first of her parents, rather than the jilted groom. He could hardly wait to hear what had caused her to bolt.

"Josh, are you still unbuttoning back there? I can't feel your fingers moving."

BONUS FEATURE

She used to *love* to feel his fingers moving—all over her body. "Just finished." He resisted the urge to smack her lightly on the bottom, just a teasing little pat, like he used to do all the time when they were dating. "You're done." He pulled the train away and backed out of the limo still holding it.

"Thanks." She stayed hunched over as she turned around, picked up her skirts and maneuvered through the door.

Tucking the train under his arm, he held her elbow to steady her descent. "Watch yourself. Don't want you tripping on your dress and taking a header."

"Believe me, neither do I. A trip to the emergency room with no ID would be a nightmare." Finally she stood on the sidewalk. "People are staring," she murmured.

"Really?" He glanced around and noticed that they were indeed the object of much curiosity. "Sheesh, you'd think they'd never seen a runaway bride before."

Pris laughed. "Earlier today I felt guilty as hell for insisting on you as the limo driver, but…I'm glad you're here."

Josh warned himself not to put too much importance on that statement. But he must have, anyway, because his heart gave a lurch and started pumping faster.

54

"In fact, I'm very glad," she said, giving him a melting look.

He gulped. A look like that always used to mean they were about to have some outstanding sex.

CHAPTER EIGHT

AS PRIS MADE her way toward the women's bathroom, she smiled at the gawkers, amazed at how little
they bothered her. Funny how that worked. She'd
always avoided making scenes of any kind, and now
that she'd made a huge scene by running out on her
wedding, she felt free to do almost anything.

But when she wedged herself into a tiny stall,
she had to amend that. She felt mentally free, but
physically, she was dragging around a lot of excess
clothing. At least she could get rid of the silk garter.
She slipped it off and hung it on the hook behind the
door.

She wondered if Josh would be interested in
helping her ditch the rest of her wedding finery. She
shouldn't be thinking in those terms, but maybe she
could be forgiven. For six months she'd gone without
sex, believing that tonight was the night.

Maybe it still could be. She wondered if Josh was
seeing anybody. But even if he wasn't, and assuming
he wanted to go along, there were risks. She'd been

hooked on him before and she didn't want to get hooked on him again.

No, it was a foolish idea. She grabbed the garter before she left the stall. After washing her hands and glancing in the mirror to check her hair, she tossed the garter in the trash on her way out the door.

JOSH TURNED ON the heater and let the limo's engine idle after he parked in the truck zone. With evening coming on, the inside of the limo was getting chilly. However, he wasn't chilly in the least, especially when he thought of how Pris had looked at him.

By the time she came out of the bathroom, though, he'd decided that sex with her would be a bad idea for many reasons. She had to be emotionally vulnerable, and that was a bad time to get involved. As for him, he was afraid he was still in love with her. Yeah, sex would be a big mistake.

He drove the car over to meet her, hopped out and went around to open the back door. "All set?"

"Much better, thanks." She hesitated by the open door. "Do you think I could ride in front with you? We could talk more easily, and I wouldn't feel so strange, being back there by myself."

"Sure. We'll have to stuff your dress in, but it should work."

She slapped her forehead. "I should have taken my slips off while I was in the bathroom. That would help a lot. Oh, well, I'll do it now."

BONUS FEATURE

"Now?" The Pris he knew would never consider taking off undergarments in the middle of a parking area.

"Just let me scoot around behind the car door, and you can block me from the other direction. Besides, I've already made a spectacle of myself. This'll just give them all a better story to tell."

"Okay." Which is how Josh ended up watching Pris shimmy out of three petticoats. He wondered if she realized how much the movement made the tops of her breasts quiver above the low neckline of her dress. Finally he had to look down at the pavement to keep his erection under control.

"There." She tossed the petticoats into the back of the limo. "I should fit in the front seat much better now."

She used to fit him like a glove. He swallowed and opened the front-passenger door. "In you go."

She glanced up as she tucked herself into the car. "You can take off that cap if you want, Josh. It's only me."

"Yeah, but you're paying for a chauffeured limo. That rates a cap."

She held his gaze. "Then let's pretend we're friends, out for a drive."

"All right." He took off the cap with a feeling of inevitability. He'd never been just friends with her. He doubted he could hold that line now, even for one night.

CHAPTER NINE

"MUCH COZIER," Pris said as they cruised along the highway in the twilight. More like the old days. They'd never made out in Josh's vintage T-Bird, but she had fond memories of his New Haven apartment.

Then she noticed a cell phone clipped to the dash. If she called her folks now, she'd probably get their machine. "Can I use the cell?" she asked.

"Be my guest."

Picking up the phone, she dialed and, fortunately, got the machine. She told them she was fine, she was with Josh, and she'd talk to them in the morning.

Josh made no comment on the call. "Are you hungry?" he asked, finally. "It's getting close to dinnertime."

"A little bit, but a hamburger from a drive-through is fine." She thought of how they used to grab fast food on their way to his apartment to make love.

"I guess we'd make an interesting couple going into a regular restaurant."

She laughed. "We'll make an interesting couple at the drive-through window."

"Good point. I can park the limo and go in to pick up the order."

"And spoil the fun? Josh, if I really wanted a restaurant meal, I'd say so. Being outrageous is starting to appeal to me."

He glanced at her. "Then I guess you've changed in the past six months."

"Try the past six hours. Until this morning, I was the same old conservative Pris. And then Brad's ex called."

Josh groaned. "Don't tell me he's been fooling around on you with the ex."

60

"Nope. She asked if I'd had sex with Brad, and I said no, because—"

"What?"

"Brad thought we should wait until after we were married." Which sounded dumb now.

"Are you saying you've gone six months without sex?"

"It hasn't been easy."

His laugh was bitter. "Tell me about it."

She looked at him in shock. "You mean, you haven't—"

"Yeah, well, I've been busy with work." He seemed embarrassed that he'd let the comment slip. "You know me, trying to get lots of hours in. So what's the story on your fiancé?" he asked, as if wanting to shift the attention away from himself. "Don't tell me he's gay."

"Nope. According to his ex, he's very quick on the trigger."

Josh coughed. "She could have been making that up out of jealousy."

"I know, so I asked him. And from his reaction, it's true. But he said he hadn't told me because he didn't think it was important."

"The hell he didn't think it was important!" Josh looked ready to spit nails. "That's why he put off having sex with you! No wonder you ran out of that church like your dress was on fire. What a jerk!"

"I didn't know what else to do. I could either run out or stay and explain to the guests that I wasn't marrying him because he's terrible in bed."

"He deserved to have everyone know, tricking you the way he did."

"Maybe so, but there were kids in that church, and Brad's great-grandmother. I thought if I ran, I'd buy myself time to figure out how to answer the questions."

"So here we are." He paused. "And neither of us has had sex in months."

"Looks that way." The past few hours had made her much bolder. "What do you think we should do about that?"

CHAPTER TEN

WITH HIS BRAIN full of thoughts about sex with Pris, Josh decided he was an unsafe driver for this house-boat on wheels. Bedroom on wheels was more like it. And temptation was sitting beside him wearing a white wedding dress.

He put on the turn signal and took the next exit. "I think we should get a hamburger and talk about the situation," he said.

"You're right," she said immediately. "I didn't mean to come on like some sex-starved woman. I just—"

"You are a sex-starved woman." Josh watched for a hamburger joint, any hamburger joint. "And I'm a sex-starved man, and that's an explosive combo. I had no idea that you'd been living like a nun ever since we split up."

"You probably think I was stupid to agree with Brad's idea."

"Not stupid. I'm surprised, that's all." Shell-shocked was more like it. All along he'd been tormented by thoughts of Pris in bed with some other guy and nothing had been happening. "So you only kissed?"

"Uh-uh. He said if we started making out, we wouldn't be able to stop."

"Oh, sure. It's more likely he realized that once you started making out, he'd embarrass himself. I know what making out with you is like, and if this guy had no control to begin with, the first time he got beyond kissing, he'd be toast in seconds. I had my moments when I wondered if it would happen to me."

"You did?" She sounded pleased to know that. "You never told me."

"Then I should have." There were lots of things he hadn't told her, including those three all-important words of love. "You're very hot, Pris."

"I thought I was that way because of you."

"I'm flattered. But I think you're naturally hot-blooded, especially if you're with a guy who appreciates that quality."

She sighed. "I guess Brad didn't."

"Oh, I think he did appreciate it." Josh spotted a drive-through. "I think he was hoping that you'd help him solve his problem. But not telling you and disguising it by saying you should both save yourselves for the wedding night is despicable." Satisfyingly despicable. He had no remorse for helping Pris escape from Brad-baby.

But now he had a decision to make, and it wouldn't be an easy one. Beside him sat a powder keg of sexual needs, and he wasn't in any better shape. This fast-food run would give them a little time to consider their actions. He eased the big car off the street and swung it into the order lane, miraculously without running over any curbs.

"I still feel like a fool for letting Brad get away with his little trick," Pris said.

"It's just that I know how important sex is to you, so I would think you'd have wanted to make sure all the spark plugs were firing before you said *I do.*"

"I probably agreed because I felt the need to put space between having sex with you and having sex with him."

"Oh." He'd felt exactly the same way, and that's why he hadn't dated anyone for six months. "I get that."

"Josh, was sex between us really that good, or has all this deprivation made it seem better than it was?"

"I don't know." But he could think of one surefire way to find out.

CHAPTER ELEVEN

PRIS COULDN'T SPEAK for Josh, but she was going crazy thinking about the possibility of having sex with him again. He, however, seemed to be relatively calm. Or so she thought until he spoke into the intercom on the menu and asked for two Big Macs.

"Josh." Laughing, she shook his arm.

He glanced over at her. "What? You want chicken instead? I thought you said hamburgers, and we always used to get—"

"Josh, this is Burger King."

"Oh." His face grew red. "I knew that." Clearing his throat, he turned back to the board and asked for two Whoppers, a large order of fries and two chocolate shakes.

It was the meal that had become a tradition with them on nights they could hardly wait to get back to his place and strip naked. They used to eat in the car on the way to his apartment, so they wouldn't lose any time. Any of the fast-food hamburger places had been fine with them, whichever one had the shortest drive-through line.

Pris wondered if Josh remembered all that. Tonight they weren't anywhere near his apartment, and even if they had been, the days of automatically assuming they'd go there and have sex were over. Six months ago she'd given him an ultimatum—either marry me or I walk. He'd chosen option B.

No matter how hard he'd worked in the past six months, he wouldn't have saved enough to realize his dream and buy a limo company of his own. She'd had time to think about that goal of his. Giving her up to pursue it hadn't been easy for him, and she grudgingly admired him for sticking to his plan.

66

So if she and Josh had sex tonight, it couldn't be about anything except mutual gratification, a roll in the hay for old times' sake. She didn't know if he'd want that. She wasn't sure if she could handle it, either.

For the time being, they couldn't talk about it because Josh had his hands full inching the car around the sharp curve that led to the delivery window. "I don't think they figured on a stretch limo when they built this part," he said.

"No, and the kids who are working this shift are getting a real charge out of watching you struggle." Pris saw two of them hanging out of the delivery window, big grins on their faces. Pris decided to wave.

At last they drew alongside the window. "Awesome," said the teenage girl who handed them their food. "Did you, like, get married in your chauffeur's uniform?" Other crew members crowded around her to peer at the limo.

"Uh, no." Josh handed the bags over to Pris and gave the girl some money.

"So you changed into your uniform for the trip? That is so cool! Chauffeuring your bride on the honeymoon! I love that!"

Pris leaned down so she could see the girl's face. "Actually, we're not married. I ran away from the wedding, and he helped me escape."

The girl's mouth rounded in a big O. "Wow," she whispered. "Just like Julia Roberts."

"Except Pris is better looking," Josh said. "Hey, thanks for the food." He hit a button and rolled the window up.

"Oh, yeah." Pris grinned at him. "Better looking than Julia Roberts. You are so full of it."

"Actually, I meant every word. You're gorgeous."

Her heart warmed in a way it never had with Brad's compliments. "I could kiss you for that."

He glanced at her. "Better be careful. One kiss, and it's all over but the shouting."

CHAPTER TWELVE

"So, WHERE DO YOU want to eat this?" Josh asked. He had an idea, but if they did that, he could predict the results. He could predict the results anyway. You could cut the sexual tension in the car with a knife.

"How about if we drive out toward the water?"

Bingo. Just what he'd been thinking. "Then I need to make another stop before we do that."

Pris took a deep breath. "Have we decided then?"

He thought they had, but he still wanted to talk it out for a little while and make sure they had an understanding of what tonight was all about. "I'm not sure if we've decided or not, but like I said, we're not going to stop with one kiss. And this limo comes equipped with quite a few things, but that's not one of them."

"Then maybe you'd better stop."

His heart pounded faster. A decision to buy condoms didn't have to mean a decision to use condoms, but in his experience, it usually meant exactly that.

He pulled into the parking lot of a drugstore. There were no spaces that would take the full length of the limo. "I'm going to have to block some cars while I run in." He left the motor going and unfastened his seat belt. "If anyone wants the limo moved, just tell them I'll be back in a minute."

"Wait. Let me go in."

"You?" He couldn't believe she'd said that. Not Pris Adams.

"Me." She unfastened her seat belt. "It's better if they see a bride buying them for her honeymoon than a chauffeur from Red Carpet buying them while he's on duty."

He hadn't thought of that, maybe because he didn't feel as though he was on duty. But the limo company had a reputation that stretched from New York City to Boston, and Pris was absolutely right that he shouldn't be caught buying condoms in one of these small coastal towns. People loved to talk, and word could get back to his boss.

Still, he hated sending Pris out to get them. "It's chilly out there." But if he gave her his jacket with the Red Carpet logo on it, then he might as well go in himself.

"I'll be fast. But I need to borrow some money." She held out her hand.

He started to reach for his wallet and hesitated. Having sex with Pris again could be the dumbest idea he'd ever had. He'd probably end up wanting her more than ever, and he couldn't have both Pris and a secure future.

She dropped her hand back in her lap. "Second thoughts?"

The lights in the parking lot allowed him to see her expression, and she looked…wistful. Need gripped him in an iron fist. "Oh, yeah," he said. "Second, third and fourth thoughts. But I still want you." He pulled his wallet out.

She took the bills he handed her and folded them neatly. Now that was more like the Pris he remembered. Then she looked at him. "Maybe this will help with your decision. Six months ago I wanted us to get married, but no matter whether we have wonderful sex or not, I couldn't marry you now."

He clutched the steering wheel as a horrible thought occurred to him. "You're not telling me that you'll go back to your trigger-happy groom."

She smiled at that. "No, but before I think of getting married to anyone else, I have to repay my folks for this wedding. On my salary at the tax firm, that'll take a long time. So you see, you're safe."

Josh didn't think so. But looking into her eyes, he no longer cared.

CHAPTER THIRTEEN

PRIS WONDERED how far this newfound spirit of adventure would take her. She'd never bought condoms in her life, let alone while wearing a wedding dress. But all she was risking was embarrassment, while Josh could be risking his job. And it wasn't as if she hadn't already been embarrassed today.

As she walked toward the front door of the drugstore, she congratulated herself on coming up with something to put Josh's fears of marriage to rest. In fact, she'd spoken the absolute truth. She felt horrible about spending her parents' money on a wedding that had fizzled. She'd repay every cent.

A man who looked like a college professor held the door for her. "Need something for the reception, do you?" he asked with a distinct British accent.

"Not exactly." She smiled at him and clutched her skirts so she'd fit through the door. "I'm a runaway bride."

"You don't say!" He peered at her from behind his wire-rimmed glasses. "I've never seen one of those in real life, just the movies."

"The opening sprint was quite dynamic, actually." She glanced around at the shoppers that had stopped in their tracks to stare at her. "Hi, everyone." She gave them all a little wave.

Some of the customers continued to ogle her, while others gave her shy smiles and went about their business. Trying to look as if she shopped for condoms every day of the week, she located the display and stood in front of it, tapping her finger against her mouth. She wanted the brand Josh had always used. Finally she spied a familiar box and grabbed it.

At the counter, the female clerk grinned. "Honeymoon supplies, huh? I'll bet the groom will hear about this for the next fifty years."

Pris had become quite fond of her new persona, so she trotted it out again. "There is no groom. I'm a runaway bride."

The clerk's mouth fell open. "No joke!" She bagged the condoms and gave Pris her change. "Looks like you found someone to run away with."

"Did I ever." Pris winked at the clerk.

"You go, girl." The clerk gave her a thumbs-up. "How far into the ceremony were you when you cut out?"

"It had just started."

"And you ran for the hills?"

"Yep, I sure did."

"I wish I'd been there to see that. A little gumption, that's what I'm talking about. If it's not right, then skedaddle. Vamoose. Let 'em eat your dust."

"That's what I decided." Pris was beginning to feel like a superhero, a champion of women who had been unfairly tricked by devious men like Brad.

"Damn straight. You have a good night, now. Enjoy your purchase."

"Thanks. I will." When she emerged from the drugstore, she was ready to jump Josh right there in the parking lot. She was woman, and she was ready to roar.

He got out and came around to help her into the car. "I see you found something."

"I did." Before she got in the car, she grabbed him around the neck and kissed him hard. It felt incredibly good to be kissing Josh again. But they had places to go and each other to do. She let him go and noticed that he looked sort of dazed. "Are you okay?"

He blinked. "I'm exceedingly okay. And I now realize that I should have asked you to buy the condoms a long time ago."

BONUS FEATURE

CHAPTER FOURTEEN

THE SENSATION OF Pris's mouth pressed against his stayed with Josh as he kept bearing east, looking for a road that would take them out to the water. A couple of times he wondered why he was bothering to find a scenic spot. Once they tumbled into the back of the limo, they wouldn't care where they were.

But he'd always been a bit of a romantic. Oh, hell, he'd always been a huge romantic, and parking the limo in view of Long Island Sound really appealed to him. The wind was whipping up a little, and with luck they'd be able to hear the waves while they were rolling around on the leather upholstery.

And they would be rolling around. Her kiss had left him no doubt of that. The only question was how soon after they parked the limo they'd be in the back, naked.

Beside him, Pris opened one of the food bags and dug around inside it. After a moment she held out a French fry dipped in ketchup. "Here."

He leaned over and took it in his mouth. "Thanks," he said as he chewed.

"Want your hamburger?"

He knew it was more than a simple question. If they ate their food on the way to the parking spot, that left nothing to do once they got there except the obvious. "Are you going to eat yours?"

"No fair. I asked you first."

His erection began to strain the material of his slacks. "Yes, I want my hamburger," he said.

"Coming right up." She sounded breathless, as if she might be getting eager, too.

He had some vivid memories of how eager she could be. "You know, we always had a bed, Pris. Would you rather find a place to stay tonight?"

She handed him his hamburger, carefully wrapped around the bottom so it wouldn't drip on his clothes, the way she used to do it. "You're bound and determined to get yourself in trouble, aren't you?"

He thought about the suggestion and realized she was right. The Red Carpet limo would be noticed whether they found a motel, hotel or B and B. And all he had to wear was his uniform. All Pris had was her wedding dress. Without turning this night into an elaborate shopping expedition at a discount store, they were confined to the car.

"I guess you're right," he said at last.

"Those leather seats are very comfy," she said. "Or maybe you know that already."

"If you're wondering if I've ever had sex in the back of this limo, I haven't. I haven't had sex in any car since high school." And his memories were of cramped quarters and lots of fumbling. Ever since he'd discovered the joys of an innerspring for this particular activity, he'd never longed for vehicle sex.

But he was longing for it now. Apparently he was oblivious to anything else, because he'd devoured his hamburger without tasting it, wadded up the wrapping and handed it to Pris before he realized what he was doing.

"Want your shake?"

"Later." He glanced over and discovered she'd nearly finished her hamburger, too. Turning down a narrow road, he saw the opening in the trees at the end of the lane. Beyond that was nothing but sand and the inky darkness of Long Island Sound. "We're here."

CHAPTER FIFTEEN

As Josh pulled the limo around so it stretched across the end of the beach road, Pris began to tremble with excitement at the thought of having sex with Josh again. "But we haven't talked," she said, feeling compelled to make sure they understood each other.

He shut off the engine and turned to her, his expression difficult to see in the darkness. "What do we need to say?"

"Maybe that this is simply a couple of old friends temporarily easing each other's misery." She could barely make out his smile. "Is that funny?"

"You make it sound like we're sharing a bowl of chicken soup." He unbuckled his seat belt.

"It'll probably be more exciting than that." She set their shakes on the floor, picked up the bag from the drugstore and unfastened her seat belt.

"I sure hope so. Listen, stay put. I'll come around and get you. I don't know how good the footing is on that side, and you're wearing those crazy high heels."

She didn't point out to him that she'd run down

the aisle and out to the limo in those same heels. His concern for her felt good. But then, she'd always known he cared about her. She wondered if he'd once loved her a little bit, too, even though he'd never said so.

When he opened the door, he let in the tang of salt air and the sound of waves slapping the shore. She breathed it in as he took her hand and helped her out. Their schedules had always been packed, and they'd only spent one day at the beach, but every time she thought of sand and sea, she thought of Josh.

He closed the car door and pulled her into his arms. "I haven't told you this, but I want to before I take your dress off. You look amazing in it."

She wound her arms around his neck, as she'd done hundreds of times, and looked into his shadowed face. "Thank you." Now she could admit to herself that she'd bought it knowing she wanted to impress him, not Brad. Such a spiteful girl, wanting to make him sorry that he gave her up.

She'd wanted to punish him for not being the man at the altar. Her heart hurt a little standing here with him now, because she'd dreamed of kissing Josh on her wedding day. It was about to happen, but not the way she'd hoped.

He pulled her closer, his arms keeping the chill salt air at bay. "All this talk about Brad's problem, and I'm scared I'll be in the same boat. I'll try not to

78

let that happen, but if it does, don't worry. After all this time, once won't be enough anyway."

She cupped his face in both hands. He felt so endearingly familiar. "I would never worry when I'm in your arms."

His head lowered. "I want to kiss you while we're still out here, because once we get inside, I might get a little wild and forget to do it right."

"Right?" She smiled. "I don't know what you mean."

"Before we get naked, I just want to say…hello." His lips settled gently over hers.

Emotion flooded through her at the restrained movement of his lips on hers. The memories of hot sex had made her forget his great capacity for tenderness. He kissed her so sweetly that tears pricked her eyes. When tonight was over, she could walk away from the sex. But she didn't know if she could walk away from this.

CHAPTER SIXTEEN

JOSH COULD HAVE SIMPLY opened the back door, urged Pris inside and gotten down to business. He should have, because hot, fast and furious sex might have distracted him from the truth—he still loved her.

And because he loved her, he didn't want to give her anything less than the best. Right now all he had was a slowly growing savings account and a dream that wouldn't become a reality for a while yet. Pris needed a guy who could pay off her debt to her parents plus give her the house and babies right away.

For some reason he'd been granted one more night with her, and he'd better enjoy it, because when morning came, they'd part again, this time forever. Nothing had really changed. But at least he'd helped her escape from Mr. Wrong. And he could ease her frustration...and in the process, his.

The kiss he'd meant to keep under control became hotter. He wasn't sure whether that was her doing or his, but tongues had become involved. When she took his hand and placed it over her breast, he decided that

80

Pris was the one deliberately turning up the thermostat.

The dress's plunging neckline made it easy for him to slip his hand inside. As he cupped her bare breast, they both moaned. Touching her felt incredible. He lifted his mouth from hers. "Time to get in the car."

She was breathing faster. "Yes. I have an idea. We'll take off the dress, turn it inside out and put it on the floor, on top of the petticoats. We can lie on it."

He stroked her breast and knew his brain cells would stop working any second now. "I don't know if that's a good—"

"It'll be wonderful. My body heat has warmed it up. Instead of cold leather, think warm satin."

"I can't think." He released her and wrenched open the door.

She fumbled with the buttons at her wrists as she turned her back to him. "Undo me before we get inside."

Thank God it was a zipper and not little buttons like her train. But first he had to navigate a hook and eye that didn't want to yield.

"Pull it free," she said, her voice tense.

"No." He finally unhooked the doggone thing and unzipped her dress.

"The bra, too," she said.

He'd had more practice at bras, and he had hers unfastened in no time.

BONUS FEATURE

Before he knew what she'd planned, she'd stepped out of the dress, flipped it inside out and laid it with a rustle of material on the floor of the limo. Good thing he'd picked a deserted beach road, because she stood outside wearing nothing but panties, thigh-high stockings and her four-inch heels.

They'd never ventured into semi-kinky play because straight sex had been so wonderful and he'd thought Pris wouldn't go for dressing up in black garter belts and peekaboo bras. Now he wasn't so sure she wouldn't, and he wished they had the time to find out.

But for the moment, she'd climbed into the back of the limo, and he was way behind the program. Shucking his jacket, he decided if she could strip out here, so could he. Soon he was down to his briefs, which were stretched tight by a major erection. Throwing his clothes on a seat, he got in and closed the door.

"Want one of these?"

He squinted in the darkness and realized she was holding a condom. "You read my mind."

She laughed. "No, I read your body language. Now hurry up. I want you so much I can't see straight."

CHAPTER SEVENTEEN

ONCE THE DOOR WAS CLOSED, Pris couldn't see very well, but that didn't matter. The next few minutes would be about her other senses—hearing the waves outside, the rhythm of Josh's breathing, the snap of latex as he put on the condom.

She breathed in the remembered scent of him. That alone would have been enough to arouse her. Then he found her in the darkness, his hands caressing her face, her breasts, her inner thighs as only he knew how.

"I've missed you so much," he whispered, his mouth moving over her throat and down the slope of one breast.

"I've missed you." She stroked the muscled expanse of his back and wondered how she'd survived without being able to do that. Then his tongue swept over her nipple and his hand slid between her thighs, and the pleasure was almost beyond enduring.

When he discovered how ready she was, he groaned. "Pris, forgive me." He braced himself above her, poised between her thighs. "I wanted to take more time, but—"

She clutched his hips and guided him closer. "I need it, too."

He probed her heat with an ease created by many nights of loving her. "I thought…I would never…ah, Pris. Sweet Pris." He dragged in a breath and thrust home.

Heaven. She wrapped her legs around his, holding him tightly inside her to savor the moment. There was no feeling like this, and no other man had ever completed her. Only Josh.

His breath fanned her ear. "I love being inside you."

84

"I love having you there."

"Maybe, if I stay very still, we can hold each other like this for a while before anything happens." He nipped her earlobe. "Do you think it will work?"

"No." The tension coiled within her. "Something's already happening."

"I should have known." He brushed his lips over hers. "You always were on the brink from the minute I kissed you. What if I do this?" He rotated his hips.

She gasped. "Keep doing it and you'll find out."

"I believe I will." The movement was subtle but devastating. His chest brushed lightly against her taut nipples and his lips grazed hers. "How's that?"

She moaned and arched against him. "You've developed some…new tricks."

"You inspire me."

"And you…you drive me crazy." The smooth satin shifted beneath her, caressing her bare skin. She began to pant as her climax hovered near.

"Good. Go crazy, Pris." He rocked forward, launching her into the most explosive orgasm of her life.

Months of pent-up frustration and longing erupted in waves of unbelievable pleasure. She called out his name and clung to him as her anchor in the tempest.

And then he was moving again, stroking quickly, gulping for air until at last he shuddered in the grip of his own climax. Long moments later, he nuzzled her throat. "Better now," he murmured.

"Mmm." She hugged him tight. "I'm sure better now."

"No." He sighed. "I meant this was even better than I remembered."

She had to agree. And that meant she had one heck of a problem.

BONUS FEATURE

CHAPTER EIGHTEEN

AT FIRST JOSH had been grateful simply to have access to Pris's luscious body, but after taking the edge off his hunger for her, he wished he could feast his eyes on her, too. Back when they were lovers they'd had sex with the lights on, and he had become used to that.

But turning the lights on in the back of the limo would be asking for trouble. He didn't want any trouble tonight—he just wanted to enjoy every minute he could with Pris.

Once he'd recovered himself enough to move, he kissed her softly. "I'm going up front to get our milk shakes and turn on the heater for a little while, so we won't get cold."

"The shakes would be nice, but believe me, I'm not cold."

"Me, either, yet, but the wind's picking up out there. I won't be long."

Moments later he had the engine running, the heater on and the bag of shakes in his hand as he climbed into the back again. While the door was still open he located Pris sitting on the floor propped against one of the leather seats, but once he closed the door, he had to feel his way.

"Gonna take off your pants again?" she asked in a husky murmur.

He laughed. "There's only one sane answer to that one." He put the bag down and peeled off his slacks. Then he picked up the bag and groped his way over to her. "To help you keep up your strength." He put the bag in her lap.

She opened the bag. "I never drink a chocolate milk shake without thinking of you."

"Same here." When he took the cup, he knew it would already have the straw shoved through the lid, because that's the way Pris did things.

His hand brushed hers, and his fingers came in contact with her engagement ring. "You're still wearing your diamond."

"Oh. Well, I can fix that in a jiffy."

Although he couldn't see her clearly, he realized she'd wedged her shake between her knees while she pulled off her ring. "Wait a minute," he said. "You should probably leave it on, so you won't lose it."

"I won't lose it." She dropped the ring into her shake. "And I definitely don't want to wear it anymore. Thanks for reminding me about it."

Saying something had been pure reflex, because he didn't want to make love to Pris while she wore

BONUS FEATURE

another guy's ring. Hell, he didn't want her to wear another guy's ring, ever. Too bad, unless he planned to put one there himself.

"It's not a very expensive ring," Pris said. "He didn't think spending a lot of money on a diamond was practical. Mmm, this milk shake tastes great."

"He discussed the cost of the ring with you?" Josh found the idea ludicrous. Talk about taking all the romance right out of it.

"Yes, and I told myself that meant he was a good money manager. He also bought a life policy on himself in lieu of an expensive honeymoon, but—"

"Hold it. Run that one by me again."

"Three nights ago he said he had a surprise for me. It was this single-pay life policy on himself. He thought that was much better than the trip to the Bahamas we'd talked about. Instead we'd go camping for our honeymoon."

Josh groaned and shook his head. "What an idiot."

"It's unromantic, I know, but he meant well. He wanted to make sure I'd never be in financial need in case anything ever happened to him."

Brad's logic hit Josh right between the eyes. It sounded absolutely stupid to him. And yet it was exactly why he hadn't asked Pris to marry him six months ago.

CHAPTER NINETEEN

"But I don't want to talk about Brad." Pris sipped her drink. "The ring reminded me of him, but he's history. Deciding to marry him was a big mistake, but at least I didn't go through with it out of fear of embarrassment."

"That was quite a thing you did, running out." Josh reached over and rubbed her knee. "Facing your parents tomorrow isn't going to be easy."

She'd forgotten that he used to rub her knee when they were in bed talking. And they'd talked a lot. They'd connected on more levels than physical pleasure, but that had been spectacular enough to take center stage most of the time.

"I can face my parents," she said softly. "I know they love me and want the best for me. Once they realize Brad's not the person I thought he was, they'll understand."

"Are you going to tell them the whole story?"

She smiled. "Um, I'll tell my mom, and I'll let her decide how much to tell my dad. I'm getting braver, but not enough to discuss my sex life with my dad."

Josh laughed and squeezed her knee. "Don't blame you."

The gentle pressure was having a predictable effect on her. "And speaking of my sex life, remember that trick I tried once with my milk shake?"

His breath caught. "As if I'd ever forget."

"Let's see if you still like it." Drawing some of the cool shake into her mouth, she put her cup on the seat and moved astride his knees. Leaning over, she discovered he was more than glad to see her.

Pulse racing, she lowered her head and slipped her mouth over his erection, all without losing any of the milk shake.

He moaned. "That's…incredible."

As she took in even more of his smooth shaft, his breathing grew labored. "Be…careful," he murmured. "I don't want to come."

She didn't mind if he did. She liked being in command. The only other time she'd tried this with a milk shake, he'd lost control almost immediately. But that had been after two days without each other, and she'd been happy to give him an extra treat.

Holding him firmly with her mouth, she moved her head slowly up and down.

"Ah…Pris…that's so good…too good." He grasped her head and drew her away. "Not this time," he murmured. "Come here." He guided her to his waiting mouth and they shared a chocolate milk-shake-flavored kiss.

"Your hair's coming undone," he whispered against her mouth.

"I don't care."

"You look so sexy with it up like that." He nibbled her lower lip. "But I wish I could see you with it falling down, too. Especially considering what I have in mind. Can you reach one of those little raincoats?"

"Uh-huh." She fumbled blindly for the box and pulled out a foil packet.

"You know what to do."

She did. They used to love this position, especially in the light when they'd been able to watch each other. Drawing back, she opened the packet and rolled the condom on. Then she held on to his shoulders, positioned herself over him and slid down, taking him in up to the hilt.

"I wish we had light," he whispered.

"Use your memory," she murmured. And then she made love to him. If memories were all he'd have of her, then she'd make this one special.

BONUS FEATURE

CHAPTER TWENTY

JOSH HAD ALWAYS cherished making love to Pris, but never more than he did during the hours they spent in the back of the limo. He could have kept it up until dawn, but she began to show signs of getting tired. No wonder. She'd been planning a wedding for weeks, with no rejuvenating sex to keep her going.

Sometime after four in the morning, he gathered her close. Creating a blanket from the train he'd removed from her dress earlier, he urged her to sleep. She insisted that she didn't want to, but in no time she'd drifted off.

Josh lay in the darkness holding the only woman he'd ever loved and thinking about the series of events that had brought them to this moment. Thoughts whirled in his head, each one more confusing than the last. Finally, needing to move, he eased away from Pris and located his clothes.

When he was dressed, he opened the door and climbed out. Making sure he had the electronic key

92

in his pocket, he locked the doors and headed toward the sound of the waves.

He walked the beach, getting sand in his shoes and feeling the cold salt air on his cheeks. The wind had died, leaving only the crunch of his footsteps and the whisper of gentle waves. A thin line of gray light bisected sea and sky by the time he had everything sorted out. He started back toward the limo.

WHEN PRIS OPENED her eyes, she had no idea where she was. Then she remembered and sat up to look for Josh. From the faint light coming through the tinted windows, dawn was on its way. Josh's clothes were gone, so he must have taken a walk. She wondered when he'd left.

Just then the limo door opened and he ducked in, looking rumpled and sexy. "Hi."

"Hi. Been for a stroll?"

"Yeah." He came over and knelt beside her, his expression very intent. "Priscilla Adams, will you marry me?"

She blinked. Maybe she was still asleep and dreaming this.

He took her hand. "I called Brad an idiot, but I'm a much bigger one. I wouldn't marry you because I couldn't offer you financial security. I called that love." He cupped her face in both hands. "But love isn't about financial security. It's about needing someone beside you, and them needing you."

Her throat tightened. If only he'd realized that six months ago. "Josh, it's no good. I made a mess of things, and I have to repay my parents for the—"

"*We'll* repay your parents. I have the money. We can do it this week."

"No! You're saving for your business. That's your dream, and I won't let you sacrifice it for me!"

"Pris, don't you see? You're my dream. If we're not together, the rest of it means nothing. I thought I had to have everything proceed according to some master plan, but if I lose you… I can't lose you. I love you too much."

Her eyes filled with tears. "I love you, too. But I can't take your money."

94   "It's nothing. I didn't know that before, but I do now, thanks to that jerk you almost married." His gaze searched hers. "And you. You showed me that risks are worth taking. Please…forgive me for… Oh, Pris." He swallowed. "I can't live without you," he murmured, his voice husky. "Please marry me."

"I will," she whispered, tears spilling from her eyes. "Oh, Josh, I will, but I'm so worried that I'll be a financial burden."

His eyes glowed with happiness as he gently wiped the tears from her cheeks. "Not a chance, my love. In fact, thanks to you, I'm the richest man on earth."

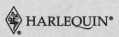

HOTEL MARCHAND

**Four sisters.
A family legacy.
And someone is out to destroy it.**

A captivating new limited continuity, launching June 2006

The most beautiful hotel in New Orleans,
and someone is out to destroy it. But mystery,
danger and some surprising family revelations
and discoveries won't stop the Marchand sisters
from protecting their birthright…
and finding love along the way.

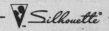

SPECIAL EDITION™

Welcome to Danbury Way—
where nothing is as it seems...

Megan Schumacher has managed to maintain a low profile on Danbury Way by keeping the huge success of her graphics business a secret. But when a new client turns out to be a neighbor's sexy ex-husband, rumors of their developing romance quickly start to swirl.

THE RELUCTANT CINDERELLA

by CHRISTINE RIMMER

Available July 2006

Don't miss the first book from the Talk of the Neighborhood miniseries.

If you enjoyed what you just read,
then we've got an offer you can't resist!

Take 2 bestselling
love stories FREE!
Plus get a FREE surprise gift!

Clip this page and mail it to Silhouette Reader Service™

IN U.S.A.	IN CANADA
3010 Walden Ave.	P.O. Box 609
P.O. Box 1867	Fort Erie, Ontario
Buffalo, N.Y. 14240-1867	L2A 5X3

YES! Please send me 2 free Silhouette Romance® novels and my free surprise gift. After receiving them, if I don't wish to receive anymore, I can return the shipping statement marked cancel. If I don't cancel, I will receive 4 brand-new novels every month, before they're available in stores! In the U.S.A., bill me at the bargain price of $3.57 plus 25¢ shipping and handling per book and applicable sales tax, if any*. In Canada, bill me at the bargain price of $4.05 plus 25¢ shipping and handling per book and applicable taxes**. That's the complete price and a savings of at least 10% off the cover prices—what a great deal! I understand that accepting the 2 free books and gift places me under no obligation ever to buy any books. I can always return a shipment and cancel at any time. Even if I never buy another book from Silhouette, the 2 free books and gift are mine to keep forever.

210 SDN DZ7L
310 SDN DZ7M

Name	(PLEASE PRINT)	
Address	Apt.#	
City	State/Prov.	Zip/Postal Code

Not valid to current Silhouette Romance® subscribers.

Want to try two free books from another series?
Call 1-800-873-8635 or visit www.morefreebooks.com.

* Terms and prices subject to change without notice. Sales tax applicable in N.Y.
** Canadian residents will be charged applicable provincial taxes and GST.
 All orders subject to approval. Offer limited to one per household.
 ® are registered trademarks owned and used by the trademark owner and or its licensee.

SROM04R   ©2004 Harlequin Enterprises Limited

Life.
It could happen to her!

Never Happened just about sums up
Alexis Jackson's life. Independent and
successful, Alexis has concentrated on
building her own business, leaving no
time for love. Now at forty, Alexis
discovers that she still has a few things
to learn about life—that the life unlived
is the one that "Never happened"
and it's her time to make a change....

Never Happened
by Debra Webb

Available July 2006
TheNextNovel.com

HN49